The
Secret Shopper
Unwrapped

The Secret Shopper Unwrapped

KATE HARRISON

First published in Great Britain in 2009 by Orion Books,
an imprint of The Orion Publishing Group Ltd
Orion House, 5 Upper Saint Martin's Lane
London WC2H 9EA

An Hachette UK Company

1 3 5 7 9 10 8 6 4 2

A CIP catalogue record for this book is
available from the British Library.

ISBN (Hardback) 978 1 4091 0730 9
ISBN (Export Trade Paperback) 978 1 4091 0731 6

Typeset at The Spartan Press Ltd,
Lymington, Hants

Printed in Great Britain by
Clays Ltd, St Ives plc

The Orion Publishing Group's policy is to use papers that are natural,
renewable and recyclable products and made from wood grown in sustainable
forests. The logging and manufacturing processes are expected to conform
to the environmental regulations of the country of origin.

www.orionbooks.co.uk

The
Secret Shopper
Unwrapped

November 6 –
Shopping Days to Christmas: 48

There's blood on the High Street. So how do you avoid falling victim to the worst recession in a lifetime?

Well, today's the day to start. Bonfire Night is over, but the fireworks are just beginning. Clear out the sparklers and the Halloween pumpkins, hang up the tinsel, stick on *Now That's What I Call Christmas Shopping*, and prepare for the fight of your shopkeeping life.

From *Surviving the Credit Crunch Christmas:
a Day-by-Day Guide for Retailers*

Chapter One

Emily

Once upon a time, there were three little girls.

(Can you still call yourself a girl at thirty-three? Maybe I'll never feel like a grown-up.)

Life was tough. The lowest point came three Christmases ago. One of the girls lost her childhood sweetheart to a Swiss banker and took far too long to work out that Heidi the husband-stealer had done her a massive favour. One girl lost her job, before landing a better one. And one lost her brilliant artist husband to the great gallery in the sky, and with it her purpose in life . . . before she found herself again.

Most important of all, we three girls found each other, when we became mystery shoppers. We were Charlie's Shopping Angels, using our secret cameras to record the best and worst in customer service. Along the way we happened to become the best of friends.

And we all expected to live happily ever after. Because isn't that what's supposed to happen?

'Mummeee! Done a poo! Wipe time!'

'Will?' I call out. 'It's your turn to sort Freddie out.'

'I'm in the middle of decorating the shop.'

'But I'm in the middle of something too.' OK. Maybe being in the middle of an idle daydream and a Kit Kat doesn't trump being eight feet up a ladder hanging dried cranberry garlands, but my secret shopping buddies would stand up for my right to enjoy a moment of Me Time. Sandie would say it's my duty to be assertive, to make up for centuries of female oppression, and Grazia would insist that a woman must be adored for mystique, not mundane tasks. All the same, I feel a little guilty.

The love of my life grunts. I hear heavy footsteps down the treads of the ladder and then up the steps to the flat.

'Mummeee!'

'Will's on his way, sweetheart.'

I take another bite of the Kit Kat. Where was I? Oh yes. Happy ever afters. The trouble is, fairy tales are so much more clear-cut than real life. In my wildest dreams, I never imagined I'd end up with an ex-husband (Duncan Prince, as far away from charming as it's possible to be) or that my son would have a stepdad who is anything but wicked. Unless you mean wicked in the cool and brilliant sense, willing to wipe bottoms and mop up midnight tears.

But happy ever after has not turned out to be what I expected at all. In my mind, happiness was like a tableau at Madame Tussaud's: me, Will and a toddler-sized Freddie, on the steps of our newly purchased shop, laughing, ready to sell dreams and beautiful things. We're looking our best: I'm a size ten (which I haven't been since Long Before Baby) and my hair's more blonde than mousy in the sun, with a designer fringe I've never quite managed with kitchen scissors. Will towers over me, cute as ever, and for once he's lost that permanently anxious look of his. Like waxworks, we were fixed in time, forever smiling.

But life's not like that. Instead we're a work-in-progress. Freddie is no longer a toddler. He's three and a half, with more personality than the entire line-up of *Britain's Got Talent*. He knows he's adored, not least because he has two male role models: the wonderful Will, plus Daddy, who is good for rough-and-tumble but would never be caught wiping anyone else's bottom (or tears, for that matter).

And two years after opening the shop, Will and I are still smiling, but we're not selling nearly enough of anything. In fact, the profits at Bell's Emporium are now lower than they were when we started out, which was definitely not the business model.

Then again, no one predicted the credit crunch would bugger up our happy ever after.

'Wheee!'

A pair of arms envelops my hips, using my body as a brake.

'Hello, Little Londoner. I hope you've washed your hands.'

Keen eyes stare up at me. He sidesteps the question completely. 'I'm not from London. I'm from Heartsneeze!' And then he fakes a sneeze, our little joke. Everything's a joke to Freddie.

We giggle. Heartsease Common is a funny place, a village in search of a purpose, with a few too many commuters and not quite enough community to connect us all together. Though the Emporium has helped. It used to be a dusty, loss-making hardware store that Will kept going despite the best efforts of his head office to close it down. And when the suits finally handed down the death sentence, the two of us brought it back to life, and renamed it Bell's Emporium after the original Mr Bell, who opened his first store on this spot almost a century ago.

'Shall we have a look at what Will's done in our shop?'

'Okey dokey,' says Freddie.

We head down the stairs from our flat, via the staffroom – more of a cubby-hole really – and then go through the door that always reminds me of Mr Benn's, onto the shop floor.

Will frowns when he spots us. 'Shut your eyes! I haven't finished yet!' He runs his hands through his dark curls – his hair needs cutting, as usual, but when would he find the time? – and tries to block the window display with his long body. He's a perfectionist, and we both know that more than ever before, getting this right *really* matters.

'Wow!' says Freddie, unable to keep his eyes closed.

I open my eyes, too.

Freddie's right. It is *very* wow. Thank Donner, Blitzen and the spirit of Father Christmas for that.

It could have gone either way. I'd decided on a classic red theme this year, before realising that Christmas comes in many shades of red: cranberry and poinsettia and holly berry and Santa suit and blood orange and reindeer-nose red. And then all the decorations arrived yesterday and they all clashed horribly, but it was too late to get new ones from the wholesaler's (and I think they're about to go bust anyway), so Will said he'd do his best with what we had.

So now we only have today, our precious Sunday off, to transform the shop from the haunted Halloween Hovel theme we'd adopted in September, into an irresistible Christmas Crunch-busting *destination* store. It's something we still haven't cracked: everyone agrees that the Emporium is fabulous fun. Big-hearted. The best shop for miles around. They're just never quite sure what we're selling . . . which I have to admit is a bit of an issue when you're trying to get the customers through the door.

We took down the fake cobwebs and the rubbery spiders this morning, and when I explained to Freddie that we had to pack them away neatly, 'for next year,' Will raised his eyebrows.

'What's that meant to mean?' I said huffily.

'Just that I love you for your optimism. As well as for everything else,' he said, and kissed me on the forehead.

We make a good team, Will and me. When one of us is feeling jaded or touchy or just plain knackered, the other one can normally summon up enough positivity for both of us. But we're having to face facts: optimism doesn't pay the rates, or the VAT man, or our suppliers (who're demanding payment up front: they say it's nothing personal, but when I can't sleep, I wonder if they've seen the writing on the wall for us).

'William Michael Powell, I do believe you've cracked it.'

He blushes, as he does at every compliment. Other women like a man with a brooding stare or abs of steel, but Will's blushes do it for me every time. Number one, they're so sweetly boyish. Number two, they, um, remind me of other blushworthy moments . . . and the fact that it was Will who made me feel like a sexy momma again, after so long feeling just like a frumpy mum.

'You think it'll do, then?'

I take another look. Even though it's not quite finished, it's riotous. The reds clash vibrantly, like a crimson and fire grotto. The smell puts the sneeze into Heartsneeze, a potent and spicy perfume of cinnamon, cloves, oranges and gingerbread. Will put on one of Freddie's Sing-along Christmas CDs on to help him get on with the decorating, and the manic cackling and warbling adds an additional dimension to the sensory overload.

OK, so it's nothing like the tasteful displays at the West End stores. It's more like the best pantomime bazaar in an opulent production of Aladdin, stuffed with festive treasures, from ruby red candles and sparkly tree decorations, to crystal tableware and jewel-studded bedroom slippers. How could anyone *not* know what we're about? We sell all the things that make a home feel like a home, a family feel like a family, and a life feel worth living.

'It's brilliant.'

He picks up a piece of shocking pink tinsel, shapes it into a circle and places it on my head. 'I now crown you the Queen of all things Christmassy.'

He leads me to the mirror. Oh, it was love at first sight when I saw that mirror at the wholesaler's. It's like something from a French courtesan's boudoir, a fur-coat-and-no-knickers affair, with gilded, blowsy roses carved into the wooden frame. I can't believe that someone hasn't bought it yet.

Then again, I'll be gutted when they do. It's been here eleven months, it's part of the furniture.

'See, it's your colour,' says Will, and I'm about to protest that shocking pink has never been my colour, too harsh against my fair hair and pale skin, when I see the two of us reflected back. I've never seen myself as beautiful, but when he looks at me like that, I can almost imagine that this short, plump, West Country girl really is a princess.

'Perfect,' I say.

He leans forward to kiss me, and when Freddie protests at being left out, Will lifts him up and kisses him too. 'It will make people buy, won't it, Em?'

Ah. There's the catch.

'Of course it will,' I say, though what do I know? Will's the one who has retail in his blood, who worked so hard to try to keep this place going when it was Bells & Whistles, the doomed hardware store. And he still failed.

7

That's another thing that keeps me awake at night. What if the store is cursed? Since I moved into the village, I've heard a few stories about the previous occupants: the original Mr Bell, who lost his wife on the Titanic. Or the son who drank himself to death.

I'd never say anything to Will, of course – he'd tell me off for letting my notorious imagination run out of control – but maybe even Mr Selfridge himself couldn't have made this place work.

I look up through the window, past the garlands and the holly and the berry-shaped fairy lights, and I see Sandie crossing the common. She marches towards the store, like a sergeant major coming to inspect the troops. I feel myself standing to attention, tucking a misbehaving curly strand of hair behind my ear and trying to pull the creases out of my T-shirt.

'Right, boys. Time for you two to go off and play football or darts or whatever other manly pursuits you want to enjoy. The girls are taking over.'

'Pub or poker, Fredster? What do you reckon?' Will winks at me.

'What's poker?' asks Freddie.

'It's a very, very boring card game played by men with whiskers and women who smell of wee,' I say hurriedly. Even though that's bridge. I don't want bloody Duncan accusing me of filling Freddie's head with gambling terminology.

'I reckon it's got to be the pub, then, mate,' Will says, taking my son's hand. 'Don't change the display too much while I'm gone. I don't want to come back and find it all girly.'

'I wouldn't dare. Not when I'm already outnumbered by the men in my life.' I give Freddie a quick hug before letting the two of them go upstairs to get mittened up. Then I go outside to view the displays from the front. Though of course, I'll adore it whatever it looks like, just like I adore everything about the shop, except for its takings.

I have to hope that it gets the Customer is King Consultancy's seal of approval . . .

Sandie is a big softie at heart, but you'd never know it to watch her now. Her face is set into a steely expression, and even though

8

she's let her hair grow a little from the helmet-head crop she had when we first met, there's something inscrutable about her. She's not working today, but she's still dressed for business, in a chocolate brown trouser suit a shade or two lighter than her skin. I catch a glimpse of leather boots at the ankle, polished to military standards.

Really, if I didn't know better, I'd be terrified.

'Hey, Sandie,' I say, waving at her. She smiles but holds up her hand to stop me getting closer. All her concentration is focused on Bell's Emporium – friendly greetings can wait. And as I'm getting her £120-an-hour expertise for the price of a cup of tea, I'm not arguing.

She begins her appraisal in the middle of the road, walking up and down to check the display from all angles. Then she takes several paces towards the store and pauses again, standing on the pavement in front of the window pane for a good two minutes.

'Can I hug you yet, Sandie? Or are you still carrying out your inspection?'

'What?' she looks confused. 'Oh. Yes. Yes, sorry, you know what I'm like. I can never find the "off" switch.'

I lean in to kiss her. 'That's what we love about you.' I breathe in her perfume. 'And what's that? It's fabulous.'

'Isn't it? Bought it in Paris last weekend. New limited edition Chanel. So secret I can't even divulge the number.' Her eyes widen with excitement. Fragrance and retail are her twin passions. OK, there's Toby too, and she's awfully fond of him, but I suspect he'd come a poor third if she was asked to choose.

'Well, whatever it's called, it smells like heaven. Are you coming in now, or are you going to give me the Customer is King verdict out here?'

'I'll come in.' She walks ahead of me, into the store. The first time we came here, when this was still a spit-and-sawdust hardware store, there was nothing welcoming about the entrance at all – in fact, I could barely manoeuvre my way in without knocking over mops and buckets and tins of paint. Now we've de-cluttered, with just one or two seasonal items at the door. Except, they're *last season's*. She looks down at the broomstick and pumpkin display and frowns.

'Sorry it's not quite finished. We're midway through the re-dressing.'

'First impressions, Emily. You'll never get a second chance to make a first impression.'

'Point taken,' I say, feeling suitably scolded. Sandie keeps walking and once she's in the main shop area, she closes her eyes, sniffs, then opens them again, before turning three hundred and sixty degrees. She inspects the shelf displays and, as I follow her gaze, I suddenly notice gaps between the reindeer tea-light holders, and an ugly lack of symmetry in the way the pine-cone table decorations are arranged.

I move towards them to even them out, but she shakes her head.

'That's easily fixed.'

Something in her tone makes me stop. 'But you've spotted something else that isn't?'

She turns her back on me, pretends to inspect further. Finally she sighs. 'I think . . . you've done a great job.'

'But?'

'I know I sound like a broken record, Emily, but it's the same problem as before.'

I sigh. 'Why would people come all the way out here unless we're being clear about what we're offering?'

She nods. 'It's not the products you've chosen. They're great. You have a terrific eye . . .' She tails off.

And now suddenly the smell is cloying and the colours seem to clash again and I feel a fool for imagining that Christmas could save us. The door opens behind me, and I turn to see Grazia striding into the shop. She is dressed extravagantly, in red and black – I do hope that's *fake* fur on her collar – with deep crimson lipstick and a wild halo of curly black hair.

'Emily! Sandie!' she cries, and is about to embrace us when she looks around the shop. 'This is magnificent! The colours, oh, they make me feel so festive, immediately.'

My mood is restored instantly. I am ridiculously susceptible to other people's opinions. We air-kiss.

'You are looking splendid, Emily. Your hair is so wonderful with that wave in it, you are the twin of Marilyn Monroe.'

There is, of course, no way I look like Marilyn's twin. More like Little Miss Muffet, after too much curds and whey.

'And Sandie, so smart as always. Really! Do you ever let your hair down?'

'Not if I can help it,' says Sandie, smiling.

But Grazia doesn't hear her, because Grazia is already in shopping mode. She places item after item on the counter by the till. 'I must have this napkin ring set, and the napkins to accompany it . . . oh, and this centrepiece for the table is so *English*. Adorable.'

Sandie and I watch her whizz around the small space, her stiletto heels tapping against the wooden floor like a crazed metronome.

'You know, Grazia, you don't have to,' I say.

'Have to what?'

'Buy our entire stock from us. Apart from anything else, there's no room for all this in your flat.'

'Pah!' She dismisses me with a flick of the hand. 'I have had enough minimalism to last my entire lifetime. This winter, I am choosing excess!'

I don't believe a word of it. Ever since Will and I set up the shop together she's been acting as fairy godmother. She loaned Will the money for the lease and the stock, pulled favours to get us write-ups in the glossy mags, and press-ganged wealthy friends into visiting us out here in the sticks. OK, she's had money to burn since she sold off her late husband's paintings, but she can't keep bailing us out for ever.

Eventually she runs out of steam. She leans on the counter, looking slightly flushed.

'I'll check those out for you later, Grazia. I think we could do with a drink first. Shopping's thirsty work, after all. And then there's the small matter of a forthcoming birthday to be celebrated.'

We head up to the flat, but before I can get out the tea-bags, Grazia's produced a bottle of Cristal from underneath her coat. I can't find any wine glasses in our cupboard, so she runs back downstairs again and brings up three rose pink crystal flutes from the glassware display. 'Add it to my account,' she says, with a wink.

'Cheers, girls,' I say, as I open the bottle, letting the cork pop up to the ceiling, missing the glass light fitting by millimetres.

Sandie gives me a reproving look. 'You know how many people lose their sight every year from champagne corks?'

'Party pooper!' says Grazia, and her vehemence makes me giggle.

We clink glasses together and take a sip – I've gained quite a taste for the finest champagne since Grazia turned into the merry widow.

'How long has it been?' I say, once we've each downed the best part of a glassful.

'Too long,' says Sandie. 'And before you say it, yes, I know it's all my fault. I'm just completely run ragged. Can you keep a secret?'

'We *are* secret shoppers!' I say indignantly.

'I'm in final negotiations to take over one of Charlie's biggest contracts.'

'Bloody hell! Go Sandie!' I say. Charlie used to be our boss at the old mystery shopping company, though he was the biggest mystery of all, hiding behind a shadowy Internet alias.

Grazia frowns. 'He will not like that.'

It's true: he even threatened to sue Sandie when she first set up the Customer is King Consultancy, but he backed down when he realised she wasn't the type to get rattled.

Sandie shrugs. 'I've left his work alone for over a year, but it turns out most of his contacts don't trust him any further than they can throw him. Which means I'm picking up more work than I can handle. I even sent Gramma on an assignment the other day.'

I've never met Sandie's grandmother, but she has a formidable reputation. 'Where?'

'Couple of burger takeaway joints.'

How did she get on?'

'Actually she was great. Very picky. Her toilet inspection was the most thorough I've ever seen. And she was very hot on trans-fats. Only problem is that she's so intimidating that even the kid behind the counter gave her service worthy of the Ritz. Speaking of which. Grazia?'

'Not more hotels, Sandie,' sighs Grazia. 'I am so tired of sleeping in someone else's bed.'

I giggle. 'Now that sounds interesting.'

'Alone. Alas. Though I am planning to make changes in that direction.'

'Who is it? Who?' I clap my hands together – when we started secret shopping we were all single, and now that I've found Will and Sandie's got Toby, there's nothing I want more than for Grazia to find someone and live happily ever after too. Widowhood just isn't her style – she's far too passionate.

'No one in particular. I have decided that as tomorrow is a *milestone* birthday, shall we say, it is time for me to move on from Leon.'

'A milestone?' says Sandie. 'You told us you were forty-one. Though, now I think of it, I'm sure you told us the same last year. And the year before.'

'I will be forty-five,' Grazia says. 'I did not mean to lie. I have been in denial. But enough of this denial! Time to act.'

'Who are you going to *act* with?' I ask.

She shrugs. 'Let us say, I am considering a number of candidates.'

They've never gone in for confessions, my colleagues. They take the bloody secret bit far too seriously. 'Go on. Give us a clue.'

'I cannot say. But it will be someone distinguished. A gentleman.'

'You still can't resist that posh Englishman thing, can you?' I say.

'Leon was hardly the epitome of posh. He was definitely nouveau riche. Which is why I am, this time, ruling out any man who has not attended one of the major public schools. I do not want to be reminded of my late husband. And a privately educated man should have good manners, at least.'

'I wouldn't bank on it,' Sandie says ruefully. 'And they tend to have very close relationships with their mummies, who are usually quite terrifying.'

Now I turn my gossip antennae towards Sandie. 'Has Toby finally told his mother about you, then?'

'Only because she was trying to matchmake him with yet another highly suitable girl from the Home Counties. She really has no idea at all that he's already been propositioned by half of them. That is, she didn't have any idea until he put her right.'

'And does she know . . . um . . .' I tail off, unsure how to put it.

'That I'm a Brummie? That I'm a shop girl? Or that I'm black?'

'Er. All three, I suppose.'

She groans. 'He's told her we met at work. She threw enough of a wobbler over that to be going on with, he said. He insists she's not racist but there's a big difference between observing cultural diversity on BBC documentaries from the comfort of your Gloucestershire estate, and seeing it in your own living room, holding your darling son's hand.'

'Drawing room, surely?' says Grazia.

'So when are you meeting her?'

Sandie groans again. 'She's only gone and invited me for Christmas. The *whole* of Christmas. The full Christmas Eve through to Boxing Day stately home experience at Bambourne Manor.'

I gulp. 'But what about your grandmother?'

'That's what I said to Toby. She'll go ballistic if I leave her alone at Christmas. He said she could come too.'

'You could always say no to the lady of the manor . . .' I suggest.

She exhales loudly. 'I tried that. Toby sulked for twenty-four hours before admitting he's pretty terrified of his mother himself and wouldn't want to cross her. He thought she was about to put him over her knee and give him a spanking when he admitted that we'd been seeing each other for almost a year without her knowledge.'

'I think it is a marvellous opportunity,' says Grazia. 'The roaring fires, the dinner, the carol service in their own chapel, the Boxing Day hunt. I take it they do hunt?'

'I've no idea. They probably hunt down lower-middle-class interlopers with the gall to get ideas above their station.'

'It might turn out OK. I thought it'd be bloody awful when I met Will's parents. You know his dad was high up in the Army? I was convinced I'd be frogmarched off the premises for being a divorced mother-of-one from the wrong side of Somerset. But they were good as gold.'

'From what Toby has told me about Mother Garnett, I have this horrible feeling I won't be welcomed into the bosom of the family.'

'One of the best things about being a foreigner is that I escape definition,' Grazia says. 'Which is why nothing you say will put me off the landed gentry.'

Sandie smiles. 'Don't worry, I'll see if I can scout out any gentlemen of a certain age for you before I get thrown out of the house party.'

'Ah, I plan to have got the whole troublesome business of sex out of the way well before then.'

Sandie and I stare at each other. Grazia never fails to amaze me. 'What's the rush? I mean, you've been widowed for four years now. Shouldn't you wait till you find Mr Right?'

'You always were the great romantic, Emily. But I am simply being realistic. Every day when I wake and examine myself in the mirror, the truth stares back at me. I must shift myself, while I still have a vestige of my former good looks to attract a man.'

'Don't be daft, Grazia, you're gorgeous.' And she is. She is the most glamorous woman I know.

But she holds up her hands and for the first time, I look beyond the French manicure, and see that the skin on the back of her hands is crepey. 'Emily, Emily. I am simply being realistic. Beauty has a best-before date. Even the most stunning Italian frescoes show their age and then crumble to dust. In my case, it may be time to consider restoration work, though it will never be quite the same.'

'If you say so,' I tell her, 'but if I was a man I'd shag you, no worries. And I hope you'll tell us after the event. In the meantime, shall we do a toast? To Grazia getting her groove back on her birthday?' I hold up my glass – Grazia's glass, really, I must remember to charge her for it – and the others join in.

'To Grazia's groove,' says Sandie.

'To my long lost libido,' says Grazia. 'But enough. We have wasted too much time on men now. You mentioned assignments?'

'Yup.' Sandie puts her glass down. 'Actually I think I have the perfect ones for both of you.'

I shake my head. 'I can't take the time off, Sandie, not when the shop is at such a critical point.'

'It won't count as work. Freddie will love it—'

'You can't get round me that way.'

'—and so will you. It might even give you ideas for the shop.'

I sigh, feeling my resistance melting away. 'Go on then, tell me. I know you won't stop until you have.'

'It's Operation Grotto Fabulous. I need a mother and child to tour the major Christmas displays and grottos across London and the South East. Rate-my-Santa. Come on, Em. I know you're a sucker for tinsel.'

'Well . . . I couldn't do all that many.'

'As many as you can take on. Even a few would help. And there are some gorgeous ones this year. The Snow Queen. Hansel and Gretel's Gingerbread Feast. The Wind in the Willows. Even Garnett's is on the list. I'll save the best ones for you.'

I nod. Actually I can't imagine anything more fun than touring the loveliest winter-themed stores, and watching Freddie's face as he meets more Father Christmases than a little boy has any right to. It certainly beats standing in our own shop, trying to do a Derren Brown on the passers-by to hypnotise them into coming in. 'Send me through the details.'

'And what do you have for me, Sandie?' asks Grazia. 'I mean it about the hotel rooms. I already have another five booked in before Christmas. Room service becomes so samey. If I see another Club Sandwich, I may go loco and stab the poor waiter with the cocktail stick.'

Sandie pretends to look hurt. 'And there was me thinking you liked that life. Right. I'll send Gramma next time. No . . . what I have in mind for you, well, I hope you won't take this the wrong way. It's based purely on your profile. And, um, well, you did say . . .'

'Spit it out.'

'The Operation is called Deep Freeze. It's about beauty salons. The, um, medical kind.'

A muscle twitches in Grazia's left cheek. But then she laughs. 'You would like me to check out cosmetic surgery?'

'You don't have to go through with it,' Sandie says hastily. 'It's one of Charlie's old contracts, from the people who regulate the clinics. They just want to check on standards, including over-selling. But they specified a glamorous woman over forty as the mystery shopper, and while Gramma is certainly over forty, she fails the other stipulation quite comprehensively.'

Grazia smiles calmly. 'Stop. No more. I will do this Deep Freeze, of course. I was considering the non-surgical options in any case so this will be a piece of cake.'

'Thanks. Both of you. I feel better now I have my top shoppers on board. All I need now is the perfect person for my third festive project.'

'And it's not something we could do?' I ask, feeling slightly hurt that she doesn't trust us.

'Em. You're impossible. A minute ago you said you didn't have time for anything else. Besides, you don't have the qualifications, I'm afraid.'

All my insecurities flood back: I took my GCSE Maths three times before admitting defeat. The fact that a) I worked in a bank and b) my ex-husband was a prodigy who did mental arithmetic in exchange for drinks in our local made my incompetence even more shameful, as he never failed to remind me. *'Well, with me around, babe, you don't need a head for figures. You just need a figure that turns heads.'*

Ha. And I fell for those lines for more than a decade. Shame they didn't teach common sense to GCSE level.

'So what is this oh-so-bloody-tricky assignment that's beyond Grazia and me?'

'Operation Christmas Crunch. And unless either of you have a secret history as a store security guard, then you don't have what it takes. Because this one involves tracking the prevalence of the

17

only seasonal figure who pops up more often at this time of year than Santa Claus.'

'Simon Cowell?' I guess.

'I'm talking about the Shop Lifter.'

Chapter Two

Christmas. Hate it. Hate every last breath-freezing, mince pie-eyed, Rudolph-the-red-nosed moment of it. Oh, and it brings out the worst in the bloody customers. Which then brings out the worst in me.

'I don't suppose you have any quinces?'

Yeah. Sure. Hidden down the front of my top. One in each bra cup. I stare at the woman – a slim, suited-and-booted type who is probably only slumming it here with the common people because hubby's lost his job in the City – before shrugging. 'What?'

'Quince. It's a fruit.'

'What's it look like?'

She sighs. 'You're the greengrocer. You should be telling me.'

'I'm just filling in. So you could shove a quince up my arse and I still wouldn't recognise it. You're gonna have to describe one.'

'Oh. Well, in the recipe book, the picture shows them already made into a jelly. I don't know. Green, maybe? With tiny seeds in it?'

I look down at the stall. 'I could do you an apple.'

She tuts. 'What about a pomegranate?'

I tut back. I want to tell her this is Shepherd's Bush Market, not Harrods Food Hall. But instead I make a big show of poking around between the bananas and the pears. 'Sorry. I thought it might be shy.'

She runs her fingers through her hair, which is showing far too much regrowth. I give her my nastiest mad-chav face and she backs away, gripping her *I am not a plastic bag* holdall to her skinny waist.

'That's it,' I say, barely under my breath. 'Off you pop, back to Waitrose, where you belong.'

And then, seconds later, I catch sight of myself in the metal bowl of the scales. *Shit.* My face is twisted in hate: I look like a bitter, scrawny fishwife.

Now I feel ashamed. I've lost Mickey a customer who might have spent hundreds over the years on posh fruit and veg. He doesn't pay me to put them off: he pays me because, when I'm on top form, I could sell hummus to the Lebanese supermarket, or hash to Dad's dealer mate, Woody.

I almost want to run after the woman and be nicer, explain that I didn't mean to be rude, I was just . . .

But what is my excuse? A bad day at the office? Pre-Menstrual Tension? Pre-Yuletide Tension?

The truth is that I'm jealous. I want her struggles. I want a City husband who is using his extra free time to train for a triathlon. I want her fridge full of premium brands instead of own-brand food. I want her wardrobe of last season's quality designer labels that will stand the test of time. And her network of buddies from her boarding school, and her good degree from a good university, and her well-bred children, who're trying not to whinge too much about the cut in pocket money.

I want her life. But the ugly me in the scales is scowling back, saying, forget it, Kelly, you had your chances. You blew them. Everything about you is downmarket: your weed-stunted ex-boyfriends, your quince-free junk-food diet, your dumb clothes and your pointless Grade D GCSE in Food Technology (which never even touched on quince). You're going nowhere. You've had twenty-four years to get used to it.

This is *your* life.

'Dad? Dad, where are you?'

The flat is in darkness, but I can smell him. Not BO – there are some things no one can put up with in a housemate, even if they're family – but the distinctive Eau de Terry Wright. He smells of Cidal antibacterial soap, Superdrug Musk aftershave, and a malty sweetness, like just-baked whisky cake.

'Shhh.'

I step into the living room, tripping over someone's shoes. OK, my shoes. Can I help it that I've sunk as low as he has?

'Dad, why are you sitting here in the dark?'

'Don't turn on the light.'

I hesitate, my hand halfway to the light switch, then decide it's better not to antagonise him if he's in one of his moods. And there's just about enough light coming from the dodgy bulb in the cooker hood, the record-breaking one that we can't turn off. Ever. That bulb has been on for nine years now, almost as long as we've lived here. I lost my virginity under its miraculous glow, back in the days before I decided that men weren't worth giving the time of day to.

As my eyes adjust to the gloom, I see Dad hunched in the far corner of the sofa. Cowering, almost.

'At least let me put the heating on. It was freezing on the stall today, they reckon it'll be minus two tonight. Unless the card meter's run out again?'

'No. There's still credit. I'd just rather people thought there was nobody home.'

Oh shit. 'People in general? Or somebody in particular?'

He says nothing. I switch on the kettle, then turn up the thermostat. My fingers are already tingling from the cold. Though it'd be ten times worse if we didn't have people below us – the family downstairs bicker constantly and noisily, and their cooking smells can be hard to bear on the nights when all we've got in the cupboard is out-of-date beans. But they save us a fortune in gas bills: since the elderly mother came over from Argentina to live with them, they have to keep the flat heated to tropical levels.

'Like the effing United Nations, our block,' Dad always says. Well, thank Christ for that or we'd freeze to death some nights.

I sit down next to him on the sofa. The malty smell is strong. He's been drinking. I can't see his face and he's wearing grey tracksuit bottoms and a grey sweatshirt pulled taut across his belly, camouflaged into the darkness.

'Who is it this time?'

'What?'

'Dad. Don't dick me about, yeah? I live here too. I think I deserve to know who's after you.'

He grunts. 'Why d'you always assume the worst?'

I stand up to make the tea. 'I can't imagine. Oh, hang on. It might be something to do with the time Big Eddie came after you for three hundred quid and wouldn't let me out of the flat until you found it.'

'Now, that was a fuss about no—'

'Or then there was the time the bailiffs turned up and wanted to take the telly Mum bought for my eighteenth birthday.'

'Don't bring her into it.'

'Why not, Dad, because— owww.'

'What?'

'I've just poured boiling water over my hand. That's what comes of making tea in the dark.' I run the cold tap over my palm until I can't feel it any more.

'Oh, do me one, will you, Kelly? I'm parched, haven't wanted to get up all afternoon, in case they're watching the flat window.'

'What about using the toilet?'

He holds up his whisky glass. Full to the brim with brown liquid . . .

'You didn't? You dirty sod—'

'Course I didn't. What do you take me for?'

I carry over the teas. 'I'm not going to answer that.' He reaches out for his tea but I pull it away. 'You're not getting this till you tell me the truth. How much do you owe?'

'Well . . . it *was* a grand.'

'A grand?' A deep chill goes through me.

'It's gone up. Interest, according to Phil.'

'Phil? As in, Phil the Cheat? Oh, Dad. Will you never learn? How much has it gone up?'

'Five.'

'Oh, well, that's quite reasonable, by Phil's standards . . .' I stop. 'You don't mean a fiver, do you? You mean five hundred.'

He nods, and takes his tea. I'm too gobsmacked to resist. Instantly I begin the kind of calculation that's become second nature for me. How much are we worth? I've got forty quid in my purse, my payment for manning the fruit and veg stall. We've pawned the telly before, and the DVD player and the Xbox and my computer, but each time it gets less: maybe four hundred, if we're lucky. And how many days filling in on the market will it take to get them back?

I give up.

'How could you mess up like this again, Dad? You promised you'd get help.'

He shrugs. 'It was meant to be the last time. I had this system, found it on the Internet . . . it was guaranteed.'

'Except it wasn't, was it? No one ever wins playing against Phil. You should know that.'

'I just wanted . . . I thought I could buy you something nice.'

'Don't pull that one. We both know it's got bugger all to do with the money. It's the buzz. Always has been, always will be. You're a lost cause.' I put down my tea, without taking a sip. It's served its purpose – my hands are warmer now. Though my palm stings like hell. I stand up, pull on my coat, grab my bag, and head for the door.

'Where are you going, Kelly love?'

'Out. To sort things. Like every other time.'

'Be careful, yeah?'

Despite my irritation, I feel touched. He's not a hundred per cent self-centred. 'Yeah.'

'Make sure no one sees you leave. They might have seen me. They'll come in after me if they realise I'm alone.'

I take it back. One hundred per cent me, me, me.

The pavement outside the flats glistens with newly-formed ice. A cloud of white steam puffs from the extractor fan on the wall of the chippy, like the breath of an asthmatic dragon. The gaudy lights of second-hand shops and off-licences make even the Goldhawk Road look festive, if you're that way inclined.

What the hell do I do now?

I could walk, couldn't I? There's nothing keeping me here except sentiment, and nothing I would miss from the flat except bad clothes and bad memories.

23

My mother's words from eight years ago echo round my brain, as they always do when Dad goes back to Square One. 'No one could judge me for leaving, Kelly. I've done my share. And you could still come with me. No one would judge you, neither.'

And I don't have to go as far as bloody Australia, do I? I could get on the Tube right now, take a train from Marylebone or Euston or King's Cross. Find out how far my forty quid would take me, off-peak. I might not have any qualifications but I know how to survive . . .

Yeah, right, Kelly. If you're such a survivor, then how come you're shaking like a junkie on a detox? How come as soon as you walk outside the flat or the safety of the market your cockiness disappears and you spend so much time looking over your shoulder it's a wonder you don't have a permanent black eye from walking into things?

So no Australia for me. Instead I walk towards Westfield Shopping Centre, the glass palace of retail excess that seems to mock all of us poor sad sods who live nearby. Then I change my mind. You don't shit on your own patch, and anyway, the place is deserted half the time. No good for me. I need it to be busy for my kind of shopping trip.

I walk towards the bus stop, where a dozen people are already waiting. A mum and a kid, a couple of old fellas, a gang of teen-age girls. All heading for the West End, where the stores stay open late, even on a Monday, desperate to attract in the customers.

For a spot of late night shopping . . .

Garnett's is packed. I dunno if anyone's buying, but they're definitely browsing. Carols play, the smell of gingerbread floats out of the air con vents, and the decorations are themed, just like they always are. It's Peter Pan crossed with Winter Wonderland this year: Tinker Bell fairy lights and pirate ships and fake snow. Mum and me used to come up here with her mates every November around this time. Just to look, of course. Looking costs nothing, Mum said.

I start in the beauty department, buy a cheap lipstick from the teen range, and ask for it to be gift-wrapped, in a lovely big glossy red bag. I keep my hood up.

'Still freezing out there, is it?' the girl behind the till asks me.

'Yeah. I just can't seem to get warm.'

Then the real work begins. The top brands are hopeless, everything's kept behind the counter, but the mid-ranges sell better in the pubs, anyhow. No one believes that your Estée Lauders aren't faked. But off-the-shelf serums, eye-creams, eye-liners, lipgloss, mascara. They're the bankers.

I lose myself in the crowd, and head towards women's fashion accessories. Don't think. Keep moving. Stay on automatic pilot. I'm doing this one last time. Then it's time for an ultimatum – another ultimatum but this time I mean it – to my father. Get help, or I'm off.

I look round the shelves: hats, tights, gloves, bags. Big bags. I'm up there with the fashion trends this season. My bag's enormous.

A beret. I'll have that. And so many lovely colours. I can't choose between them. Devore scarves. Great for Christmas presents. Leather gloves in black and burgundy: so much warmer than fleece, and much more classy and discreet. They squash up lovely and small in your pocket. No bulk.

Don't think, Kelly. Just do.

Wolford tights. They don't ladder, ladies, like the cheap ones do. And couldn't we all do with a nice new wallet? Even if there's nothing to put in it? I know I could.

A quick glance over my shoulder. I've been shopping so long, I need a wee now. Ladies is on the third floor, always nice to have a bit of privacy. Examine your shopping, make sure there's nothing wrong with them, and that there's no tags attached. Wouldn't want an embarrassing scene at the exit . . . I'll take the escalator, see if anything else catches my eye on my journey.

'Excuse me, miss? I hope you are intending to pay for your items.'

The voice is male, Spanish-sounding. Firm. Not hostile but not friendly either. Even before I turn around I can picture the uniform: navy blue jacket with faked military gold-braid epaulettes and a white shirt and black tie underneath. I take a deep breath. I might need to run for it. How far is it to the main doors? Once I turn I have a split second to decide, on instinct, whether I

25

can outrun the security guard. Please God I've got a fat wheezer on thirty a day.

But when I do turn, I flinch. Because he is fat, this guy, with short legs and a chubby, toffee-coloured face, his cheeks already flushed from the nervous tension of catching a thief. I could run rings around him. But it wouldn't do me any good, because . . .

'Kelly?'

'Luis?'

'Oh, Kelly. What are you doing?'

Luis, my downstairs neighbour. Luis, the man who keeps us warm when we can't afford the heating. Luis, whose raucous family singalongs and Latin American music give Dad and me an all too vivid idea of what life could be like if he wasn't a gambling addict and I wasn't a petty criminal.

So much for not shitting on my own patch.

Chapter Three

Grazia

'More fizz?'

The man sitting opposite me doesn't wait for an answer, but fills my glass with a little too much enthusiasm. Foam bubbles over the brim. I wonder if this is any clue to what I should expect later.

'Thank you, James. This is *such* a treat.'

'My pleasure, my dear.'

Is it my imagination, or did he wink after saying *pleasure?* Oh, this is too, too difficult for me. I do not flirt. I am too direct for that. When I see what I want, I go for it. When I met my husband, he recognised that – and knew instantly that we were kindred spirits.

But Leon was not the typical Englishman and I have to face facts: I have no idea how to behave around the real thing. I sense that I may scare off the quintessential gentleman, unless I find the right approach. Even at twenty, I would have struggled to be a coquette. At forty-five, it is surely laughable. Instead, I will employ flattery.

'Tables at this restaurant are gold dust since that review in the *Sunday Times*,' I say, even though I have eaten here – and paid for dinner myself – twice since it opened. 'Was it terribly difficult to get a reservation?'

'Oh, my dear, it's been a few years since my name alone could bump Madonna off the top table, but I like to think I still have influence where it matters.'

James smiles. Or perhaps the correct word would be 'twinkles'. He is attractive, for a man of . . . well, he claims to be fifty-five, but my Internet research suggests a decade has slipped his otherwise razor-sharp mind. And, after all, I have shaved six years off my own age.

He wears it well, every inch the newsreader he used to be. Tanned and fit from golf, a generous head of unashamedly black-and-white hair, a firm jaw. The only surprise is that he isn't still appearing on early evening bulletins, as everyone knows a distinguished man has double the on-screen life expectancy of a woman. I looked for clues on our previous two dates, but he appears to drink for pleasure, not oblivion, and though he acknowledges the supermodel beauty of our waitresses, he still pays more attention to me.

Yes. He is perfect for what I have in mind. Of course, Emily and Sandie think I am crazy, but they do not understand. I identify a problem, I take action to resolve it. In this case, my problem is of an intimate nature, but that does not mean it should be ignored. I was never a cold woman, yet since Leon died, *that* side of me has been dormant. It is not that I lack the company of attractive men, so perhaps I have simply forgotten how to experience these feelings. And the best way to kick start them is to allow myself to be seduced . . . or, as the English say, to get back in the saddle.

The streamlined sommelier hovers discreetly.

'Will you be taking wine with your meal, sir?'

'I do hope so. You will be drinking, my dear?'

'Oh yes.'

He twinkles again. 'That's what I always love about the more . . . mature woman,' he says, addressing the sommelier, man-to-man. 'Not ashamed to reveal their *appetites*.'

Dinner is over too soon. The earthy Italian food is every bit as delicious as it was on my previous visits – and thankfully nothing at all like Mama used to make – but my mouth is dry and no matter how many glasses of wine I drink, it is still difficult to eat.

I began to suspect halfway through the starter of bread and tomato soup that he knew I had made up my mind. By dessert, he was making schoolboy innuendoes about the pick-me-up-powers of the tiramisu. And now the bill is paid, the petits fours are eaten and I am dragging out my coffee – difficult when I was stupid enough to order only my usual espresso. The last sips are cold and I try not to flinch at the bitter taste.

'How was that, my dear?'

'Wonderful.' I cast my eyes downwards, attempting coyness.

'I agree. The food was outstanding. But the company even better.' He looks theatrically at his watch. 'You know, the only thing I miss about being married was the rare evenings like these, when everything seemed quite perfect, and yet I knew the best was yet to come . . .'

He is, I will admit, a little cheesy. But my doubts are probably more to do with the fact that James is not Leon. All widows must go through this rite of passage, to become used to another man's way of speaking and way of loving . . .

Loving?

Ah, Grazia, this is what you came here for, after all.

'Grazia?'

I look up in surprise – he has used my name so rarely tonight that I wondered whether he had forgotten it. 'I am sorry. I, too, was thinking of the past. It is self-indulgent, however. One must keep ones eyes fixed forward.'

He chuckles. 'Right now, my eyes are fixed forward, my dear.' And he nods towards my breasts. 'And what a delightful view I have of . . . what I hope might be the immediate future.'

I attempt a flirtatious smile, and hope I have no spinach between my teeth.

'Now. Call me a naughty boy if you like, but I have taken the perhaps overly-confident step of checking my favourite room is available in my club. I wondered whether you might join me there. We can talk, drink, get to know each other even better . . .'

I hesitate. For two years after his death, it felt as though I could

29

hear Leon's voice in my head at difficult times, advising me in typically opinionated fashion what to do. A temporary madness brought on by grief, I realise now, but sometimes I do miss it. I had spent so long doing what he wanted, that it is still so difficult to make my own decisions.

I take a breath: my head is swimming from the wine. 'James. We are both adults. You do not require privacy for talking. But yes, I will be delighted to accompany you.'

He winks. 'Direct, aren't we, my dear? I appreciate that in a woman.' He stands up, lands a kiss on my cheek that then gravitates towards my left earlobe, and then gestures towards the waiter for our coats. 'Time to go, I think.'

At his club, the receptionist gives me a knowing look. How many women has he signed in before – this year, this month, even this week? I have to work hard to stop myself leafing back through the visitors' book and finding out for myself.

But no. The decision has been made.

The room is small and the most favourable description I would give it in a secret shopping report would be shabby chic. Clubbish, of course, in browns and creams, with two dark leather armchairs, a bookshelf of second-hand Penguin novels, and, in the corner, a too-small TV that says, *if you are boring enough to want to watch television while you're staying here, then you don't deserve your membership.* The room is not dirty, exactly, but I am not sure it would pass the 'check under the bed test'. The bed itself – the centre of attention, I suppose – is a queen-size, with fresh white linen and a reassuring woollen blanket that probably reminds guests of cold, homesick nights in their dorms at boarding school. The bathroom will almost certainly be equipped with vintage Armitage Shanks and—

'It is rather cosy, isn't it?' says James, mistaking my scrutiny for approval. His arm snakes around my waist and I try to relax into it, to focus on his subtle aftershave and the confident pressure of his hand.

He releases me, gestures towards the chairs, and as I sit down, he retrieves a bottle of cognac from inside a hollowed out copy of the Bible. 'This is one of the reasons why this is my favourite room. It's not even my booze, it's my friend Arthur's, but we play this game where we stash bottles about the place. Hide and seek for alcoholics.' He disappears into the bathroom, reappears with two crystal tumblers and pours generous measures into each. 'Oh, and they have a better class of tooth mug here.'

He hands me the cognac, we clink glasses, and sip simultaneously. It delivers a warm shock to my tongue and throat.

'Excellent cognac.'

'Arthur always has good taste in brandy,' says James, standing close to me now, or perhaps it simply seems that way, 'though not in women. I am the opposite.'

And he leans down, and kisses me on the lips, so gently that I am almost more aware of the vapour and taste of the cognac than I am of the kiss. I close my eyes, and I hear him put the glass down, and as he begins to kiss more fiercely, it occurs to me that perhaps I should put my own glass down, too.

Then it happens. Nerve endings that had been snoozing for two years begin to wake up, and James seems to sense it, because his arms rest on my shoulders, then begin to pull me up from the chair, and I feel infused with light. I think then of Leon, and have to swat away memories like mosquitoes in summer.

And then I allow myself to slip towards a place where thought does not matter, although I do fleetingly worry about what he will think of my forty-five-year-old breasts and my forty-five-year-old skin and all the rest.

But then I put James back in his place. He is my gateway lover, a staging post on my return to the dating world. All that matters is that we should both enjoy . . . ahem . . . the ride.

Afterwards.

James has opened the window and is smoking, poking his head out through the gap to breathe away the smoke.

I would join him – I have a strange, unexpected desire for a cigarette myself, even though Leon and I gave up together five years ago – but I sense he needs his space. And so do I.

I am not one for graphic descriptions of sex: Emily will have to wait a long time for details of my lover's prowess or anatomy. I cannot think of sex in this way.

But my mood now is agitated, unsatisfied. James is a different man from Leon, physically and mentally, and what we have just done was different in sensation and meaning to what I did with my husband. It was good to feel such feelings again, and he wanted to make sure I experienced pleasure, although I sensed this had more to do with his own ego than any particular concern for my well-being.

And then, an instant after we finished, the spell was broken. He got up from the bed almost immediately, to find his cigarettes, and has now smoked three. Even though he is nothing to me, I feel vulnerable. Naked, despite the cover of the sheet.

'Is it cold out there?' I say eventually.

He turns, seemingly surprised I am still there. 'Is there a draught? One feels it more at our age, don't you find?'

I bristle. *Such rudeness.* I can only think that he is one of those men who feel vulnerable, not invincible, after sex. 'Yes. Perhaps I should be wearing one of your British bedjackets to keep me warm.'

He scowls, closes the window with a sulky slam, and then heads for the brandy bottle, pouring himself a measure. I try to remember where I put my own glass, and find it by the side of the bed. I hold it up, and he refills it with a slight sneer. 'We like a drink, don't we, dear . . .'

Why does *dear* sound so much nastier than *my dear*? I don't answer him. He climbs back onto the bed beside me, but leaves a chilly distance between us.

Leon used to cling to me afterwards, as though I was his energy source.

'Been a while, then, eh, Grazia?'

I am beginning to wish I was anywhere but here. 'Since what?'

He shrugs. 'But you're in decent shape. To be honest, I don't tend to date women my age—'

I am about to point out that, according to my research, he is at least twenty years older than me, but I do not think he is listening to me any more.

'—but you were intriguing. And now I must say that in the dark, I don't think I'd have known the difference.'

'Only in the dark?' I say it before I think.

32

An 'and finally' newsreader smile spreads across his face. 'I wouldn't wish to be unchivalrous, but none of us is immune to gravity. Or a certain *loosening*.'

I cannot help myself. I look down. Loosening? Is that a nice word for sag? I like to think I have a realistic view of my own shortcomings, but when I examine my chest, I now see stretch marks and mottled skin where previously I simply saw me.

He slaps me on the thigh, through the quilt. 'But don't be down in the dumps. You're not short of money, are you? There is so much to be done these days. You don't even need to go under the knife. Lasers are good.'

'Lasers?'

'The wife swore by them. Great for the neck and titties. And though that olive skin of yours wears better than English pallor, it does risk looking somewhat sallow. But a quick zap, and you're fixed in your lunch hour. Then there are fillers to plump out sunken cheeks. I'm not a fan of Botox personally, but that frown of yours has the unfortunate side effect of making you seem awfully cross the whole time. If you look in the mirror now, for example, you look absolutely livid.'

I try not to listen – to screen out his words, to dismiss them as the peculiar obsession of a man who hates women – but it is hard not to conclude that the nips and tucks I had seen as a vague possibility are, in fact, urgently required. 'You seem to know a lot about this, James.'

'Ah.' He taps the side of his nose. 'Ah, well. I don't make a habit of admitting this, but I have had the odd *tweak*.'

'I am surprised. I thought you looked exactly your age.'

He gives me a strange look, trying to decide whether I am joking. He smiles. 'I am lucky that not much is required, thanks to my God-given bone structure, but every six months, I do attend a certain Harley Street clinic for a touch-up. A few vials of youth serum in the right places and ten minutes later I have a spring in my step again.'

'I would never have guessed.'

'Precisely the point, old girl. Now. Don't take this the wrong way, but I'd be happy to give you my dermatologist's number. Here.' He tears a scrap of paper from the pad on the bedside

33

table, and scribbles something down. 'That number's like gold dust, I wouldn't normally share it, but under the circumstances . . .' He leers at me.

I take the paper, and reach out of bed to put it in my handbag. 'I do not know what to say.'

'You're embarrassed. Don't be. You said it yourself, we're both adults.' He takes a sip of brandy. 'And while we're being grown-up, you don't have to stay, you know? I'm sure we're of an age where we don't have to do the whole "spending the night together" thing. The lure of one's own bed can be powerful, eh?'

It takes me a moment to realise I am being dismissed. And another moment to realise he is right: I do not wish to stay here with him for a moment longer. My own Egyptian cotton sheets have never seemed so appealing. 'Quite,' I say.

'Lizzy on reception will get you a cab, let me call down.' He picks up the phone but I wave him off.

'Please do not worry,' I say, leaning down to pick up my clothes from the floor, and then clutching them towards my body as I head for the bathroom to dress. 'I need some fresh air.'

And when I finally escape into the raw London night, I am thankful for the anonymity that the fog affords.

There! It is done.

Admittedly, my choice of suitor was an appalling one, and my ability to judge character has let me down. Then again, at least I have no desire ever to see that man and his loathsome, smug, injected face again.

So I am middle-aged. I cannot kid myself any more. His comments have caused a shift in me, one that is not welcome. Whereas before I regarded cosmetic 'work' as a hypothetical possibility, something to consider one day, I now know I will be taking Sandie's latest task, Operation Deep Freeze, more seriously than I would have liked.

But with age come some benefits. One, at least this encounter is an end in itself. I am hardly going to end up pregnant and ruined. Two, I know what while I might be showing my age, at least I have integrity – unlike that man and his missing decade.

Regrets are for cowards. I will move on. The single regret I will permit myself is that I did not ask James why, when he invested so much in his appearance, he had not asked the dermatologist to eliminate his jowls.

Chapter Four

Sandie

'Your turn.'

'No way, Brains,' Toby mumbles from under the duvet. 'It's yours. And you've got to get up anyway.'

We lie in bed, waiting for one of us to break the stalemate. Normally I'd give in first, because he's right, I do have to get up anyway, to begin my daily quest to reach the summit of Mount To-Be-Done. Knowing before I even switch on the laptop that I won't make it past base camp, because some other crisis will inevitably arise.

After two years running the business on my own, it's getting more exhausting, not less. Still, today I'm interviewing for my first ever employee: part Person Friday (the classifieds people wouldn't let me put *Girl* Friday) and part professional secret shopping operative. My problems could be solved by this afternoon.

The thought gives me just enough energy to get up.

'OK, Toby. You win. You layabout toffs are all the same. Expecting to be waited on hand and foot.' As I push slippers onto my feet, the dog jumps off the bed and begins to take terrier-sized leaps into the air next to me. 'But you can take Monty out this morning. I have far too much to do.'

I follow the dog into the kitchen, and watch the river while the kettle boils. Mist rises from the water like steam from coffee. The first time I saw the view from Toby's penthouse, he threw me out because he thought I was a thief. And even though I've lived here for a year now, I still can't quite believe that this fabulous view is mine to enjoy over my morning Earl Grey.

But for how much longer? Only six weeks until I meet Mother Garnett. Toby claims she's a pussycat, but I've googled her and one profile of the dynasty describes her as 'a matriarch who stays out of the limelight, but considered by many to be the string-puller behind the scenes. Reportedly determined to continue the Garnett's dynasty by finding her only son – a well-known playboy on the London circuit – a suitable society wife.'

OK. I have tamed Toby's playboy tendencies since I moved in, but I doubt she'll give me credit for that, never mind see me as wife material. And that scares me. Love makes you vulnerable. My life would stop being fun without him.

I make the tea and take Toby's into the bedroom. 'Are you intending to get up today, oh light of my life?'

He opens one eye. 'Oh, I don't know if I'll bother. Though Rafe was talking about a game of tennis.'

I pull the quilt off the bed and reveal him in all his boxer-shorted glory. That's another view I never thought would be *all* mine. His tanned body is tennis-honed, though to be fair, the idleness is an act, put on for friends like Rafe who really don't have any responsibilities and for whom a knockabout game of tennis at Chelsea Harbour Club is one of many ways of filling their privileged lives. I could never be with Toby if he was like that. 'I'd reconsider your plans for the day if I were you, mate.'

He yawns extravagantly. 'I suppose I could pop in on the corner shop.'

The corner shop is Garnett's, the best department store in London and quite possibly the world, and it is Toby's birthright, courtesy of his great-granddad. It's where we met – when I tutored him in spreadsheets and retail basics in exchange for nice lunches and my nickname, Brains. It was my life for seven years and, if I'm honest, still my first love.

He pretends to Rafe and the rest that the store is no more important than the old train set he also inherited from Great-Grandpa Garnett. But I know it means the world to him, and

37

that if he takes time off for tennis, he puts the hours in afterwards.

'Good idea, Toby. All play and no work makes you a very dull boy. And do consider getting dressed.'

'Wouldn't want to distract you, eh?'

'Quite,' I say. 'Plus those pants are so full of holes that you're playing with fire. You *know* how Monty loves chipolatas.'

I manage to duck out of the way as he throws one, two, three pillows at me. Life is always a game to Toby.

After my shower, I dress in a business suit. I always do, even if I'm not due to see another soul all day – it makes a distinction between home and business. Especially as my commute is ten paces long, to Toby's third bedroom.

Moving in with Toby was one of the few things in my life that wasn't meticulously planned. For the first few months we were together, we were still pretending that we were 'just mates'. The kind of mates who always seemed to end up in bed together and then spent the morning after trying to remember quite how we got there.

It was one of those morning afters, when I was about to drag myself out to buy *Loot* and try to find a flat share without loons or smelly people, that he suggested we lived together. 'Makes sense, while you're building up the business. Keeps your expenses down. And there's plenty of room for two.'

There is room for an entire rugby team in Toby's flat. But I still wasn't sure. 'What if we fall out?'

'I'm so laid back I never fall out with anyone, and you're a pussycat underneath. And I'm almost as house-trained as Monty. Never leave the loo seat up.'

'I can't contribute much.'

'I'm sure we can come to some arrangement,' he said, kissing my neck.

Resistance was futile. Then, on the day I moved in, embarrassed by how little space my possessions took up in the back of the black cab, Toby told me he had a surprise and insisted I kept my eyes closed while he led me into the flat.

'You can open them now, Brains.'

He'd transformed the second guest bedroom into the new base for the Customer is King Consultancy. I don't know how he managed it, because I'd only been round there two days before, but I guess being on the board of Garnett's means you can skip to the front of the queue for home deliveries.

The desk was all glass, to make the most of the space. The far wall had been wallpapered with a vintage print featuring boutique shop fronts. Another wall was lined with white-painted wooden shelving units, with primrose-coloured lever arch files, ready to be filled with business plans and mystery shopping reports. A year planner and whiteboard were attached to the third wall, and my desk faced the river. He'd even put a jasmine plant alongside the new perspex in-tray.

'I can change it for another one, if you don't like the smell. I know how fussy you are about fragrances.'

'No, it's perfect. Quite, quite perfect.'

It's the most romantic thing anyone has ever done for me (though that's not hard, as I've never been the kind of woman who attracts big gestures or bouquets).

I fire up the computer, check my schedule for the day, put a coffee pod into the machine and make myself a decaff espresso. As I answer a few emails, I can hear Toby pottering loudly around the flat. It's taken a while to get used to living with someone, not least because I was brought up to think it's a one-way ticket to Hell. Gramma, who raised me as a good Christian girl, thinks I live with a flatmate in Holloway, and that this is my office address. If she knew the truth, she'd accuse me of being no better than my mother, with the morals of an alley cat.

I shake my head, to shake away my gramma's words. She loves me, no question, but her own morals belong to another century.

Toby pops his head around the door. 'Can I play butler again this morning?'

I smile. No one could mistake him for a butler. The Garnett genes are too strong. In the boardroom at the store there are gloomy portraits of his father, grandfather and the great-granddaddy himself, and every one is a blond bombshell, the dark suits and formal poses not managing to disguising the twinkle in their eyes and the bouffant luxury of their flaxen hair.

But Toby does like playing a role, perhaps because his own role in life was forced upon him.

'Butler's too formal, but you can be my secretary if you like.'

By the time my potential client has arrived, Toby has plated up some chocolate biscuits, restocked my coffee machine, and poured fresh milk into a bone china jug from his antique tea set.

'Very good, Garnett.'

'Ma'am,' he says, doffing an imaginary cap. I giggle. It's good for me when he punctures my seriousness with his silliness.

I hear his booming voice in the hallway, and he knocks. 'I'll just double check that Miss Brai— Miss Barrow is ready to see you.'

I come to the door. My visitor is what I expected: a slightly tweedy man in late middle-age who runs a once-exclusive chain of five stores selling male-oriented gifts – shaving gear, hip flasks, pipes and snuff. He smells sweet and clean, of leaf tobacco and cologne, and he is acutely embarrassed by his financial difficulties.

'I've been told by my daughters that we need to do more with our website,' he says, after Toby has served coffee and then withdrawn.

I already know that. In fact, I know exactly what Mr Tweed-and-Snuff should be doing with his store, including beefing up his web presence, closing down all but the flagship shop, and perhaps arranging a tie-up with an airline I know who've just abandoned their in-flight grooming supplier over quality issues.

Half an hour later, I've overcome his reluctance to take advice from a *slip of a girl*, and he's signed up for three months of 'store survival' consultancy. Thank goodness. I don't think I'm big-headed but I do know I'm his only hope. Toby shows him out, and winks at me over Mr Tweed's shoulder.

'*Another satisfied customer?*' he whispers, and when I nod, he blows me a kiss.

The Person Friday interviews begin at two. The candidates aren't coming to the flat – it's too intimate. Instead, I've invited them to a café nearby.

It must be the last caff in this part of London to avoid yummy-mummification. It's dark and low-key, and the Lebanese owner has shocking customer service skills, but today I don't want to be fussed over. I order a coffee, because I feel tired again, but it tastes funny. Too used to Starbucks to handle the real McCoy, I guess. After ten minutes I manage to capture the guy's attention and he brings me a fresh mint tea, which goes down better.

The first candidate comes highly recommended by the agency: a sweet little thing, with perfect whitened teeth and French-manicured nails. But I'm not looking for a nice view across the desk. I want initiative, drive.

I guess I want a version of me, ten years ago (though with better dress sense and sense of humour. I like to think both have developed in the last decade).

The second agency candidate is a man in his mid-twenties. His CV suggests he has an ego the size of a Routemaster, which is a worry. OK, so I do want drive, but I also need a willingness to get the teas in.

He leans forward, arms carefully positioned on the table to avoid messing up his shiny suit.

I straighten up and look him in the eye. 'I'll be frank with you, Ben. This is an unusual position. The person I recruit will be both my deputy *and* my dogsbody.'

'Right,' he says dubiously. 'The agency said there was plenty of scope for the right candidate.'

'Absolutely. My business is thriving. But I can't take on someone who thinks doing the photocopying is beneath them. How do you feel about photocopying?'

He shrugs. 'I guess someone's got to do it.'

But not you, I think. And I want to bark out *next!* But I don't. 'Where do you see yourself in five years, then, Ben? In my position, maybe?'

He smiles. 'I like to think I'd be employing more than one person to do my photocopying by then . . .'

I sigh. 'I really do admire your frankness, so I hope you won't mind complete honesty in return. I think this is a job you'd outgrow very quickly, so let's call a halt to this right now, shall we?'

Ben stands up almost before I've finished my sentence. 'I was thinking the same myself. And, between you and me, I'm down to the last thirty for a place on this year's *The Apprentice*. So I wouldn't have wanted to let you down.'

I'm hungry, suddenly, and with twenty minutes to go before the next candidate, I order a falafel salad. But when it arrives, I manage two bites before I need to run for the café's toilet and throw up what feels like everything I've eaten and drunk in the last twenty-four hours, including an entire field's worth of chopped mint leaves.

And as I stand up again, leaning against the tiled walls to steady myself, I have a moment of terrifying insight. I do some calculations in my head, and I *know*.

I feel the urge to vomit yet again, even though there's surely nothing left to bring up.

How?

But of course I know how, even if I don't know quite when, or what went wrong. So much for the pill being foolproof. Seems Gramma was right all along when she warned me that the only true contraceptive was abstinence – 'Look at your mother, her reputation lost before she was even out of her teens.' I bought my grandmother's line that unplanned pregnancy was the ultimate in feckless, hopeless, low-class behaviour.

It never occurred to me that it might just be down to plain old bad luck.

As I clean myself up, I catch sight of my face in the cloakroom mirror. I look for changes: plumped up cheeks, a maternal softening of my features. But all I see is panic.

Self-employed, business-loaned to the hilt, and pregnant by a fun-loving ex-playboy with a terrifying mother.

Though not as terrifying, surely, as my own gramma. *What is she going to say?*

I turn the rusty tap and splash icy water across my face and hands. I need to carry on with the interviews as planned, deal with this later.

I walk out of the toilets. A slim, drawn girl is sitting at my table already, fiddling with the sachets of sugar. I know on sight that she's wrong, wrong, wrong. She doesn't seem to have made any effort with her appearance – she's wearing jeans, for *a job interview* – and even though her hair is shorter than mine, it's messy, which is an achievement in itself.

I only agreed to see her as a favour to my old colleague Luis, the world's soppiest security guard, but I can tell I'm wasting my time.

'Kelly?' I hold out my hand.

'Yeah. Hi.'

She doesn't get up, but touches my hand briefly. Her hand is pale, with thin fingers and bitten nails. Her expression is defiant *and* desperate, and I am exhausted at the prospect of going through the motions. Then I remember what's happening inside my body, about the tiredness that's steamrollered me over the last fortnight. At least now I understand why, though it's no comfort whatsoever.

How can I have been so careless?

I pull myself back to the here and now. 'Thanks for coming. Shall I start by telling you about the job, then you can tell me about yourself?' I say, glad that this is the third time I've been through it, so that I can rely on autopilot while my brain processes this staggering new information and what it means.

A baby? *A baby!*

I know it happens. People have sex, they fall pregnant, babies are born. But it doesn't happen to me. Until now I thought I was immune to real life. I must be even more stupid than I thought.

Chapter Five

Soon as I see her, I know it's a total bloody waste of time.

Course, I'd guessed that already. And in case I hadn't, Dad told me so this morning, as I set up the ironing board. It creaked because it hasn't been used since my Auntie Feen's funeral in 2002 – not that Feen would have cared about the state of my blouse. She preferred vodka to ironing.

'Job interview? Who's going to give you a job?'

'Cheers, Dad.'

'It's nothing personal, Kelly, love. Just the way we are. Wrights don't take to working for other people. We're free spirits.'

'So that's what we are. Glad you told me that. For years I've been thinking we're born too stupid and too lazy to get a job, but it turns out we're actually born free, like big cats.' I shook the iron, trying to get it to steam.

'Don't tell me you're not proud to be a Wright.'

I groaned. 'I don't have time for this now.' I gave the iron a final, brutal shake – and rusty water shot out across the front of my white blouse. My *only* white blouse.

'No, Kelly. Come on. Out with it.'

When Dad's in a mood like that – determined to get a rise out of me – sometimes it's easier to go along with it. 'OK. You win. What am I meant to be proud of? That you can go back three generations of your side of the family before you find anyone who managed to hold down a proper job? Or that being a Wright means that by the time I'm thirty, I'll either be an alcoholic, a gambling addict, or if I'm really lucky, both?'

'You're an ungrateful bitch, sometimes, aren't you, Kelly?'

I held up the shirt, and inspected the stains. Hopeless. And I saw that one of the buttons was hanging onto the fabric by a thread. Like my sanity . . .

I reached forward and pulled off the button. Then I grasped the next button, and the next, wrenching them away from the shirt so angrily that I heard the cotton tear. I liked the sound.

'Ungrateful? Me? What about you, Dad? What about the times I've rescued you from bars and punch-ups and certifiable fucking loan sharks?'

'You've always been terrible for exaggerating.' He looked the picture of injured innocence, which made me even more furious. 'Bloody drama queen, like your mother.'

I looked at the shirt. I wasn't going to wear it now, anyway. I took one sleeve in each hand and pulled as hard as I could. It tore with a satisfying synthetic screech. 'That's right, Dad. I love conflict. I'd much rather have grown up hearing flaming rows than in a loving, stable family.'

And I dropped the shirt on the floor and ran out of the flat. I didn't even remember my handbag.

'. . . the role isn't for everyone. In fact, the person I'm looking for might not exist. They'll need to spend fifty per cent of their time doing the most basic tasks – organising my diary, answering the phone, that kind of thing – and then fifty per cent showing initiative and helping me to build the business.'

This woman is waiting for me to say something, but I don't have a clue what it should be. I haven't been through anything like this since I was sixteen and the school made us do 'mock interviews' with local business people they'd brought in for the day. I did what they wanted: I mocked the interviewers, until the careers teacher threw me out. 'You'll never come to anything, Kelly Wright. Not with that attitude.'

And guess what? She was right. None of the jobs I've had since school have involved interviews, unless you count a quick chat down the pub or word of mouth down the market. But they've had no prospects, either.

'So?' asks Sandie Barrow. 'How does that sound to you?'

'Um. Yeah. Good.'

She doesn't seem to be listening to me. Not that anyone ever bloody does. She's weird, not what I was expecting. Didn't think she'd be black, for a start: I thought she'd be a typical Chelsea housewife, all blonde and Botoxed.

Oh, and she's moody. Sipping water like she's got the mother of all hangovers, even though she dresses like she's in the Sally Army.

I bet she doesn't rate me much either. I'm still in my jeans, my hair's gone flat because I stormed out before I got chance to wash it, and my T-shirt's sweaty because my Oyster card's in my bag back in the flat, and I had to run from Shepherd's Bush to Chelsea to make it on time.

'So how do you know Luis, then?' she asks eventually.

'He's my neighbour.'

'Right. Right. He was very keen that I saw you, even though I did explain I was looking for someone with . . . well, some qualifications. Relevant experience.'

Maybe I should just do a runner. I've done what Luis wanted me to do. I came for the interview. He never said how long I had to stay here, did he?

'Luis is a good bloke.'

She looks at me properly for the first time. 'Yes. Yes, he is.'

The way she says it sounds really genuine. Like he's her guardian angel or something. Maybe he's her security guardian angel . . . the idea makes me smile. Apart from anything else, he'd need bloody strong wings to fly around with that beer gut of his.

'What's funny?' she says.

'Oh. Just thinking about Luis. Whether he makes a habit of rescuing people.'

'Is he trying to rescue you, then, Kelly?' Her voice is quiet and serious, like she really wants to know.

'Maybe. 'Just for a second, I'm almost tempted to tell her everything. The way Luis ushered me off the shop floor and I thought I was completely screwed. But he didn't take me into an office. Instead we went to the little room where the security guards go to eat their sandwiches and read the paper. I want to explain to her how he told me he'd heard the rows between me and Dad, and the way he'd wanted to come upstairs and sort him out, but his wife had told him that British people didn't do that, didn't interfere, but he'd felt terrible about it, and he hoped that if his own daughter back in Argentina was being bullied, he hoped someone would help her.

Maybe I should tell her that he said he'd never let someone go before, but he wanted to help me turn my life around. Told me he had an old friend who was looking for an expert in store security who'd asked him to recommend someone. And that maybe the best expert in store security would be someone who could beat it.

'But I haven't beaten it. You just caught me.'

'By accident. You are good shoplifter, Kelly. But it is time to turn your hand to a more honest way of living.'

I actually felt a bit weepy then. One of the only compliments I'd ever been paid, even though it was for my shoplifting. He told me he'd put me forward for the job – though I'd have to stay vague about my previous experience – as long as I stayed on the straight and narrow in future whether I got the job or not. I said yes – of course I did, I'm not stupid – and breathed a bloody great sigh of relief when he let me go. Without asking me to give back the stuff I'd nicked. He was so carried away with the idea of saving me from my life of crime that he forgot. I felt bloody guilty, but I still had to pay off enough of Dad's gambling debts to allow him to hang onto his teeth for now . . .

But I can't tell Sandie any of that, can I?

She's still looking at me. 'You know, Luis didn't just ask me to see you, Kelly. He begged me. He said there was something about you that made you different. I'll be honest, I'm not seeing it yet.'

'How am I meant to show you?'

She shrugs. 'I don't know. I'm not a charity, but I've had my difficult times. Luis knows I'll give someone a chance if they can convince me they want it. But if you're not even going to try, we might as well call a halt to this.'

She waits. Wants a sob story, I guess. Do-gooders are all the same. Pretend it's all about you, but really they want to feel better about themselves.

'What do you want to know?'

Sandie sighs. 'Relevant experience? Some kind of interest in retail. A spark of any kind would be good.'

She's annoying me now. Talking down to me like I'm a sulky kid. 'Luis has seen me working on the market, yeah? I cover different stalls, when people are on holiday, sick, whatever. I'm reliable. I handle money for other people. I'm . . .' I stop short of saying I'm honest. '. . . good with customers. Always having a laugh and a joke.' Except if they want a quince, that is.

'What do you mean by good?'

I close my eyes. 'I dunno . . . it's like, markets are like the world, aren't they? There's so much life, all these people searching for something. I love the challenge of finding what that is, and selling it to them, knowing what makes them tick. Our market's like a family, too, everyone looks out for each other.' I open my eyes again and realise she's staring at me like I'm interesting, not like I'm a rambling idiot. 'I feel at home there.'

Sandie takes a gulp of water. 'And what about security? Luis explained I was looking for someone who understood how security works? I've just won a new contract to report back on security at major stores, and so I need someone who can recognise flaws and blind spots, but doesn't look like a security guard. What can you bring to that?'

'I've never worked as a store detective myself,' I say, 'but I can spot them a mile off. A . . . relative used to be involved in security. She used to point out how they worked. Turned into a bit of a hobby of ours, spotting them.'

'This isn't a hobby for me, you know.'

'Sure. Yeah. I didn't mean—'

'This isn't just my living. It's my . . .' she pauses, 'my *baby*. My own business. It's about more than money. For a while, well, I won't go into details, but I was a write-off. Even I believed that, once. And now, I'm never going to allow anyone to write me off ever again. I wouldn't expect you to understand.'

I stare back at her. She's got a feisty side, under the shoulder pads and helmet hair. A side I find myself liking far more than the poker-up-her-arse side I saw before. Even weirder, I think I do understand, just a tiny bit, even though the nearest I've come to running my own business is selling nicked stuff down the pub.

'I've had a few people write me off in my time,' I say. 'Are you going to write me off too?'

'Um . . . I don't think it's appropriate at this stage . . .'

'S'all right. I won't blame you if you do. Tell you the truth, I don't think I can promise you anything. Reckon Luis is the only one on the planet who thinks I can actually do this job.' I stand up. 'But thanks for seeing me. That was your good deed for the day, eh?'

I walk out before she has time to slag me off for wasting her time. Then I remember I haven't got any money on me. If only I hadn't stormed off, I might have been able to ask her for the Tube fare home.

Shit-for-brains Kelly strikes again.

November 12 –
Shopping Days to Christmas: 42

Are your tills starting to ring like a campanologist on speed? If not, you're in trouble. Everything's to play for, but start with the shop floor. Are your staff dedicated to the highest standards of customer service? If not, ditch them. Scrooge had it right: Christmas is no time for sentimentality.

Chapter Six

Emily

It's so quiet in Bell's Emporium you could hear a pin drop.

Except there are no pins dropping. But there is the infuriating sound of Jean's knitting needles clicking together, at a hundred-and-thirty stitches per minute. This week the mad blur is turning into an unidentified sludge-brown item, in cable knit. I just hope it's not another scratchy cardigan for Freddie.

I'm not good with quiet. On Monday, when we had a customer who actually *bought* something (a sugar-pink vintage tea set and cake-stand I'd had my eye on myself), the woman told me it must be lovely living in the countryside. 'I crave peace and quiet and time to just . . . think. And bake home-made biscuits,' she said, before speeding off in her Jag, the tea set carefully wrapped up in the boot. I think we both knew it would never be unwrapped.

One woman's fantasy is turning into *this* woman's nightmare. I imagined our shop would be a bustling place, gossipy and mildly chaotic, like the world's most glamorous jumble sale.

These days, it's more like a funeral parlour. The only gossip comes from Jean, and consists of gory bulletins on the health of her church friends, grim house price news from her estate agent fancy man, and out-of-date rumours about Hollywood A-listers gleaned from old *OK!* magazines she's read in the doctor's waiting room. When she *does* come out with a nugget of something genuinely interesting – like the rumour that started in the Post

Office that Heartsease Common is being used as a location for the latest Keira Knightly movie – I am usually too stunned to respond.

'I'll make a tea, shall I, Jean?' I say, when the sound of the needles threatens to push me over the edge.

'Lovely,' she trills, without looking up.

I go upstairs to the flat, even though there's a kettle in our staffroom. I find Will on the sofa with Freddie, reading a story about a ship full of female pirates.

The Fredster smiles up at me. 'Look, Mummy. This pirate is just like you.'

I peer over his shoulder at the book. The pirate in question is a plump blonde pudding with mad hair under her skull-and-cross-bones hat. 'Thanks, sweetheart,' I say.

'Oh, Fred, she looks nothing like Mummy,' insists Will loyally.

'Is it possible to sack someone you don't actually pay?' I whisper to him.

'Not sure that would be cricket,' he says, handing the book to Freddie, before standing up and giving me a hug. 'She means well, you know that.'

'Makes me feel worse about wanting to garrotte her with her own three-ply wool.'

Jean was one of the old store's fixtures and fittings, though she's a lot harder to shift than the antiquated shelving systems. She's in her seventies – no one's allowed to know quite how close she is to the big eight-oh – and her customer services skills are limited. When the hardware company closed down the old Bell's store and we took over the lease, we told her we couldn't afford to pay her, but she still turns up with her knitting whenever she fancies it, sitting behind the till, and putting browsers off with her nosiness.

'Have you worked out what it is she's knitting yet? My money's on a bed jacket for the vicar's wife to take into hospital for her hysterectomy.'

I shake my head. 'Whenever I see her clicking away, I think of those women who used to knit at the guillotine during the French Revolution. And then I think it must be an omen.'

He laughs. 'We're all doomed, doooomed, I tell you! If the guillotine doesn't get us, then the zombies will. Or the vampires.'

'It's not a joke,' I protest, but I'm already smiling. He snakes his long arms around my waist and then pretends to sink his fangs into my neck. Pretty soon the fake-bites turn into tiny kisses, and I look up quickly to check on Freddie, but he's absorbed in the pictures of the girl pirates.

'Shall I ask Jean if she can mind Freddie while we do . . . the accounts?' he suggests. 'While it's quiet in the shop?'

I consider protesting – it seems indecent to fiddle with Will while the Emporium burns, but then again . . . there are enough bad bits about self-employment: the tax return, the VAT return, the endless calculations. Shouldn't we enjoy the freedom, too? And, it just happens to be the perfect time to make another baby . . .

'But she's expecting a cup of tea,'

'I'll take her a glass of sherry instead,' he suggests. His eyes are deep blue right now – they change colour every time I look at them, but the darker they are, the more I fancy him.

My mind is made up. 'Freddie. How would you like to do some of that knitting with Auntie Jean for a while?'

'Okey dokey,' he says happily. For some unfathomable reason, he adores Jean, and he loves knitting, too. Even though he ends up as tangled as a kitten when he takes hold of the child-sized needles she's bought for him.

'I'll take him down, 'says Will, giving me a final squeeze before disentangling himself. 'See you in a moment. Be ready to reveal those figures, will you?'

'Is this it?'

My son took the words right out of my mouth. The first location in my Grotto Fabulous Secret Shopping Project consists of a small shed erected on the second floor of Reading's third largest department store (the signs outside proclaim that 'small is beautiful' but actually, the whole store is depressingly run down and not a place to linger).

The shed has fake snow covering the felt roof, and Alpine-style flower-boxes filled with plastic tulips against the window. I doubt you get tulips in Lapland. I move my handbag-camera up and down to capture the full effect.

'Is this *really* it, Mummy?' he repeats, his voice small with disappointment.

I know how he feels. Disappointment seems to be stalking me right now. The impromptu 'accounts' session with Will this morning ended in a big row, because he's changed his mind again about babies. Well, he claims he never actually said yes to babies in the first place, despite our lovely cosy fireside conversation a few weeks ago when he said he'd love another Freddie in the house.

'I meant, in theory. One day,' he explained this morning, stroking my hair. 'But even you must realise that this is not the time, Em. We're struggling as it is. One thing at a time.'

'But I want a baby we make together. To make us a proper family.'

He sat up in bed. His chameleon-eyes had turned cool blue, shot with an even chillier hint of green. 'I think we're already a proper family, aren't we?'

'You know what I mean. Duncan's always rubbing it in that he's Freddie's dad, not you. But when we have a baby together, he'll back off.'

'Em. He'll always be Freddie's father. You can't erase bits of the past just because they don't quite fit the fairy tale. Life's not like that.' He was using his patient voice, the one that makes him sound saintly and me feel a total tit.

'I'm not a fool.'

'I never said you were, did I?' He leaned down to the side of the bed and put his T-shirt back on.

'Don't go.'

'Em, I'm not in the mood any more.' He leaned across to kiss me on the forehead. 'We'll make up for it later, eh?'

'Okey dokey,' I said, very quietly. Actually, I wasn't really in the mood any more myself. He rubbed his temples, as though he had a headache. 'I think you need to focus on what we have got, instead of always chasing perfection.'

I *do* try to focus on what we've got. I have a bright, beautiful son, and a wonderful, caring, sexy man, and we're working together on building our dream life. So why do I feel it's not quite enough?

Freddie tugs on my arm. 'Look, Mummy.'

A listless elf in a bottle-green ballet tunic is chatting to an assistant at the toy counter. I try to catch her eye, but she ignores me. 'Wait by Santa's shed . . . um, grotto,' I tell Freddie, and then walk towards the elf, repositioning my handbag so the camera lens will point upwards to catch the conversation.

'Hi,' I say. 'Are you part of the grotto experience?'

The girl is about seventeen, and very thin: her knees are so sharp I'm amazed they haven't torn her red tights. 'Nah. I always dress like this.'

The other assistant laughs.

'Very funny, ' I say. 'But I have a three-year-old boy who has been looking forward to meeting Father Christmas.'

'Oh.' She looks over my shoulder at Freddie and her pale face softens a little. 'Well, you'll have to wait. Santa's on his fag break.'

'He smokes?'

'He is trying to give up,' she says. 'It's worse this time of year, because it's early. So quiet. A fag relieves the boredom, he says. But he always brings his own *special* mouthwash to get rid of the smell before he comes back.'

This makes the other assistant snigger again.

'Any idea how long he'll be?' I ask. If I were a normal customer, of course, I'd have given up by now, but I'm a professional. I will see this through.

'Oh. Talk of the devil. Here he is now.'

I turn and see a bearded figure heading towards us. He's properly plump in his tatty uniform, and he seems to have a limp.

I hear a squeal and see Freddie's face: he's just spotted Santa and he is utterly enthralled. He runs towards the red-suited man and almost knocks him flying as he grabs the patent leather boots.

'Have you been waiting to see me, young man?' says Santa.

'Yes!' The expression on my son's face makes my heart feel like

55

it might burst with love. Even now, the strength of my feelings for him knocks me flying.

'I do hope you've been good . . .' Santa looks up at me and winks. 'And that Mummy has too.'

'Oh, Mummy's always on her best behaviour, isn't she, Freddie?' I say, as I follow the two of them into Santa's garden shed.

It's claustrophobic and dingy inside, but I know from experience that my secret camera can manage even in the darkest conditions. I can't smell nicotine, but the stink of mint mouthwash is overwhelming. I'll put that in my written report, as covert filming technology doesn't yet include smelly-vision.

Santa sits down on a wicker chair, and he helps Freddie onto his lap. I stand under the eaves of the pitched roof, my neck craned to one side, because the shed is under five feet high.

'So, young man,' says Father Christmas in a weary, said this a million times before voice, 'what are you hoping I'll be bringing down the chimney?'

Freddie looks at me anxiously. 'Mummy,' he whispers. 'Do we have a chim-iny?'

'Yes, of course we do, Fredster.'

'What is it?'

'Well, it's . . .' Have you ever tried to describe a chimney to a child? Not as easy as it sounds. '. . . the big hole in the living room wall that sticks out.'

'Where Will lights the fire?' Freddie looks down at Father Christmas's plastic boots. 'Don't your feet get very hot?'

Father Christmas chuckles, though the sound stops very abruptly, as if someone has flicked off his Ho Ho Ho switch. 'Oh, don't worry about me, young man. I am fireproof. So. What do you like? Trains? Trucks?'

Freddie's forehead screws up in concentration. 'I like shoes.'

I stifle a giggle. I wish my ex-husband was here. He'd be outraged.

'Shoes? Right. What kind of shoes?'

'Wellies are nice. But my favourites shoes are pink. Like mummy's.'

Santa peers down at my shoes – a pair of rather cute courts with pink bows, picked up from the supermarket – and gives me a worried look. 'So, you'd like pink shoes for Christmas?'

'Maybe,' says Freddie, thinking it over.

'What else do you like, young man?'

I do wish he'd bother to ask Freddie's name. It's the least he can do.

'Shopping.'

I smile to myself again. Shopping – or rather '*shuupppy*' – was Freddie's first word. Duncan was, and still is, horrified by the idea that his son likes girly things, whereas I can think of a thousand things worse than my boy growing up in touch with his feminine side.

I have a feeling Santa will side with Duncan. He seems lost for words. 'Shopping . . .' he mumbles. 'Not many little boys like shopping.'

'Not ord'ny shopping,' Freddie explains. 'Ord'ny shopping is boring. Only shopping when Mummy brings her camera along.'

I freeze.

'Her camera?'

'Shhhh!' says Freddie. 'It's a secret.'

I gulp. 'What about a drum kit, Freddie? Weren't you saying the other day that you'd like a little drum kit?'

But Santa is staring at me, eyes narrowed. 'I'm very good with secrets, young man. Go on, whisper in my ear.'

Freddie reaches up to bury his face in the upper reaches of Santa's synthetic beard, while I wonder whether I should snatch him away, or try to bluff it out. 'Mummy . . .' he pauses dramatically, 'is a spy! Like on CBBC.'

'Ha, ha,' I laugh. 'Where do they get their crazy ideas from?'

'Cept Mummy spies on shops,' he continues gleefully. 'She has a spy camera in her handbag and she films all the shop people and sometimes they get cross with her, and then she gets them into trouble.'

'What a vivid imagination he has,' I say, still hoping Santa might dismiss this as the incoherent mumblings of a child with too much imagination. Even though, in fact, Freddie's description of my job is pretty much spot on.

'There was a rumour they were gonna send someone,' says Santa, his voice no longer quite so jolly. 'But I thought it was a wind-up. I couldn't think where they'd get someone who'd be willing to use their own kid as a decoy.'

'I don't know what you're talking about—'

'Out of order, that's what it is. We're just normal people, trying to earn a living, and they send people to spy on us.'

Freddie is frowning, confused by the old man's sudden change of mood. 'I would like a train set, please, Father Christmas,' he says, trying to calm Santa down, 'that's if you don't have any shoes in my size. But post it through the letterbox, because if it comes down the chim-iny it will burn.'

'Freddie, it's time for us to go now,' I say, bending over and taking his hand to help him off Santa's knee. But then Santa makes a lunge towards me.

'That it, is it? The camera? Can't we go anywhere or do anything these days without being filmed? Police state.' There's a crazy glint in Santa's eye now.

'It's not going to do you any harm. You were doing fine. Honestly. I'm sure your bosses will be entirely satisfied.' I try to open the door. Santa lunges forward for a second time, and as I drop the bag, he smashes his head against the roof.

'Ow, bollocks!'

He stops in his tracks and I turn to give him the dirtiest of looks – how am I going to explain to Freddie why Santa would use foul language – as a bottle falls from his inner pocket, onto the floor. It smashes, and the smell of peppermint rises from the fragments.

'Mouthwash,' he says, as I instinctively point the handbag cam at the broken bottle.

And realise that the label reads, *crème de menthe*.

'You're a disgrace,' I hiss, before ducking under the shed doorway. 'Freddie, Santa's hurt his head. But we'll write him a proper list and post it to Lapland tonight.'

'Bye, bye, Santa,' my little boy waves through the space at the man, whose beard has slipped slightly, revealing ruddy cheeks and spittle all over his lips. 'Get better soon! And watch out for fires in chim-inys.'

Chapter Seven

Sandie

There's a limit to how long you can sit in the lobby of a three-star hotel before you begin to look like a prostitute.

And I passed that limit, oh, about half an hour ago.

I get out my BlackBerry and try to look businesslike, though it occurs to me that escorts have BlackBerries too, these days, to juggle their appointments. Let's hope that the average madam is more efficient than my new PA . . .

I dial the office number for the fifth time and *finally*, she answers.

'Yvette. Where the hell have you been?'

'Asleep.'

'*Asleep?* Are you ill or something?'

'No,' she says, cheerily, 'but it's been scientifically proven that siestas are highly beneficial. I'm so much more efficient when I have a nap after lunch. My last boss didn't mind.'

She didn't mention *that* at her interview. 'Well, while you were grabbing forty winks, I've been sitting at the Three Lions Hotel waiting for my contact.'

'Oh. Did you try his mobile?'

'Of course I did. It's unobtainable. You must have sent me the wrong number.'

'Hang on, the answerphone's flashing, let me just . . .'

In the background, I hear the electronic beep, and then a muffled message. 'Hi, this is Phillip Finch from the Midlands

Retail Consortium, I've been waiting at the Three Crowns Hotel now for twenty minutes—'

'Yvette. Did he just say the Three Crowns? Where the hell is that?'

The machine beeps again, and Phillip Finch comes on again, now sounding exasperated. 'It's been an hour, now. I am leaving to avoid wasting the rest of the afternoon. Do return my call. If you can be bothered.'

'That's so weird,' Yvette says. 'I swear he told me the Three Lions.'

'Really? Because it's so much more likely that this top flight businessman, who knows the area intimately, would tell you the wrong place, than that *you would write it down wrong,* isn't it?'

'Errr . . .' I think the sarcasm is lost on her.

To be fair to Yvette, she landed the job not because of any particular aptitude but simply for being the least worst of the candidates. I had hoped she might rise to the challenge, or make up in accuracy for her lack of spark. Wrong. 'It's not as though it's the first time, is it, Yvette? There was the incident with the hampers . . .' where she managed to send a crate of vintage wines to a teetotal client, and the teetotaller's holistic vegetarian selection to my booziest. 'And the lost videos.'

'I swear I posted them, Sandie.'

'I believe you. But you were supposed to courier them so they couldn't get lost in the post.'

'If you'd seen the queue at the post office, though . . .'

My inner grizzly bear, the unseemly anger that rises inside me sometimes, is beginning to growl. I want to shout and swear at Yvette, ask if she has the faintest idea of how much this business means to me, and the damage she's doing with her careless stupidity.

But I'm better than that, aren't I? And anger can't be good for the . . . thing growing deep inside me. Thing. There, what kind of a mother would I make? It's not a thing. It's a person. Isn't it?

I take a deep breath. It's not Yvette's fault she's clueless. I've laid people off before, when I was at Garnett's, but this feels much more personal. 'Yvette, I'm sorry but this isn't working, is it? I don't think my expectations are the same as yours and so I think we ought to call it a day.'

'You're sacking me?'

'I'm afraid so. And actually you're still on your trial period.'

'Give me another chance. I'll ring Mr Finch, explain—'

'I doubt he'd be too impressed with your afternoon nap. No, I'm sorry, my decision is final.'

I hear Yvette harrumph down the phone. 'Well, I'll sue you for unfair dismissal.'

'On what grounds exactly?'

'Errr . . . racism.'

'But you're white, Yvette.'

'Yes, and you're black. You're biased against me on the grounds of skin colour.'

This is all I need. 'No. I'm biased against you because you're not very good.'

'But—'

'There's nothing more to say, Yvette. Just leave the office now, please. Don't finish anything off. I'll pay you to the end of the week, but it's one of those things. We'll both put it down to experience, eh? Yvette?'

But it appears I'm talking to thin air. Yvette has hung up on me. Perhaps she's decided to award herself another little lie down. I know I could do with one myself.

By the time I've instructed Toby to escort my former PA off the premises (after a quick frisk for stolen stationery), and placated Phillip Finch, I'm late for my next appointment. It's one I almost cancelled, given the circumstances, but I don't believe in letting people down.

The toyshop should be busy at this time of year. It's in one of the commuter villages outside Birmingham that's come up in the world since I lived in the area: the Post Office window is full of adverts for yoga-lates and breast-feeding support groups, and the coffee shops are all full.

But The Rocking Horse looks uncared for and dark from the outside, and you'd never know it was coming up to Christmas.

There are dolls in checked summer dresses in the window display, as well as dusty jigsaw boxes and faded board games.

The owner, Sally, was so stressed on the phone when she booked the consultation that I couldn't get any sense of who she might be, but now I meet her and it's making more sense. She's in her early thirties, I guess, rather dowdy for her age, and she won't shut up.

'. . . and I thought it would change my life, I mean, how hard could it be to run a toyshop, but it's like a millstone . . . Oh, and the customers. So rude. Their children have no manners and . . .'

As she chatters away, I inspect the interior. It used to be her aunt and uncle's shop, but the uncle's died, and the aunt's in a home, and Sally thought she'd found herself a new career. But instead the bills keep coming in, and the profits falling.

'. . . and I thought the retro thing was big, you see, but kids these days only want computer games. That's what the problem is,' she whimpers.

'No. That's not what the problem is at all.'

She frowns at me. 'Isn't it?'

'Retro is good,' I say, pointing towards a high-up shelf lined with boxed porcelain dolls. 'Those are Sasha dolls. Very retro. They sell for a hundred plus on eBay.' Then I take a few steps towards the clothes rail, where fancy-dress costumes hang limply from metal hangers. 'But time warp is bad.'

'I quite like this,' she says, taking out a polyester Superman costume.

I take it from her, sniff it. 'But it smells worse than a charity shop. No one's going to buy this for their child, *and* they make the whole store stink. Do you know how hygiene conscious parents are these days? And what's this meant to be?' I unhook a huge tent made of floral smocked material.

'That's from the maternity range,' she explains, and pulls on the fabric to show how far it stretches. It could happily cover a family saloon.

'Do women really get that big?' I say, casting a disbelieving look at my own belly.

'Hmm. Revolting, isn't it?'

I walk away. 'You've got a captive market, Sally, there are

thousands of mums in this town alone who'd like to give their little darlings something more durable and traditional than a Wii game. Who want to recapture their own childhoods. But they're not going to pay top whack in a place that's slightly less inviting than the Red Cross supplies tent after a major disaster.'

She takes a sharp intake of breath. OK, maybe I should have been more careful in my phrasing.

'But all is very far from lost. Let's put the kettle on, shall we, and I'll explain what I think could be done.'

It's coming up to rush hour by the time I've told Sally what she has to do, i.e. clear eighty per cent of the old stock via a Christmas giveaway and eBay. Then gut the place completely, and make it a sleek, chic toy boutique full of Steiff teddy bears and Hornby train sets for yummy mummies and nostalgic daddies and baby-boomer grandparents. Or she could decide to switch completely online. Which, given her attitude to the 'snotty mothers and their snottier brats', might be the preferred option. If you want to run a shop, it does help to like customers.

I get in the hire car, resigned to the fact it'll take me forty minutes to get to my gramma's house.

I programme the satnav to find another route. That's better. That'll take me at least an hour and a quarter. The longer I can put this off, the better.

The new route takes me off the main roads, and round the suburbs. I'm still twenty-five miles from where I grew up – but the territory feels familiar. Three-bed semis with white wooden frontages, and a lot of pebbledash. Grotty shops selling a bit of everything, but nothing you could truly covet. And gangs of kids doing nothing, but malevolently. Even now, the sight of more than three teenage girls gathered on a street corner makes my mouth go dry: that's what comes of being a 'stuck-up' grammar school girl.

As I drive, I fret. I don't plan to tell my grandmother about the baby, but she has the gift of second sight where I'm concerned. She knows when I'm hiding something, and pregnancy is the biggest secret I've ever tried to keep.

As the satnav takes me closer to home, I try to imagine what it *would* be like if she could be pleased for me . . . a hug that lasts for ever, tears of surprise and joy, reassurances that it'll be fine, that we'll get through this unexpected but still quite wonderful development together.

It seems as fake as a made-for-TV movie. The more likely outcome involves a devastatingly long pause, an expression of terrible disappointment, and a series of probing questions about Toby's intentions towards me, my own plans, and my attitude to adoption.

I don't know what Toby's intentions are, because he doesn't know about the pregnancy; I don't know what my plans are, either, and as for adoption . . . well, that involves acknowledging that I'm having a baby, which is too extraordinary a thought. I've never had a maternal instinct. It's not that I don't like kids – Freddie's terrific – it's just that when I've heard other women talk about that desire, I've had to take their word for it, because my dreams were always different. To be the first female store manager at Garnett's, or to run my own business. OK, maybe there are quiet, mortifying moments when I catch myself fantasising about a grand wedding to Toby . . .

But there's no baby in my picture of wedding bliss, just Toby and me and Monty the dog. My gramma would probably see it as immature and selfish, but fortunately there's no law saying everyone has to produce two point four children and live in a cul-de-sac.

A cul-de-sac like this one.

I'm here. Home. I take a deep breath, pull my stomach in (even though there's not even a hint of a bump yet) and apply blusher to my sallow skin. The glow of pregnancy certainly hasn't kicked in so far.

'Sandra! You're late.'

'Lovely to see you too, Gramma.' And despite my anxiety, it *is* lovely to see her. She stands at the front door, hands on pink-aproned hips, as stout and uncompromising as the teapot I know will be ready on the kitchen worktop. For all her harsh moralising, Gramma has always been a reassuring figure. In her ordered world, right decisions are rewarded, wrong ones attract punishment, and everything can be solved by common sense.

'You look peaky,' she says, and I brace myself for further inquiries. But instead she gives me a brief, tense hug and ushers me into the hall. 'We've got company, come into the kitchen.'

'Oh.' I feel mildly put out. Don't I merit her undivided attention any more? Then it occurs to me that undivided attention is exactly what I don't want today. 'Is it someone from church?'

She gives me an odd look. 'No.'

'The WRVS, then?'

She turns away. The kitchen is spotless, as always, and a freshly baked tinned-pineapple upside-down cake is cooling on a wire tray. 'Put that onto the serving plate, will you, Sandra, please?'

As she takes the milk out of the fridge and pours some into a jug, I notice her hand is shaking. 'Gramma. Is something wrong?'

She doesn't turn round. 'It's hard to know what the right thing is, sometimes.'

'What are you talking about?'

'Promise me you won't be angry with me, Sandra. Promise me you'll try to understand that there are no rules for this situation.'

No rules? Coming from my grandmother, this is heresy. 'What have you done, Gramma? If you've messed up the Pizza Palace home delivery shopping assignment, it's fine. I probably shouldn't even have asked you, at your age.' But even as I garble on, I sense this has nothing to do with secret shopping.

She shakes her head, then puts the milk down, and reaches out to take my hand. Her grip is steely, but her skin is clammy. She pulls me into the living room and I don't have time to catch my breath before the guest rises from the sofa. Not an easy job, I'd have thought, as she's a bulky woman, crammed into the tightest of jeans.

And then I look up from the jeans and part of my brain lights up, the area that handles memories and faces and emotions.

As the woman launches herself at me and cries out, 'Oh Lord, look at you, look at you,' I already know somewhere very deep in

66

my consciousness who she is . . . even though it takes me a few more seconds to speak.

'Mum?'

My last memory of my mother is mundane, one of those recollections that only becomes significant in retrospect.

I was about six, already so unnaturally keen on school that I liked to keep my uniform on way past home time. It must have been November, because that was when my mother always came over from Jamaica. The flights were cheaper than over Christmas and she'd always loved Bonfire Night, because my late grandfather had been a demon for the fireworks.

I knew she was my mum, but even at that age, I knew she wasn't like other mothers. She didn't live with us, for a start. Then there were her clothes, which were startlingly tight and bright, in primary colours which clashed with each other and the grey landscape where I lived. She was younger than most of the mums, so on the few occasions that she turned up at the school gate, my friends thought she was my big sister. Also, she swore copiously, played loud reggae tapes 'to remind me of home,' and left wet towels on the bathroom floor for my grandmother to pick up. She was stuck in a teen rebellion time warp, although by this time she must have been twenty-three.

Gramma bore it all with grim fortitude, though I heard them arguing some nights, or rather I heard my mother's high voice through the floorboards, though never my grandmother's muttered responses.

That final year, we went to the illuminations at Walsall, and my mother seemed more childlike than ever, whooping and giggling at the lights. I felt more grown-up myself, I didn't even cry when I fell over and chipped a tooth. The next day, Mum went with me to the dentist on the edge of Birmingham. I suspect now that Gramma made her take me. We sat in the surgery waiting room for hours before they called me in for my emergency appointment, but my mother refused to come into the treatment room – 'I hate needles, Sandie, they'll make me go all funny.' Then she took me for chips and cherry soda in a café afterwards. I'd been crying, and she made up a poem about teeth, which made me laugh, even though my mouth was numb and I was dribbling cherryade.

She put me to bed, and the next day she was gone. Back to Jamaica. It wasn't unusual for it to happen like that – Gramma didn't believe in tearful airport goodbyes – but it turned out this was her last visit.

Well, her last visit for twenty-three years.

My mother is crying, and I'm trying to think of something to say that will make her feel better. But none of the things I want to say, like *why did you go and not come back?* or *what have you been doing for all these years?* or *how did you get so fat?*, seem to fit the bill.

'My baby,' she howls, and I have a strong hunch that she's enjoying being the centre of attention. Then I realise that's exactly what my grandmother is thinking too.

But maybe my mother is the one person on earth who can understand what's happening to my body. She was so much younger, yet she had the strength to go through with the pregnancy and give birth. Even though she didn't quite have the strength to be a full-time mum afterwards.

I'm seized by a desire to tell her the truth, but I sense my grandmother standing behind me. One dramatic revelation is enough for a single afternoon.

'Gramma?'

She is very still, her arms rigid at her sides, her eyes wary. No. Not wary. Fearful.

'Marina wanted to see you. She was worried that you would refuse unless we did it this way.'

'Because you turned her against me, Ma.'

'I did nothing of the sort,' says Gramma, but my mother gives her such a contemptuous look that she flinches. 'It certainly wasn't my intention.'

'You sure about that, Ma?'

'Marina Barrow, don't you dare try to rewrite history. We made an agreement, based on what was best for Sandra.'

'An agreement? Has old age affected your memory? You didn't give me a choice.'

'You didn't have the maturity to know what was right,' says Gramma, 'and it doesn't seem to me that much has changed.'

'I'm forty-six years old, Ma. If I'm not a grown up now, I never will be.'

'Exactly.'

'You evil witch—'

Being caught in the crossfire is making me feel faint. I hold up my hand. 'Please. Will you stop shouting and say something that makes some sense?'

They stare at me, then each other. 'Go on, Ma,' my mother says, 'you always did know the difference between right and wrong. Explain away.'

My grandmother sighs, then sits down abruptly, as though she's lost the strength in her legs. 'Before you say anything, Sandra, just remember I did what I did because I thought it was for the best . . .'

'And what did you think was for the best?' I ask.

'Your mother was always unreliable. Even as a child. But you weren't like that, Sandra. You were a quiet, studious girl, except when your mother showed up once a year and disrupted our routines. I didn't want to risk your going the wrong way too.'

My mother shakes her head. 'Your stupid rules didn't work with me, so you thought you'd have another shot at it with Sandie.'

'It's Sandra,' Gramma says.

'I never even wanted to call her that. I wanted to call her Amber Loretta.'

'You'd have been better off going after her father than coming up with ridiculous names.'

'Who says I didn't go after the father?'

I look at her now. *My mother*. It doesn't sit right with this voluptuous, still young-looking woman wearing too much make up and too little clothing for the occasion. 'Did you?' I ask. 'Go after my father?'

'Honey, I tried. But it's complicated.'

'She means she doesn't know who your father is, Sandra.'

I look at my mother. She doesn't say anything.

'And that is why I wanted you to grow up free of . . . malign influences.'

'You make me sound like Satan, Ma.'

'A bad influence doesn't need a tail and a pitchfork,' Gramma says. 'But even you, Marina, can't have wished your lifestyle on your only daughter. To be a single mother, with all the stigma that goes with it? No home, no husband, the Lord alone knows what else.'

'No, but I didn't want her to live without fun, either.'

'I am *here*,' I remind them. 'None of this is making sense. I thought you were the one who left, Mother . . . sorry, do you mind if I call you Marnie? Mother seems weird.'

'Sure, honey.' She nods. 'Look, I did agree to let your grandmother raise you while I was away. But she was the one who decided to change the terms of the deal, after it had been agreed.'

'Deal?'

'It wasn't like that, Sandra.' But my grandmother sounds hesitant.

'Did you ban my mother from visiting us?'

'I never used that word.'

Marnie shrugs. 'She said there were two ways of settling things. The easy way, where I got on with my life in Jamaica, and maybe some day, when you were older, I could come back. Or the hard way, which would involve social services and the police and a whole lot of other people she knew I'm not keen on . . .'

None of it makes sense. I look from one woman to the other. What happens now? Am I meant to choose, like a tug-of-love child?

'Why wait till now to come back, though, Marnie?'

'I know I'm weak, Sandie. I pushed the idea of you away. Thought it was better for you. But then this year I kept thinking how you'd be thirty soon – thirty, my only daughter – and I wanted to get to know you, now I could no longer influence you badly. Better late than not at all?'

'That's a matter of opinion,' Gramma says.

I stand up.

'Don't go. I've come a long way, Sandie.'

I walk over to where my mother's sitting, and lean in to kiss her on the cheek, an action that feels awkward. I catch her perfume.

'Is that Le Jardin de Max Factor?'

'Yes,' she says. 'Yes. I've always worn it.'

And I've always wondered why I liked that scent, even though it's seen as cheap and cloying in certain circles. I hadn't realised it was the most powerful reminder of the mother I'd lost.

'I'll be in touch. I promise. I just need a bit of time to . . . rewrite everything in my head.'

I leave, now, before my inner grizzly bear roars at Gramma. I realise that by ignoring her, I'm already siding with Marnie, but if there's ever been a time I can be allowed to be selfish, surely it's now.

November 22 –
Shopping Days to Christmas: 32

Remember the good old days (well, it was only 2007)? Back then you could flog any old rubbish if you marketed it right.

But these days, the customer must be cajoled, persuaded . . . even bullied into the belief that what you're selling will change their miserable life for the better.

Chapter Eight

Grazia

I am sitting in a marshmallow of a waiting room, with a woman who resembles a deep-tanned gargoyle, and a man who would make Liberace look understated.

The room has no sharp edges. It would be perfect for a mentally unbalanced person hell-bent on self-harm, because it would be impossible to hurt oneself on the white feathery cushions and puffy pink sofas and this strange, spongy flooring that gives a little with each step. Even the doors have rounded corners, and soft-closing mechanisms that make them impossible to slam.

The irony of this is not lost on me (though it may be lost on the gargoyle, whose face is so rigid that I suspect even a raised eyebrow would cause a tsunami of Botox and filler). Because the only reason you'd come to this adult's soft-play area is to be prodded and injected and hurt.

'Miss Verdi?' Liberace calls my false name out from behind the pearl-encrusted reception desk. 'The consultant will see you now.'

And this time it is a *real* consultant, rather than the frighteningly unqualified girls who advised me on my previous two missions. Their uniforms were crisp and spotless, hugging surgically trim bodies, but the aura of medical knowledge was entirely bogus. Unless knowing how to pluck eyebrows or shape toenails counts as medical knowledge.

So when I left the two clinics in question with a list of treatments costing more than a year's rental on a St Tropez apartment, I told myself that this was no reflection on me, they were simply operating the hard sell. But Dr Target's advice will be harder to ignore or explain away.

The treatment room dispenses with the pretence that this is a glorified spa. There are locked drug cabinets, a trolley, a couch, a yellow box for sharps, and a bin for clinical waste. Since this consultation is costing me – well, costing the cosmetic surgery regulators who have ordered the assignment – a cool two hundred pounds, there is no reason to pretend we are not here to do serious business.

'Miss Verdi. A pleasure,' says Dr Target, rising from his white leather chair to shake my hand warmly. He is shorter than I expected, and younger, no more than forty-five. Though the youthful appearance may be due to his own treatments, of course. I would not describe him as good-looking – his features tend towards the bland – but he has the aura of a man who knows what women want, and also knows he can provide it. I would guess this makes him attractive to many of my sex. I read on the Internet that he was recently and expensively divorced: there can be no shortage of women pursuing him, and his secrets of eternal youth.

I sit down, and a serious-looking nurse in her fifties enters the room, switching on a Dictaphone to record Dr Target's pearls of wisdom. So that makes two of us taping him. I am suddenly conscious of the tiny camera lens hidden behind the button of my black linen shirt, and the recording device strapped around my waist. I hope he does not intend to examine my body as well as my face.

'What can I help you with today?' asks Dr Target. He has a soothing, transatlantic voice that could earn him serious money as a TV voiceover artiste, should the bottom ever fall out of the liposuction market.

'It is my face,' I say. 'I appear tired, even when I wake after a good night's sleep feeling refreshed.' The line is the one I was instructed to use by my mystery shopping assignment briefing, but ever since my encounter with the beastly James, it feels very apposite.

'Specifically where on your face gives you most concern?'

I try not to think of James's comments. I must remember that I am playing a role . . .

Albeit a role that the mirror Dr Target is now holding confirms I am well qualified for. The lighting above the patient's chair is cruel, the opposite of the lighting favoured by expensive boutiques. My reflection makes me wince momentarily, which makes the lines still worse.

'I wish I looked a little more like me. Like the me I have always known. And not an old woman.' As soon as I have said it, I regret it. People I do not know will be reviewing this footage and making judgements about me.

'You brought the photographs of you as a younger person as requested?'

I nod and hand them over. It was hard to find a photograph that showed me in any detail, because in most of them I was the adjunct to Leon, in the shadow of his greatness. But there were a couple from our wedding day, where my strong features – my dark eyes and my well-shaped lips and oh, those cheekbones I always took for granted – are displayed to good effect.

The consultant examines them, looks up at me, down again at the pictures. 'I have some observations myself, but it would help to understand your concerns in more depth,' he says. He holds up the nicer of the two photographs, and the nurse holds the mirror up, too. 'Perhaps you'd care to compare now and then for me, and tell me what you see.'

I want to say that, no, I wouldn't care to compare the past with the present. But I promised Sandie I would complete the mission, so I do as he suggests.

'The eyes . . .' I say. 'The bags under the eyes. That is what I see first. Then the loss of my cheeks. The thinness of my lips, now. And the brown marks across my forehead, and the way my skin has begun to drape and hang in the wrong places, like one of those dreadful throws people use to hide an ugly old sofa. And . . .'

And then I stop. The nurse is looking at me with a mixture of curiosity and sympathy. She has a plain, calm face, one that has probably changed little over the years.

'Perhaps you would get Miss Verdi a glass of water, Helen. And then I will be very happy to outline the possible treatment options.'

Dr Target emerges from my mystery shopping assignment with a clean bill of health.

I, on the other hand, am feeling almost tearful.

He was very nice. There was no pressure. Not for Dr Target the three-for-two-procedures deal I was offered at the more downmarket clinics, or the personalised full-colour image of how I could look if I signed on the dotted line without delay.

Instead he suggested fillers here and there, perhaps a touch of Botox, and possibly a mild chemical peel. I said he sounded as though he was suggesting dishes from a tapas menu, and he laughed and said, yes, a little bit of this and that could make all the difference. He did say he'd be happy to fill my naso-labial folds – the haggish lines running from my nostrils to my lips – right now, but equally I was welcome to wait for his letter and call him once I'd had time to consider.

Then, as the newspaper reporters say, I made my excuses and left. Left in the direction of a cocoon-like hotel I know, where I could repair my make-up and my self-esteem in the kindly light of their cloakrooms, before restoring my equilibrium with a glass of Barolo.

Could this be the right thing to do? I can afford it, after all, and the pain and bruising are both minimal, according to the entirely trustworthy Dr Target. I will still be me, just retouched and restored in key locations.

If I were still moving in the art circles I frequented with Leon, there would be no question. I see the photographs in *Tatler*, and the women who once told me how ageing was simply a new aesthetic are now rejecting the idea of doing it gracefully and are instead embracing every preventative measure known to medicine. And they are not stopping at the injectables, either. More than one has lost a chin or two. Something which Dr Target confirms is currently not possible without a scalpel.

So why not improve? Is there a moral difference between this strange plumping substance they would inject in the right places, and lipstick (which has been as important to me as oxygen since I was twelve)?

And yet . . . and yet. Since I lost Leon, I have tried so hard to shed this need for approval. Can I truly argue that if I had this done, it would be for me alone? And not to silence that pig James, and the voices from a thousand magazine articles and paparazzi shots of women my age who have had the audacity to show in their faces a hint of having lived for longer than two decades?

'Oh. Yes.' I notice the dark-suited man hovering next to my corner armchair. Actually, another drink could be just the thing. 'Barolo, large, please. Put it on my tab.'

As the waiter retreats, I admire his youthful physicality. Broad shoulders, the perfect V to his waist, the pert buttocks.

I allow myself a laugh at my own expense, surprised at how much longing I feel, not for the waiter especially, but for those days. I cannot regain *that* through medical intervention, unless the excellent Dr Target invents a time machine that erases more than wrinkles. True, the night with James did show that I can still respond physically to a man but I cannot see myself trusting one again for a long time.

The waiter returns promptly with the glass, and this time I notice his face, too, slightly soft, more Leonardo di Caprio than Vin Diesel. He smiles, a genuine one, that lights up pale silver eyes. My mystery shopping training has equipped me with the ability to see the difference between fake smiles and the real thing: employers expect the best waiting staff to let their eyes crinkle at the edges with excitement at the prospect of serving customers.

The sweet boy is trying hard. I will make sure I tip, when I settle my bill.

'Thank you. Do you want me to sign for the wine?'

His smile grows broader, more than a hint of amusement. I give him the benefit of the doubt, deciding it falls just the right side of insolence.

'That won't be necessary,' he says, pulling out the chair next to me, 'provided of course, that you allow me to keep you company while you drink it.'

I am lost for words. An *escort*? Here? It is not what I would have expected from this hotel. As I look around the packed bar, I remember something I have noticed before about this place – that they only seem to employ female waiting staff, and pretty ones at that, presumably to give the male guests an appealing view at all times.

'You're not a waiter . . .'

'No. I'm not. I am, however, rather on the thirsty side,' he brings his left arm from behind his back, and he's holding a glass of champagne, 'and I was rather hoping you wouldn't make me stand at the bar.'

'Uh.' I feel myself colouring, until I realise why he asked: the bar is packed. 'Oh, of course not. Yes. Do take the seat. It does get extremely busy in here. Are there really no other seats already? It's only just past five.'

'Oh, there are other seats,' he says, and now his smile seems to have another agenda. 'But none quite as desirable as the one closest to you.'

I blush. 'You flatter me. Are you drunk?'

'Not even slightly. I just have a talent.'

'For what?'

'Instantly spotting the most attractive woman in a room.'

I look around the room. 'Where are they?'

'Who?'

'Your friends. You Englishmen like japes, am I right? This is a little game, flirt with the older woman, before moving onto the next place.'

'No. You're wrong. I am here alone.'

'Really?'

He shakes his head. 'Ah, I get it. This is the brush off, right. That's fine. You win some, you lose some. But it was nice to meet you . . .' He holds out his hand.

'Grazia.'

'Oh, that's beautiful. It makes me think of sunsets with a glass of Chianti – or maybe Barolo, I like that too – and a plate of fresh mozzarella di bufala.'

His accent is not bad. 'You like Italy.'

'I like Italian women more, Grazia. Give me your number, and I will prove that I am absolutely serious.'

I used to think I was a good judge of character, but after the James experience, I have sworn to take no one at face value again.

And yet, this man is irresistibly handsome. Too good to be true, almost certainly, but there is always a chance. I reach into my handbag and draw out one of my visiting cards.

He takes it. 'I will call you. But now I have something highly embarrassing but necessary to admit.'

I try not to let him see me sigh. 'What?'

'My name . . . is Nigel. There. It's the bane of my life.'

'And that is all?'

'If you'd lived with the name Nigel for as long as I have, you would not see it as a trivial issue.'

'If I had lived with the name Nigel, you would not be chatting me up.'

And I feel something. Excitement. He has what James did not – how did I miss it – a sense of humour!

Chapter Nine

I'm standing at the fridge, considering leftover pizza for break-fast, when she calls.

'Kelly? It's Sandie Barrow. From the Customer is King Consultancy.'

I shut the fridge door. Didn't ever expect to hear from that uptight bitch again. Maybe Luis told her the truth about me, and she wants to give me a head-girl telling off for wasting her time. 'Oh yeah?'

'I'll get straight to the point. The person I recruited as my assistant hasn't worked out, and I wondered if you were still interested in the role?'

I take the phone away from my ear and stare at the display to make sure it's not one of the idiots from the market trying to wind me up. No. Definitely the right number. 'You're offering me the job?'

There's a slight pause, and I realise how gobsmacked I must have sounded.

'Yes. I am. Subject, of course, to the usual terms and con-ditions, trial period of four weeks, discussions about salary . . .'

I've got the job! Kelly Louise Wright, the girl least likely to make anything of herself, is being offered a proper job – with a *salary* instead of cash in hand – for the first time in her hopeless life.

'. . . and, naturally, the provision of two satisfactory references.'

'References?' *Shit.*

'But as I'd like to speed the process up, I'm happy to take those on the phone, if you can give me details of your referees.'

'Oh. Yes. Sure.' I begin a mental run-down of my mates, working out which of the people from the market can put on the poshest accents and use the longest words in return for a pint. There should be no shortage of volunteers . . .

Must make sure they mention how brilliant I am at thinking on my feet.

'So you'll take it, then?' Sandie sounds so relieved that I realise I've gone and missed a trick here, one that should come naturally, after my years of life on the market. It's all about bargaining power.

'We-ell, I'll have to think it over . . .'

'Only I do want to be honest, Kelly. I reckon I might be taking a gamble with you, because you're not what I'd call *traditionally* qualified for the job.'

'What, on account of me having no qualifications at all?'

She laughs. 'That'll be it. I'm operating on a hunch here, and the longer you leave it, the bigger the risk that I might—'

'Come to your senses?'

'— go back to the safer option. Up to you, Kelly.'

She leaves it hanging, and I realise that for all her nasty clothes and good manners, this woman has the deal-making instincts of a stallholder. And what's the alternative? Today's cold pizza breakfast is the highlight of my entire week. My only other appointments are signing on and possibly filling in for Pam on the handbag stall, if her bunion op hasn't been cancelled again.

'I'll take it.'

'You will?' She sounds surprised. Or could it be pleased? She doesn't have a clue what she's letting herself in for. 'Good. Great. Welcome to the team. When can you start?'

'Obviously I need some time to organise myself.'

'Obviously,' she agrees. 'So shall we say tomorrow morning, nine o'clock?'

After she hangs up, I lean against the oven, staring at the phone. This *is* for real.

Of course, it won't last. She'll find out pretty soon that I am unreliable and moody and disorganised. Oh, and dim. All the reasons why I was never going to amount to anything, and never have.

But still, I wish I had someone to tell. Dad's asleep – he had a big night last night. I could try calling Mum or my brother in Australia, but they're bound to be out, doing whatever it is ex-pats do: drinking tinnies on Bondi or hanging out in a buzzing coffee shop, like the characters in *Neighbours*. And my friends . . . well, I found out who my true friends were a couple of years ago, and I could count them on one hand. Or one finger (and I haven't heard from Tina for a while). The rest would just take the piss, and what's the point in mentioning it now, when I can't see me lasting till the end of the week.

A determined salsa beat pulses up from the flat below me, and I remember that there is at least one person who'd be pleased to hear my news.

Luis's mother opens the door when I knock. She reminds me of a little bird, light-boned and weightless, except for her ankles which are as thick as cricket bats. She smiles at me, which is a bit gross as she hasn't got any teeth in, and I manage to explain through sign language that I'm looking for Luis, and she invites me inside.

I've never been here before, but it makes our flat upstairs look even sadder. No grey carpet, no brown walls, no kitchen cabinets with the doors falling off. Down here, everything's yellow and red and parrot green, and the shelves are crammed with knick-knacks, and the floor is covered in rugs and shoes and books. And, of course, the temperature is tropical.

Luis's mama shuffles into the hall, and a few seconds later, Luis appears in T-shirt and tracksuit bottoms, his hair sticking out at odd angles, and a deep crease across his cheek.

'Sorry, Luis. I didn't realise you were asleep.'

He yawns. 'Is OK. Was getting up soon, anyhow. Double-shifts.'

'To pay the heating bill?'

82

He smiles. 'Ha, ha. Funny girl.' He says something in Spanish to his mother, who shuffles away again. He sits down on one sofa and points to the other. 'You sitting?'

'Thanks. I came to tell you my news. Your friend Sandie has offered me the job.'

Luis beams at me. Really beams, like a ray of bloody sunshine. 'I knew you and she would be good together. I knew this! Now you go straight!' And he gets up and pats me heartily on the back. 'I knew you good girl underneath, for sure.'

'Dunno about that, Luis. But . . . well, I am grateful that you didn't grass me up at Garnett's. I know it was a big risk for you.'

He shrugs it off, walks towards the kitchen, which has units painted the colour of tangerines. 'Ah. You had not even left the shop. Sandwich?' he asks, as he begins to spread pieces of bread with a brown fudgy stuff.

I'm about to refuse when I realise I still haven't had breakfast. 'Thanks.'

'So. I am now Luis the lifesaver, yes? It was worth the risk.'

I sigh. 'Maybe. Listen, Luis. You're not going to be gutted if it doesn't work out, are you? I did what you asked me to, yeah? Went for the job. Got it. But I don't really *do* regular hours. Not like normal people.'

He turns back towards me from the sandwich-making. 'What makes you so special that you no need to work, huh, Kelly?'

Cheeky bastard. 'I'm not saying I'm special. I'm just crap at getting up. Crap at sticking to stuff. Not the way I was brought up.'

'Ah! You blame your parents.'

I think about Dad, snoring his life away upstairs. 'Why shouldn't I?'

'Because you're grown woman, Kelly. You smart, I know that. Why should I double-shift so you have big lay-in every day?'

'Um . . .'

He brings over a plate of sandwiches, the brown stuff oozing out of the crusty edges of the thick white bread. 'Don't worry. You're safe, I no grass you up now. But there is no mystery working for Sandie. She is tough, tough cookie on outside, but sweet inside.' He bites into the sandwich. 'Like this. You try.'

I pick up mine, and bite into it. The brown stuff is toffee, so sickly sweet it makes my face wrinkle. 'How can you eat this stuff, Luis?'

'Is my favourite. Remind me of home.' He smacks his lips in approval. 'So. You giving up before you begin?'

I shrug. 'Quicker to give up on myself, instead of waiting for her to give up on me.'

'Ah, self-pity is so unsexy, Kelly. You don't have boyfriend?'

Sexy? That's the last thing I want to be. 'I'm . . . in between men.'

'So you can focus on your career?' And then he twinkles at me again. 'Try your best, please? Show I was right to give you a chance, huh?'

I put down my half-eaten sandwich. 'Do you still think you were right?'

'I hope I am right. Gambling terrifies me.'

'And me.'

He hesitates. 'Ah, if I understand about your life, you have more reason to be terrified than me, Kelly. But also more reason to make this happen.'

I don't know how he knows, but he does. Other people know, too, but they don't get involved. Why would anyone sane get involved in the bloody mess that is my life if they didn't have to?

Luis doesn't have to, but he has. Kindness confuses me. I'm looking for the ulterior motive but I can't think of one.

'I'm going to try, Luis. It's all I can do.' I stand up and he gives me that beam.

'You will be surprised at what you can do,' he says, like he's some kind of mystical South American guru. Instead of a short, fat security guard.

But he cares. That's more unusual round these parts than Aztec gold.

My first day at work. I haven't bothered to tell Dad I got the job. He'd only have set his alarm to get up early so he could take the piss.

So I'm alone as I creep around in the November darkness, and stub my toe on the telly cabinet and have to bite my hand to stop myself screaming.

And I feel sick as a dog. How unfair is that? I didn't even have a drink last night, although I was gagging for one to help me sleep.

After my motivational talk with Luis yesterday, I went to the market as a customer for a change. Talked Polly into lending me a suit with a pencil skirt (she'd had it hanging round since about 1982, judging from the shoulder pads). Said I wanted to try it on at home. Not sure she believed me, but she says so long as I take it back within two days she'll give me the money back. No problem. I might not even get through the day. Had to buy the shoes outright, though they only set me back seven quid. Ray did me a deal.

I leave the dark flat at quarter to nine and instead of turning left to go to the market, I go towards the bus stops on Shepherd's Bush Green, joining the stream of commuters. The office workers, the shop workers and the rest. At first I'm convinced one of them might point at me, as if to say 'She's not one of us,' but they don't, and I catch sight of myself in the charity shop window and you know, I look good. Weird, but good. Older. Really, I need a bun to go with the secretary look, but I don't have long enough hair, or any clue how I'd do a bun even if I did.

The bus is packed and sweaty, even though it's cold out. I'm worrying about getting Polly's suit dirty, and then some fat cow stands on my foot, and I really, really want to swear at her, but somehow the suit stops me, because that's not what you do when you're dressed like this. Instead, you apologise too – even though it's obviously fat cow's bloody fault – and shuffle a bit out of her way so she can't do it a second time.

Remind me why the hell I'm doing this again?

At Chelsea I get off, and wonder why I feel high as a bloody kite, till I realise it's because I'm getting my share of oxygen, after having my lungs squashed to buggery on the bus. No way can I do *that* every day.

But the river looks pretty, if you like that kind of thing, little waves reflecting the pale sky. Mum always called them white horses. I follow Sandie's directions, though my feet are starting to hurt, what with the walking and the bus incident. Finally I find her apartment block – these are definitely *not* flats – and the concierge lets me in without question.

Shoulder pads really do have their uses.

Sandie warned me she works from home but I can't see her being the type to loll round all day in her pyjamas, and sure enough she comes to the door in smart navy trousers and a cream shirt. She looks at my outfit and nods approvingly.

'That's an improvement. Welcome aboard, Kelly.'

She leads me briskly through the apartment and I catch glimpses of huge leather sofas and an antique globe and several well-chewed dog bones. It's very male, very clubbish. Her office is different – more feminine and airy, and too small for two of us.

'I know it looks cramped,' she says, reading my mind, 'but I spend a lot of time on the road, and if you prove yourself at the mystery shopping, then so will you.'

'Great,' I say. Prove myself? What a joke.

She's right down to business, explaining filing systems and voicemail and email and current priority clients and contracts and, finally, how the coffee machine works.

Once my induction's over, I sip my coffee as slowly as possible, to delay the moment when I have to sit down at the laptop and she realises that my 'touch typing' consists of using my two index fingers.

'Oh. I almost forgot,' she says. 'Don't worry about getting stuck in just yet. I've made you an appointment this morning with my secret camera guy. The sooner you're all tooled up, the sooner you can go undercover and put all that store security expertise of yours into action!' And she smiles, like this is something I should be looking forward to . . .

Secret Camera Guy is called Alan, and works from a tiny office behind a watch repairer's in Soho. It's just like the Harry Potter movie, and I'm half-expecting to have to give a password to the old guy behind the counter but instead he lifts the wooden divider and gestures out back.

I take one look at Alan and I know he's ex-Filth. There's something seriously upright and uptight about him, even though he's hunched over a workbench, slicing into a leather briefcase with a scalpel.

'You're Sandie's new girl?' he says, glancing up briefly, before returning to his cutting. 'Let me just finish this then I'll be with you.'

The workshop is crammed full of equipment, but ruthlessly organised. A place for everything and everything in its place. I bet the bloke can't even leave the house without making sure his shoes are so shiny that you can trim your nose hair in their reflection. And I bet he has plenty of nose hair. He's pretty old. Thirty-three, minimum.

He lifts the briefcase onto a shelf – a place for everything, like I thought – and scrutinises me, like I'm a problem to be solved. I feel hot and bothered, suddenly convinced that he'll see what Sandie didn't. That my 'security expertise' comes from walking on the wrong side of the law.

'I'm Al,' he says holding out a chunky hand and giving me the 'I was in the Vice Squad and I haven't lost my grip' shake.

'Kelly,' I mutter, giving him my 'hard as nails meself, mate, so you don't impress me' handshake in return.

'You're a bit different from the last one,' he says, with a tough guy smile he obviously thinks is sexy. 'Not surprised she didn't last. She was more interested in flirting than learning how to operate the kit.'

Oh, so he fancies himself, does he? 'Don't worry. I won't be flirting. No offence, Al, but I've never gone for short, past it guys.'

His eyes narrow. Ha. 'Shall we get on? Sandie said you need to get a quick lesson in operating the standard bag cam, plus I'm going to measure you up for a shirt with a button camera. But I'm only going to fit out the shirt if you last your trial period, and now that I've met you, I'm not going to put that to the top of my priority list, if you get my drift.'

He's lucky I'm on my best first-day behaviour, or I'd smack him one. Cocky sod. Why are coppers *always* like this? Full of themselves and in your face when you don't want them around, and fucking nowhere to be seen when you actually need them. 'Whatever.'

He opens a drawer behind him, and pulls out a tape measure. 'Shall we get this bit over with first? I prefer to get the measurements myself, as ladies have a tendency to lie in my experience. But if you're going to accuse me of sexual harassment then I can just watch.'

I raise my eyebrows. 'Go ahead. Believe me, there's no way on earth I would make an association between you and anything sexual.'

He shrugs. 'Close your eyes. Raise your arms. And shut your mouth.'

'What, that's going to affect my chest size?'

'No. But it's going to make my job a hell of a lot easier.'

Chapter Ten

Emily

What's a girl to do when her shop is emptier than Damart in a heat wave, her relationship is in the doldrums, her ex-husband is refusing to pay maintenance on the grounds of the global downturn, and her son seems hell-bent on taking the secret out of her secret shopping sideline?

Why, bury her head in the sand, of course. Or, in my case, in the dirt.

'What do you think, Blanche?'

'More soot, definitely. And perhaps some more stains on her teeth.'

I peer at myself in the trailer mirror. I've often dreamed of being an eighteenth century heroine, floating around in a fetching bodice, and being mildly manhandled by Regency gentlemen. Which is what I thought I was signing up for when Jean's rumour about the film company coming to Heartsease turned out, against all expectation, to be true.

And when they posted notices asking for locals to act as extras, I thought my luck had changed. I imagined my hair coiled around my neck in delicate ringlets, rosy colour on my cheeks and lips, a cleavage to die for.

It was only when I joined the queue for the costume fitting this morning that I realised that the crowd scene they're filming on the green isn't a Frost Fair or a Hog Roast.

It's a public hanging.

89

'OK, that's you done,' says Blanche, the make-up supervisor. She leans down to check Freddie, who has already been transformed into the cutest urchin I've ever seen. 'And you were born to be grubby, weren't you, petal?'

'I do love dirt, actually,' my son says.

'So do I,' says Blanche. 'Right, if you can line up with the others to be checked by casting, then we can confirm if we'll definitely need you tomorrow.'

She points towards the other end of the common, where several dozen inhabitants of Heartsease are milling around, looking severely impoverished, clad in various shades of grey and shit-brown. I spot Jean – she gave herself the day off from the Emporium – in a shawl and long black dress. Her estate agent 'fancy man' Bob is there, too, as is the bank manager, the dentist, and Wendy who runs the playgroup. Normal life has been suspended in Heartsease, while we play at being movie stars.

Even though we're not filming till tomorrow, the common is vibrating with the sound of a dozen diesel generators, firing up the trailers and vans and even the ancient double-decker buses with steamed up windows where the crew are hiding, drinking cups of tea. There's an enormous catering van belching out the smell of hot oil from the back, and supplying enough food for a regiment from the serving hatch. Not that we're allowed to have any: until we're officially part of the cast, we're second class citizens.

At the furthest end of the common, the set designers are rigging up a gallows, using weathered-looking wood and canvas. There's another refreshments stall, too, but this one is for show, selling slices of meat and mugs of mead. I guess watching public hangings was hungry, thirsty work.

'Is that a fairground ride, Mummy?' Fredster points at the gallows.

'Something like that,' I say, hurrying in the other direction.

'Oh, doesn't he look a poppet?' exclaims Jean as Freddie and I get closer to the other extras.

'Quite the little tyke,' says Wendy. She's not fond of the Fredster. I think it's because she likes girls to be girls and boys to be boys, and can't get her head around the fact that my boy is equally fond of shoes and trains and, even worse, that I don't seem to care so long as he's happy.

Despite the lack of tiaras, we do look great. It's pauper chic – in truth, my voluptuous figure looks better in lowlife, low-cut rags, than it would ever have done in an empire line frock.

Will wasn't interested in acting, which is a shame as I bet he'd have looked super-fanciable a bit roughed up. Could have been the lift we needed for our love life, which has taken a nosedive since our big row over Babies. He says he feels under pressure to perform, when he's not even sure that he wants a kid, and in return I feel rejected. I know that logically what he says makes sense: there's no rush, we have too much on our plate with the shop, we can barely afford to pay the bills for the three of us.

But since when have logic and biology gone together?

My fellow paupers have gone silent. I look up and see the casting director, a chic woman in a red suit, followed by a young male assistant with a clipboard and an anxious expression.

'OK, guys,' says the casting director in a London drawl, 'you know what this is, yes? A public execution. So after three I want to hear your best jeering and whooping. Hangings were the eighteenth-century equivalent of a *Take That* gig. Or, judging from the age of some of you, an early performance by Elvis Presley. So give it some welly, please.'

The assistant steps forward. 'One . . . two . . . three . . . GO!'

We begin. I try to whistle through my fingers but I've never managed that in my life, so instead I join in with roaring. Freddie looks nervous, until the bank manager winks at him, and he giggles. Jean's facial expression is utterly terrifying: she bares what's left of her teeth (they asked her to take her falsies out for the occasion) and her eyes are authentically hate-filled.

Ah. Maybe I just need to think of someone I loathe.

That wasn't hard. I imagine that we're lining up to watch Duncan be punished for his many misdemeanours. Not hanging, perhaps, but I'd be very happy to see him in the stocks, being pelted with rotten cabbages. There! Take that, for running off with Heidi. And here's a turnip for trying to do me out of any money for selling our house. And a mouldy potato for trying to suggest to my parents that it was *my* fault we broke up. And a rotten egg for being a tightwad with the maintenance.

That's better. I'm really thinking myself into the part now . . .

The casting director is inspecting each of us individually, and whispering to her assistant. As she reaches Jean I hear her say, 'Bit old, isn't she? Don't think they ever lived that long in this period, so make sure she's in deep background if we do need to use her.'

The assistant looks even more concerned. 'Shall I stop make-up putting through anyone over sixty, then? Only I'd lined up the entire Churchwomen's Guild.'

'Unline them.'

Casting woman nods through the bank manager and the dentist – 'though tell him to keep his gob shut, his teeth are too bloody good' – before reaching me and Freddie. I give her a nice big roar, and she winces.

'Bit plump for a bloodthirsty pauper, do you think?'

'OK.' The assistant nods, scribbling something down.

'And the hair looks like it's out of a bottle.'

'Excuse me,' I say, 'but I'm a natural blonde.'

'But the child's good. I don't suppose we can have him and not her?'

'She's the mum, so we'd need to get in a chaperone.'

The casting director sighs. 'Good point. And at least the mum's short. She's through, but again, deepest of deep background, except for the kid.'

I stop wailing, lost for words, or wails. I can't believe the way that woman spoke about me, as if I wasn't even here. I'm on the point of arguing or telling her to stuff it, when I notice that Wendy gets nodded through without comment.

If I pull out of the film, I'd never hear the last of it at Tiny Tykes. I'm just going to have to grit my teeth, swallow the insult and think of Duncan.

Freddie and I get home just as Will is shutting up shop for lunch. We used to stay open all day, until we realised we'd never had many customers between one and one thirty. Now we compromise with a sign on the door saying THUMP HARD IF YOU WANT TO COME IN, WE'RE ONLY UPSTAIRS.

But today I am in a funny mood, and this suddenly seems like the height of stupidity.

'Couldn't you have waited till I got back to make lunch? There are dozens of people out there from the film company. Hundreds even. They might have been searching for a . . .' I look around the shop for the right product, '. . . a snowman-shaped frying pan to change their lives.'

He looks at the pan, then at me. 'You think so?'

I put the pan down. 'OK. Maybe not. Maybe that's our bloody problem. If we sold something people actually needed—'

'I can't believe you're saying that in the pan's earshot. Imagine how hurt it will be . . .' He leans forward and rubs my nose: his finger comes away black. 'Oh, I love you when you're dirty.'

'Don't think you can get round me with flattery,' I say, but I'm already blushing. 'They think I'm too fat to be a peasant anyway.'

'Who said that? I'll punch him.'

I laugh. 'It was a woman. And don't punch her, she adores Freddie.'

'Aha.' Will kneels down to seize the Fredster, who whoops with delight. 'Hey, matey. Maybe you're the key to our future billions. We can put him on the stage, Em. Watch out Daniel Radcliffe.'

'Hmmm. Can you imagine Duncan's reaction? He'd be in court fighting for custody faster than you can say Harry Potter, insisting he gets half the money.'

Will turns Freddie upside down, to further whoops, and then peers at me from between my son's feet. 'Right little ray of sunshine today, aren't we? Still, I know a good way to cheer you up.' And he winks lasciviously.

'Will!'

'Must be the costume. I haven't seen a comelier wench in years.'

'Oh, shit, I forgot to take it off.'

Will puts Freddie down, and then pinches my bottom. 'Do you think you might need some help with that?'

I'm in a much better mood this morning. Last night Will and I made up in spectacularly enjoyable fashion (although he made a big thing out of using a condom). The sky is clear, and the forecast is for a brilliantly crisp November day. And the smell of fried breakfast is wafting its way across the green, thanks to the film company's location catering van.

It's still not quite six o'clock, but I've been peeping out of the window since five (which, due to the extremely poky nature of the flat above Bell's Emporium doesn't even require me to get out of bed: I just move the curtain to one side) when the crew began to arrive. It's a mini-village in its own right down there, with even more trailers at one end, and the other side cordoned off and completely cleared of all modernity. Cars have been moved away, lamp-posts uprooted and the bus stop temporarily shifted out of shot. Apparently Heartsease Common was chosen by the location manager because we were the only place he saw within travelling distance of London with a whole row of unextended houses opposite the common. I never thought that the relative poverty of our funny, rundown little village would be a bonus.

And it's been a small boost for the shop, too: yesterday we managed a week's takings in an afternoon. Will even claimed to have sold the snowman frying pan, though I wouldn't be surprised if he'd just hidden it to make me feel more cheerful about the shop's prospects.

I throw myself under the shower. Can't quite get the fake dirt off, but then I'll be back in make-up within the hour. I try to wake Freddie, and manage to manhandle him into his clothes as he stands with arms outstretched and eyes firmly closed, like a sleepwalker.

'Off already?' says Will, when I kiss him goodbye.

'Yes. We've got a "call time" of six thirty.'

'Oh, we've got all the lingo now, have we? Well, happy extra-ing. Make sure you come back lovely and grubby again.'

'That's another thing I learned from the pros yesterday. We're not extras. Freddie and I are supporting artistes!'

I leave him snuggled under the duvet and head downstairs with Freddie, who is beginning to wake up. I'm banking on the fact that he won't be able to see too much of the drama, but maybe I ought to warn him.

'Now, the most important thing to remember today, Fredster, is that we're pretending. When they bring the lady up and put the rope around her neck, they're just playing. OK?'

'Like at the adventure playground? They have ropes at the adventure playground, don't they, Mummy?'

'Well, yes,' I say, suddenly terrified that he'll start acting out *The Highwaywoman's Destiny* with his pre-school pals. Wendy would not be pleased. 'But ropes and necks don't go together. OK? They're *very, very* dangerous.'

'Whatever.'

My jaw drops. 'What did you say?'

'Whatever.' He looks guilty. 'Thomas says it to his mum.'

Thomas is one of the rougher kids at Tiny Tykes. 'Charming. Well, you don't say it to me.'

'Why?'

Oh no. Why? is Freddie's new favourite game. He can play it for way, way longer than I can, until I give in around the seventh or eighth time he asks. I have – to my shame – even found myself groaning, 'Because I say so, and I'm your mother.'

'Ooh, Freddie, can you smell breakfast? I bet they have bacon sandwiches.'

Food is the only way to distract him from the Why? game, so we follow our noses towards the fabulous smell of sizzling fry-up which is wafting irresistibly across the green. A red-haired guy with a clipboard – even younger than all the other guys and girls with clipboards – intercepts me.

'You extras?'

'Supporting artistes, yes.'

He shrugs. 'Whatever.'

I look at Freddie, who is trying not to giggle.

The man consults his list. 'Who are you?'

I peer over the clipboard. 'Emily there . . . and Freddie there.'

He ticks us off. 'I'm Kevin, the second Assistant Director,

which means you do what I say, OK? You go where I tell you, you do what I ask.'

I have to suppress the urge to laugh at his self-importance. 'Your wish is my command.'

His eyes narrow suspiciously. 'Good. You can get some breakfast now that most of the crew and cast have had theirs, and then straight to costume and make-up. But remember when it comes to lunchtime, you have to wait until they've got their food in case we run out. It's the way it works.'

And he strides off before I have time to reply. 'Right, Freddie. Breakfast time!'

The queue is short now, and we're standing behind a bloke dressed as a soldier. He looks very familiar – I can't work out whether I've seen him around Heartsease or on *The Bill* – and I'm checking him out in between reading through the breakfast choices. It's better than the posh hotel where Duncan and I stayed on our one-night honeymoon: eggs every way, two types of sausages, home-baked beans, fried bread, mushrooms, hash browns. Plus tables running along the side of the van with more cereals than Mr Kellogg could ever have dreamed up.

BANG!

For a moment, I can't tell what's happened. Soldier man is falling backwards and there's a powerful smell of burning flesh coming from the catering van.

And then I'm running away from the van, and somehow Freddie's ended up in my arms, though I don't remember lifting him, and he feels quite weightless, and I don't stop to look back until I am on the other side of the common.

'Mummy, why did the van go bang?'

'I don't know.' Finally I look back. The van is surrounded by people but it hasn't turned into a fireball. In fact, I can't see any flames at all. We walk back slowly. The closer we get, the stronger the charred smell becomes and I wonder if that's human flesh. A pall of thick smoke is rising above the crowd, and the original silence has turned into a loud chattering and shouting.

'Mummy! Fire engines!'

I hadn't heard the sirens until he said that, but I look across the green and two are speeding towards us.

'Is anyone hurt?' I ask a pretty girl dressed in a long, muddy black dress.

'I heard the chef's singed his eyebrows.' She tuts. 'It's terrible.'

'Yes. Lucky escape, though, if that's all that happened.'

She gives me a funny look. 'No. I mean it's terrible that it bloody blew up before I had a chance to get my breakfast. I knew I should have eaten before I went to costume. I'll have to make do with cereal now. It's going to be a long time till lunch.'

'Out of the way, coming through, coming through.' A man in a first-aider uniform pushes through the crowd, leading a man in chef's whites to safety. Sure enough, his forehead is pink and he only has tiny remnants of eyebrows left, but otherwise he looks unscathed. Thank goodness: I don't think I could ever have eaten a fry-up again if that smell had been anything other than scorched sausage.

I look for the soldier actor who was just in front of me. Finally I spot him sitting in a director's chair, a small gaggle of extras listening intently.

'. . . one minute I was waiting for my bacon, and the next I was literally sent flying, at least thirty feet into the air. It's a miracle I didn't break anything . . .'

Kevin the second AD appears with a loud-hailer. 'OK, everyone, settle down, settle down. We're just waiting for the fire crew to check everything's safe, so if you could all clear the area, and anyone who hasn't been to costume or make-up yet, then please head in that direction. We'll update you as soon as we know what's going on.'

My stomach grumbles loudly and I stare longingly at the remaining food at the side of the van, now out of bounds. Green dress girl has nipped in ahead of the announcement, and is skulking away with several mini-boxes of Coco Pops.

'. . . well, that'll be that for today,' I hear one extra saying to another. 'Have you ever known a production carry on without catering?'

An hour later, there are still a few firefighters on site, making sure there's no further risk (oh, and sipping the remaining tea and coffee from the flasks, and scoffing the cereal, and eyeing up the actresses). A recovery vehicle is trying to get into position on the green to tow the catering van away. I've been through costume and make-up, and so has Freddie, but there's a lot of milling around and no work whatsoever being done.

I'm trying to earwig a conversation between red-headed Kevin, and the first AD, when Will appears.

'Didn't that fire start within minutes of you getting onto the set, Em? Is there something you're not telling me about your pyromaniac tendencies?'

'Shh!'

He smiles and adopts an expression of innocence as he too listens in.

'Reckon that's it for the day, now,' says the first AD. 'All that money down the drain, thanks to a dodgy sausage.'

'I thought it was the gas cylinder,' says Kevin.

'I never rated that cook, anyway. But thank Christ it didn't happen earlier. Can you imagine if boiling fat had exploded all over Keira and James?'

'Yeah. Actually, if it had been a bit worse, it might have saved make-up the trouble of doing the extras. A few scars here and there would have added to the authenticity.'

They laugh, as Will's eyes widen. I put my finger to my mouth to stop him saying anything.

'Seriously, though, we can't carry on without food,' says the first AD. 'Though I did suggest that you could get in the car and drive round Berkshire to fetch a few pizzas. Kev'll do anything to help, I said.'

'Cheers, mate. As if babysitting the SAs isn't bad enough. This lot are awful, talk about village idiots.'

Will's had enough now. He turns around and walks towards the two clipboarded ones, his face serious. 'Excuse me?' His voice is unfailingly polite, but I'm not fooled. Mild-mannered Will has been known to turn all *Incredible Hulk*. He flattened his boss with a single punch when the bloke turned up to tell him the old hardware store was closing for good.

'We're kinda busy, mate,' says Kev.

'I noticed,' says Will, and I tighten my grip on Freddie's hand.

'Will, it doesn't matter—'

'I couldn't help overhearing, you see, and I think I might just be able to help out. I'm Will Lewis, from the Emporium over the road.'

'It's OK, mate, we don't need any saucepans today,' says Kev, already turning his back.

'You might not need saucepans, but you need food, don't you?'

The first AD looks up at Will for the first time. 'Yeah, you got that right.'

'Only I have a background in catering, and I think that with a little help with some friends in Heartsease we might just be able to rustle up some lunch. But of course, if you're not interested . . .'

A background in catering? That's news to me. Although he does make a very tasty cheese and pickle sandwich.

The first AD is suddenly all ears. 'Follow me,' he says and I watch as Will is whisked off in the direction of the location manager. I am, if I am honest, a teeny weeny bit disappointed that he didn't get involved in a punch-up to defend the honour of me and Freddie and the rest of the Heartsease Common 'village idiots'.

But I'm also seriously impressed. I just hope he realises that he's got them over a barrel when it comes to naming his price.

I don't think Heartsease Common was ever a prime target for the Luftwaffe but by ten o'clock the spirit of the Blitz is recreated in our kitchen, and half a dozen other kitchens throughout the village.

'Will Lewis to Margaret Clark. Are you receiving me, over?'

'Receiving, go ahead.' Margaret Clark's voice trills down the walkie-talkie handset (requisitioned from Wendy at playgroup, who uses them for outings). We now have one in every kitchen, connected to Will, Commander in Chief, Operation Feed the Hungry Film Crew. If we can pull this off, we'll make enough money to keep us solvent all the way until January.

'Can you confirm plans for soup, over?'

'We're making carrot and coriander, and leek and potato. With bacon bits for the non-veggies. Over.'

'Any ingredients needed? Over.'

'Ten pints of double cream, and eight bunches of fresh coriander. Over. Oh. And bread. Over. Again.'

'Cream and coriander added to the list. Bread being taken care of by Patricia Bailey. Roger, over and out.'

I add the ingredients to the master shopping list. We've managed to get hold of a lot of food already by taking everything undamaged by the explosion and knocking on doors to beg, borrow and steal the contents of the village larders. 'So that's all? Shall I get going to the supermarket?'

'Yes. You'd better. Keep checking your phone, though, I'll text you updates. We're bound to be missing something.'

'Like our marbles?'

He smiles. 'Oh, ye of little faith, Em. Don't you believe we can do this?'

I consider the question. In two and a half hours' time, we're meant to be serving two soups, three choices of main course with four veg, unlimited fruit crumble and chocolate fudge cake and a selection of salads and cheeses to one hundred and fifty people, including several Hollywood A-listers, and an Oscar-winning director.

'I'm just worried . . .'

'What's worrying you?'

'Well, there's food poisoning for a start. Allergies. Cold soup. Hard bread. Broken teeth. Hygiene. And that's before we worry about what the food tastes like.'

'Oh, Em . . .' He puts down his walkie-talkie, and heads over to give me a cuddle. 'We're on track. Nothing is impossible for the folks of Heartsease Common. Remember the fete.'

It's true that there hasn't been an event like this since we staged the Save Our Shop fete on the village green two and a half years ago. OK, so we didn't actually manage to save the shop at the time, but it was a catalyst for so many things. Romances began that day, babies have been conceived as a direct result. And it was also the day when I realised I'd fallen in love with Will, even though he didn't know it . . . back then, it seemed impossible that I'd ever break free of Duncan's influence, or find a man who'd be willing to look twice at a plump, downtrodden single mum.

'Em?'

'Sorry. Yes, I was just remembering the fete. Like you said. And you're right.' I lean across to kiss him. 'Absolutely anything is possible.'

November 28 –
Shopping Days to Christmas: 26

Service and value: in a recession these words should be somewhere you can see them all the time. Like tattooed on your deputy manager's forehead . . .

Chapter Eleven

Sandie

' . . . And then Keira kissed Will on the cheek, and said it was the best blackberry crumble she'd ever had! It was amazing. Oh, and the director was trying to make a deal to ship forty jars of spiced shallot pickle over to his beach house in LA.'

I nod across the table at Emily, but I'm not really listening to her story about the Day the Movie World Came to Heartsease and Wonderful Will Saved the Day.

I'm watching her, and watching Freddie, and wondering how she does it. And whether I could ever do it too.

'But you had to sacrifice your appearance in the movie to provide the food?' asks Grazia.

Grazia is more like me. OK, so she looked after her husband for years, but she also has a selfish streak. She never had kids, and somehow I always imagined myself the same in my forties. Travelling the world, doing my own thing.

But if I go through with this, I will have a stroppy teenager to deal with at Grazia's age. I touch my stomach, still unable to believe that this is really happening to me.

No, those maternal hormones definitely haven't kicked in yet.

'Ah, that's the brilliant bit. I was worried that Will wouldn't realise what a strong bargaining position he was in, but I underestimated him. He did the deal for more money than I would have dared suggest, and then he threw in the final condition. That me and Freddie would be in the front row of extras during the big scenes!'

Freddie claps his hands together. 'I patted a horse, actually!'

As Emily explains the movie's ludicrous plot, I study Freddie, who is chomping his way through his early Christmas dinner. We're on assignment in a family 'fun' pub, though there seems to be a lack of families or fun-seekers.

It's not the kind of place I'd normally choose for lunch, and I only agreed to take on the job today because we've got to test our new secret cameras; and surely with three on the go we're bound to cover all angles. Plus I thought it'd be fun to have an 'office party' with my fellow secret shoppers and it's a novelty to be able to relax. Now that Kelly's joined me, I can afford to nip out for a while. She doesn't have the certificates that Yvette had, but she's a heck of a lot more streetwise. And her references were absolutely superb. Almost too good to be true.

Al's not sure. Funny bloke. He had words when he delivered the new cameras, warning me to be on my guard. Toby thinks he's got a crush on me, but I can't see it: Al could have his pick of women, he has that macho ex-forces aura about him. Anyway I thanked him for his advice, and then ignored it. It feels good to be able to leave the office for a change and I'm not going to let paranoia spoil it for me.

First impressions at the pub were mixed. When the waitress realised we were here for the Festive Frolics Menu – 'you're the first we've had this year' – she switched the Christmas music compilation to full volume, despite the groans of our fellow customers. They're mainly office workers and besuited lone men making half a pint of lager last all afternoon. I suspect some of them have been made redundant, but haven't yet got round to telling their wives. They must be desperate, to put up with *Stop the Cavalry* and *Last Christmas* on a half-hourly loop.

'Mummy?' Freddie says, while Emily's explaining the highway-woman's miraculous escape from the gallows. 'I loathe turkey with a passion.'

We laugh: he sounds exactly like Will. Freddie is adorable, despite having bread sauce down his chin. And in his hair. Oh, and a father who has the positive personality traits of Hannibal

Lecter. Maybe I *could* do this. Maybe, unlike my mother, I have the determination. The stubbornness.

'Try to have just a little bit more, it tastes nice once you're used to it,' Emily urges.

He gives her a strange look, then regurgitates a mouthful of white poultry onto his plate, and I have to look away, it makes me feel so sick.

'Oh dear, Fredster,' she says, reaching out automatically, fresh tissue in hand. Tissues. I never have a tissue to hand. I travel light. 'Never mind. Turkey can be a bit dry. But you've done very well with your sprouts.'

And that's the thing. Emily's made up for her husband's awfulness with unlimited supplies of patience and kindness and optimism and bloody-mindedness. But what hope do I have? The maybe-baby inside me will inherit my stubbornness and bad temper and control-freakery.

And then there's Toby himself. I suppose he does expect to have children one day, though we've never discussed it (which is proof that he doesn't see me as a long-term prospect). No, he'll succumb in the end to one of those well-bred girls selected by his mother, and the girl and he will procreate tidily, a couple of male heirs and then perhaps a female for decoration. And the children will come out at tea-time and gymkhanas, and Toby will perhaps conduct affairs from the Chelsea flat. Maybe in the back of his mind he has me lined up for the mistress role. So far, so Edwardian.

'Anyway,' says Emily, once she's described every detail of the costumes and pudding preferences of a bunch of actors I've never heard of, and told us how she got autographs of every member of the supporting cast for her dad and her nephew, 'enough about me. What's the news from you two?'

I hesitate. Telling someone will make it real. Luckily, Grazia jumps in.

'I appear to have acquired a toyboy.'

'No!' Emily claps her hands together with delighted shock, and even I am momentarily distracted from my problems. 'How toy is your boy, exactly?'

Grazia hesitates. 'Well . . . he will be thirty in August.'

'Twenty-nine! A whole fifteen years younger. Wow. You fox! Or should that be a cougar?'

'Cougar?'

'That's what they call women who prowl about looking for younger men. It said so in the *Daily Mail.*'

The *Daily Mail.* What would they make of me? Gold-digging Afro-Caribbean single mum?

'. . . and I could not believe he was approaching me at first, in fact I thought he was a waiter. He must have some kind of strange mother fixation. Though I explained that I have never been the mothering kind.'

I gulp. How does anyone know? I never even liked dolls when I was little. I preferred my plastic cash register.

'Toyboy?' says Freddie, trying the word out. 'Mummy, am I a toyboy? I am a boy and I have lots of toys.'

Emily leans over to kiss him. 'You're my toyboy, that's for sure, lovely Fredster. So, go on then,' she whispers to Grazia, 'details.'

As Grazia obliges, explaining her uncertainty about exposing her body to this much younger man, I find myself growing impatient. Such a trivial worry, compared to what's happening in *my* body. My face is becoming hot, and I feel that familiar rage grumbling inside me.

It's not just the pregnancy. There's also my mother's reappearance and the revelations about why she left. Maybe if it weren't for what's happening to me right now I'd side with Gramma, but instead I think of Marnie, cajoled into severing ties with her little girl. Perhaps she could have been stronger, but I know from experience that my grandmother can be an unstoppable force, especially when she thinks she has best interests at heart.

Whose best interests? Right now, I can't even bring myself to speak to Gramma.

'And what about you, Sandie? How is his Lordship?' Emily never wants to hear any bad news about my relationship with Toby.

'Oh, you know. Same as usual. Charming but immature. Although . . . I have other news. Big news.'

Emily smiles. 'Don't tell me, let me guess. Is it work or personal?'

'Personal.'

'Right . . . well, there's no engagement ring to be seen. I'd have spotted that straight away, so—'

'No games, Emily, OK? My mother's turned up.' I was so tempted, then, to confess. But I have to be strong. A problem shared is not a problem halved.

Grazia raises an eyebrow to signify surprise. So at least she hasn't had Botox yet. I rather suspected she might, once she got going on Operation Deep Freeze. But Emily is staring at me.

'What now?' I ask.

'Oh. Oh, you see that wasn't what I was expecting at all.'

'That makes two of us.' And I describe the inglorious reunion.

'Why has she come back now?' asks Grazia.

'She says she just felt the moment was right. But . . . well, if I'm honest, it doesn't make sense to me that she'd let me get to twenty-nine before deciding to do this. Surely when I was sixteen or eighteen or twenty-one would have been the time to do it?'

'And you've seen her since?' Emily asks.

I shake my head. 'Not yet. She's been catching up with old friends in the Midlands, but she's planning to come and stay with me once she's done. Toby thinks it's great, he can't wait to meet her.'

'And you?'

'I'm half-excited, half-terrified. It could be the start of something great, but the way Gramma's indoctrinated me, I'm also expecting my mother to have a wild party and wreck Toby's flat. Or plant cannabis seeds in his window boxes.'

'You done here?' The waitress comes to the table and all three of us instantly turn our cameras towards her. We're never off-duty.

'Yes, thanks,' says Emily.

'You'll be wanting pudding? We've got traditional plum, chocolate yule log, or cheese and biscuits. And ice cream for the baby.'

'I'm not a baby,' says Freddie, sticking out his bottom lip. 'And I don't like ice cream.'

I look at him again. How would we feed a child? Toby's fridge usually contains only vodka and last night's takeaway leftovers. And anyway, I can't rely on Toby being around, can I?

By the time the waitress has agreed to a special dessert of Frosties and golden syrup for Freddie – and unknowingly earned herself extra points in her secret-shopping write-up – I'm glad I haven't told anyone. My body might be capable of bearing a child, but I am not capable of bringing one up. I don't know why I ever thought any different.

'You know, you really did surprise me when you told us about your mum,' says Emily, after the waitress has cleared away our main course dishes.

'Why's that?'

'Because . . . oh, I know this sounds daft, but you know what a vivid imagination I have. The minute you walked in earlier, there was something about your face, and I had this strange vision . . .'

'Emily!' barks Grazia, 'Get to the point and put us out of our misery, if you please.'

'OK. Sorry. I just had this hunch that you were . . . well, pregnant.'

I stare back at her, momentarily speechless.

'Pah, your imagination, Emily, it will get you into very big trouble, one day?' says Grazia.

But Emily is staring back. 'Sandie?'

'I . . .'

'Oh, bloody hell. I'm right, aren't I? And forgive me for saying so, but you don't look best pleased.'

'Is this true, Sandie?' Grazia looks appalled.

I nod. 'It wasn't part of the plan, put it that way.'

Emily leaps up from her chair and envelops me in a hug. When she lets go, she says, 'Planning's overrated, Sandie. You'll make an amazing mum. And Toby will be such a fun daddy!'

I break away. Her reaction makes me feel even more ashamed of my own. I was right: troubles should not be shared. 'Maybe.'

Emily looks at me. 'He does know, doesn't he? About the baby?'

I look back, trying not to blink. 'No. The . . . time hasn't been right yet, and I haven't made any decisions.'

'But it's not just your decision, Sandie, is it? You're not seriously saying that you'd consider getting rid—' She checks herself, working out whether Freddie is listening.

'It is Sandie's life,' says Grazia, quietly.

'Not just hers,' Emily hisses back.

I hold up my hand. 'I will tell him . . . when I'm ready,' I lie. 'But please don't say anything if he's back at the flat this afternoon. Promise me.'

Emily won't look at me now. 'I promise. At least for today. But I think you're making an enormous mistake, and I won't keep a secret for ever.'

I nod, pay the bill, and then watch her as she takes Freddie off to the toilet.

Grazia stands next to me. She places her beautifully manicured hand on mine, just for a moment. It's cool to the touch and oddly calming. 'It is too personal to her, you know, Sandie. She cannot be uninvolved.'

'It's pretty personal to me too.'

She smiles. 'Men are entitled to their rights, of course. But it is a woman who knows what is right for her. Instinct will tell you what to do. Do not be swayed as I was swayed.'

'Do you regret it, Grazia? Agreeing to Leon's demand not to have kids.'

Her eyes become distant. 'Sometimes yes, sometimes no. We live with the consequences of what we did not do, as well as what we did.' She turns back to me. 'But there would be no toyboy if I had babies, I think. Trust yourself. As the great English saying has it, there are swings and roundabouts.'

And then Emily reappears, carrying Freddie, and every kiss she plants on his rosy cheeks feels like a reproach.

Chapter Twelve

So. Sandie has been caught out by life. She looks shell-shocked, perhaps even haunted, as we walk from the restaurant to her flat.

There is nothing anyone can say to help, but this does not stop Emily trying to pour oil on troubled water. She has become bored with sulking and is instead beginning a campaign to convince Sandie that this is the best mistake she has ever made. So far she has talked about web support networks and *The Contented Little Baby Book*, and how the first year is a doddle as soon as you find the right routine. What she seems to have forgotten is that we met her right in the middle of Freddie's first year, and she was like the washed-up victim of some appalling natural disaster.

Perhaps I should have been more definitive when Sandie asked me about my own situation. But there are no easy answers. On one day I feel free, on another I feel barren. Motherhood is not like dyeing one's hair to discover whether blondes do have more fun (when I did that, I attracted far too much attention from transvestites wanting to know where I got my wig). I made my choice. That is that.

'And the thing about babies is they're so portable. Before they can walk, that is,' Emily says, as Freddie attempts to pull her into the path of a BMW speeding out of the basement of Toby's apartment building.

'Terrific,' says Sandie wearily, 'but please will you shut up about it now? I promise I will tell him, but not now.'

She waves at the security guard on the gate and we follow her into the lifts. I find Toby's home soulless and plasticky, but Sandie seems happy here. However, with all that floor-to-ceiling glass, it is patently no place for a baby.

The door opens before she puts the key in the lock. Toby is on the other side, all blond hair and bonhomie. 'My lovely girl-friend,' he says, leaning forward to plant a kiss on her lips, 'and her lovely colleagues.' He high-fives Freddie, before hugging me and then Emily. She looks incredibly guilty at knowing Sandie's secret, but luckily Toby is too excited to notice.

'Got a surprise for you, Sandie,' he says. 'Big surprise.'

'I don't like surprises.'

He leads us into the living room. The only part of his apartment I covet is here, with the stunning panorama of the river. If I could transplant it to my land-locked apartment in South Kensington, all would be perfect.

'Hey, honey.'

A woman who could only be Sandie's mother is silhouetted against the window, holding a large glass of white wine. She is the mesmerising pear-shape of a bottle of Lambrusco, and is proof positive that after forty a woman must choose between her bottom and her face. I opted for a pert derrière, and so I must suffer sunken cheeks. She has a filled out face, and an even more filled out bottom that is testing the seams of her denim jeans almost beyond endurance.

Sandie and her mother approach each other a little warily. They manage the briefest of hugs, the older woman's arm lifting high in the air, to stabilise the contents of her wine glass.

'Marnie,' says Sandie, withdrawing instantly. 'What brings you down here?'

'Ah, Ma was driving me crazy so I got myself onto a train down to the Big Smoke. Train seats have gone and shrunk since last time I was here.' And she slaps her own behind. 'Worth the journey, though. Nice place. Even *nicer* man.'

Toby beams. 'Marnie and I have been getting acquainted,' he says.

Sandie looks disapprovingly at the wine. 'So I see. Well, I can't wait to catch up myself, but we have secret camera footage to review.'

'No problem, honey. Your man's already warned me that we can't clutter up the place while you're looking at *top secret* material, so he's taking me to the pub. Join us when it's over. You and your friends, and that nice Kelly. I can't believe my own daughter has *staff* . . .'

Sandie nods. 'We'll see. Aren't you due at Garnett's?'

'Yes, but I couldn't leave your mum on her own. One afternoon won't hurt.'

'I suppose not,' she agrees. 'And where is Kelly anyway?'

'At the bank,' says Toby, 'but she's been working like a maniac. You have to bring her too.'

'Maybe. I don't pay people to drink, though.'

Toby kisses her again. 'All right, Sandie, we get the message. But try to come along later.' He holds his arm out, and Marnie links arms with him, and they walk away, giggling like children. After they close the front door behind them, we stare at each other.

'Your mother is . . . a live wire,' I say, after a pause to choose the correct word.

'Well, I thought she was rude. She didn't even notice Freddie. Did she, darling?' Emily is indignant.

'My mother isn't really into babies,' Sandie says, and unspoken questions hang in the air. We stare out of the window, trying to find something uncontroversial to say.

'Mummy?'

We look to Freddie, whose face is very serious. 'Yes, Fredster.'

'There's a poo coming soon. Very soon.'

Emily grimaces at the rest of us before whisking him off in the direction of the toilet. 'Ah well. At least we didn't capture that little gem on camera.'

'Let's hope we captured *something* on camera,' says Sandie, setting up her laptop on the coffee table and switching on her new handbag-cam. 'Al claimed that the wireless uploading is so simple that Freddie could do it, but that doesn't necessarily mean we adults will find it as easy to—'

But before she can finish, the first images have appeared on the computer screen. 'Sandie, look.'

The image of the outside of the pub is so much sharper than the pictures from the old cameras. Almost *Hollywood* quality, I would say.

'Great,' she says, switching on the TV and connecting a lead to the front. The footage is now playing on Toby's giant plasma screen, the colours bright and the details so defined I am sure I can see the regrowth around the barmaid's recently plucked eyebrows, and even sense the beery breath of the man who leered at us all from his bar-stool. The sound that emerges from the surround-sound-speakers is wonderfully clear, so I can hear the chatter about share prices from the unemployed men to the right, as well as I can hear Freddie's giggles. And then, as the barmaid leads us to our table, Sandie's camera turns on me . . .

Oh, my face! My poor, lived in face. The lines, the discolouration, the saggy parts, the poorly applied make-up . . . and as I begin to ask the woman questions, I see my uneven yellowing teeth and the affected way I form my words with lips that have lost all their original plumpness.

I cannot even follow what I am saying – something about whether the turkey stuffing is nut-free – because I am too horrified. Dear God, what can Nigel the toyboy possibly see in this weathered tan handbag of a face? Is he quite deranged? I almost feel a little sympathy for the unchivalrous James and his attempts to persuade me I should go under the knife. Perhaps he did have my best interests at heart.

There is something too familiar about the woman on the screen, however. I cannot quite make the connection.

'Hey, you look brilliant, Grazia,' Emily gushes as she walks back into the room. She takes the remote from Sandie, and rewinds so that a spectacularly unflattering freeze frame of me with my mouth half open is on the screen.

And then the connection is made. My *mother* is staring back at me in full digital detail. The small-mindedness of eyes that never wanted to see beyond Liguria, the pursed lips that only ever muttered petty gossip or complaints, the coarseness of the hair where she constantly pulled it back from her face in frustration. Even when she died, she wore that scowl in her open coffin.

And now it is as though she is speaking to me: *what did I tell you, daughter? You may think you can run away but we catch up with you in the end. Forget your ridiculous fantasies about younger men and hang onto whatever little dignity remains.*

'I do not think so,' I say.

'Yes, you are. You're so photogenic, too. Isn't she, Sandie?'

Sandie's expression is more guarded and I know then and there that Dr Target is my only option. 'Very striking.'

I have been so foolish to think that heavy make-up and defiance could protect me from the signs of middle-age. The recordings play on and my fellow mystery shopping musketeers moan and groan about their own appearance – Sandie hates her hair and her thighs and her lips, and Emily hates 'my chipmunk cheeks and, oh God, those mammoth boobs, I never used to have mammoth boobs. In fact, I am one big pile of squidginess.'

And I have to bite my tongue because I would kill for Sandie's lips, or just a fraction of Emily's squidginess.

'I could do with a swift brandy after that,' Emily says, when it has finished.

'It would take more than brandy for me,' I say. 'Absinthe at the very least. Or perhaps cyanide.'

'Oh, it's just unfamiliar,' Sandie says. 'It's just that we never see ourselves on screen, do we? This time we were bound to get each other on camera and these new cameras, sadly, don't lie.'

'Even so, I want to go to the pub and so does Freddie, don't you, my boy? So are we going to find out how far Toby and your mum have got on their pub crawl?'

Sandie looks fed up. 'Well, of course, I'm not drinking at the moment.'

'Why not? Oh!' The penny drops for Emily. 'Oh, yes. Which means you haven't made a decision, have you? I'm so relieved, Sandie, I can't tell you—'

'It doesn't mean anything, Emily. Sorry.' Sandie stands up.

'You could have a soft drink. Come on, it'll be a great chance for us all to get to know your mother. See if she can resist Freddie's charms this time.'

'You go if you like. My mother's been in no great hurry to get to know me for the last twenty years, so I think she can wait another couple of hours while I finish off here. Plus I need to wait for Kelly.'

'How is the new girl?' I ask, trying to distract myself from those damning images.

Sandie shrugs. 'Too early to say. She's keen, but rough around the edges. Awful typing. Al, you know, who does the secret cameras since Bert retired, he's got a real downer on her.'

'In what way?'

'Says he gets "dodgy vibes" from her. But then he's ex-forces, isn't he? The sort who'd think my grandmother was slovenly because her socks aren't ironed. Anyway, Luis trusts her, and I trust her, so—'

The buzzer sounds. 'Hi, Kelly. I'll just buzz you up.' She puts the intercom down. 'You can see for yourselves.'

'So you trust her, but she does not have her own key?' I raise my eyebrows.

'Not yet. Just to be on the safe side . . .'

As we wait for her to come up the stairs, I wonder if *dodgy* means tattoos or a hard stare.

'All right, Sandie? Sorry I'm a bit later than I said—'

But she is simply a girl. A slight creature with an under-nourished physique and an unkempt pixie haircut of the kind last modelled by Mia Farrow. When she sees us she starts, wariness in her dark eyes, like an animal surprised by a hunter. Then she checks herself and her face changes. She seems to be challenging me.

'These are my friends, Kelly. Well, we started as colleagues at Charlie's Shopping Angels, but now we're thick as thieves. Emily, Freddie and Grazia.'

Kelly nods at each of us. Is she shy, or defiant? I can find no reason not to trust her, and yet despite her size and her low-key presence, she has a strange aura.

I struggle to pinpoint why I feel this way after I leave the apartment. It is only when I hail a cab, and catch sight of myself in the driver's mirror, that I realise.

That defensive shiftiness reminds me of myself, twenty-five years ago.

Chapter Thirteen

Every morning, I pinch myself.

I, Kelly Louise Wright, notoriously unreliable bitch and chip off the idle block, have been employed now for two weeks and one day. I haven't been late once. I have managed to keep my terrible touch-typing a secret. I haven't yet broken the computer, photocopier or fax machine.

And I think that Sandie and I are beginning to understand each other. She is tough but fair, like an inspirational school-teacher from an American movie (in real life, all my teachers were tough *and* vindictive, constantly blaming me for things I hadn't done). I bring her in a coffee from Costa every morning. She makes me a sandwich at lunchtime if she's eating in. Best of all, she actually seems to rate my secret filming.

There's just one fly in the ointment.

'Oh, well, if it isn't the wage slave on the way to the office.'

Except that's unfair to flies. Flies might regurgitate their food to eat again, and carry ten billion bacteria on each foot, but at least they don't hang around the house in filthy tracksuit bottoms, scratching their balls and hurling insults at their offspring.

'Fuck off, Father.'

'That how you talk to your clients, Kelly?'

'No, Dad. Because they're polite to me in the first place. That's how it works out there. You know. In the outside world. Where people don't look over their shoulders the whole bloody time in case someone's after them for money.'

'I know more about the world than you ever will.' Dad sinks down into the sofa, sighing deeply. Well, it is a bit exhausting, getting out of bed at eight thirty in the morning. He retrieves the remote from under his fat arse, and switches on GMTV. 'Oh, that new girl's tasty. Make us a cuppa while you're up, would you?'

I don't know why he pisses me off so much more right *now* than before. He's said a thousand worse things, yet that stupid comment, *I know more about the world than you ever will,* echoes inside my head as I flick on the kettle, pull out the teabags and sniff the two out-of-date bottles of milk to see which is the least off.

And by the time the water has boiled, the echo is more like the howl-round of speakers at a dodgy gig. I stand behind him. 'What do you mean?'

'Eh?'

'*I know more about the world than you ever will.*' My imitation's pretty good: holding my nose gives my voice the authentic Terry Wright whine. 'What's that supposed to mean?'

'Christ, Kell, bit early for this, isn't it?'

'I just want to know what you mean.'

I study the crown of his head, and I swear I can see the brain cells moving under the mottled skin of his scalp as he tries to think of something.

'Well, you're still a kid, aren't you? You've never been inside, you've never been in a punch-up or carried a blade, you've never had to run for your life . . .' He's in his stride now, Man in Pub Setting the World to Rights Mode.

Never had to run for my life? I wish I could forget the past as easily as he can.

But still he's blathering on. 'Those are the times that you learn about yourself, and about life.'

'So it doesn't count that I've spent most of my life watching *your* back. Trying to keep you one step ahead of the debt collectors and everyone else who fancied a go? You don't think I might have learned the odd thing from shitting myself every time you were late home. Or fixing you back up again those times you didn't run fast enough?'

He takes a big fat breath. 'You're blowing this up into something massive, Kell.'

I am so tempted to empty this tea over his head. Or maybe just the sour milk. But then what would be the point? It'd be me that had to clean up the sofa, and he could wash the globs of milk out of his barely-there hair, but it wouldn't change what's inside his thick skull.

'It is pretty massive, though, isn't it, Dad? What I've had to do for you over the years?' I wait for his answer, hoping that maybe, *just this once*, he might pick up on the seriousness. When he says that I judge him more brutally than any magistrate he's ever come up against, he's so wrong. Every day I long for him to prove that he's more than he seems to be.

'It's tough, yeah, but that's what families do. And I've helped you out once or twice, haven't I?'

I freeze. *Don't say any more. Please. I don't want to remember.*

'Anyhow, Kell, you needn't worry no more. Because I found a way out.'

I stop on my way back to the fridge. There are no words that could possibly freak me out more than the ones he's just spoken.

'A way out? Like all the other way outs and guaranteed solutions and foolproof plans you've had before?'

He chuckles. 'No. Because this one will work. Can't let you in on all the details, but trust me, Kelly, this is the one. You're never gonna have to worry about me again.'

Secret camera on? Check.

Bag wedged into correct position under armpit, facing out? Check.

Innocent facial expression? Check.

I do this every time I go on a mission, but I need to do it extra-carefully today, as I know my mind isn't fully on the job.

You're never gonna have to worry about me again.

Jesus. If there's a sentence more likely to make me worry myself silly, it's that one. And I have a horrible feeling he knows it, too.

I did try to get the info out of him, but he was acting like a small boy with a dirty secret, and he wasn't letting go of it. I left him humming to himself and travelled straight to my assignment, at a large branch of a childrenswear and toy shop on a retail park in the gloomy outskirts of north London.

My task is weirdly familiar from my previous life: I'm on a mission to steal. But there's a crucial difference. If I am caught, I have a get out of jail free card. Literally, a card that asks the store detective to call their head office, to confirm that I'm not actually a shoplifter, but a mystery shopper.

It's only happened to me once, so far, and for the first time in my life, I really felt for the poor bloody store detective. He'd been so excited to catch me pocketing a small bag of nails, and a bundle of seed packets (the mission briefings always stipulate the value of the items we take, but honestly – who the hell would risk lifting a bag of nails from a DIY store? No, if it was me, I'd go the whole hog, walking out of the doors with the kitchen sink or maybe a barbecue, and if anyone challenged me, telling them I just wanted to check I could get it in the car). When I produced my card, he was almost in tears, and I found myself trying to console him over a cup of tea and a biscuit in the staffroom.

But the other missions have been a resounding success. The score's been eight-one to Kelly Wright Shoplifting Services. Really, I can see why the stores are so desperate to review security, because it is piss poor. If Sandie and I fall out, then I know where to target.

Except the proceeds of a week's hardcore theft would scarcely make a dent in the debt Dad generally runs up in a single night of gambling. Like today. This store wouldn't be top of the list for any pro: there's so little value in these polyester-mix baby socks, or packs of nipple guards. The expensive stuff, the pushchairs and baby-seats, are triple-tagged. In other words, anyone who resorts to stealing from here does so for one reason and one reason only: they bloody need to.

I step through the sliding doors, into the store. The guard on the door is young, green-looking, but I guess he'd be fast on his feet if he had to chase some waddling desperate pregnant woman, or a wretched new mother who can barely focus thanks to three weeks without sleep.

But he's just window-dressing. Not the real threat.

'Need any help, love?'

I swing around, aiming my camera at the woman who has just spoken. She's going through the motions, and she isn't a security guard, either. But the acknowledgement would certainly be enough to let customers know that they've been noticed . . . and that customers who don't intend to pay for their goods might be noticed too.

'Just browsing, thanks.' Stay anonymous. Polite but not chatty. Be a body in the crowd, but not a face. For today's mission, I've dressed the part, in a wintry grey fleece, and jeans, because everyone goes shopping in jeans. Well, maybe not everyone. Here the customers wear leggings. Comfy, elasticated leggings, with room for post-baby weight or plain lazy weight. Leggings don't judge you for eating too many Dunkin' Donuts. And leggings don't give you a muffin top where your waist used to be.

Some of my class mates have had kids now, and I see them in the market, the same but different. Most of the blokes round our way don't think it's macho to change a nappy, and so the work falls on the girls, making them look old before their time. Same round here, I think. The security guard is the only man in the place, though to call him a man is pushing it.

But that won't be me. I don't like babies, and I don't like parents either. People don't have kids for the kids' sakes, they have them for their own selfish reasons. I read in the paper about designer babies, created as spare parts for sickly brothers and sisters, and I think, what's the difference between that and my dad, who uses me as a bouncer and a bank?

I do a circuit of the store, orienting myself and filming the displays so the HQ management can make sure all's in order on the shop floor. Cute stuff at the entrance, to tempt you inside: frilly toddler dresses, chunky cord dungarees, even a sailor suit. Cheap soft toys in pastel fleece. The aisles draw you round towards more toys and games, mainly gaudy action figures with body parts that detach bloodily or transform into robot limbs, and fake babies that cry and wee to order. The centrepiece of the store is a display of baby hardware, different makes of pushchairs and cots and playpens all laid out in a strange fake landscape complete with zebra crossing and postbox and village green.

Then in a far corner there's the maternity stuff; hideous bras designed for women with boobs as big as udders, and breast pumps and paper knickers and other things I'd rather not think about too much.

But it's not really the product range I'm interested in. It's the staff. As well as the guard, and the woman at the door, there are two girls on the tills, school-leavers, I'd guess. The skinny one has a bump under her waist, like an alien invasion, and I guess she'll be using her staff discount before too long. The fat one with the nose stud probably isn't expecting, but you never know. She looks like the women in the papers who say they didn't know they were pregnant until they gave birth while watching *EastEnders*.

There should be a comedy sign behind the till. *You don't have to be knocked up to work here, but it helps.*

And then I see the security operative. A ruddy-faced woman with red hair and a lightweight fawn trench coat is in the next aisle, trying to look casual. The eyes give it away. Beady, bright blue and slightly squint, they patrol the store while she stays put, like an ancient mummy in a horror film. She's been pretending to examine the instructions on a rattle (I mean. Come on. Instructions for using a rattle: Pick up. Shake. Repeat till your head explodes) for a couple of minutes now but she is using her thick fringe as cover, her head bent but her eyes wide open.

She's aware of me for sure, but I don't know if she has me down as bona fide, or the kind of customer who pushes the concept of 'best value in town' to extremes by awarding herself the odd free gift.

I feel a slight buzz. When I was a teenager I stole for pleasure as well as profit. I was good at it, simple as that. I used to choose awkward things to lift, bulky bubble bath instead of pocketable lipgloss. Once I took a turkey for Tina's mum because her dad had drunk the Christmas money. The value was the same, but the thrill was bigger. The fun stopped when it became a necessity.

But this is me against The Mummy. Something of the old

thrill is there, the battle of wits. I've done enough general filming of shelf display and point-of-sale, so I head back towards the pants and vest multipacks. Light, small, *needed* by growing kids. No wonder they're disappearing faster than anything else, a fact which The Mummy knows because her dead eyes linger longer over that department before swivelling over towards Sun Protection and Outdoor Fun.

I could cheat. The briefing only specifies taking an item under the ten pound mark, so it'd be easier to take a tube of posh chamomile cream 'for soothing Baby's softest places'. But no. That's not realistic. The women round here wouldn't bother taking the risk for something they don't need . . .

I stop. The reality of what I'm doing hits me like a belt round the ear on my birthday. I've been treating this as a lark, a crack, a funny story to tell the girls on the market some day, when Sandie's sussed me out and sent me packing. Kelly Wright, poacher turned gamekeeper.

But this is no funny story. It's serious. Every incompetent guard I uncover will be retrained or, more likely, given the push, and replaced by someone who can actually do the job. Who'll catch the thieves. The thieves stealing for their babies, even though they might lose their babies if they're caught.

It's doing my head in, thinking this through. Instead I spot a pack of farmyard-themed baby socks, a pair for each day of the week, and scoop it into my handbag with my left hand. Simultaneously I pull out a hankie with my right and blow my nose, in case The Mummy has seen the swift movement and looks up. She hasn't, and she doesn't.

Now I need to take care of the security tags. They're the magnetic ones, smaller than a postage stamp, and pre-packed into the cellophane. My nails – sharpened to scary points earlier this morning – rip through the wrapping, and I grope around for the tag. Got it! I pretend to replace the hankie in my bag, and quickly retrieve the tag from between Sheepdog Sunday socks and Moo-cow Monday. I fold it under the nail of my thumb, then when I pick up another pack of socks to read all about the fibre content (ninety per cent man-made? That's a recipe for sweaty baby feet, surely?), I let the tag fall out onto the shelf.

Done.

Shan't hang around and let my ginger nemesis get suspicious.

No matter how good I get at this, approaching the exit always makes my guts gurgle and my heart rev. One step in front of the other, that's how you do it. The boy on the door in the gold braid isn't a problem. It's the tags. Every now and then they chuck two into the package instead of one. I guess it's their idea of fun, like the women in the condom factory who keep a pin handy to keep the birth rate up. It's a laugh a minute, work.

Right foot, left, right, left, the carpet changes to crunchy door mat, and the security lad gives me a half-look as I step between the two sensors and . . .

I'm out. Of course I'm out. I've nicked frozen birds and thigh-high bondage boots, so socks are a piece of piss.

I am Kelly. I rule.

'You eaten all the pies?'

I am standing in the workshop of Uptight Alan the Secret Cameraman, being fitted for my undercover shirt. Yes, after completing my latest assignment, Sandie has taken me on as a bona fide mystery shopper, and the shirt is my prize.

Only trouble is, my prize gapes open at my chest. Acceptable on a footballer's wife, distracting on a professional shoplifter.

'Er, no. You obviously screwed up the measurements. Must have been when your hand was trembling with the thrill of touching a real live woman. Go on. Admit it. How long's it been?'

Uptight Alan gives me a bored look that's meant to show that he doesn't care what I say. Which only proves that he does. Ha. One-nil to me.

Not that he seems to know much about wearing clothes that fit. He's got this T-shirt on that clings to his pecs and his abs and the rest. As if anyone's interested . . .

'I've often wondered what makes grown women think it's either acceptable or attractive to behave like schoolgirls.'

'And I've never understood why ex-coppers still behave like dickheads even after they've left the force.'

'Actually, I was in the Army. Though it's interesting that

you've got a chip on your shoulder regarding the police. Any particular reason?'

'No.' I begin to unbutton my shirt and Alan turns away. 'Still, the Army figures. I guess you're used to seeing men naked, but not women. All boys together in the barracks, eh?'

He takes my shirt silently, averting his gaze from my body. Then he places his fingers around the buttonhole where the tiny camera is concealed and rips, suddenly and violently, through the fabric. 'You'll have to come back when I've bought another shirt.' He throws my own sweater back to me without looking round again. 'If you last that long . . .' It's spoken in a whisper that I am meant to hear.

'Just what have you got against me, arsehole?'

Now he does look at me, a snide smile on his taut, Action Man face. 'Oh, I can't possibly imagine. Your perfect manners? Your refined use of the English language?'

'You're just covering up for the fact you've got the hots for me, aren't you, Al? The depth of feelings I've unlocked.' And I pout at him.

'I'm trying – and failing – to cover up the depth of loathing I'm feeling for you, Kelly. And also failing to work out why a sensible woman like Sandie would have hired someone like you.'

'Because . . .' And then I stop. The truth is I don't know why she's hired me either.

Al takes a step towards me and the workshop feels even smaller. 'However tough she looks, Sandie has blind spots. That boyfriend of hers is one, and I have a horrible suspicion you're another.'

'What it's to you? Fancy her, do you?'

He sighs. 'No. But you need to know I am looking out for her.'

'Isn't that sweet? Though you're a bit short for a bodyguard, aren't you, mate?'

That's got him. He shakes his head. 'You can joke all you like, but I know what you are.'

I feel cold, despite the heat in the workshop. Has he seen through me? 'Meaning?'

He smiles. 'Work it out for yourself.'

I try to think of a smart reply but nothing comes. I grab my bag and leave the workshop without looking back. As I walk onto the street, I wonder what it is he thinks he knows about me. My petty criminal tendencies?

Or the other stuff. The stuff that I won't let myself think about, the shameful, terrifying memories that will always be part of me, however hard I try to banish them.

December 10 —
Shopping Days to Christmas: 14

When was the last time you slept with a *Big Brother* runner-up?
Surviving this recession takes dedication. Focus on product place-
ment: it's not what you know, but who you know. Has anyone
working in your store dated a footballer? Did your niece go to
school with an *X-Factor* contestant? The most fleeting celebrity
endorsement could save your Christmas.

Chapter Fourteen

'**M**ummy, Mummy! It's the Batmobile!'

It's completely ridiculous that Duncan's arrival still makes me jump. It's not even a surprise: he's here the second Saturday of every month (well, except when he isn't, like last month, because of some *'high level catastrophe'* in the insurance world) and takes Freddie off for thirty hours. At night I can't stop myself waking on the hour, every hour, thanks to my internal alarm clock.

I join Freddie at the flat window as Duncan climbs out of the car, squinting against the wintry sun. The Batmobile is a swish black BMW coupé, which he assured me he bought second-hand, 'for way below the book price, thanks to the credit crunch.' But when I looked it up online I worked out it had cost eighteen thousand pounds minimum – the equivalent of nearly two years' maintenance payments, even though he only uses the bloody thing when he's over here from Switzerland. The rest of the time it sits in a climate-controlled garage and for all I know is sponged down and buffed up on a daily basis by a scantily clad model dressed in purest chamois.

Whereas our battered white van is lucky if it gets topped up with windscreen washer fluid. We call it the Snowvan, because whenever we leave it parked somewhere, it sheds a little blizzard of flaked paintwork on the road around itself (actually, I think it looks more like catastrophic dandruff).

But Freddie loves the Batmobile. And he loves his dad, too. Of course, I am pleased that my son is so well-adjusted, but I do hope he loves me more.

'Daddy!'

Freddie is tearing down the steps towards his father. I follow at a distance, but close enough to see him leap up and see Duncan catch him and groan with the weight of him, before he swings him up into his arms.

'Hey, big lad! Look at the size of you,' he puffs.

'He seems to be growing a centimetre a day at the moment,' I say, and Duncan looks up at me. His boyish face is an odd yellowy colour, as though he's about to throw up, and I notice strands of white hair in his highlighted crop for the first time.

'If you're planning to ask for an increase in the maintenance, then you've picked the wrong weekend,' he grunts.

I turn around, so he can't see that he's still capable of hurting me. 'I wasn't planning to ask you for anything.'

'Can I come up?'

That's worrying. He always races off after the most cursory of hellos. He's been in such a hurry to leave that he's forgotten Freddie's overnight bag twice: the second time he got the whole way back to Somerset before realising. Freddie was hysterical on the phone at the absence of Pingu, and I drove to meet Duncan halfway (well, slightly more than halfway, I realised later, after trusting him to choose the handover location) with the missing penguin, because I knew that for all his three-year-old's bravado, my baby would never sleep without it.

'Sure.'

I know that Duncan's going to think our flat's a mess. A very *Christmassy* mess, admittedly: I've gone overboard on the décor this year and personally I think it looks fabulous, if a bit multi-coloured. I'd started out planning a purely purple theme, based on the most stunning blackcurrant-coloured glass baubles I snaffled from the shop. But then we got these amazing green glass lanterns in, and somehow one of them got cracked, and it would have cost more to try to send it back than we'd get as a refund, so that came upstairs too. Then there were the pink angel fairy lights. And the little peg Santas and white pom-pom snowmen that Freddie and I made together at Tiny Tykes. Coordinated it is not, but it's so festive.

I do admit the flat needs a tidy up, but there's never enough time when Freddie's around, so a thorough going-over is the next glamorous task on my to-do list. Duncan thinks I spend my off-duty weekends in some kind of sex-crazed Bohemian orgy with Will. The truth is that while Will mans the shop, I scrub with manic ferocity.

But, to my surprise, Duncan doesn't mention the mess. He slumps into the sofa, while Freddie tells him everything that's happened in his small world. 'And I think Lara is going to be my girlfriend, except her hair's too short, she looks like a boy. But she is pretty. Oh, and Daddy, I am going to be a movie star . . . and I'm a donkey in the Tiny Tykes nitty play.'

Duncan looks bemused. 'He means nativity,' I say.

'A donkey, eh? That's my boy,' says Duncan, winking at me. The first sign of the old Duncan I've seen this morning. 'Like father, like son.'

Freddie looks puzzled. 'Did you play a donkey too, then, Daddy?'

'You could say that.'

Duncan was always very pleased with himself in that department. Though in retrospect I think that it's all about proportion: even a button mushroom would look plus-sized when you're as short as he is.

'Why don't you fetch that photo of you with Keira?' I suggest, and Freddie runs off to his room. When he's gone, I turn to Duncan. 'Come on. What is it?'

He looks at me, and his expression really reminds me of Freddie's when he's caught in the middle of doing something he shouldn't: half guilt and half indignation.

'They let me go, Em.'

'Who?'

'The fucking company, of course. Who else?' He hisses. 'They've bloody well gone and made me redundant. Me!'

I stare back at him. 'When?'

'Last night. Waited until the end of the day, didn't they? Knew I had a plane to catch, called me up to the management office about ten minutes before I was due to get a cab to the airport, and said I didn't even have to come back on Monday.'

'What?'

'The HR woman is such a bitch. "We can arrange to have your personal items packed up and shipped to the UK",' he says, in a falsetto, accented voice. ' "Why don't you use your return ticket to come back and deal with the apartment, Duncan? As a measure of our appreciation of your work for the company, we will continue paying the rent until the end of the year." Till the end of December. Three weeks. Thanks a fucking bunch.'

I have so many questions. But before I can ask them, Freddie returns and plonks himself onto his father's lap so heavily that Duncan cries out. 'Watch where you're going, Freddie,' he snaps.

Hurt crosses my son's face and I feel it like a punch in the belly. I'm going to have to toughen up but how? 'Come here, Fredster. Daddy's feeling very tired, he'll look at your pictures later. Won't you?'

'Yeah. Sorry, Fred. Bad day. Sometimes daddies have bad days.'

Duncan has more bad days than most. His temper has always been on the short side. Just like him.

'Why don't you go down and see if Will needs help on the till, Freddie? You know how good you are at it.'

He nods, and disappears. We hear his heavy tread as he gallops down the stairs, in donkey mode.

'I'm not the only one,' Duncan says. 'They're axing twenty-five per cent of the workforce. Rumour is that it might be fifty per cent by the end of the year.'

'And Heidi?'

'She's safe. I didn't even have a chance to see her because of the bloody flight. I rang her and . . .'

'What?'

'She didn't sound as surprised as I expected. I know she's above me in the pecking order, but if she'd known, wouldn't she have warned me?'

'I suppose it's difficult for her. Being your boss and your . . . lover.'

'Partner,' he corrects me.

The word hangs in the air between us. We were once husband and wife, but I don't think we were *ever* partners.

'And the money?'

'The least they could get away with. Two months' notice. I could try for more, but they have an entire fucking floor of lawyers so . . .'

Two months' notice. I feel sick. 'What will you do?'

He stares at the floor. 'It hasn't sunk in yet. I could look for something else out there, but they're one of the last companies to make lay-offs. Financial services isn't exactly a growth area at the moment. I just didn't think . . . well, you never think it'll be you. Do you?'

I shake my head. 'No.' Just like I never thought my husband would leave me for his boss a few months after I had *our* baby. Or that he'd try to trick me into accepting a lower divorce settlement by forgetting to tell me he was turning what was meant to be our family home in London into luxury rental flats. I learned the hard way, and I guess it's his turn. But Duncan's led such a charmed life – the playboy of Western Somerset – that I guess it's going to be a harder lesson than it was for me.

'I guess I'll probably come home.'

'To Somerset?'

He gives me a sarcastic look. 'Come on, now, Emily. I'm never going to find a job to suit someone of my calibre there, am I? No, I'll move into one of the flats. Heidi can probably wangle a transfer to London. It'll be fine.'

'But won't the rent be your only income?'

'Thanks for the vote of confidence. I know all you're thinking about is your precious maintenance, to keep you and your bloke in the style you've become accustomed to,' he waves around the squalid flat, unaware of the irony, 'but there are going to be changes, aren't there? I can't keep supporting your dumb venture now, can I?'

'But you're not supporting us, Duncan,' I say, trying to stay calm. One of us has to. 'The maintenance has been worked out based purely on Freddie's needs, we don't use a penny of it.'

'Yeah, right. Well, let's see what changes now that I'm not

earning. Anyway, the top flat's available from January. The tenants have given notice. Going back to Gdansk because there are no opportunities here any more. The one stroke of luck I've had.'

'Right. And I guess there's always the car, too.'

He scowls. 'Meaning?'

'Well, you always said that you don't need a car in London. That's why I wasn't allowed to get one.'

'*Allowed?* You make me sound like some fucking Victorian husband. As I recall, you made most of your own choices without my permission. Besides, I'll need the car for picking up Freddie. I'll have more time to spend with him, till I find the right job. No point hurrying into something just to keep the wolf from the door. I quite fancy spending some time hanging out at the galleries, seeing new bits of London . . .'

I close my eyes for just a moment, hoping this might be a dream. When I open them again, he's still there, talking about all the museums he's never been to, the possibility of joining a private members' club for the networking opportunities, *ninety per cent of vacancies these days come from word of mouth,* and I realise that I'm witnessing Duncan re-inflating into his bubble of utter self-belief, and I also realise with absolute certainty that he's not going to learn a single thing from this brush with reality.

'Good,' I say, interrupting him. 'Well, I'm glad you have all these exciting plans, but you're missing out on time with Freddie, so why don't we talk in more detail when you drop him off tomorrow?'

'Can't wait to get shot of him so you can spend *quality time* with your Willy, eh?'

I take a deep breath. 'I have a more pressing engagement with a mop and bucket.'

He looks around him. 'Yes. It is looking a bit grubby up here. Can't be great for Freddie.'

And he stands up, brushes the imaginary dirt from his designer jeans, checks his hair in the mirror, ruffling it so that the grey seems to disappear, and heads downstairs.

I wait until he reaches the bottom before I kick the sofa. Once, twice, three times, so hard that dust motes fly into the air, dancing in the beam of sunlight.

But it doesn't make me feel any better.

I wasn't *exactly* lying when I said that we only spend the maintenance on Freddie. But it does make up a pretty high proportion of our income, and pays for shoes and clothes and playgroup and petrol and food and . . .

I go down to tell Will what's happened. 'We're going to go bust, aren't we?'

He gives me a big hug. 'Oh, Em. You and your imagination.'

I sink into his chest, my cheek against the fleece of his shirt, breathing in the scent of him mixed with the scent of bluebell fabric conditioner. But, for once, it doesn't soothe me at all. I pull away.

'No. It's not just my imagination this time, is it? Look around you, Will. What do you see?'

He smiles patiently – probably the wrong thing to do as it makes me even more ratty – and does as I say. The shop's still looking abundantly festive, but I wish it wasn't. A few more gaps on the shelves would be nice.

'Um. All the things we love, the items we've chosen with so much care. Decorations and housewares and gifts.' I nod at him to continue. 'And, um, candles, and pot pourri and jams and teddy bears and fairy lights and . . . oh, come on, Em, tell me what you're thinking. I'll never guess on my own.'

'Can you see any customers?'

He slaps his forehead in mock horror. 'Aha! I knew there was something missing.'

'Very funny.'

'But actually, we've had loads more customers this week, haven't we?'

He's right. We have had a sudden dramatic increase in customers, for no apparent reason. I even went on the AA website to see if we were benefiting from a traffic diversion through the village. 'Yes, we have. But how many of them actually bought anything?'

'Ah. Well, Rome wasn't built in a day.'

'It's not a day, though, is it, Will? It's seven hundred days.

And, apart from the money we earned from feeding the film people, can you tell me how many of those days we've actually broken even on takings?'

'You can't expect me to keep those kind of figures in my mind, Em.'

But I know he has a photographic memory, and could recite not just takings but breakdowns by product, gender of customer and payment method.

I lean against the counter. 'We need to face facts. It'd take an imagination far more developed than mine to pretend that we're doing OK. That we can survive this . . .'

He takes a step towards me now and holds me in a different way. No 'there, there' pats on the back. More an acknowledgement that we've failed. I feel tears pricking behind my eyes, more from relief than anything. 'Emily, Emily, Emily,' Will breathes my name into my hair and suddenly the idea of cleaning the flat disappears from my agenda. 'If we're doomed anyway, maybe we should take a long lunch hour off . . .'

I close my eyes as he kisses me. I forget all about takings.

The sound of an engine – a beast of an engine with a deep roar – makes me open my eyes. Right outside the shop a silver car pulls up, as long and shiny as a hearse, with smoked windows and a chrome woman – or is it an angel? – mounted on the bonnet. If it wasn't for this kiss, I'd probably go out there and tell them to park their swanky motor somewhere that it wouldn't block the view of our festive products.

But what's the point? I close my eyes again, until Will pulls away and I hear the front door of the store open. We jump apart as a greying man in a peaked cap and long felt chauffeur's coat comes in.

'All right?' he says. 'I'm looking for pickle.'

Will is immediately in sales mode. 'Ah, we can do you pickle, no problem,' and leads the way towards the shelf. 'Mrs Bridges, Thursday Cottage, Tracklements. Any particular flavour?'

I peer over my shoulder. The chauffeur has definitely come from that car. I try to make out the figure in the back. Male, I think. Not that tall, but it could just be the deep bucket seats making the passenger almost horizontal.

The chauffeur frowns. 'Those don't look very home-made. That's my brief. Home-made. Local.'

Will picks one of the jars up. 'Well, these are from Wiltshire, that's the next county down.'

The chauffeur's face darkens further. 'Don't waste my time, sunshine. Are any of these made in the village?'

'No, but—'

The guy's already heading for the door. I step forward, pulling on my most dazzling smile and shifting my elbows up and in, to boost my cleavage. I need to distract him for long enough to find out what he wants. 'I'm sure we can help if you can just give me a little more information. Like where you heard about us. It doesn't sound as though you were just passing through.'

He looks at me, then down. Good. Got him. 'No . . . um, no. It's something that someone mentioned to Tom . . . um, to my client, last week. That there was this weird village in the middle of nowhere where they sold the most authentic pickles and chutneys and home-made produce. He forgot the name and we were passing through on the way back to London and he saw the place name, Heartsease, and he ordered me to take the turning. I've already been to the Post Office and they said they thought it might be you.'

Tom? I take another sneaky look into the car. Could it really be *the* Tom? Short stature? Short hair?

'Who might have mentioned it?'

Finally the chauffeur looks up from my cleavage. 'Look, love, no offence, but I don't have time for twenty questions. It would have been someone from the industry, I guess. Weren't they this way recently? On a shoot?'

'The film industry?' And then I realise. 'It wouldn't have been Keira, would it?'

He's sizing me up. 'Dunno. Might have been.'

'I know exactly what you're talking about now.' Will gives me a questioning look. 'It's such an exclusive range that we don't have it on display. How long can you wait?'

'We're behind as it is.'

I rack my brains for something I read in *Heat*. Or was it *Hello!* 'Tom's a big fan of English tea, isn't he? Could we maybe offer him a tasting of some of our favourite brews, while we check the stock position?'

'He won't get out the car. He's got a bit funny about people since the last set of pap shots tried to make out he'd had a hair transplant.'

'He doesn't need to. We'll bring it on a tray for him to have in the car.'

'It's a limo.'

'And maybe if you'd like something stronger? For your trouble?'

He hesitates. 'He did say he really wanted some of that pickle . . .'

'We'll be two minutes,' I say, all but shoving Will back through the door and up the stairs.

'Either you've lost it completely, or you're seeing something I'm not,' he mutters.

'It's from the film company, isn't it? One of the stars has been putting the word round in the Grouchy Club, about this artisan pickle shop they found.'

'It's the Groucho, surely.'

'Doesn't matter what it's called. I'm going to brew up, you run round all the usual suspects from the church and take *every single jar* of pickle you can find. And chutney. And jam. And biscuits. Anything that's there. Doesn't matter if it's dated pre-millennium. They'll love that. This is not just artisan pickle. This is artisan *vintage* pickle.'

'But don't we need a license to sell food—'

'Can you see a health inspector? Don't think. Do! We'll worry about that later. This is our chance to go A-list, Will. We've got to grab it by the bollocks.'

And as he nods and races off, and I rip open a packet of PG Tips, I consider for a second that I might have got completely the wrong end of the stick, and be about to humiliate myself utterly.

But since when has humiliation ever bothered me?

Chapter Fifteen

Sandie

'How much have you told your mother about me, exactly?'

Toby grins at me, the big cheesy charming grin that disarmed me on the day we met in Garnett's, nearly ten years ago now, and normally still works a treat. But not today. It would take a truck-full of tranquillisers to calm me down today.

'Just the best bits. Well, the decent best bits. There are some things that a gentlemen never divulges.'

The taxi pulls up outside the mock Tudor frontage of Liberty and, as Toby pays, I have to work hard to suppress the urge to run in the opposite direction. I think Toby realises this, because he grabs me by the hand.

'Have you told her . . . warned her about the most important thing?'

He squeezes my hand. 'You mean, where you're from?'

I nod.

'Honestly, you've no need to worry at all, Sandie. She might not like Birmingham as a place, but you hardly even have an accent. She'll be fine with it.'

And before I can hit him, he pulls me into the store.

I am, momentarily, distracted by the Christmas finery and sheer showmanship of the place. This store is festive whatever the date, but now it's breath-taking. I look up at the enormous modern glass chandeliers which hang from the ceiling of the central light well, four floors up, like a cascade of baubles. Then I notice how each balcony is themed in a different seasonal colour: purple, berry red, emerald. For me, it was always Garnett's or Liberty, though when Garnett's offered me a traineeship first, I was almost relieved that I wouldn't have to come here for the interview. Somehow it seemed impossible that this grand dame of British retail would ever extend a bejewelled hand to an anonymous girl from the suburbs.

Not so anonymous today, not with Toby at my side. The salesgirls are nudging each other, probably because they recognise him from the gossip columns. Though they might also recognise him if they sneak into Garnett's in their lunch hours – he's really been putting the hours in lately because the board are in a state about falling sales.

'Weird, isn't it, that your mother wanted to meet us here?'

He heads for the stairs and waves vaguely at one of the managers. 'Is it? Mother's virtually a fixture and fitting here when she's in town. She thinks Garnett's is too common.'

'Right.'

I feel sick most of the time at the moment, but the nausea I'm feeling right now has nothing to do with my *condition*. As I climb the steps, my head's floaty while my legs are leaden and everything feels distant . . . I grab hold of the carved wooden banister.

'Come on, Brains, old thing,' he says, pulling a funny face to make me smile. 'The worst thing you can do is let her know you're afraid.'

'What, because she'll spot my weak point and go for the jugular?'

'She's a human being, not a Pit Bull.'

An image pops up in my head of a densely built, brutish dog, wearing a tiara and kid gloves. It must be hormones. I never used to have a vivid imagination.

Toby puts out his hand. 'Look, I was worried about meeting *your* mother too. It's natural. But now me and Marnie get on like the proverbial house on fire, despite our many differences.'

'Differences? You've got more in common with her than I have. The drinking. The loud music. The dirty jokes. It's like living in a barracks.'

My mother's presence has done nothing to clarify the

pregnancy situation. Except possibly to convince me I can expect precisely no help from either her or the father of my—

It's not even a baby yet, though, is it? I have to keep telling myself that. Even when – and I know how mad this is – I feel the urge to talk to it. Because, face it, I have no one else to talk to. Gramma hasn't called me, and I haven't called her. I'm too scared that my inner grizzly will roar down the phone.

'Your mum's a gem, Sandie. Quite fancy her, actually.'

'Toby!'

'Oh. OK. I suppose that did sound a bit like a story from the *News of the World*. Anyway, she's our guest. I just like to make sure she's happy. And if that happens to involve the odd trip to the pub, well, it's the least I can do.'

We're outside the tea room now. 'I don't want to do this.'

He takes my hand, pretends to kiss it but then nibbles on my finger. 'She's not going to eat you. The cream tea here is far tastier than you are.'

'Ha ha.' I try to smile. I wish I could tell him, really I do, but until I've made my mind up what I'm going to do . . . Because there might be no reason to tell him at all . . .

'Anyway, I bet she's as nervous as you are. You're the girl who's threatening to take her little boy away from her. There's a lot riding on this.'

And that's when I acknowledge to myself for the first time why this matters so much, and why I've been putting off the biggest decision of my life, until after I meet Laetitia Garnett.

'Yes,' I say quietly. 'There is.'

I see her a fraction of a second before she sees me. It's long enough.

The elegant dining room is busy but that could *only* be her. I've seen Toby's paternal ancestors in the portraits that hang on the Garnett's boardroom wall, and it's been obvious that he inherited his clotted-cream blond quiff and his strong jaw from that side of the family.

Mrs Garnett is blonde, too, but the expensive platinum kind. She doesn't get *those* highlights done at the village hairdresser back in Gloucestershire. Toby has always insisted that she keeps a low profile, 'she can't bear the ladies-who-lunch set, she's more of a homebody.' Because of that, I expected a certain roundness in her figure, the insulating curves of a woman who needs to keep warm through winters spent in a draughty stately home.

But she is model-thin. I can count three rows of ribs above her shimmery eel-coloured blouse, and you could shave Parmesan on her collar bones. Toby has her eyes, the same perfect ovals, except on her face they dominate because she has none of his boyish padding. Instead she has puffy wine-coloured lips, jutting cheekbones, and a perfectly sculpted nose. She's like a Japanese Manga doll, though considerably less cute.

And now she sees me, and the eyes flicker away, and then she sees Toby, and then the eyes swivel down towards his hand in mine, and then back up again to my face and her burgundy lips thin as they make a little o, before she regains control and pulls them apart into a smile.

'Mums!' Toby has spotted her now, and pulls me towards her table.

'Gannet!' she says, leaping up from the table. The huge bow at the front of her blouse shimmers like a waterfall and draws the eye downwards. In her tailored trousers, her hips are Paris Hilton slim, and as we get closer, I hear the jingle-jangle of a dozen silver bracelets on her left wrist. No watch. No need when you have a driver at your beck and call.

'Mums, this is Sandie. Now, do please be kind. She's been rather nervous about meeting you.'

'Oh, my dear,' she says, and suddenly her eyes – the same mercury blue as her son's – show what appears to be genuine sympathy. 'You poor thing.'

She air kisses me and I smell Youth Dew. It's a classic fragrance, warm and spicy. One I had earmarked in my head for when I pass forty, though I suspect elegance will be as elusive to me then as it is now. But right now it's overwhelming, almost odious. I can no longer tolerate perfume, on myself or on other people. Without it, I feel disarmed, like a soldier who has lost his rifle.

I pull away as soon as I can without seeming rude. 'I've heard so much about you, Mrs Garnett.'

She sits back down. 'Don't believe a word of it. Idle gossip I'm sure. Now, let's get you tea and cake, that's just the thing for nerves.'

And then she *winks* at me.

Winks.

It could still be a ruse, of course. She's hardly going to reveal her true colours this early, or in front of her adoring boy. Instead, they're catching up on Bambourne village gossip. The dogs, the horses, the vet, the WI, the cleaning lady . . . I wait for the bitchiness, but there's nothing there. Well, perhaps the comment about the cleaning lady's daughter being pregnant again – 'aiming for the hat trick before she's eighteen, I suspect' – is a little barbed. And although she's not actually spelled it out, I pick up so much from the tone of her comments: that the vet is gay and the groom is interested, and the leading light in the am dram group is playing away. Nothing escapes the lady of the manor.

'And you, Mums? What have *you* been up to?'

'Ah, well, you know how much time it takes to run the house. I barely have time for my roster of lovers.'

Toby laughs heartily enough for me to realise that Mrs Garnett does not have lovers, or at least not that her son knows about. 'Mums, you know, you could. It's been two years and I don't expect you to join a convent.'

Toby's father died shortly after we got together. He grieved discreetly, which I put down partly to his public school upbringing, but also to the fact that the family had already 'lost' Garnett Senior fifteen years previously. He'd suffered a devastating stroke after discovering that his own brother had been stealing systematically from the family firm for over a decade. Toby has a very low threshold for dishonesty . . .

I need to tell him. Really I do. After today. Once I've got through this, I will give him the news. Maybe it can work after all.

'. . . I think old Sourpuss is on his way out, Gannet. Kidneys. You know how cats go.'

'Not poor Sourpuss.'

'Well, he is the wrong side of twenty.'

'Are you letting him sleep in your bed?'

Mrs Garnett nods. 'Hmmm. Even though his bladder isn't in tip-top condition.'

'You're a softie, Mums. Isn't she, Sandie? I told you there was nothing to fret about.'

I look up at the woman opposite. She seems lonelier than I expected, behind that brittle beauty.

The waiter arrives to take our order. Mrs Garnett orders a cured and smoked meat platter, Toby wants a slice of Victoria sandwich, but I can't face a rich cake or cream tea, so I order soldiers with Marmite.

'Do you know, my dear, it's never occurred to me to have Marmite after breakfast time. Isn't it funny, the differences between people's habits?' Mrs Garnett laughs softly and Toby joins in.

I wonder what she'd make of my mother's breakfast habits – how she finishes off cocktails she made the night before, glugging them the way other people drink Tropicana? Maybe now is not the time to share that particular quirk.

'So Toby tells me you're running your own business now?'

'Yes. Mystery shopping and retail consultancy. It's a growth area, despite the recession. Stores know they have to fight just to retain the customers they've got, so they need our services.'

'Of course, the retail game is all about connections, isn't it, my dear? So the Garnett connection can do you no harm.' She pats Toby on the hand. Hers is sinewy, the skin bright white against the latte-varnish of her nails.

I stare into her eyes. Does she mean what I think she means? I decide she can't. 'Ah, well, of course, my ten years' experience at Garnett's does count for a lot.'

Her eyes stay steady. 'Of course. So. Is it at this point that I ask whether your intentions towards my son are wholly honourable?'

Toby chuckles and I smile. OK, so she has a slightly odd sense of humour, but then my old colleagues at the store often questioned whether I had a sense of humour at all.

Before I manage to think of something light to say to her in reply, she speaks again. 'Oh, sorry, no. That's your father's role, isn't it? So when should we expect to meet the members of your tribe, my dear?'

Again she chuckles, but I don't. Even Toby looks slightly embarrassed . . . 'Mums, I'm sure I mentioned it. Sandie's father isn't on the scene.'

She raises her hand to her mouth. 'I am *so sorry*. Gannet, my mind is like a sieve these days. I honestly cannot remember you mentioning that. My dear, when did you lose him?'

I could lie. What difference will it make? A dead father is so much easier to explain than an unknown one, and it's not as though I plan to let her meet *my* mother.

And yet . . .

'I don't think you can lose what you never really had, can you, Mrs Garnett? Unfortunately, I never knew my father. My mother had me when she was a teenager and she chose not to reveal who he was.'

There! It only occurs to me after I've spoken that perhaps this is the ultimate test, that of all the things she says this afternoon, her response to this could determine my entire future.

'Ah,' she says, as the waiter arrives with three teapots. 'Ah. How . . . liberating to be able to be oneself, without the tiresome responsibility of familial expectations. No wonder you've made such an impression, my dear.'

I escape to the toilet before the toast soldiers arrive.

My skin is greasy from stress so I fumble about in my bag for the little book of powdery blotting paper that Grazia bought me, but I can't seem to tear one out because my fingers are too clumsy and sweaty.

Could this woman ever become my mother-in-law, or the grandmother for my maybe-baby?

I feel something then. I don't know whether it's physical – it can't be, surely, not this early on – so it must be psychological. A movement or a twinge below my belly button. My imagination, of course, that's probably where my kidney is, or my bladder.

But still . . . I place my palm against the flat of my stomach and imagine what's beneath, as though this bundle of cells – because that's all I will allow it to be – can offer some kind of guidance.

'What's the right thing to do?'

And then the door opens behind me and I jump as the Manga face of Mrs Garnett appears in the mirror over my shoulder. I move my hand away instantly, and then pretend to be brushing lint off my suit.

She couldn't have seen me, could she?

'He's already pining for you out there, my dear,' she says.

'Oh. Well, we can't have that, can we?' And I walk for the door, while she smiles and fishes lipstick out of her tiny clutch bag, even though the wine colour on her lips looks as perfect as it did when I arrived.

Home. I slump onto the sofa, closing my throbbing eyes. It doesn't help. At least my mother's not here. She's left a note saying she's gone out with some of her new friends from the Ruddy Duck.

'How do you think it went, Sandie? I was very pleased. And so much better that you met her now, takes the worry out of Christmas, eh?'

I open my eyes again. He's scooped up Monty in his arms and is holding him in the crook of his left arm, like a baby, and tickling the dog's bald pink stomach with his right hand.

'She's very . . . elegant.'

'You should see the photos of her from when she met my father. If it's not too Freudian to say it about one's own mother, she was awfully hot stuff.'

He puts the dog down and sits down next to me. 'Mind you, so are you. I don't know what it is, but you're looking even hotter lately. Extra luscious . . .' He reaches an arm around me. 'I can't remember the last time we were on our own in the flat, without your mother. I mean, I adore her, of course, but, um. Nice to have some privacy, don't you think?'

'Mmm.'

He begins to stroke my neck, the way I like it. Except, just like perfume, I don't seem to like it any more. I think of those same fingers on Monty's tummy.

'She won't be back for ages, will she?'

I shrug him off. 'No. Actually, while we're alone, I wanted to talk to you, Toby.'

'Talk? Aww . . . seems like an awfully wasted opportunity.'

The hand sneaks back onto my neck, and his eyes are pleading with me, like a schoolboy wanting a second slice of Victoria sandwich, but all I can see now are *her* eyes and I feel that twinge again. Did she see me, making that gesture that only a pregnant woman ever makes?

I pull away from his hand. I need to be on my own. 'I'm going out.'

He looks affronted, just for a second, but then he shrugs. One of the things I like most about Toby is that he never bears grudges. 'Oh, OK. I'm sure Monty would appreciate a walk . . .'

And at the mention of the magic word, the dog launches himself at me and I groan in defeat. 'OK, Monty. Lead!'

He trots off to the corner and returns with his lead in his mouth. I stand up, and so does Toby, and he kisses me, a big full-on smacker on the mouth. But I'm too distracted to enjoy it. His mother has unsettled me completely: I can't shake the feeling that she's toying with me.

'Don't be long, Brains. Monty isn't the only one who wants his share of Sandie Barrow . . .'

Chapter Sixteen

Grazia

D r Target works on my face in complete silence. He has jettisoned the charm and the chat, and his determined expression reminds me of Leon's when he squared up to a new blank canvas.

My canvas is not new or blank, alas. If it were, there would be no need for any of the vials and needles laid out on Dr Target's metal tray. One of the vials will send my frown on holiday for six months. One will plump up my cheeks, and the third will smooth away my crow's feet ('although we may require an extra ampoule for that area, which will increase the cost. One does not want to end up with an asymmetrical distribution of lines,' the doctor explained before I signed my consent form).

I do not care about the money, thanks to Leon. I care about having my old face back, though the doctor has warned me not to expect too much. 'What we can achieve is a fresher look, but that doesn't mean you'll see the same reflection as you did twenty years ago. However, without exception, my patients report that the subtle changes I can make allow them to face the world with more confidence.'

And that is what I am trying to keep in mind as the first needle comes closer to my eyes. Dr Target has used anaesthetic cream to numb my face, which makes me feel even less connected to reality.

'Ugh.'

'That's usually the only slightly sore one,' he says. 'The other needles are much finer.'

I see his pink fingers in soft focus at the edge of my vision. He takes the needle away and begins to massage whatever it is he's injected under the skin. The pressure is firmer than I expected and I close my eyes because, frankly, it hurts now.

'I know this is a tad uncomfortable but I need to make sure the filler is even, otherwise you may end up with lumpy areas,' the doctor says, 'and we wouldn't want that, would we?'

I try to imagine myself somewhere else, somewhere that does not stink of disinfectant and vanity. Beaches have never relaxed me – they remind me too much of Italy – so I picture an English garden, and try to replace the ticklish medical smell with the scent of tea rose.

The injections follow, one after the other, and each one as unpleasant as the last, albeit in subtly different ways. I manage not to moan again, though I am at the edge of my endurance.

'Done!'

Dr Target steps back to admire his work, then nods. The nurse proffers a glass of water, which I drink, and then proceeds to place cool cloths across my face. I feel like a mummy.

'Do move back into the comfortable chair for a couple of minutes, Miss Verdi, and once the cloths have reduced the immediate redness, I will show you my handiwork. I hope you'll be as pleased as I am.'

Right now I do not feel pleased. Right now I feel vulnerable and faint and extraordinarily foolish. 'The other women who have this done? Why?'

'Ah, an interesting question. I am no mind-reader, but I probably understand the female psyche better than the average man. Most patients insist they are doing it for themselves, of course.'

'But you do not believe them?' I open my eyes and I can just see his smile through the damp, cooling cloths.

'It is complex. If a woman were to be cast away on an island with no people and no mirrors, I doubt she would prioritise Botox. But a woman sees her reflection – even, dare I say it, her worth – in the eyes and reactions of other people. When they're younger, they take a positive response for granted, yet when it stops coming, they feel invisible.'

I think of the shock of seeing the secret camera footage and therefore seeing how I must really look to other people. 'Invisible. Yes. And I suppose there is often a man involved?'

'Sometimes, although you might be surprised to know that most often the opinion that matters most is not that of the husband or the boyfriend, but of the girlfriends. Women, I sometimes think, can be their own worst enemies. Now, fascinating as this topic is, I believe your face should be nicely *cooked* by now, and I am sure you are curious about the outcome of your investment . . .'

I can still recognise myself.

But only just.

I mumble appropriate words of approval but they are clearly not effusive enough. Dr Target looks solemn and perhaps a touch hurt. What is it with men needing so much reassurance? I am the one with a numb face and delicate ego.

He takes away the mirror. 'It often takes a while to settle into your new appearance. Very common. Wait until the swelling has subsided and let me know how you feel. It's simple enough to dissolve the fillers with a second injection, if you can't live with it. I've done it for the patients of other less experienced practitioners, with excellent results. But I have never had a single client ask me to neutralise work that I've done.'

I leave the office with my aftercare sheet, and the December wind slices into me. It's just after four and I am grateful for the dark, even though I know rationally that no one but me and Dr Target would notice the changes.

As I enter the department store, I wonder if this is the definition of loneliness? That only my doctor knows my face well enough to notice it has been altered.

'Pah!' My self-pity is pathetic.

I didn't mean to say it out loud, and the teenager in the lift with me looks at me askance. *Another batty old woman.*

The lavatories are empty. I walk to the furthest mirror and force myself to look again.

I am half-Grazia, half-Barbie. It is horrible.

No. I look again, but with some objectivity. It is not horrible. There is redness and perhaps a little too much plumping up, but that will settle down. I step a little closer, and there is something impressive about the tautness of the skin around my eyes, the way the fans of lines, and the years of smoky bars and late nights that caused them, have been cancelled out.

There is no change yet to my forehead, as it will take a while for the muscles to forget to work, and I feel a sudden wistful fondness towards my frown and the experiences that created it. The love I felt for Leon and the pain I felt when he died are still recorded there, between my eyebrows.

But the memories won't go when the lines melt away, will they, silly soppy Grazia? And the procedures are an investment, part of the plan to create new memories as vivid as the ones that I have now. Memories that may include Nigel.

It's about the future. I nod at myself in the mirror, resolute.

And that's when it occurs to me. It isn't actually the fillers that are making me unrecognisable. It's the complete lack of make-up.

Of course . . . the nurse removed every trace before the doctor got to work on me.

I shudder – I have not been out in public without make-up since I was thirteen years old. No wonder I was so traumatised.

I lift my handbag onto the counter and line up the contents of my make-up bag. Time to draw in the details of my brand new face . . .

I wake next morning feeling like a young girl, but my mood has nothing to do with Dr Target and his youth drugs.

And everything to do with my toyboy.

It is ridiculous, really. Nigel knows so little about me, yet I feel he understands me completely.

There is something old-fashioned about him, even though he is not yet thirty. The reason I mistook him for a waiter was the classic cut of his suit, but when he joined me that afternoon I realised the fabric was too fine and the tailoring bespoke. He thinks it is the funniest thing, and wants me to call him 'garçon'.

'Nigel is such a bloody dull name. I've been trying to escape it for my entire life,' he says with the intense seriousness of youth, which just reminds me that I have lived fifteen years longer than he has. So I call him garçon, the French for waiter, and try to forget that it is also the French for boy.

This evening is our second proper 'date', and that is the reason for my skittish mood. But I feel less skittish when I look in the mirror. My face is still swollen in odd places, but those lumps are now accessorised by cornflower blue streaks of bruising underneath.

However . . . if I narrow my eyes to blur away the lumps, and imagine the bruising gone, then there is a change there, a certain evenness that I am not sure I had twenty years ago. It is a very subtle change, and it is only now I examine myself that I realise what was wrong before, the way that age twists one's features until symmetry seems the very best one could hope for.

I sit in the harshest daylight and try out different make-up, the way a young girl tries her first lipstick and eyeshadows. I discover that it takes less blusher to enhance newly boosted cheeks, and my eyes are more awake, despite the bruises.

By lunchtime, I am still surprised by my reflection, but not shocked. And by teatime – as date-time approaches – my brain has adjusted and I find it hard to believe that my youthful good looks are due to anything other than my strong Italian genes.

We meet in an intimate members' bar in Bloomsbury. It is very dark and my last moment fear that he might spot the pin-pricks on my face is assuaged. Though I do wonder whether he has chosen this place so there is no risk that he might be spotted *with an old woman*.

I order a margarita, and he orders the same, and the drinks are perfect, from the artfully salted rim to the hefty kick of tequila and lime. We toast to the night ahead, and when he lifts the glass to his lips he looks like a blond, baby-faced Bond, and I feel like a femme fatale, and I am suddenly struck dumb by the most powerful feeling of desire. I almost lose my balance, and am relieved that there is a bar stool immediately behind me.

'Grazia! Have you been drinking already?'

'No, of course not.' My voice sounds odd, almost like a growl.

'Why don't we try the sofas instead, just in case you feel wobbly again?'

Part of me does indeed feel extremely unsteady at the thought of sitting so close to him. During our first meeting, in the bar, there was a table between us, along with my disbelief that a man his age could possibly feel attracted to me. Last time, we ate at a trendy fusion place, sitting opposite each other in sunken oriental tables that made my knees ache. Despite the sake, and a little footsie when I could still feel my feet, we ended the evening with a chaste kiss on the cheek. Although if he hadn't been so skilled at hailing a taxi, I had a feeling it might have been more.

The sofa is in a corner alcove, under a low red light. I position myself slightly to the side of the lamp, so that the glow will be at its most flattering. Such knowledge is important for a woman over thirty-five, even after two thousand pounds' worth of dermatological intervention.

He ducks to avoid the light, and as his body shifts, I can smell his aftershave. Ozonic, almost salty, with a dash of lime, as tempting as our margaritas.

He smiles at me and the blood rushes to my face.

'So, Grazia.'

'So . . .' I do not want to call him garçon. I feel too self-conscious.

'Do you like the bar?'

I nod. 'It is cosy.'

'Cosy? They'd hate that. They think the look is brothel chic.'

'Ah. I have never been to a brothel.' I feel foolish now, a middle-aged woman with no stories to tell.

'Nor have I,' says my toyboy, and I believe him of course. A man like him would never have to pay. 'I prefer cosy. Especially with you.'

I blush more deeply and my face hurts in the places where I am bruised. Sandie and Emily would not recognise me like this, coy and lost for words. 'Thank you.'

We sip our drinks. I do not look at him because every time I do, I find myself imagining him with no clothes on – and I am convinced he might be able to see that in my eyes. I try to think of something that will cool me down, as men do to improve their sexual staying power, and the loathsome James pops into my head, with his oily chat-up lines and his hastiness to despatch me after he'd finished. *That* does the trick.

'Is everything OK, Grazia?'

'Uh?'

'You seem distracted.'

And I look at this man, and I have an urge to giggle. James and Nigel are like representatives of two different species. To think I all but forced myself into bed with James, out of some misguided belief that it would help me find closure . . . when all the time there was a man like Nigel who could make me feel so girlish and yet so wild. Unfamiliar feelings, *terrifying* feelings, and yet ones I embrace as a sign I am still alive.

The rush makes me brave. 'I am distracted, yes. Distracted by wondering why you want to spend time with me.'

He laughs. 'Ah, fishing for compliments? Well, let's see—'

'No. I am not fishing for compliments. It is evident that I am older than you, and that you would have no shortage of pretty girls delighted to date you. Why choose me?'

'Seriously?'

I nod, bracing myself for tales of a crush on a schoolteacher that was never realised.

'Because you were the *hottest* thing in that bar that night. Well, the hottest thing I had seen for a very long time. Your poise, your expression. I wanted to know the person underneath. And I fancied you like crazy.'

I look up at him, waiting for a punchline, the jokingly insulting phrase to bring me back to earth. But he seems to have finished.

Perhaps it is the margarita hitting my bloodstream, because as I look at his face I allow myself to believe he means what he says.

'That is excellent. Because I "fancied you like crazy" also, Nigel,' I say. 'So, tell me, what were your plans for the rest of the evening?'

He looks flustered. 'Um. Well, I had a table booked at a little French place I know.'

'And are you hungry?'

He smiles. 'Not really. But it's what you do, isn't it? To get to know each other.'

I smile back. 'I can think of a better way.'

He gulps, and so do I, still surprised at my own nerve.

'My flat's not far, um, if I haven't got the wrong end of the . . .' He blushes and I wonder how far the blush has spread.

I shake my head. 'No misunderstanding, Nigel. Cancel the reservation. There is always pizza.'

And in his hurry to stand up he stumbles, and ends up falling towards me, steadying himself on the back of the sofa, his arms either side of my shoulders, and I lean forward just a centimetre or two, enough to make him kiss me, and I hold my breath, hoping that the first real kiss will not be a disappointment.

It is not.

Nigel's apartment is on the very top floor of a block in a road behind Marylebone High Street. There is no lift, and he looks back as we climb the stairs to check I am not struggling. Does he really think I am *so* old?

To keep my confidence up, I focus on the kiss. If our lips are such a perfect fit, surely it bodes well?

By the time we reach the door to his apartment, my breath is a little shorter than I would like it to be. It is quite dark inside, and he darts around switching on lamps, and I am relieved that there is no central light to cast the most ageing of glows.

But my bravado has deserted me. Instead I stand at the edge of the room, clutching my handbag like a comfort blanket. 'What a pretty place.'

It *is* pretty, if small. This is a living room and kitchen combined, with sweet little windows at one end offering an enchanting roof-scape of London by night. The décor is more feminine than I expected, with chintzy sofas and buttermilk walls, and I wonder suddenly whether he already has a girlfriend, and intends to make me his mistress. I am struggling enough with the idea of having a toyboy.

'It's nice, isn't it? If a bit girly. I moved in two years ago and still haven't got round to painting it black and red, installing a dartboard, table football machine, PlayStation.'

It takes me a moment to realise he is joking. 'I like it as it is.'

He steps towards me. 'It was different in the bar, somehow, wasn't it? I feel quite nervous now.'

'Nervous?'

'Being here with you. Any man would be nervous.'

'I had never realised I was so terrifying.'

'Not terrifying,' he says, taking another step forward. 'Terrifyingly attractive.'

'Now you are being silly.'

Nigel shakes his head. 'I cannot believe you have so little self-awareness. A man could lose himself just looking at you.'

I laugh, but he seems quite serious. My bravado returns. 'And is that what you are planning for tonight? Looking at me?'

'I . . .'

And then he kisses me again and all the awkwardness is gone. As, soon, are our clothes. It is as effortless and natural as the best kind of dream, though the sensations make me feel wide awake.

I do not even laugh when the moment comes for him to release a catch in the wall, and a bed moves smoothly down into position.

'It's my James Bond bed,' he says. 'Which makes you my Bond girl.'

And as we sink down onto the exquisitely soft mattress, I realise I do, against all possible odds, feel like a girl all over again.

Chapter Seventeen

Never thought I'd love feeling this knackered.

I used to feel knackered after a day on the market, of course. Sore feet, hands all scaly and red like a pensioner's, skin and clothes smelling of overripe bananas and cabbage. I used to avoid looking at myself in the bathroom mirror after a fourteen-hour day, but when I forgot, my ground-down old bag expression used to shock me. Twenty-four? More like forty-four.

But now I like being squashed into this sweaty bus with the other commuters. My wrists ache from typing, and my eyes are sore from the screen, and my head throbs from the mental effort, and my feet are blistered from traipsing around stores and my shoulders are uneven from the weight of the secret camera. Like the teenager with the too-tight suit and the woman in the crumpled bank uniform, I have my battle scars. I am a paid-up, weary member of society.

I stop to empty the post box in the entrance hall of the flats. As usual, it's full of red bills and junk mail, but now my first two weeks' money has come in, I might be able to afford to pay more than the minimum off my credit card. Not *much* more, but it's a start.

'Hey, working girl!'

I turn to see Luis coming down the communal staircase, in his Garnett's jacket with the ridiculous gold braid and lapels. Except today it doesn't look ridiculous. Despite his belly and his bad teeth, he wears it well.

'All right?' I mumble. It's the first time I've seen him since I got the job, and I hate the fact he knows so much about the *old* me, because I already feel like a completely reformed character.

'You look very, very smart, Kelly. Is very good. You standing different and everything.'

I can't remember the last time someone paid me a compliment. Then I do. It was Luis last time, too, telling me I was a skilled shoplifter. I don't know how to react this time either. 'Must be the backache making me walk funny.'

He shakes his head and his jowls shake too. 'And the job? You like it?'

'Oh, you know. Beats a life of crime, making a nuisance of myself in department stores.'

He steps closer to me and touches my arm. 'No. No more.' He taps his forehead. 'Is forgotten, yes? Is all in past. How do you say it? Washed the slate clean.'

'Really?'

'Yes, yes, yes, never seen you before in my life.' He chuckles. 'My name is Luis. Delighted to meet you!'

And he walks off, smiling to himself, and I find that I am smiling too . . .

The corridor bulbs have blown again, or been nicked, so I look for the crack of light under the front door of our flat. It's swings and roundabouts – the gap lets in the cold draughts, but it's stopped me breaking my neck after dozens of night on the piss.

I hear voices as I approach. Dad's is higher than normal, and he's chattering away like a neurotic monkey in a cage. Every now and then there's a rumble. I can't make out the words, but it's definitely an argument.

Shit. Is this what Dad means by 'you're never gonna have to worry about me again'?

I pause by the door. I want to throw off my shoes and clothes and jump into the shower and then change into leggings and a fleece and lie on the sofa with my tray of beer and beans on toast watching *EastEnders* followed by Nigella Lawson telling me how to stuff my Christmas goose.

I don't want to walk into some fucking confrontation between Dad and a debt collector or bookie or pub landlord. I want to be normal.

Maybe I should go to Tina's and help put the kids to bed and roll up a fat spliff and forget about Dad. He's a grown man, he shouldn't expect me to come and rescue him time after time.

Except who else will? And he was there once, when it really mattered, and that kind of debt is one you never repay.

I put my key in the lock and the chattering stops. When I open the door, I see Dad first, sitting in the armchair facing me. The light is bright and unforgiving, and his eyes are shiny with fear.

The man on the sofa has his back to me, but he doesn't turn round. Smoke is rising around him, and though it's coming from his cigar rather than the fires of hell, his silhouette is definitely sinister.

'Kelly. You're early.'

'No she's not,' says smoke man. He turns around now. He is completely bald, except for oddly bushy brown brows above eyes so fleshy that I can hardly see the whites. His skin is tanned and he's got a mouthful of too-perfect crowns. He's dressed for the golf course, but Dad doesn't play anything that doesn't involve cards, dice or horses. 'You're normally back between six fifteen and six thirty-five, aren't you? Depending on the traffic on the Cromwell Road.'

He wants me to feel spooked, and he's managed it. 'You my stalker, are you?'

He stands up now. He's bulky, but not fat. A bouncer's build. Weird shiny skin so he could be any age from fifty to seventy. 'No. I'm Charlie. Charlie Flack. Good to meet Terry's girl at long last.' He reaches out his hand and gives me a brief bone crusher of a shake. I don't let him see how much it bloody well hurts. I hear a cough behind me, and it's only now that I notice another bloke, twice as broad as Charlie, standing guard behind the front door.

'Ah. Lads' night in, is it. I won't cramp your style,' I say. 'I'll just go and get changed, then I'm off to Tina's, yeah, Dad? Won't be back till late.'

'You still in touch with Tina then?' asks Charlie casually. 'Only I heard she'd moved on, towards Dalston way I think.'

'Tina Bird?'

'Tina as in First Class Tits Tina, yeah?'

I nod. Tina's first boyfriend bought her a boob job in cash for her sixteenth birthday with the money he made robbing a post office in Middlesex. She dumped him when he got sent down.

'Like I say, I heard she'd moved east. Weekend before last.'

'I didn't know . . .'

'I guess you've been busy. With your new job and that.'

I stare at him. His eyes have crinkled at the edges. I think he's enjoying this. 'What's this about? Did you come here to see Dad, or me?'

My father is inspecting his hands, picking at rough skin on his palms.

'Both,' says Charlie, 'but I've caught up on old times with your pa, now, so why don't we leave him to it? Let me buy you a drink, bet you could do with one after a hard day's work.'

'I'm not going anywhere with you.'

He sighs. 'Fuck me, Terry, she doesn't just look like your ex-wife, she moans like her too.' He pulls out his wallet, fishes out a twenty pound note, and leans across to pass it to Dad. 'You go and get a drink, will you, while we have a chat?'

My father stands up.

'You're not leaving me, Dad? You don't know what could happen.'

He shuffles along: I notice for the first time that his trousers hang off his hips, like an old man's. Not like him to go off his food. 'Charlie's all right. He's not like that.'

'No,' says Charlie. 'Why keep a dog and bark yourself, eh?'

'I'm not staying here—'

Charlie stands up now. 'Listen, love, I'm not going to hurt you. I just want ten minutes, little chat, then you can settle down with your beans on toast like I was never here. Bye, Terry, see you soon.'

I turn round just in time to see the door slam behind my

father. His shoes are still by the door. 'Silly sod's gone out in his slippers,' I say, and I'm about to call after him when Charlie places a large warm paw on my shoulder.

'Leave him, Kelly. He's only going to the Anchor, anyway. They're not going to chuck him out on account of his footwear, are they? Most of the lowlifes in there have trouble remembering to put their trousers on. Just sit down and I'll tell you what you need to know.'

'I'm not going to like it, am I?'

'Just sit down, please. Women. Tell me again why I deal with 'em?'

I sit where Dad was. The cushion's still warm and I can smell the Cidal soap and the whisky. 'I don't know what you do with women.'

He pauses. 'OK. Here's the deal. I've known your dad a few years. Well. Thirty odd. Not best mates or anything, but I came to his wedding. Good do, it was, he knew how to throw a good party—'

'You're not here to go down Memory Lane, are you, Mr Flack?' I know I shouldn't wind him up but I can't seem to help myself. Maybe it's because I'd rather he thumped me than told me whatever it is.

'Right. Well, word came to me a while back that he wanted some help. Money help. We both know that he's not the best with money, don't we?'

'Half of Shepherd's Bush knows he's not the best with money.'

'Which is why he came to me. I'd turned him down before because, well, I know what you're thinking about me, I can see it in your face, but I've got strong feelings about gambling. Not everything I do is a hundred per cent above board, I admit, but I don't do stuff that breaks up families and I don't dole out cash if the debtor is going to throw it all away.'

'That's big of you.'

'But this time it was different, you see, Kelly. This time I checked a few things out and I realised there was something he could offer me in return. Or, rather, something the Wright family might be able to do to return the favour.'

'There isn't a family any more, Mr Flack. Haven't you noticed? Just me and Dad.'

He nods. 'That's enough family for anyone, isn't it, though? But you're right. Terry's got nothing I want, but you have.'

I shiver. Jesus, he can't mean—

'Not like that, love. You're young enough to be my granddaughter. Great-granddaughter even, round these parts. Plus, no offence, but I never have liked scrawny birds. No, this is about you being a career girl.'

'A what?'

He clasps his hands together. They really are too huge to be human, and the knuckles crack louder than the exhaust on a bus. 'OK. I'll get to the point. It's your boss, darling.'

'Sandie?'

His eyes pop open and I see pure loathing. 'Yeah. Sandra Barrow.'

'What's she done to you? I mean, she's . . . and you're . . .' I shake my head. 'I just don't see how your paths would ever even have crossed.'

'Well, they did. I helped her out, when no one else would. And she crossed me and went after my business associates. On the back of what she learned with me. And I don't like that. So I've got a simple proposition for you. I bought your dad's debts. All of them. Not just the recent ones, but the ones that go back to before you were born, the loans he took out to repay the gambling debts and then the ones he took out to pay off the loans on the loans he took out to repay the gambling debts. I've got the paperwork back in the office if you want to see it. It makes what the fucking banks have been up to look like a kid's game.'

'He always said it wasn't that bad . . .'

'But you were too clever to really believe him, weren't you, love? Anyway, I'm offering to clear the lot. Only money, isn't it? Clean slate. Maybe even a bit of a bonus on top. You could take him out of London. I know a place where there's no bookies. Up in Scotland. Quite a little club of guys like him, escaping. Trying to keep each other on track. They grow potatoes and raspberries and chickens. They do still bet on the number of eggs laid every morning, mind you.' And he laughs.

'And what do you want me to do? In return for you saving Dad from himself?'

'Open a few doors, love, that's all. Leave a note with the security code lying about where someone might be able to copy it down. Nothing illegal. Just a little bit of carelessness. She'll never even know it had anything to do with you.'

'It?'

'You don't need to worry. I promise no one gets hurt. Do I look like a violent bloke?'

I don't answer that. 'Why?'

'I'm not a vindictive man but I can't have people taking advantage of me.'

The light bulb hanging from the ceiling feels like it's scalding my eyes, and my brain is tired. 'I don't get how you and Sandie could be in the same world. Never mind get my head round the idea of her cheating you in some way.'

He shrugs his enormous shoulders. 'Not really your business, love. But I'm big on natural justice. Sandie Barrow causes me trouble, I cause her trouble. I help your daddy out, you help me out.' He pushes himself up from the sofa.

'And if I don't want to help you out?'

'Then the bank of Flack withdraws credit. And I don't think I need to spell out to you what that means.' He reaches into the pocket of his golf trousers and pulls out a card. There is no name on it, just a number, embossed in black ink. 'I don't want to rush you. After all, longer you're there, more trust you're going to build. Let me know by Christmas Eve, eh, Kelly? Jobs like this are best done when everyone else is busy stuffing themselves.'

The fucker strides towards the door, like he owns the place. Which I guess he does, in a way.

'What will you do to her? To Sandie?'

'Oh, don't worry, darling. Like I said, I don't get mixed up in nasty stuff. Nothing physical. Mental lasts longer, eh?'

And he leaves, and his heavy follows, closing the door carefully behind him.

December 17 –
Shopping Days to Christmas: 7

If your store is not attracting the crowds by now, then even Santa can't save you. But you might as well keep trying, I suppose. Blow up balloons, dress as Santa, offer to cook Christmas lunch for your customers, auction your granny as the perfect companion for the big day (just don't mention her flatulence). Do whatever it takes to get people through the door, and keep them there until they buy . . .

Chapter Eighteen

Emily

It's too early.

I *know* it's too early. I have more than enough on my plate today, what with launching the first ever Heartsease Emporium Festive Foodie Festival, but I can't help thinking about it.

I can't go to the chemist anyway, because as soon as I do the news will be round the village faster than if I'd put a sign in the shop window saying, WOO HOO, there might be a little Emily or a little Will on the way. Wendy from playgroup would be round to add the embryo to her petition for a new primary school for Heartsease before I had a chance to pee on a stick.

And anyway, my period's only thirty-six hours late. And it could be stress. I mean, it has been ever so stressful lately, getting ready for the relaunch and for Christmas, and then getting the letter from Duncan's lawyer threatening to take most of the maintenance away due to my ex-husband's 'changed circumstances'.

Still. A woman knows, doesn't she? I swear I feel nauseous already, though that might be the quality control tests I did this morning of Mrs Ingalls' rum and chocolate Christmas pudding truffles. Just to see whether they really do live up to the hype (they do. Oh, yes, they *really* do).

'Em! I need a hand with the trestle tables.'

Will is going to be so excited. Though I know I need to choose my moment. He does look a bit stressed.

'Coming!'

Oh, it's the perfect day for our launch, really it is. Blue sky weather, but chilly enough to create puffs of white breath and sizzling smoke from the chestnut brazier.

Our luck's changing. I can feel it.

Downstairs the store is busier than I've ever seen it, though sadly no one's here to buy anything. I know most of these people not by name, but by what they make: there's Mrs Bramble Jelly and Mrs Treacle Tart and Miss Vanilla and Cranberry Fudge and Mrs White Chocolate Brownie and Mrs Rye and Cranberry Bread and the Christmas Pud and Mince Pie Sisters, and of course there's Miss Sloe and Cranberry Gin, whose rosy cheeks suggests that she too takes quality control very seriously indeed. Then there are the blokes, bringing holly and mistletoe and herbs from their greenhouses. And the farmers turning up with all manner of cheeses and cold meats and tubs of stuffing, and even a few *live* turkeys for the kids to gawp at and the adults to feel guilty about.

If it weren't for the Boden wellies and the Range Rovers and the fact that finest imported American cranberries are in pretty much every second recipe (our home production lines have actually caused a Thames Valley shortage of both the fresh and frozen varieties), the scene would be positively medieval.

Will weaves his way through the crowd, and gives me a brief kiss. 'Right. We need to get the tables out front; the non-perishables are stacking up and we need to get them off the ground or the health and safety will turn up and bloody well shut us down.'

He is magnificent when he's in action. I can forgive him the brevity of the kiss and the tendency to bark orders, because he is tall and gorgeous and commanding and . . .

Oh, what a baby we're going to have together.

Possibly.

'Em?'

'Sorry. Just a bit overwhelmed by the scale of it all.'

'Hmm.' He looks at me in that schoolteachery way of his, and I am convinced he's about to challenge me. But then I think he decides that whatever it is that's up with me, it's bound to be time-consuming to deal with now. 'Let's get moving.'

It must be the hormones because I feel quite emotional as we get everything ready. This is our big chance to build the future for the three . . . no, the four of us.

And we have Tom Cruise on our side. OK, so I am not entirely certain it was Tom Cruise in the back of that car – are Scientologists allowed to eat pickle anyway? – but the visit really was a breakthrough.

We'd been living in cloud cuckoo land before that. The cutesy Christmas decorations and the trinkets and the quirky kitchenware were nice enough but why would anyone make a special trip to the sticks to find the same stuff, made in the same factories in Eastern Europe, that they could buy in the big department stores? Entrepreneurial spirit is fine, but to set ourselves up against Garnett's and Selfridges and Harrod's was retail suicide.

But the pickles and chutneys are different. The reputation of those preserves has travelled all the way up the M4 and back again. Even in a downturn, people want to eat as well as they can, especially at Christmas, and the foods produced by the ladies of Heartsease Common are made with love. Suddenly our location seems an advantage, not a disadvantage. It's harder to feel that love if you're buying your pickle in a glossy food hall, but no one can question the homespun authenticity of the Emporium . . . and we're not stopping at food. Oh no. We've made DIY paperchain packs, and used the Tiny Tykes pompom snowmen design as the basis for another traditional family activity set.

'Emily!'

Sandie is coming towards me across the Green. She doesn't look blooming yet, in fact she looks madly grumpy. Oh! We're going to be pregnant together. I missed out on ante-natal group bonding the first time because I'd only just moved to London, and Duncan said he was too busy in his new job to 'play silly buggers in a church hall with a knitted womb and a plastic foetus'.

But this time I'll be the expert. I'll be able to tell her what to eat and how to breathe and which painkillers to go for during childbirth (all of them). And our bumps will grow up together.

I'll have a girl, she'll have a boy, both in time for *next* Christmas and we'll sit with them sleeping in our arms on the common and . . .

'Earth to Emily, are you reading me?'

I hug her, wanting to whisper the news in her ear, but I ought to tell Will first. But there's something different about her. Something missing . . .

'Why aren't you wearing perfume?'

She pulls a face. 'Makes me feel sick as a dog.'

'Oh, thank goodness. For a minute I thought you might have got rid—'

She shakes her head and then I see Toby coming up behind her, carrying boxes, along with Sandie's mum and Monty the dog and that waif of a girl she's employed as her assistant.

'You still haven't told him?'

'It's complicated.'

'No it's not. It's the most straightforward thing in the world.'

'He's not ready, Emily,' she whispers, her voice increasingly desperate. 'You know how Duncan wasn't ready for Freddie? Well, Toby makes your ex look like a model of maturity.'

'I'm sure that's not true . . . hello, Toby, have you got a present for us?'

He leans over the box to kiss me. 'Ho, ho, ho, little girl. I might have. Depends if you've been good all year. Or if you'll sit on Santa's lap.'

'For God's sake, Toby.' Sandie snatches the box from him and groans at its weight. I just stop myself telling him to take it back because she's pregnant. She strides off in the direction of the shop.

Toby shakes his head. 'She's definitely got out the wrong side of the bed this morning. Is the filthy temper a family trait, Marnie?'

'Must be from my mother. She can be a complete cow. I am pure sweetness and light.' Sandie's mother grins. She's attracting plenty of attention from the farmers, thanks to her seasonal outfit: a clingy red dress that ends mid-thigh, with white fake-fur scarf and long black patent leather boots to complete the Mrs Santa Claus look.

'Where shall I put these?' The new girl is holding a bag full of bright check paper, for gift-wrapping. She's not exactly dressed for the country in her cheap suit and scuffed heels, and that dark eyeliner makes her pale face look old. I want to dress her in my fleecy pyjamas and fatten her up with tea and buttered toast.

'I'll take them. Let me get you all a cuppa?'

Sandie's mother looks up. 'I don't suppose you've got anything stronger?'

'Just to keep the cold out,' says Toby, 'because Marnie's really not used to the British weather again yet.'

'So I see,' I say, looking at the expanses of uncovered flesh. 'I'll see what I can do.'

It's all going swimmingly – the pickles are selling like hot cakes, and the hot cakes like pickles – until I realise I can't find my son. I spot Jean scoffing away on a hog-roast roll with apple sauce. 'You're meant to be looking after Freddie. Where is he?'

'Oh, he wanted to go upstairs. Kids are watched all the time these days, aren't they, so I thought it'd be nice for him to amuse himself for a bit.'

I smile sweetly and tear upstairs, already scared that he's gone walkabout, and imagining all the awful things that could have happened to him, involving bad strangers and angry turkeys and sizzling chestnuts. But he's in his room, chatting away to the hideous plus-sized teddy bear Duncan bought him last weekend.

'. . . and then the train driver was going too fast down the mountain and all the passengers were screaming and—'

'Freddie! What are you doing up here?'

'Big Ted wanted a story,' he says, 'so I was telling him all about the runaway train.'

There's something almost satanic about that teddy. It's bigger than Freddie, with bristly synthetic hair and stiff limbs. But the worst bit is its face – it has the latest animatronic features to make it extra realistic, including an authentic bear growl and creepy yellow eyes that seem to follow you around the room.

It must have cost an absolute bomb, even though Duncan is playing the poverty card. I loathed the thing from the moment Freddie made me shake its creepy rigid paw. Will thinks I'm projecting all my unresolved anger about my marriage onto the bloody thing. He's probably right, but I still hate Big Ted, and it's way too big for me to 'accidentally' throw it in the washing machine.

'Why don't you just bring Pingu down instead? Then you can tell him a story and watch what's going on?'

Freddie casts a contemptuous look at the much-loved penguin, lying abandoned in the corner of the room. 'Pingu is smelly, Mummy. And his nose is coming off.'

I feel stung on poor Pingu's behalf, even though he has, admittedly, started to whiff a bit. Freddie is growing out of his baby things, which makes me feel quite emotional. Then I remember that soon I'll be reliving that all again, and hopefully with Sandie to share the fun. And I have an idea.

'Come on, Fredster. Big Ted is fine, but he can't play football, can he?'

'I'm more of a rugger chap, myself,' says Toby when I present him with a football and a small boy who wants a kick about.

'Same difference but without the physical violence, isn't it?'

He looks nervous. 'He still might hurt himself.'

'Freddie's a lot tougher than he looks.'

And to prove it, Freddie tries to kick the ball, misses, and strikes Toby hard on the shin.

'Sorry!'

Toby winces. 'I'll take that as kick-off shall I, David Beckham?' And he reaches down for the ball and limps off towards the middle of the common, followed by Freddie and by Monty.

'I know what you're doing,' Sandie hisses.

'What's that then?'

'Trying to awaken his paternal instinct. Prove to me he wouldn't be a dead loss with a kid.'

I smile at her. 'Don't know what you're talking about.'

We watch as Toby crouches down to listen to Freddie, who is chattering away. After a minute or so they go off to search for sticks and place them in position at the far end before Toby stands in between them in goal. Freddie takes aim, kicks, and Toby leaps to make a save, landing awkwardly on the ground.

Freddie giggles uncontrollably and ends up rolling on the earth alongside him. Then Monty picks up one of the 'goal posts' in his mouth and both boys run after the dog.

'Anyway. Just because he can act like a three-year-old does not mean he'd make a good father.'

'It's a start, Sandie.'

We watch them try again. 'I think his mother's guessed.'

'No!'

She nods. 'She caught me touching my stomach in the ladies. You know that thing that pregnant women do? I'm sure it's just conditioning that made me do it, but she gave me this *look*.'

'Did you say anything?'

'No, I just did a runner before she could get out her purse and offer me a fistful of money to get out of his life and never darken her door again.'

Toby is still in goal, but he's texting someone. He lets three goals through before the Fredster realises he's not even bothering to defend any more. Hmm. Maybe this isn't quite going as planned. Time for Plan B.

'Can you keep a secret, Sandie?'

She turns to me. I look down at my own, fairly flat stomach, and wink.

'No! Shit, Emily, what a nightmare.'

I scowl. 'Well, not really. Actually I'm rather chuffed.'

'Yes, but what about Will? He's such a worrier.'

'Is he?'

She gives me one of her serious looks. 'I think he keeps a lot of it from you, Emily. He knows that you can take things to heart, so sometimes he calls me. Just to talk things through.'

'He's going behind my back?'

'No, no. And only business stuff. Nothing intimate. He never even hinted about the baby.'

'Ah. Um, that's because he doesn't actually know.'

'EMILY! After all the lectures you've given me about the father's right to know.'

I shrug. 'Well, to be fair, I only worked it out this morning.'

'How pregnant are you?'

'My period's forty hours late. Don't look like that. I'm always so regular.'

She shrugs. 'You're pleased, then?'

'Thrilled. It's what I've always wanted. A baby with Will, I mean. I know the timing's tricky, but there's never a perfect time, and I think we've really turned a corner with the shop, I mean, look at it.'

We turn back towards the Emporium. The queue stretches all the way onto the pavement, and cars are double-parked outside while people load boxes of food into their boots. It's what I always wanted – a buzzy, festive, fabulous store, with us at the heart of it all . . .

'It's definitely a breakthrough, Emily, but one day like this won't clear all the debts you've been building up. And have you thought how you'll restock when your suppliers are all pensioners with loyalty cards at the hospital—'

'Now you're being ageist.'

'No. Realistic. Will might be too scared to tell you the truth but I'm not.'

I turn away. Across the grass, Freddie and Monty are chasing after Toby, who is clutching the ball to his body. So he got them playing rugby after all. Freddie tackles him, grabbing hold of his ankles like a determined terrier, and Toby crashes down again.

'Keep an eye on them, would you? I think I need to talk to Will.'

'Oh, Emily, not now, surely it can wait . . .'

But I'm already heading for the shop.

I lead Will upstairs and into Freddie's bedroom. It feels like a good place for sharing the news.

'All right, Em, out with it. Whatever *it* is.'

I feel nervous, as what Sandie says suddenly sinks in. 'How bad are things exactly?'

He looks at the floor, spots Pingu, picks him up and places him back on Freddie's bed, tucked under the pillow. 'Not now, eh?'

'Sandie seems to think things are terminal. You've never told me that.'

'You know how blunt she can be, Em.'

'So she's exaggerating, is she?'

He sits down on Freddie's Charlie and Lola duvet cover. 'I don't know. If you'd asked me before this food idea then, well . . . yes. I was going to tell you after Christmas. I wanted us to have a great one, didn't want to spoil it.'

'But the food makes a difference?'

'Maybe. But then again it might not. Not if Duncan is serious about cutting the maintenance for Freddie.'

'I thought we didn't need his money.'

'It's the only cushion we have, Em. We can't keep asking Grazia.'

I look up at Big Ted. I know it's my imagination but I swear his creepy eyes are looking straight at me. It's like there are three of us in this relationship. 'I could do more secret shopping?'

'It pays peanuts, you know that. Look, I'm not saying we're going under. If we can keep the takings up, do a bit of mail order after Christmas, *and* if we can argue the case for keeping the maintenance at the same level *and* if nothing unexpected happens, then . . . well, we can probably ride it out.'

'Unexpected?'

'It'd be just our luck if the roof fell in or the rum truffles gave someone food poisoning, wouldn't it?'

Or if we had another mouth to feed . . .

'Hey.' Will stands up and comes over to put his arms around me. 'It's not over yet. Emily's Emporium could have many years ahead yet.'

'Will . . .' I know it's bad timing, but I want him to say it'll be all right. I breathe into his shirt, whisper the words. 'Will, I think I might be pregnant.'

I feel his muscles tighten under his shirt, and he seems to have stopped breathing. When I pull away from him, he has his eyes closed.

'It's not the end of the world, is it? You'll be a brilliant dad, and a baby costs nothing when it's little, and I can keep it under the counter in a Moses basket, and we'll probably have even more customers because everyone in the village is so nosy so they'll be in and out all the time—'

'How?'

I laugh. 'Accidents happen—'

'Accidents? Jesus Christ, Emily, you're not a Victorian serving wench with a randy master, are you?'

'You think I've done it on purpose?'

'Well, you've been on about having another bloody baby for months now. A child doesn't arrive with its own fairy godmother and a lifetime's worth of magic money. Didn't you learn from your bloody marriage that there's no such thing as happy ever after?'

'Will, *please*. Don't shout. You never shout.'

But he's already opening the door. 'I need time on my own.'

'Where are you going?'

'Somewhere I can calm down. Somewhere I can think.' And he slams the door behind him. I bet he's going to sit in the shed and play the old *Space Invaders* game his brother bought him for his birthday, like he always does when he needs to calm down.

But now isn't a time for playing games.

'OK. Off you go! We'll manage on our own. I was on my own with Freddie, better to know right now that you're not going to be around . . .'

I stop. There's no one in here except me. And fucking Big Ted, whose ruthless eyes meet mine, before I look away. I'd throw the bloody thing out of the window, except I'd never get it through the gap.

And then I feel an all too familiar loosening in my belly. Even as I open the door and head for the toilet I feel foolish and ludicrous and confused and relieved, yes, relieved.

Which doesn't explain why I have to take the Tampax packet out of the bathroom cabinet with one hand, because I'm having to hold my other hand to my mouth to stop myself crying out loud.

Chapter Nineteen

Even as Emily sobs into my jumper, I find myself wishing we could swap places.

I don't want Will, or Freddie, or an ex-husband. But I do wish I had my period again. Never thought I'd miss my 'monthlies' as Gramma calls them.

'There, there,' I say, patting her on the arm. I'm not good with crying women. I'm more like a man. I do practical solutions, to-do lists, constructive criticism, reality checks. I do *not* do shoulders to cry on.

'I shouldn't have told him before I knew for sure.'

'No, you probably shouldn't have.'

Emily detaches herself. 'Well, thanks a lot for your support, Sandie,' and stomps off. Ah well. At least being cross with me has stopped her crying.

It's getting dark, and the queues have died down outside the Emporium now, though the store glows prettily. I'd defy anyone to pass without wanting to go in. I do think it's their best chance – their only chance, really – of keeping the shop open, but there are no guarantees. Everything's an uphill struggle at the moment, for everyone.

Time to head back to London, before my Scrooge spirit spreads through Heartsease like a nasty dose of chicken pox. I'll round up the troops and once we get back, I might lock myself in my office and try to lose myself in the paperwork I've fallen so behind on.

I haven't seen my mother or Toby and Monty since Toby collapsed in a heap after the game of rugby with Freddie. I bet they're in the pub *and* I bet they're also expecting me to drive home. Isn't it meant to be the other way around – the mother ferrying the daughter from bar to bar? I call Toby's mobile as I walk towards the car.

'Hello, my darling!' In the background I can hear my mother's laughter above a hubbub of male voices. Yes, definitely the pub.

'Having a nice afternoon?'

'A *lovely* afternoon,' he says, missing my sarcasm. 'Just needed to quench my thirst after all that running about.'

'Well, your taxi to Chelsea will be leaving from outside the pub in four minutes' time. Otherwise you'll be running all the way home.'

And I hang up before he tries to charm me into letting him finish his drink.

I click the remote to turn off the car alarm, and phone Kelly: she's been in the store helping out. Well, running the place, more or less, with Will gone walkabout over Emily's phantom pregnancy, and Emily herself mourning the loss of a dream.

Kelly's a revelation, the only person I can rely on right now. I feel unjustly proud of the way she's developing. To think that I nearly didn't appoint her at all. She's a grafter, and approaches every new task with a set-jawed determination that reminds me a little of my gramma. Not that that is necessarily a positive thing. Not the way I see her now. I try not to think about Gramma at the moment. Too much of a toxic mix of rage at her, and guilt at myself for not wanting to call home.

Kelly. Yes. There's more to Kelly than hard work. At her interview, I thought I saw a feral, fox-like cunning in her eyes. But now I think she's more like a stray cat, watchful and wary. Kelly watches and listens and learns – she's already outwitted some of the best store security set-ups in London – and at times she's so sharp that I am relieved she's on *my* side and not a competitor's.

She comes straight out of the store and crawls into the back of

Toby's convertible, and then we sit outside the pub until I get so frustrated that I lean on the siren-loud car horn. I can feel disapproval from the residents of Heartsease but I keep at it till Toby and my mother emerge with the dog. They're laughing at some shared joke. I can't remember the last time I felt like laughing.

I can't bring myself to speak to either of them as we head back to London. Instead I keep my eyes on the road and my mind on planning which invoices I am going to spend the evening typing out.

'I bet you're exhausted after all *your* work, Kelly,' I say pointedly as we approach the Chiswick flyover. 'I'll drop you off. What's your address again?'

She catches my eye in the mirror and I see the wariness again. Perhaps she's embarrassed about where she lives. I want to tell her that it's not where you start, it's where you finish, but maybe that is too patronising. 'You can drop me on the Goldhawk Road if it's not too far out of your way.'

By the time we get there, Toby and my mother have insisted on retracting the roof – even though it's now heading for zero degrees – and Mum is working her way through a karaoke-style performance of Bob Marley's greatest hits. When Kelly climbs out of the car and heads off down a side street, I wish I could do the same.

'I have a headache, could the two of you *please* keep it down?'

'Oh, come on, Sandie. Don't be boring!' says Toby.

'BORING!' my mother shouts.

Maybe I should be pleased that Marnie and Toby have hit it off. How many potential mother-and-son-in-laws are so close?

I grip the steering wheel, trying to talk away my growing irritation. Can I blame Toby for wanting some fun? I admit I haven't been a barrel of laughs myself lately – I haven't been able to relax in case I accidentally let something slip about the baby – and as a result he's been working longer and longer hours at Garnett's. Maybe getting drunk with Marnie is his safety valve . . .

But I don't have a safety valve, so why should he? I feel a switch tripping and the full force of the Barrow rage unfurling from somewhere deep inside me.

I launch the car towards the pavement, almost crashing into a Bendy-bus, and when the driver shakes his head at me, I give him the finger.

'Right. Out! The two of you! Out!'

My mother blinks, looks around her, blinks again. 'But we're not here yet.'

'Well spotted, Marnie. We're not home, but this *is* where you and Toby are getting out.'

Toby leans forward from the back seat. 'Come on, Sandie. We were only singing.'

'It's not about singing. It's about being taken for granted and excluded and . . . oh, never mind. Your chauffeur is resigning, and as you're both too drunk to drive, that means you are taking the long way home.'

A handful of passengers are watching us from the bus stop.

'Wouldn't mess with her, mate,' says a young lad in a beanie. 'Better to walk it, I reckon.'

I turn to look at Toby and he puts on his best little-boy-lost expression but I am unmoved. 'You heard the bloke,' I say. 'Just be glad I'm letting you off at the bus stop.'

'Ah, she was like this when she was little,' says my mother, 'stubborn as hell.'

'And how the hell would you know?' I whisper. It comes out with such ferocity that she flinches. She doesn't say another word, just swings open the car door and totters out onto the pavement. The beanie kid and his mate give her a round of applause when they see her legs.

'Don't you think you're being a bit childish?' Toby mumbles as he pushes the seat forward and clambers out, holding Monty in his arms.

'Me?' I laugh bitterly. 'No. Not me. I'm just fed up being your surrogate mother. I want a relationship of equals. Monty is more mature than you are.'

I lean over to slam the car door behind him. He looks utterly bewildered. 'If you're looking for the pubs, they're that way,' I tell him, before putting my foot down and pulling out towards the roundabout, pressing the button to close the hood because it's too cold to drive open-topped when you're sober. I indicate for the far right-hand lane, wondering how long it will take them to get back to Chelsea, how long I will have in peace.

And then it occurs to me. I don't have to go home. Chelsea isn't *my* home, anyway, it's Toby's. I have a credit card, a phone, a car that can top a hundred miles an hour without breaking a sweat.

I veer back across the lanes, towards the left-hand link road leading back out of London. I don't have a clue where I'm going and at this moment, that feels seriously, unbelievably good.

For the first hundred miles I'm expecting to spot blue flashing lights in my rear-view mirror. I'm not quite sure why, as I'm pretty sure Toby won't report his car stolen, and I have stuck to the speed limit so far . . .

But what I am doing feels illicit. I suppose it could count as running away. The radio is off and all I can hear are the wheels against the tarmac and the soft puff of the heater. I keep looking at the seat beside me and panicking slightly at my lack of luggage. I never go anywhere without my trolley case, carefully packed with travel-sized items for every eventuality: French soap leaves and the special quick-dry hair turban and tiny pots of temporary filling and crown cement in case of dental disaster, and at least two perfumes, of course.

Right now I don't even have a hairbrush.

Do I need a hairbrush where I'm going? I don't know *where* I'm going. I found myself on the M40, because that's what happens when the A40 runs out, but then I realised that if I kept going I'd end up near Gramma's, and I am not ready for *that*. I don't want to hear her reasons for banning my mother from seeing me, because she might just have a point: from what I have seen of my mother so far, it's hard to believe I've missed out on much.

No, I prefer to hang onto my anger at Gramma and Marnie and Toby and even this pregnancy because that anger is giving me more energy than I've had in weeks. And it's stopping me from getting angry with myself.

I keep going, ignoring the signs that say Birmingham. I drive past IKEA and the RAC headquarters and the road signs now read *To The North* and tiredness hits me like a hot desert wind depositing grit in my eyes, but still I drive. Is Manchester far enough from everything to give me perspective on my life? Or Scotland? I've never been to Scotland.

And then I see the sign for Liverpool. It's where Gramma and my grandfather arrived in the fifties, with suitcases full of expectation . . .

And then I realise I know exactly where I want to go. Not Liverpool, but not a million miles away either. For the first time in this journey, I switch on the satnav, press in the location, and relax a little as I follow the virtual woman's husky-voiced instructions.

Blackpool was the seaside choice of most of my schoolmates. The Pleasure Beach and the Lido and the pubs serving underage drinkers were the perfect hang-out for teenagers.

Gramma and I always went to Southport.

'It was the first place that looked the way I thought England was supposed to look,' she used to tell me. We'd take the coach from Digbeth to Liverpool, to meet her friends who lived in an airless two-up, two-down dwarfed by tower blocks. Then they'd drive their ancient Vauxhall Cavalier through the strangely flat countryside towards the coast. There were always endless traffic queues and it was a race against time to get there before the car overheated.

And, once we were there, it was our special place. Not the distant sea, or that pier that goes on for ever, but the shops, oh, the *shops*. Not what was in them, even, but the wonderful promenade, with the pillars and the roofs to keep the rain off as you window-shopped, and the ironwork, intricate as a lace doiley.

It's not so familiar now. I don't remember this much suburbia on the way to the coast, but the satnav is insistent. Then finally I take a right turn and there she is. Southport could *only* be a woman, fussy retired woman who smells of Yardley Lavender perfume, dignified but old before her time. The kind who will greet you after a long journey with tea made with loose leaves, and a home-made cake, served on matching crockery.

A little like my gramma? I put the thought out of my mind.

The satnav offers me a choice of six hotels, and I select the 'star pick', which turns out to be unsettlingly hip-looking and very unlikely to offer home-made cake, but before I can drive off a uniformed man opens my car door for me, and welcomes me to Southport, and takes my key. He doesn't bat an eyelid when I explain I have no luggage, but tells me he can provide pretty much everything I need, from a toothbrush to a reflexology appointment.

I can hardly straighten my legs, after so long in the driving seat. I don't have the energy to try to cut a deal with the receptionist, and I don't even take a note of her name badge or the sincerity of her greeting as she prepares my keycard and outlines the breakfast times.

'There's an office party on in the bar tonight, I'm afraid,' she says. 'You're very welcome to have a drink in the bistro on us, though.'

I shake my head. A drink is the last thing I need. As I walk past the bar, I can hear cheering and singing. When the lift arrives I have to lean on the mirrored walls until I reach my floor, and then I put the keycard in the wrong way once, twice, three times before the little green light lets me into the room.

All I can see is the enormous bed. I throw off my shoes and climb in, fully clothed. There's a menu of romantic comedies and thrillers and music on the plasma screen but I can't even figure out how to put the receiver on standby. The blue glow is almost soothing and I know that sleep won't take long to arrive . . .

Sunday. I could probably order room service breakfast, but I didn't come here to skulk in my room feeling sorry for myself. I make my way to the brasserie, picking up a newspaper on the way in, and hiding behind it as the waitress serves me dry toast and the weakest tea, exactly what I asked for. Still makes me feel sick.

'You could try lemon marmalade,' the waitress suggests.

'Pardon?'

'For the morning sickness.'

I stare at her.

'Sorry, love,' she says. 'It's just that you've ordered exactly what I used to eat when I was pregnant, so I assumed . . .'

I nod.

'You're not showing, don't worry. But do try the marmalade. It's the citrus. It helps, some of the time.' She leans in, conspiratorial. She's late thirties, mumsy, tired-looking. 'But the thing that made all the difference, what I swear by, is crystallised ginger. The best. Try the sweet shop in the arcade.'

I thank her, but I want to disappear. I go back to the newspaper, determined not to make eye contact with anyone. Why didn't I bring my sunglasses?

But the newspaper is no distraction. It proclaims on the front, *Feel-good Festive Special* and the pages are crammed with stories about family reunions and miracle babies.

Way too close to home.

I manage another quarter piece of toast, a spoonful of marmalade on its own, and a few sips of tea, and then I leave the hotel, hoping I can manage not to vomit. That fresh air will blow away this unbearable nausea.

The shops are exactly as I remembered them, and though they must have changed hands a few times, Lord Street looks the same. Except on the other side of the road there's a huge empty Woolworth's. Like every kid, I loved the pick 'n' mix and the rest and I feel sad for the poor store and the poor people who used to work there.

Will the Customer is King Consultancy will survive the downturn? To stay afloat I'm having to do things I'd never have done: pitch against Charlie for work, even though I swore I wouldn't poach (and especially not from a man like him), go into new areas like security and cosmetic surgery clinics. It's a million miles from the little girl who fell in love with Oxford Street and this very boulevard.

But then I look at the shoppers, wrapped up against the coastal breeze in Christmas reds and greens and purples, and I see the smiles on their faces as they are drawn towards the window displays, against all their sensible instincts. I see a small girl outside a toyshop, her eyes stretched wide at some unknown but utterly desirable doll or game, her mother pulling her away gently, but the girl's eyes stay fixed on the window for as long as possible before she disappears into the crowd of legs and boots and carrier bags full of booty.

I turn my back on the shops and head towards the sea. The clouds move faster here on the coast, and the early greyness has blown away so that the sky is a strong, bright blue.

The colour of baby boys.

Stop it.

I walk past the gaudy amusement arcades with their thousands of bulbs and their electronic jamming, and towards the sea. And I walk and I walk and I'd forgotten how far it was, and I try *not* to think but of course I can't stop, can I?

And even though I manage to block out the thoughts about the baby, other stuff surfaces. Like Gramma's insistent voice telling me how to behave, when all the time she had no right to take the moral high ground. No right at all.

I spoke to her on the phone, eventually, on Friday, when the guilt got the better of me. I couldn't live with myself if I'd let her spend Christmas on her own for the first time. She might have made the wrong decision over sending Marnie away, but we all make mistakes. Of course, if I promised to spend Christmas with her, it had the added bonus of letting me off festivities chez Laetitia Garnett at Bambourne Manor.

'I have made my own arrangements, thank you, Sandra. I didn't want to wait until you took pity on me.'

Her tone was so final that I didn't argue, even though I wasn't sure I believed her.

There's a long, long boardwalk towards the pier but it stretches across sand, not sea. Way in the distance, there's something that looks like water but it might be a mirage. I'm the only one on my own, surrounded by couples, old dears sucking on chips because their teeth don't fit properly, young families. Could that have been Marnie and my dad, whoever he was, and me in my pushchair? I don't dwell on not knowing who my father was, not normally, but maybe these are not normal times.

Was he good, my dad, or a wrong 'un? Is he still alive? Gramma has hinted that he could have been any one of a number of men, and that's not the kind of thing you bring up with your long lost mother, is it, not when you're only just getting to know each other again.

I reach the end of the pier, at last. This must be new, a glass building that projects out into the sand on legs as thin as a bird's. It's dazzlingly bright inside – it no longer feels like Christmas, because the glass makes it hotter than a greenhouse – and they've blown up photographs from Edwardian times on the walls. More old dears. More couples, young families. No one alone, that I can see.

But it's not the photos that take me back, it's the machines: dozens of the old-fashioned slotters. Tableaux of the Bastille prison and a haunted graveyard, operated by old-fashioned pennies; singing puppets, and the one I always loved the best, the fortune teller, who examined your palm and then 'wrote' her own prediction on a piece of coloured card.

I exchange a pound coin for ten old pennies, and I leave the fortune teller till I have only one left, so I won't be tempted to cheat and try a second time if I don't like what the card says the first time.

The penny drops and her shop dummy's hand moves across a page. Then the card pops down into the slot. Pink for a girl.

You're tired. You know what they say – a change is as good as a rest. Take a break from the stresses and strains of life and enjoy the feeling. Return home refreshed. The number 12 is starred.

I read the message five, six times before the penny drops in my head and I realise that however many times I read it, it's not going to answer my questions.

December 20 –
Shopping Days to Christmas: 4

Face facts. You're knackered, your genuine welcoming smile is so fixed that you'll probably need surgery to undo it in the new year. If I were you, I'd take a break. Leave the lunatics in charge of the asylum. There's nothing you can do at this stage, anyway, so save someone else's shop by doing your own present shopping.

Chapter Twenty

I keep wondering whether Sandie is testing me.

Four weeks ago, the guys on the market used to think twice about trusting me with the float for a fruit and veg stall, in case my dad came on the scrounge. Now I've been left in charge of a business with a turnover of over a million quid.

Four weeks ago, I thought a turnover was something you bought in Gregg's Bakery. Mind you, I still don't know what a bloody quince looks like . . .

Sandie called me on Sunday, to say she was taking a break for a few days. Not that I was surprised that she'd fallen out with Posh Boy after that awkward journey back from the weird shop her mate Emily runs. Of course he takes her for granted. That's what blokes do.

She said on the phone that she knew she was asking a lot, that I was fully entitled to say no if I didn't want to hold the fort. 'But I've been so impressed with how fast you've learned and I know you won't let me down.'

'I don't know if I'm ready,' I said.

'You underestimate yourself, Kelly. You're incredibly bright, but you don't realise it. So will you do it?'

I couldn't really refuse. 'If you really think I'm up to it. But are *you* all right? Where are you?'

'I'm fine but I'd rather not say for now . . . Toby has an uncanny ability to charm the truth out of people.'

I considered telling her that I was pretty certain I could resist his public school twat charm, but decided against it. 'No worries.'

'You'll find everything you need to know in my Outlook calendar. Times like this that being anally retentive comes in handy, eh? But just keep things ticking over. I'm sure there'll be no major crises, everyone's winding down for Christmas.'

She's right so far. It's Tuesday and nothing's gone wrong yet. Yesterday I stole several items of stationery from a major high street retailer, and today I'm making sure hampers have been received by four key clients. Tomorrow and Thursday I'll finish processing all outstanding payments.

And on Friday the twenty-third of December I'll decide whether to screw over the one person who's ever rated me, or whether to sacrifice my good-for-nothing-but-still-my-own-flesh-and-blood-father to save my shiny new 'career'.

I hate Christmas every year, but this year in particular every last holly wreath and illuminated sleigh seems to be mocking me.

Toby sticks his head around the office door. 'I'm just off to Garnett's. Everything OK?'

'Fine, thanks.' I feel I should be sniffy with him, out of loyalty to Sandie. *Funny kind of loyalty*, my conscience whines at me.

'Are you sure you're not overdoing it, Kelly?'

I stare at him. 'Sandie asked me keep an eye on things for her.'

'And where's Sandie now, if the business is so bloody important to her?'

I just shrug. In a way, I'm relieved that he cares about her enough to be grumpy about her flit. 'Anyway, you're working long hours too, aren't you?'

He shrugs. 'Call it displacement activity.'

'You haven't heard from her then?'

He steps into the room, sits down in her chair. 'The odd text. Every time I call I just get her voicemail and then after a couple of hours she'll text me saying she's fine which is a polite way of telling me to fuck off, isn't it?'

'I honestly can't imagine Sandie ever telling anyone to fuck off.'

He picks up her hole punch and takes off the back cover, sending a blizzard of perfect paper circles floating down onto her desk. 'You'd be surprised. She's got a temper on her. She might not use actual swear words, but she doesn't need to . . .' As he talks, his voice is softer than I expected. He begins to pick up the paper dots, one by one, and throw them into the bin. 'I don't know where this is going, Kelly. She's so distant. I can't get her to talk to me at all. She hasn't said anything to you, has she?'

'No. I'm sure she'll be back for Christmas,' I say. Even though I'm not sure at all. She sounded pretty lost on the phone.

Toby sighs. 'I wonder if Christmas is the problem. She seemed to get on so well with my mother when they met up, but I guess an invitation to Bambourne Manor is intimidating.'

'Maybe she just wants some reassurance that she comes first.' I feel out of my depth in this conversation. I don't have the faintest bloody idea of what it's like to be in a relationship where someone *cares about how I feel*.

But Toby nods, as though I have said something very profound. 'Hmmm. You could be right. Thanks, Kelly. Can I bring you back some mince pies, as a thank you for your wise counsel? Garnett's own are rated the best in London by *Taste* magazine.'

I smile. 'All right then.'

He winks, and then salutes. 'Will do!' As he leaves the room, he whistles. 'Monty! Time to go to work!'

I wait for the door to shut behind them, and then slump onto my desk. Why do I feel so deflated?

And then I realise. It's because I'll miss this and I'll miss them – yes, even Posh Boy and his stinky little dog – if I have to leave the Customer is King Consultancy behind.

I've just lifted a gift pack of Snowball Truffles when my mobile rings. Unknown number. I only answer it because it might be Sandie calling from her mystery bolthole.

'Miss Kelly Wright, compliments of the season! Out Christmas shopping, eh, darling?'

The fake charm of Charlie's voice is more chilling than a security guard's tap on the shoulder. 'Are you following me?'

'Oh, isn't it lovely that you've inherited your daddy's paranoid streak?'

He hasn't answered my question, but I let it go. 'What is it?'

'Just a gentle reminder, sweetheart. Only two more shopping days till Christmas Eve. And we all know what happens on Christmas Eve, don't we?'

'We go and drink ourselves into a coma and try our hardest not to get sober again till New Year's Day?'

'Ha, ha. You're funny.' He stops laughing. 'No, on Christmas Eve, you tip me the wink and your dad gets the very best present he ever had. Freedom from worry. A new start. I can see his scrawny face now, all lit up when he realises what you've done for him. It's like one of those TV movies.'

'You're making a big assumption, Charlie.'

There's a pause at the other end. 'I go on hunches, darling. Do I believe that a good girl like you is going to sacrifice her own flesh and blood for the sake of some stuck-up cow who's living off her boyfriend's money and my bloody hard work? I know what I'd want my daughters to do.'

I hadn't pictured Charlie as a family man. Or even a human being. 'How old are they?'

'Who?'

'Your daughters?'

'Oh. I was speaking metaphorically, sweetheart. I've never been blessed with kids. Maybe it's why I'm so sentimental about family.'

Sentimental isn't a word I'd have chosen. 'I'll meet your deadline, Charlie, OK?'

'Good on you, Kelly. But if you're wavering, just remember. Your daddy was there when it counted for you. Shouldn't you do the same for him?'

And he puts the phone down and I stand in the middle of the chocolate shop, bathed in prickly sweat. The fear's always there, under the surface. Who told him? Surely not Dad? Or could it just be a horrible coincidence?

No. I don't think anything's coincidental in Charlie's world. After it happened, I spent so long going over and over it in my head. What might have changed if I'd taken a different turn that night. Would things have turned out different for me? Like that film, *Sliding Doors*, with the girl who married the bloke from Coldplay. But once you start thinking like that, it's a kind of madness. What if my mum had never gone to Australia, or if I'd gone with her? Would I be engaged to a bloke called Bruce? Maybe right now I'd be buying steaks for the annual Christmas Day barbecue on the beach?

And what if Dad had never discovered how much he loved a spin of the dice, and how he could never shake the idea that Lady Luck might give him a break for once? Trouble with my father is he's got this bloody vivid imagination. He's an optimist trapped in a life that really should have convinced him by now that the fucking glass is half empty *and* has an enormous crack in the side.

It could have been worse for me. So many crap things happen to people every minute of every day – getting caught up in wars or earthquakes or floods – and maybe Dad's right, I've got no excuse for still feeling like this, so long after it happened. And not much happened, anyway, because of him. *'What matters, Kell, is being there when it counts.'*

'Excuse me?'

It's a shock to see the uniform. Never there when you need them, eh, and always there when you don't.

'I have reason to believe you may have items in your bag you haven't paid for.'

It's an even bigger shock to realise I'm on the street – I was too preoccupied thinking about Dad to realise what I was doing. I'm already charged up to do a runner – I can easily outpace this scrawny bitch – when I remember that this isn't for real. This is my job, I have my get-out-of-jail-free card, and all I need to do is flash it, and everything returns to normal.

If only everything in my life was like that.

On Thursday morning, Sandie calls me when I've just got off the bus in Chelsea. I can hear seagulls in the background, and gusts of wind whip away words as she speaks.

'You are coping, aren't you, Kelly?'

'Yes. Really, there's nothing to worry about. What about you, Sandie? Are you . . . um, getting on OK?'

'Absolutely. This was just what I needed.' Except, if anything, she sounds more anxious than she did when I last spoke to her. 'How are things at the apartment?'

189

'Toby's very unsettled. He seems very worried about you.'
Actually, I haven't seen much of him. He's either at Garnett's or
at the pub with Marnie and Monty.

'I'm planning to come back tomorrow. Briefly, well, perhaps
not briefly, I don't quite know yet. But you don't need to come in
tomorrow. Not the day before Christmas Eve. I'm sure you've got
shopping and organising to do.'

Shopping and organising. Yes, I guess that is what normal
people do. Even though it's only just past nine, there's already a
sense of purpose on the streets of West London. Rolls of wrapping paper peep out of shopping bags, and there are queues
building up as I pass the delis and the gift shops. For a few days,
the credit crunch is on hold.

'I don't mind coming in.' Because, let's face it, I have no one to
buy a gift for. Dad would rather have the money for whisky and I
gave up expecting anything from him a bloody long time ago.

'Well, maybe just the morning then. It'd be nice to see you
before . . .' She stops. 'I'd like to show my appreciation. Oh, and
Al from the surveillance shop will be popping in today to deliver
your new shirt and show you how it works. Use one of the
countersigned cheques so you can get the cash from the bank,
there won't be time for his cheque to clear before Christmas.'

She really does trust me completely. It makes me feel like the
world's biggest scumbag. And then I realise: I've already decided
what I'm going to do . . .

In the bank, the girls behind the counter are wearing party
hats.

'Would you like to pull a cracker?' the clerk says. She's about
my age, and her cheeks are flushed, and I suspect the liqueur
chocolates have already been doing the rounds, even though it's
only five to eleven.

'You're all right,' I say.

'Go on,' she says, thrusting one towards me through the
narrow security gap where the money goes. 'It's been such a shit
year, we all need cheering up, don't you reckon?'

I grasp the end, because I don't think she's going to give me
the money if I don't play along. I pull, and the cracker lets out
the most pathetic little bang, and I get the bigger piece, complete

with a joke I can't face reading, and a hat, and one of those fortune-telling goldfish made of thin plastic. 'Lucky me,' I say.

'Put the hat on,' she says, and I pretend to, but then accidentally tear it as I pull it over my head. 'Try out the fish.' She's beginning to get on my tits.

'What about the queue . . .' I protest, but when I turn around, everyone's grinning as though they're pumping fucking laughing gas out through the speakers along with the festive music. Maybe a week ago, I'd have been feeling the same, but right now I feel like an outsider. They represent the honest, fun-loving British workers, letting their hair down after twelve months of struggle. And I represent the underclass, the people who'd rip you off soon as look at you, and sell their own grannies for a fiver.

I put the sodding fish onto my palm and it curls up from the heat, and then flips over, like it's drowning. I consult the Interpretation Guide that comes with it. 'It says I'm going to come into some money in the next thirty seconds,' I say, loudly, and the queue laughs as one, and the girl claps her hands together and wishes me a merry Christmas as she hands over the cash and an individually wrapped segment from a Terry's Chocolate Orange.

I tuck the money away into my bag and leave the bank. Actually, not one of the Interpretations is a forecast about money or handsome strangers. Instead they indicate character and my flipped fish revealed more about me than I'd like, in a single word.

FICKLE.

Alan doesn't need a fortune-telling goldfish to make judgements about me.

'She left you in charge?' he says, when he turns up with my secret camera shirt.

'Took your time with that, didn't you?'

He hands it over. It smells of starch, crisply laundered to Army standards, no doubt. But then close-up, I bet he smells of starch, too. He's as rigid as a mop handle, and as humourless. Today he's all dressed up in 'smart casual wear', very dashing if you're into the whole *Top Gun* thing – which I am *so* not – and I wonder if he's gone to all that trouble for Sandie.

'I didn't hurry with your shirt, no, Kelly. Wasn't sure you'd be around long enough to need it.'

'You were wrong there, then.'

'Sandie's too trusting. She's only known you a few weeks.'

I don't reply. Maybe I should proclaim my trustworthiness, but I have a hunch he'd see through it. He already looks at me like he's one of those X-ray scanners at an airport, and it wouldn't surprise me if those glasses of his are super-specs, invented in his workshop with a microchip so he can tell if I'm lying *and* see my underwear at the same time. He has to get his kicks somehow.

'We going to go out and test it then?' he asks.

'Do we have to?'

'Part of the service Sandie pays for,' Al says. 'Of course, if you want to opt out, it's your decision.'

I shrug. 'No, let's do it.'

I go to the bathroom to change into the shirt – at least it fits this time – and then we head out of Sandie's flat, towards the river.

'So what are your plans for Christmas, then, Kelly?'

'You don't have to pretend to be interested, you know.'

'But I am interested in people,' he says. 'Other men have hobbies. Fly-fishing or stamp-collecting. I like knowing what makes people tick. And anyway, I feel a responsibility towards Sandie to know about you in particular. She's a good kid.'

'Kid? I bet she'd love that.'

He smiles as he crosses the road, and it makes him look *almost* human. 'She wouldn't, would she? She's only a year younger than me, actually. But there's something vulnerable about her. Always thought that.'

'This your famous ability to judge what makes people tick, is it?'

'If you like. It's not rocket science. Spiky people are like cacti. The sharp bits are to keep everyone else at arm's length. Don't you think?'

'Are we still talking about Sandie?'

He shrugs. 'Who else would we be talking about?'

He's messing with my head now. Something makes me want to argue the toss, but I don't need him on my back. We stop at a park bench. 'OK, Kelly, let's try some filming; outside first, and then we can go into one of the stores.'

He unbuttons his own shirt, and there, just below the very tight abs, is a wide belt with a very small recorder attached.

'You trying to impress me with your Action Man stomach, are you?'

He sighs. 'No, Kelly. I have no desire to impress you. I wore mine because I thought you'd accuse me of harassment if I started fiddling around near your nether regions.'

'Oh.'

He doesn't look at me as he explains the controls, which are so simple Monty could work them with his paw.

'So there's an on switch and an off switch, that's what you're telling me? Well, thanks for the lesson but I reckon I could have worked that out for myself.'

Al shakes his head wearily. 'You know, it might seem like a joke to you, but this is serious equipment.'

I pull a serious face. Taking the piss out of Al is the only fun I've had all week. 'Serious. Right.'

'OK, no one dies if you get caught out filming a grumpy assistant in Selfridges or wherever, but I developed this for use in dangerous situations. Where being detected because of a strange beep or an odd movement could cost you your life.'

'Ooh, my hero,' I say. 'Where has it been used then? Notting Hill? Even . . . Brixton?'

'Afghanistan. Iraq. North Korea.'

That stops me in my tracks. 'Seriously?'

'Well, not this actual camera, obviously. Most of the ones we used in hostile environments sustained catastrophic damage in the end. I had one that saved my life once.'

'Now you're just showing off.' But I'm too curious not to ask. 'What happened?'

He shifts the belt up a little and I see a pitted scar in his flesh, a good ten centimetres wide.

'Ouch.'

'Shrapnel. From our own side, which didn't make it hurt any less, I can tell you. I was undercover in Helmand when the guys I was with got bombed. If I hadn't had the belt on, it'd have gone deeper, and I'd have bled to death. Video didn't make it, though, which annoyed me.'

'It would,' I say. Despite my cynicism, I can't help being *slightly* impressed. Not just by the camera, or the story, but by the low-key way he told it.

'So there are no excuses for coming away from an assignment without the footage, eh, Kelly? Now, let's go through the basics of making sure the camera lens is facing in the right direction, shall we? If you don't mind me getting personal, it's all about being aware where your nipples are pointing.'

He demonstrates what he means, and then I try, first in the open and then inside a couple of stores. He's pretty patient with me as he corrects my posture and explains about lighting levels and how to minimise sound distortion. In fact, he's such a good teacher that about twenty minutes passes before I remember that I am meant to be taking the piss. By then we're heading back towards the office.

'So, you never told me what you were doing for Christmas, did you, Alan?' I look pointedly at his hand. 'No Mrs Army Wife to boil your sprouts for you?'

'I learned to boil my own in the forces,' he says, and I can't tell whether he's playing along. 'Actually, I'm puppy-sitting for friends up the road in Sand's End. Got to be more fun than spending Christmas with people, eh?'

'Oh no, I got it,' I say. 'You're one of those he-men who can't relate to women unless they're stark naked and airbrushed on the inside of your locker door?'

He shakes his head. 'It's a shame, Kelly.'

'What is?'

'The last few minutes I was getting the impression that there might be an OK person lingering somewhere deep under your sarky veneer. But it seems I was wrong.'

I shrug because I can't think of anything clever to say.

'Merry Christmas, Kelly. And good luck. With an attitude like that, you're going to need it.'

And he marches away, like a sentry going off duty. Except I don't think that man is *ever* off duty.

*

On Friday morning, Sandie texts to say she's on her way back and just before noon, she arrives. I come out of the office into the living room. She's hugging Toby, while Monty the dog humps her leg, but the happy threesome breaks apart when I appear. Actually, she looks relieved to have an excuse to move away. Her eyes are less tired than they were, but her shoulders still slope like the roof of a rundown shed.

'How has everything been, Kelly? Shall we go into the office? I've missed it.' She turns her back on Toby and I follow her. 'It all looks very organised in here.'

'Like you said, there wasn't much to do except keep things ticking over. Everyone seems to have packed up for Christmas.'

'And now you must do the same. Honestly, I can't thank you enough.' She reaches into her handbag and pulls out a stick of rock with THANK YOU written through the middle in pink candy. She hands me an envelope.

I smile. 'Thanks. First card I've had this year.'

She looks at me with complete sympathy and I realise I've made myself sound like a sad fucker. I tear open the envelope and pull out a hand-made card featuring a cottage at night, surrounded by glitter snow.

And then cash falls out . . . a lot of cash.

'Sandie, I can't take this. You already pay me a salary.'

'Seriously. You deserve it.'

'No.'

The dog is sniffing at the money. 'I insist, Kelly. I'd rather you had it than Monty ate it for lunch.'

I know I can't really refuse.

'Thank you so much. I'll be able to treat myself. My dad means well but he doesn't really have the knack of choosing decent presents.'

'Will it just be the two of you?'

For a moment, I'm terrified that she's going to invite me and Dad to Bamborne Manor . . . while Charlie's henchmen do their worst here. 'We like it that way,' I lie.

'How lovely. I bet you've got all kinds of rituals, haven't you?' she says excitedly, as though it really matters to her.

'Oh yeah. Proper London Christmas we have. And you're going off to the country. That'll be the first Christmas with your mum in years then, eh?'

Her smile falters. 'That's the plan. Along with Toby's mother, not to mention the entire extended Garnett family, servants, hounds, you name it. Honestly, spending Christmas holed up in London, on my own, has never seemed so tempting.'

Shit. She can't stay here. 'You've just spent some time on your own. You don't want to be alone while everyone's celebrating, do you? I'm sure it won't be nearly as bad as you fear.'

'Oh, Kelly.'

And then I realise she's crying, very discreetly, with wounded animal sobs that she's desperately trying to swallow. I move forward to comfort her, even though I don't know if she'd rather I stayed on the other side of the office. Then again the room's so small that I can't pretend I haven't noticed.

'Is there anything I can do?' I say, hoping she won't suggest tagging along with Dad and me for our turkey meal for two.

She freezes in my arms and I hear her gulp once, twice, three times before she comes back under control and untangles herself. 'No. No, you've done more than enough. I must be . . . pre-menstrual or something. I'll be fine. And now you really, really need to head off and do festive things.'

'Right. Thanks.' And I pick up my bag and my coat and scarf and this time I don't hug her. 'Have a brilliant Christmas, Sandie.'

She follows me out into the living room again. Toby is pretending to look out of the window but there's really nothing to see out there, just the Thames, flat and grey like the sky. Is it the last time I'll see this view?

Glad I'm getting out of here now, I get this feeling that there's a huge fuck-off row brewing.

He comes over to hug me. 'Have a good 'un, Kelly. Hope you get some mistletoe action.' He stops and reaches down to the floor, retrieving a branch. 'In fact, here's some I prepared earlier.' And he gives me a soft kiss on the cheek.

I leave the flat, and when I turn to close the door behind me, I see the two of them, at opposite ends of the room, like actors on the set of the latest Tarantino movie, waiting for someone to shout 'Action!'

And I know I'm the one with the machine gun, waiting for my cue to let rip.

Chapter Twenty-One

Grazia

Of all the cultural experiences I have enjoyed since moving to Britain, I have never been invited to a proper slap-up English Christmas lunch.

Leon's family had left London by the time I arrived on the scene. In fact, they had deserted him hurriedly in the summer he turned sixteen, to move to a part of Spain Leon always called the Costa del Crime. The one time we did visit them at Christmas, it was steak, salad and Rioja at every meal.

So when Nigel suggests joining him for lunch on Sunday for their annual celebration, I am almost tempted. Until I realise that there's every chance I am older than his parents.

'I really would not want to impose.'

'Rubbish. The more the merrier.' He runs his hand down my neck, but the light in his bedroom is too harsh, and my neck too scraggy, for it to be relaxing. I have been thinking of calling Dr Target to find out whether there is anything he can do to redeem the skin between chest and chin. For all my initial doubts, I am concerned that cosmetic treatments could prove addictive.

'Is there not a danger that they might read more into our . . . situation than there is? Regarding commitment?'

He looks hurt. 'Not that again. You're very keen on setting limits, aren't you? Anyway, my granny once invited a bloke she'd met at the bus stop.'

'And your mother was OK with that?'

'We-ell, admittedly she wasn't over the moon. The bloke did smell quite bad. Granny's dead now, so we don't get the dramas we used to . . .'

'I bet there would be drama if I showed up.'

He keeps stroking, but I know I am doing the right thing. It is not just the age. It is about protecting myself. I gained a glimpse of the hurt that a man can cause when the odious James ripped me to pieces after a single night together.

Nigel is no James, but surely that makes him even more dangerous. I might fall for him, and then where would I be when he leaves me for someone his own age, as all toyboys inevitably do. Losing Leon was unbearable and the more I begin to like Nigel, the more I *know* I could not bear to lose anyone again.

'You're too hung up about this age thing, Grazia. My parents are way, way older than you anyway. Different generation from us.'

I take a deep breath. 'Tell me about them.'

'OK, well, my mother works in a temp agency, placing secretaries and so on. She does aerobics once a week and she buys all her clothes from Next, except her underwear, which she gets from Marks and Spencer. Though she's very concerned about whether the quality is as good as it used to be. She writes a lot of letters of complaint.'

'And how old is she?'

'Oh. Um.' He closes his eyes to do the mental arithmetic. 'Forty . . . nine. No, forty-eight.'

I gulp. I have never actually told him my age. All I did was to maintain a diplomatic silence when he attempted to guess, and in the end he made up his mind I was thirty-seven. I never denied it. Another reason our liaison is doomed: one cannot build trust based on lies. 'She must have had you very young, then?'

'Yes. Nineteen, she was, and my father was twenty-three. It was different then, though, wasn't it? They didn't have the opportunities we had.'

'It is not as though they were born in the time of rationing, Nigel.'

'That's what Mum always says.' He frowns at me, as though he is seeing the similarities for the first time.

I change the subject. 'And your father?'

'He's in local government. Trading standards, consumer protection. A bit like what you do, with the secret shopping.' He leans over and kisses my forehead. I hope he has not noticed the slight wonkiness to my brow, where the Botox has frozen the left side just a fraction more than the right. 'You'll have so much in common.'

'I have not said yes.'

He lies on his side, resting on his elbow, and he looks strikingly young against the white sheet. Unmarked by life, even at almost thirty.

'Go on, Grazia. It's either that, or we spend the big day right here, in bed. Which I would prefer, of course, but it would upset my mother no end. At the very least, you could see it as your Christmas present to a middle-aged lady.'

I shake my head. 'We will see. In the meantime, perhaps you might consider an early present to this middle-aged lady?'

And he laughs in that appreciative way that makes me feel anything but middle-aged. As we re-entangle deliciously, I congratulate myself on taking his mind off his family.

I leave his flat a little while later, just as it is getting dark, and it strikes me suddenly that Marylebone High Street at dusk is perhaps the closest thing I have ever seen to my romantic teenaged imaginings of England. Dickens could not have conjured up somewhere so picture perfect. There is enough ice in the air to make one feel wintry, but not enough to chill the bones. Me, I like the cold, sometimes. Italy could get cold, but not like this. *This* reminds me of how far I have come . . .

There are the stores, of course, the prettiest of stores, selling the loveliest of inconsequential non-essentials. I covet everything: the lotions and potions in Space NK, the heavenly haberdashery and ribbons at Rouleaux, the huge glass jars of e-numbered delights in the window of the sweet shop, the hand-painted naïf plates and teapots in Emma Bridgewater, the thousands of classic books in

Daunt's, the jewel-coloured cashmere sweaters in Brora, the copper pans in Divertimenti . . .

And then there are the stalls, just for Christmas, with strings of fairy lights suspended from the canvas roofs. I stop by a stall selling biscuits and cakes, every single one snow white. Star-shaped meringues dusted with icing sugar. Cookies with big chunks of white chocolate melted into the dough. Marzipan hearts with a frosty sheen. I have barely shopped for the last few weeks – other sensual delights have taken priority – but I am seized by the desire to buy up half the stall. The woman selling them is suspiciously thin for a baker, but she looks thrilled when I get out my purse. The hearts are perfect for Emily. The cookies will go down well with Nigel who, like so many men, has a sweet tooth. And little Freddie will love the stars . . . oh, and perhaps those tiny snowmen, too. I add them to the pile, and the woman wraps them in glorious shimmery cellophane, with cascades of ribbon. I tip her five pounds when she hands over the bag of goodies.

It is only when I walk away that I remember I am not due to see another single soul now before Christmas. Even the other apartments in my building are emptying fast, as the ex-pats – those that have not yet taken flight from London's financial crisis – head home to Russia or New York or Tokyo. There is a danger I will be the only human being in the block: even the concierge has the day off to spend with his family. And me? I have no family. Nigel is simply a temporary diversion from the ultimate emptiness of my life.

The bag bites into my hand. I am a foolish, lonely woman and I should use the festive period as an opportunity to reflect on my shallow life and my failures and my stupidity in allowing myself to be seduced by icing sugar and bows.

And then I catch sight of a furniture shop window, the display laid out like a fairy-tale boudoir, with a huge bed draped in silk, and a beautiful armoire and white dressing table. Before I can look away, I see my own reflection in the mirror and . . .

I look alive. Far, far better than I had expected – or feared. But it has nothing whatsoever to do with Dr Target's handiwork.

No, my glow is far more to do with *Nigel's* handiwork. In this light, I could almost fool myself into believing that I am thirty-seven. I have not looked like this since . . . I cannot recall.

Do I really want to cut myself off from everything that makes life worth living? Which is more masochistic – a willingness to be hurt by people, or the determination to cut yourself off, the way my mother did?

I put the carrier-full of cakes down on the pavement and take my telephone out of my handbag.

'Nigel? It is me. I have decided . . . hmmm. Yes. If your mother has room for one more, I would be delighted to come for Christmas lunch.'

December 23 –
Shopping Days to Christmas: 1

New Year Sales are so nineteen-nineties. If you haven't already discounted your stock by at least fifty per cent, then that's why your store's like the *Marie Celeste*. Get slashing.

Chapter Twenty-Two

OK, so maybe it's not ideal to be going on a grotto secret shopping expedition at four o'clock on the day before Christmas Eve.

But I didn't do it *on purpose*. It was only when Sandie called me to ask if I was around to let a courier pick up the last tape, that I realised the problem. I'd been to the grotto with the drunk Santa. I'd been to the out-of-town-mall animatronic Christmas experience (a real hoot, where the reindeers cracked double-entendre jokes to keep the adults amused while the kids chatted to the man in the beard). I'd been to a minimalist grotto in Hoxton where Santa was played by an albino conceptual artist and 'snow' obviously had a very different meaning, and I had a lot of explaining to do afterwards when Freddie kept playing the Why? game. But I'd forgotten the last visit on my list.

To Garnett's . . .

Well, I've had a lot on my mind organising the perfect Christmas. Everything is ready. The wardrobe is full of presents for my two favourite males. Freddie's main gift is a shiny blue bike with stabilisers (which I plan to wrap in tinsel and fairy lights, because I saw them do it in a magazine and it looked dreamy), but he's also getting a bubble gum machine, a cricket bat, an 'educational' electronic cash register, new shoes and a *Beano* annual, plus about half a dozen shrink-wrapped plastic pocket-money gifts.

And though Will and I agreed ages ago that we wouldn't spend much on each other, I couldn't resist the *Carry On* movie box set – he has such a schoolboy sense of humour, and he loves Barbara Windsor. I've carried on the theme with a naughty nurse's outfit for me that I was going to save until we went to bed on Christmas night. But I must admit that I'm having second thoughts about wearing it, as we haven't touched each other since the pregnancy scare . . .

Then there are the decorations. I'm going to use cupcake cases as tea light holders (which I saw in the same magazine) – I tried it out and it looks gorgeous, the flames reflected in the gold and silver foil. I've been eyeing up the trees and bushes all around the village, and I'm planning a dusk raid with my secateurs to pick holly and eucalyptus and mistletoe. I even found a spare container of Johnson's powder from when Freddie was a baby so I can do what my dad did, and scatter it like snow across the living room before my boy goes to bed.

Then Will can tramp through it in his biggest boots, to 'prove' that Santa visited.

That's if Will hasn't gone off in a huff. He's so cross that I'm going on this final mystery shopping trip. I mean, it's a simple mistake. The sort busy women across the country would identify with. Yet he's behaving as though I've bought a one-way ticket to Lapland.

'You're really leaving me in the lurch,' he grumbles, while Freddie races around the store clapping his hands and shouting, 'We're going to see Father Christmas again!'

'Look around you, Will. It's not like we've got much left to sell.'

He harrumphs in a grudging kind of way. Even he can't deny that the Emporium's diversification into local produce has been our most successful venture yet. We're sold out of all the puddings and cakes, despite a round-the-clock restocking effort by the Heartsease ladies, though we've still got a few mince pies and Brussels sprouts and tubs of fresh brandy butter.

OK, I admit that I might have hoarded some of the nicer things for us. I've hidden the cakes in the wardrobe with Freddie's presents, and the perishables are in the shed at the back, because Will would only tell me off if he knew. But with all the rows lately, it's even more important that this is the most Perfect Christmas Ever.

'I'll be back in a few hours. And if we do have a last minute rush of customers, it'll probably be tomorrow, anyway, won't it?'

'We'll see,' he says, and then pointedly turns his back on me to reorganise the jars of Onion and Cranberry relish (a special invention concocted by the vicar's wife for the Emporium, and a total triumph served with port and Stilton).

'Like that, is it?' I whisper, and then crouch down to my son's level. 'OK. Socks?'

'Check,' says Freddie, pulling them up so I can see he's got some on. All right, so one is emblazoned with Superman and the other with My Little Pony (he must have half-inched that from his friend Abigail). But it is progress.

'Shoes done up?'

'Check!'

'Jumper, coat, scarf, hat?'

'Check, check, check, check!'

'Reindeer?'

'Mummy . . .'

'Flying sledge?'

'You're being silly!' he says, giggling.

'Yes I am! Because it's Christmas! Right glove, left glove?'

He holds up his mittened hands.

'Fredster ready for take-off, ready, launch, FIRE!'

And Freddie runs out of the shop towards the front door. When I turn round to say goodbye to Will, he's staring after Freddie, an unreadable expression on his face.

I don't say goodbye.

It takes me an hour to find a parking space, then another twenty minutes to get through to the parking office call centre to pay by phone – whatever happened to meters?

I am *not* looking forward to this. It's not just that Garnett's will be packed out. It's also that I haven't been back there at Christmas for three years, not since I went here with Freddie when he was six months old and I was the world's most miserable mother: newly single and utterly shell-shocked.

I don't want to be reminded of that time.

'You won't remember coming here, Fredster, but this is where I met Auntie Sandie for the first time.'

He shrugs – he's caught that maddening gesture from his father – and pushes at the heavy metal door to the store, which doesn't budge. A liveried doorman steps forward to contribute the necessary force and, after a second's hesitation, I step inside.

It's heaving. Of course. Only a fool would come here two days before Christmas, but there are thousands more fools like us gathered in the entrance alone.

Freddie's eyes register surprise, then fear.

'You've got to hold my hand now it's busy, darling, all right? We'll fight our way through the crowds to find Santa.'

His little hand is damp as it grips mine, but his expression as he looks up at me is one of complete trust: of course I'll get him safely to Santa. I am Mummy. I can do anything.

There are very few children about, but lots of harassed adults, burdened by too many bags and too little time. We pass through the ground floor, which is decked out as a Winter Wonderland, with lights that simulate soft falling snow, and assistants dressed as woodland animals offering free samples of reviving hot cider punch and butterscotch Florentines.

I must try that at the Emporium. Even if the customers don't go for it, it'd help the day pass more quickly.

Despite the crush, Garnett's is already working its magic on me: I don't quite know where to look first, and neither does Freddie. Now our hands are locked together, he's loving it, pointing at things with his other hand: the woman carrying a dog in her handbag, the man with a huge rucksack stuffed with gift-wrapped presents. But we tear ourselves away from the serious business of buying and head for the grotto, where it's quieter. No one else has time to linger around the Peter Pan themed displays, or visit Father Christmas. I switch my camera on, pay the ten pound entrance fee (no *wonder* it's quiet) and then hold back slightly as Freddie pushes through the grotto blackout curtains and into the cave.

'Oh, wow, Mummy!'

My eyes take longer to adjust to the semi-darkness than my

son's, but when they do, I realise why Garnett's keeps its reputation year after year. Directly ahead of us is a deserted pirate ship – maybe half life-size, but as we're in the dark, it feels full-sized – and our entrance must have triggered the show, because lightning flashes across the sky, the pirate ship disappears behind what seems like a curtain of stormy rain, and to our left we see a children's bedroom, where a mother is reading stories to her daughter and two sons. And a small boy balances on the window ledge, listening intently . . .

It's years since I've read the book and, of course, Freddie is way too young to know the story. But it doesn't matter because there's something so magical about these tableaux that Peter's longing, and Wendy's patience, and Captain Hook's wickedness makes me painfully sad and euphorically happy and utterly terrified in turn. And Freddie is entranced by the animation and the sound effects and especially by the pirates and Tinker Bell's fluttering presence.

I don't know how long we're in there, but when Wendy and her brothers finally find their way back to the nursery, I realise I've been so caught up in it all that I've forgotten to follow the action with my camera, the first time in almost three years of secret shopping.

Fairy lights appear at the far end of the room, drawing us towards the exit. But of course, there's still Santa to see.

He's sitting in the next room, beside a huge tree. He looks as though he's been there for ever, just waiting for my little boy.

'Hello there, youngster.'

Weird. There's something very familiar about that voice.

'Come on, don't be shy. Are you going to come and sit next to me and tell me what you'd like for Christmas? I can't mind-read, you know!'

I don't know what accent I expect Santa to have, but it's definitely not upper-crust old Etonian. As we approach, I look for clues. The face is covered by the best fake beard I've ever seen – I bet that's real human beard hair, knowing the Garnett's commitment to authenticity – but the eyes are silvery and amused.

'It's Freddie, isn't it?' says Father Christmas.

The Fredster's jaw drops.

Santa beckons. His hand gives him away: unlined, young, covered in downy blond hair . . .

Toby.

I wink at him, but he doesn't see it. He's too busy settling Freddie down, and asking him questions about the plans for Christmas and what he's hoping for, and nodding and chuckling in a surprisingly authentic Santa-like way.

What is he doing playing Santa? He's a senior partner, the next in line for the Garnett's throne, and here he is making little boys' dreams come true.

I watch him as he chats to Freddie, who doesn't seem to be making any connection between this white-haired man and the guy who was playing football with him on Heartsease Common only six days ago. And I realise that he will make a phenomenal father.

If he's given the opportunity . . .

After giving Freddie a very generous ten minutes – well, I guess there's no one behind us in the queue – he dispatches my son to an elf to select the present. I point the camera towards Freddie, but whisper to Toby, 'Well, you're the best one we've seen.'

'I should hope so,' he whispers back.

'But why you?'

'Our regular guy decided to spend Christmas in Australia, but didn't give us time to find a replacement. I'm probably the only person in the whole store who isn't overworked in the Christmas rush so I volunteered. Plus I don't think you should ever ask any employee to do a job you're not willing to do yourself.'

'And how's it been?'

'Um. Very hands-on. I've caught about three colds in a week. And I have a horrible feeling my beard has a nasty case of nits.' I catch a certain weariness in his voice.

Freddie has chosen his present now so I turn away.

'Only one more day to go,' I whisper, hoping I've managed to capture his performance on screen.

It might just be the most important piece of footage I've ever recorded.

*

'Is that the *real* Santa, then, Mummy?' Freddie says as he takes my hand to leave the grotto, holding his brightly wrapped present in the other.

I freeze. 'What on earth do you mean?' He couldn't have guessed, could he?

He frowns. 'I told Abigail about our trips, but she says that nobody can be in lots of places at once. Even Father Christmas.'

A chill of guilt passes over me. Has my secret shopping work spoiled the illusion of Christmas for my little boy? Bloody precocious Abigail. 'Well, what do you think, Fredster?'

His face fills with doubt. 'I'm not sure. The first Santa we saw, he smelled funny, didn't he? Not like today. Today he smelled nice. And he knew my name. So are they the same?'

I step onto the escalator, with him next to me. 'The funny thing about Father Christmas, Freddie, is that he's two things at once. He's a real man, just like Daddy—'

'And like Will?'

I smile. 'Yes, like Will, too. But Father Christmas is also magic. How many children do you think there are in the world?'

He counts on his fingers. 'Um . . . nine hundred?'

'Maybe a few more than that. But even with just nine hundred, do you think Daddy could manage to get around all the houses, down nine hundred chimneys, on Christmas Eve?'

We step off as he thinks about it. 'But more than one child could live down one chimney.'

I laugh. 'True. Very clever, Freddie, though even if it was just five hundred, I think Daddy would struggle. But Father Christmas can be in all of those houses, and more, all over the world. All at once.'

Freddie's brow relaxes. 'Oh. Oh, so he could be in lots of different shops?'

'Easily.' I feel the guilt beginning to subside . . .

'But he still smells different, in different places.'

'Yes, well, he eats different things for tea every day. Unlike you, young man. You're going to turn into a spaghetti hoop.'

He giggles. 'I'll be all red and stringy, won't I, Mummy?'

And I lean down and kiss him, and then blow a raspberry on his neck. 'You will, and I will want to eat you up, my darling.

Now, shall we go and buy a few treats ready for Santa and his reindeers tonight?'

'Will they like spaghetti hoops?'

I pick him up. 'We'll get some extra in, just in case.'

We arrive back at Heartsease later than I'd planned, thanks to mad traffic. The grotto, Toby's sterling performance and Freddie's response to it, made me feel extremely festive, and I couldn't resist a few last minute purchases. Everything seems so cheap this year, even in Garnett's food hall, with endless BOGOFs and Credit Crunched Christmas promotions, so I loaded up a trolley full of stuff we don't *need* in the strictest sense, but things that will improve our quality of life. Hand-stitched stockings for both my favourite males, and a few more bargain toys for Freddie – chosen while I distracted him by asking him to choose the brightest clementines or the nuttiest-looking nuts. Thank goodness for a son who loves shopping.

An hour disappears like *that*, and as I drive home slightly above the speed limit so I don't miss the courier, I hope that Will can be placated by the delicious port I picked up for after Freddie's bedtime (I know it's delicious as they were doing free samples and oh, wow, I swear they've invented liquid Christmas).

And then I have to remember to phone Sandie to make sure she watches the footage.

But as I turn onto the Common to park, I spot something I wasn't expecting.

'The Batmobile!' shrieks Freddie from his car seat. 'Daddy's here!'

'Hmm. Yes. Apparently he is.'

Duncan is not supposed to be coming to pick Freddie up until Boxing Day. I try to convince myself he's just popped in to wish us a Merry Christmas and drop off some presents, but the awful feeling in my stomach is telling a different story.

I decide to leave the shopping in the Snowvan for now, rather than face more accusations from Duncan that I am spending his money like some vengeful shopaholic. 'Come on, big fella. Let's see what Daddy's doing here.'

We're barely through the door when Will appears at the top of the stairs to the flat. He's mouthing something, but I can't tell what, and then Duncan appears behind him. Freddie is running up the steps but when he gets to the upstairs landing he freezes, torn between hugging his father and hugging the man who plays the bigger role in his life.

After ten long seconds of agonising, he positions himself so that he can loop his left arm around Duncan's knee, and his right arm around Will's. A diplomat in the making. It makes me feel simultaneously proud and guilty.

'Freddie boy!' says Duncan, tugging our son's right arm from Will's leg, so he can pick him up. 'Happy Christmas!'

'Don't be silly, Daddy. Everyone knows there are two more sleeps till it's Christmas.'

Duncan smiles. 'Oh. Yes. Of course. I got muddled.'

'This is a surprise, Duncan,' I say. 'Don't tell me you were just passing.'

'You're the one who chose to relocate our child somewhere hundreds of miles from home.'

I open my mouth to point out that, in fact, *he* was the one to choose to move to bloody Austria before Freddie was even born, but I decide to maintain the moral high ground. 'Not that it isn't nice to see you, but the contact arrangements are there for a reason.'

He puts Freddie down. 'Oh yes. Remind me what those are again.'

The threat in his voice is low-key but it's definitely there. Will's picked up on it too, and is wearing his *how the hell did I end up in the middle of this mess* expression.

'If we're going to have a grown-up talk, perhaps it should not be *devant l'enfant*,' I say.

'I'll take him downstairs,' says Will.

'No. You need to be here for what I have to say.' Duncan gives us an extra-malevolent stare, just to spook us.

We all look down at Freddie and, as usual, it's up to me to sort it. 'Fredster, I'm a bit worried that Santa might not know to come to the flat at Christmas.'

'Why? He knew who I was so he must be very clever.'

'Um. Yes, but our flat just looks like a shop from the outside.

Would you go and do him a special drawing, so that he knows that Freddie lives here?'

His face turns solemn. 'Yes, Mummy.' And off he trots.

'Right, let's get this over with,' I say, leading the way into the living room. I don't offer tea or biscuits, because I don't want to encourage my ex-husband to drop in unannounced ever again.

He sits down in Will's armchair and I count backwards from ten to stop myself telling him to move. It'll be over soon. He'll be gone and we can relax and I can fetch the port from the car and—

'So. The arrangements. Remind me what they are again,' says Duncan.

I sigh. 'I'm really not in the mood for game playing.'

He shakes his head. 'This isn't a game. I think it's time to check we all have the same understanding of what the deal is.'

'OK. Have it your way. The deal, as you put it, is that you can see Freddie whenever you want, in addition to your regular arrangements, so long as we have enough notice. Of course, up until now, you haven't been in the country, but as things have changed for you, we can negotiate amendments—'

'Negotiate? Well, that's fucking generous of you, Emily.'

'Don't speak to her like that,' Will says. 'This is our home, and I am completely prepared to throw you out of it if you can't be civilised.'

Duncan shrugs. 'I'm not stopping long. But you're right, Emily, things have changed, as my solicitor pointed out in the last letter.'

'Yes. And of course we'll do our best to be fair and reduce our costs, but if anything Freddie gets more expensive, not less, the more he grows,' I say.

'I've never objected to paying my share to support my son. What I do object to is supporting you and your lover in your half-arsed attempt to play shops.'

'Come on, Duncan, we've talked about this before; you know that we only spend money on things directly connected to Freddie and his needs.'

Duncan reaches into his pocket and pulls out a small digital recorder. 'I wish I could believe you, Emily, but sadly I have other information.'

He presses play on the recorder.

'Sandie seems to think things are terminal. You've never told me that.'

It's my voice, as tinny and high-pitched as it always sounds on the camera-bag recordings. I've got used to hearing myself, but this time it chills me.

'You know how blunt she can be, Em.'

Will's voice.

'So she's exaggerating, is she?'

'Where did you get that?'

Duncan puts his fingers to his lips. 'Hang on, it's just getting to the best bit.'

'Maybe. But then again it might not. Not if Duncan is serious about cutting the maintenance for Freddie.'

'So we do need his money after all?'

'It's the only cushion we have, Em. We can't keep asking Grazia.'

I stare at Will and he shakes his head in disbelief. 'You've been bugging us? You've been bugging your own ex-wife?'

Duncan switches off the recording. 'Oh, it's a bit late for the fake outrage, isn't it, Will? It's only what your lover does every day to unsuspecting store staff. Anyway, a man's entitled to know how his money's being spent, isn't he? Especially if, contrary to what he's been told, it's not going towards his son, but towards keeping his ex and her lover afloat? Oh, and the new baby. Congratulations are in order, I gather.'

I gawp. He even knows about that.

Will coughs. 'That was a false alarm.'

My brain is scrambled. *How?* I try to remember when Will and I had that conversation, where we were. And then I realise . . .

'It's the bear, isn't it? The demonic bear.'

Duncan smiles slyly. 'Good, isn't it? I read about it in the *Daily Mail*, after a woman used an earlier prototype to find out about her husband's affairs. Ordered it online and the transmitter works a treat. Crystal clear sound, don't you think? Thank goodness Freddie loved it. Terrible waste of money otherwise.'

I gulp. 'You manipulated our son so you could record private conversations?'

Will takes my hand. 'Don't give him the satisfaction. You

know this won't be acceptable in court, don't you? Judges take a dim view of people spying on their exes.'

'Ah, well, interestingly, as the technology is becoming more accessible, even the judiciary are loosening up. But of course, I don't want to have to take this to court.'

He puts the recorder down on the coffee table. We all stare at the bloody thing as though it's a ticking bomb.

'So what *do* you want?' I ask eventually.

'Obviously the evidence that's come to light does rather favour my case for reducing the maintenance payments, so I'm expecting that you won't object to my solicitor's proposal, which is for a fifty per cent reduction from January onwards.'

'*Fifty?*'

'But in the light of the changes to my work life, I do want to take a more active role in Freddie's upbringing, which will reduce the costs to you two considerably. And allow you the time to focus on your . . . hobby.'

'Hobby? Look, I've just about had enough of you. Coming in here, swearing, snooping . . .' Will stands up now and so does Duncan. They square up to one another, Will almost a head taller than Duncan. 'I want you to leave.'

'Happy to,' says Duncan, magnanimously, 'It shouldn't take Freddie all that long to pack, should it?'

I gawp. 'Freddie?'

'I'm taking him back to Somerset for Christmas.'

'Oh no you're not.'

'Oh yes I am.' Duncan laughs. 'Funnily enough, I'm taking him to Aladdin tomorrow afternoon. You wouldn't believe the black market in panto tickets, but my dad's got a contact, so we'll be in the front row of the stalls.'

'But you were meant to be spending Christmas with Heidi.'

Now he looks shifty. 'She's . . . having to go skiing from Boxing Day, with the bosses. She didn't want to, but they more or less told her she'd be sacked if she didn't. And I know you hate her spending time with Freddie, so it's the perfect chance for the two of us to bond.'

'Just like that?'

He shrugs. 'Yeah.'

I shake my head. 'You're way out of order thinking you can just change everything on a whim, Duncan. It's all arranged. We go to Somerset *after* Boxing Day and that's when he gets to see your parents and my parents and my sister and her kids. Cut our money if you have to, but there's no way you're getting your hands on Freddie for Christmas. No way.'

'Oh, Emily. You're making it sound so much more dramatic than it has to. This isn't a tug-of-love *Kramer versus Kramer* moment. I just want to enjoy my first proper Christmas with my son. After all, you've had him on Christmas day for the last three years. It's only fair, surely.'

'Only fair? The first Christmas you were with Heidi in your love nest, and the last two you were skiing. You didn't even see him till the new year.'

'I know. I feel bad. Which is why it's so important for me to give him a lovely family Christmas this year. My parents are all set. We're even prepared to ask your folks over. After all, it's not just about what you want, is it? Grandparents are a big part of a child's life.'

Will is standing very still, but I can see his hands are formed into fists. Duncan leans over and picks up the tape recorder, pretending to study the controls.

It's stalemate. I can't let him take Freddie, can I? He belongs here, with us, and the thought of his face as he unwraps his presents has been the only thing keeping me positive for the last couple of weeks, amongst all the tension with Will.

And yet I don't doubt for a second that Duncan will haul us back to the courts unless he gets his own way. He has this vindictive, determined streak that makes him pursue things to the bitter end, regardless of the consequences, and with no job to distract him, he won't let go.

'Mummy! Finished my drawing!'

Freddie comes in, clutching a sheet of paper covered in bright squiggles. He's also managed to cover his hands and cheeks in felt tip pen.

'Lovely, darling,' I say, glancing at the picture.

'There's our house, and there's Santa,' he says, pointing to a large red blob. 'And those are the reindeers. Where are we going to put the picture? To make sure Santa won't miss it? On the front door?'

Duncan raises his eyebrows at me, waiting for my answer. I close my eyes, because I can already feel tears of frustration and disappointment welling up. I don't have a choice.

'No, Fredster, not on our front door. We've had a little bit of a change of plan for Christmas. It's so exciting, because Daddy is going to take you all the way to see Granny and Granddad Prince back in Somerset, in the Batmobile. Isn't that cool!'

Duncan nods. I want to hit him. Freddie's face is confused. 'Are you and Will coming in the van?'

'Um . . . no, not this time. We can't really leave the shop empty, can we?' Freddie looks at each of us in turn, trying to work out what to make of this bombshell. It's like when he's tripped over and totters on the edge of bursting into tears or soldiering on bravely. 'But you're always there at Christmas.'

'I know, darling. But someone has to be here to tell Father Christmas where to deliver your presents, in case he gets mixed up.'

'Granny and Granddad's tree is taller than me,' says Duncan. 'And the chimney is much wider than this one, which means there's room for Santa to drop even more presents down it.'

That tips the balance. Freddie smiles. 'Really?'

'Isn't that right, Mummy?' Duncan says.

I feel faint with fury now but I try to turn my grimace into a smile. 'I'd better go and get your suitcase packed.'

'I'll come and help,' says Freddie, 'I don't want you to forget Big Ted.'

Christmas Eve —
Shopping Days to Christmas: 0

They think it's all over. It is now. Have a sherry and a mince pie and hope Father Christmas has stuffed his sack with a little quantitative easing along for you and yours . . .

Chapter Twenty-Three

Overnight, the nausea has disappeared and I want to eat everything in sight.

'Can we stop at the next services?' I'm crammed into the back of the stupid sports car with all the suitcases, my carefully selected gifts for everyone, and a snoring Monty in his basket, while Toby drives and my mother is sitting pretty in the front. She even gave a regal wave as Toby overtook a Jag a few minutes ago.

'Again? We've only got just over an hour to go before we get there.'

'I need to stretch my legs or I'll get deep vein thrombosis. This seat isn't designed for adults, is it?'

He turns off the slip road to the next services. It's so packed, I can believe that the whole country is passing through here on the way to their own ancestral homes. A small group of carol singers are standing outside in the dark, soldiering bravely through the old favourites – from a saintly *Away in a Manger* to a surprisingly raucous *Fairytale of New York* – but most of the travellers aren't giving them a second glance. Too little time to feel festive.

I take pity on them, throw a couple of one-pound coins in the hat. We were late leaving because Toby didn't get back from Garnett's till past five, claiming some last minute crisis. But he's the boss, isn't he? He can leave whatever time he likes. I bet he was 'busy' sharing a bottle of Courvoisier and a plate of mince pies with the rest of the board. They take their traditions seriously.

While Toby and my mother go round the side of the building with the dog for a crafty fag, I thank God for M&S Simply Food, and fill my basket with Snowman Mini Cakes and Sage and Onion Stuffing flavoured crisps. It occurs to me as I stand in the queue that perhaps I should be eating protein and wholegrain and essential fatty acids, but then again, is there any point? I've made my decision.

'Got enough to keep you going there, Sandie?' asks Toby when I get into the car, the bags taking up the other seat in the back. I set about chomping my way through the snowmen and a turkey sandwich. The furious movement of my jaw helps stop me thinking. Thinking is overrated.

I spent the whole time I was in Southport thinking and it got me nowhere. The harder I tried to lose myself in my childhood memories of the pier and the slot machines, the more loudly the present day interrupted: the knowledge that while my mind was working overtime, my body was quietly growing a new person.

I know I'm standing at a fork in the road, with the two women who made me what I am pointing me in two different directions. Gramma points the way towards a purposeful and self-controlled life, but one with lashings of guilt and shame and paranoia about what the neighbours might think . . .

By the other signpost is Marnie, pointing towards a chaotic existence of fatherless children and wild parties.

I know which life would be more fun, but I also know myself too well to believe that I could ever embrace chaos and uncertainty.

I realised something else in Southport: Toby can't be part of my decision process. OK, he's the father, and to shut him out isn't the most honourable thing I've ever done, but does he have the maturity to cope with this?

'Is it too cold to put the roof down for the last twenty minutes, girls?' Toby calls from the front of the car. 'Just for the fun of it.'

I groan, but he's already pressing the button. No. He's not nearly grown up enough for life or death decisions, and definitely not for parenthood.

Neither am I. Some people just aren't cut out for kids. I can't pretend that either option makes me feel good about myself, but the least worst option is the best one for me right now.

The bitter wind makes my eyes water, and the cold makes me shiver but I don't complain. My gramma would say it's no more than I deserve. I can't help wondering if she's right.

The skies are so much darker here in the countryside, and the stars so much brighter. As Toby drives through the village of Bambourne, he toots his horn outside The Pig and Whistle, a cosy-looking limestone pub with white foam sprayed in snow-flake patterns inside the windows. I can see a woman behind the bar who waves at him.

The Lord of the Manor . . .

'Great boozer. We could sneak down there later if Mother is getting a bit intense.'

I wonder what he means by 'intense' but decide not to ask.

The house is a mile from the village, up an unlit track. Toby hasn't said much about the place, beyond warning us that we should take thermals because it can get bloody draughty. That makes sense – the icy Mrs Garnett can probably exist in sub-zero conditions. But as for the house itself, I don't know whether to expect splendour or decay.

Toby's car takes the steep hill effortlessly, but he has to slow down on the bends, and I feel colder by the second. If Mrs G. has guessed about my condition, then perhaps she's planning to push me down the sweeping staircase or serve me tea with deadly herbs from the centuries-old kitchen garden?

Maybe I should tell her that I'll be taking care of things myself straight after Christmas . . .

Finally Toby takes a sharp right between two oak trees, onto a path lined with dozens more. In the distance I can see the house, and it's smaller than I expected. Limestone, of course, with perfect square windows. Lights shine from the upstairs room and it looks almost cosy.

'Bob's in, then,' says Toby.

'Bob?'

'Handyman, gardener, you name it, he does it. When he can

be bothered. He knows Mother won't throw him out because my father used to play conkers with him when they were kids.'

'That's his cottage?'

'Yup.' He catches my eye in the mirror. 'You didn't think that was the *house*, did you?'

I don't reply, because I've just seen the real thing. It's a monster. Limestone, again, but as the gravel spits underneath the car wheels, I feel dwarfed. Three storeys, six large windows on each of the first two levels, and then three more tiny windows popping up from the roof: the servants' quarters. I wonder if that's where Mrs Garnett has put me. After all, it is what I am. A shop girl.

Bizarrely, I can't see any lights on in the house, apart from a dim one past the front door. 'Your mother wouldn't have forgotten we're coming, would she?'

Toby steps out of the car and pushes the seat forward so Monty and I can get out. 'What? Oh, no. It's just the bloody electricity bills. Do you know how much it costs to heat and light this place?'

As I climb out of the back my knees crack, and I have pins and needles in my feet. 'No idea.'

'Twenty grand. And that was last year, before the bills went up. Dad was obsessive about energy saving, but my mother has a tendency to leave doors open or forget to turn the heating off in summer. I've been trying to persuade her to fit solar panels but she doesn't think the roof would stand the weight. Honestly, she's such a worrier. The house has been here for three hundred years, and it'll be here after we've gone.'

'That is one amazing pad,' says Marnie.

It is, and it isn't. It's like a child's drawing of a house, but without the charm. Instead it looks as though the façade would topple over if you pushed it gently. I cannot imagine a less Christmassy place.

'I don't want to stay here.'

'Bit late for that, Brains. But it'll be lovely and warm in the back of the house. You'll feel much better by the time we've got some sherry inside you! Family tradition on Christmas Eve. And pretty much every other eve, where Mums is concerned.'

Marnie cackles and follows Monty and Toby into the house. I feel like a prisoner entering Holloway and even though my sentence is only three days long, I already know it will feel like a lifetime.

The house smells of damp and Youth Dew. It feels as though the air in here hasn't moved for centuries. Toby strides through quickly, but he turns once, checking my reaction, so I keep my face composed and my nose unwrinkled.

There are two hall lights, both low-energy ones, barely adequate for a space this size. There's a wide staircase straight ahead and as I look up to the top of the house, I feel dizzy. It's a very long way to fall . . . or to be pushed. Paintings hang from the walls, dark hunting scenes and a single, rather sentimental, picture of a woman and a toddler in a lush garden.

Toby veers left, towards another dim light beyond the staircase, and we step through two more huge doorways, large enough to accommodate a horse, and maybe a carriage too. We pass through the dining room, which has a grand but unlit fireplace and a long table laid for five, the cutlery and crystal glasses spaced so far apart that passing the salt would constitute aerobic exercise. You'd never know it was Christmas: not a single holly wreath or any hint of tinsel. OK, so I hadn't quite expected a reception committee of carol-singing villagers, but surely the point of a house like this is to embrace the season?

And now we're in the kitchen, a room almost as big as Toby's Chelsea flat. It feels claustrophobic and institutional, thanks to the low ceiling and the flickering fluorescent strip lights. The oven's not on, and the doors on the sixties-style beige units are wonky. A plate sits on the draining board, with a dirty knife and a dried-out piece of cheese resting on top.

'She must be upstairs, getting ready,' says Toby, after a while. 'Mums! Mother?' And he leaves the room, followed by Monty.

Marnie and I look at each other. 'Is this a real house, or the set of a horror film?' she says.

I smile. 'I was wondering that.'

Marnie opens the cupboard doors at random. The shelves are mostly empty, beyond a few odd jars of marmalade or packets of crackers. Finally she finds what she was looking for: a collection of bottles with remnants of alcohol in them.

'Now we need glasses. You're having one?'

'No, I won't.'

'Oh, come on, Sandie. Your gramma's not here now to tell you off, is she?'

'No,' I say, wondering where she is right now and whether she's OK. How can I have deserted her for *this*?

'It'll help make you less uptight.'

'Who says I'm uptight?'

She laughs as she opens more doors. One falls off in her hand, which makes her laugh even louder. 'You are the definition of uptight, honey, and today you're worse than usual. Aha!' She pulls out two plastic picnic tumblers and pours some sherry into each. 'There. With added dust.'

I take the tumbler and sniff suspiciously. The grapey smell is seductive. And after all, it won't matter now, will it? Not now I've made my mind up. I sip.

'Hey, Sandie. Aren't you going to toast to health, wealth and happiness? Oh, and your entry into the aristocracy . . .'

I clink tumblers. 'I've got a long, long way to go before that happens.'

She shakes her head. 'That boy is crazy about you.'

'What makes you think that?'

'Well, he talks about you *all the time*. When you did your little flit to wherever it was, he had a face like a puppy that had been kicked. The way he looks at you, oh, girl, I remember how it felt when a man looked at me like that . . .'

I can't help smiling. 'Men look at you all the time, Marnie.'

'Not like that. Guys know what I am. I got that look. Always have. Can't help it, and it's got me in no end of trouble over the years. But the way Toby looks at you, it's like you're a princess. And he wants to lock you up in his castle—'

'Not if the wicked queen has anything to do with it.'

'You know you're the first girl he's ever brought home for Christmas?'

I look at her. 'No. No, I didn't know that.'

'Well, then. Stop this thinking that you have to prove yourself to his stuck-up bitch of a mother. If she's got any sense, she'll know you've already won.'

'I'm not so sure . . .'

Monty comes tearing into the kitchen, paws rat-ratting on the kitchen tiles, and behind him, Toby and his mother. She's wearing a kimono dressing gown, the belt tied tightly around her tiny waist, and her fragile arms poking out of the wide sleeves so she resembles a haute couture scarecrow. An even more powerful wave of Youth Dew wafts in my direction.

Followed by an even stronger wave of booze. Yes, she's definitely been at the sherry already. Then again, so have I.

'Welcome, Sandie,' she says, reaching out with her hand. I don't know whether to shake it, or whether I should curtsey while she touches my head. But before I can receive the blessing, she spots my mother and does such a dramatic pirouette that Toby has to step forward to catch her. The unobtrusive way he does it makes me wonder how many times he's had to do this before.

'Ah. Mother of Sandie. You are very welcome in my home.'

My mother doesn't hold with shaking hands. Instead she envelops Mrs G. in a luscious bear hug.

'It's fabulous to be here,' Marnie says when she finally lets go of her hostess. 'Never spent Christmas in a stately home before, Mrs Garnett.'

'Hardly stately. Like its occupier, it looked rather better forty years ago. And call me Laetitia.'

'Never met a Laetitia before neither. I'm Marnie.' She looks down at hand, suddenly remembering that she's already helped herself to the sherry. 'We needed warming up, and this is doing a lovely job.'

'Oh. Yes. One gets used to draughts, living in a house like this. But the bedrooms are cosier. Let me show you where you're sleeping.'

I suppose I'd expected separate bedrooms. I hadn't expected separate *floors.*

'I thought you wouldn't mind being up here, while us oldies sleep on the first floor. The stairs can be treacherous, and watch the carpet, as it's a little loose in places,' says Mrs G. as we take the second flight, and then veer off up a tiny narrow staircase into the attic. 'Unless there's a reason I don't know about why you need to be nearer a bathroom?'

We reach the top and look at each other and there's something steely in that look . . .

She knows. I'm certain of it. And Marnie might think I've won, but Mrs G. is not giving up without a fight.

'None at all. I bet the view's good from up here. In the daylight.' Right now I can see nothing, just a deep rural blackness.

'Yes. Though the windows are somewhat smaller than they are downstairs.'

She isn't kidding. The room is somewhat smaller too, I suspect. This dark little hole barely has room for the single bed, and there's a brown stain on the ceiling. The fireplace is bare wood, not marble, and the grate has only a few old pieces of coal, and a pile of ashes.

Mrs G. tuts. 'Oh dear. I knew I'd forgotten something. We're all out of logs but I'm sure I could ask your mother if she wouldn't mind sacrificing her electric radiator if you think you'll feel the cold?'

'No. No, she feels the cold worse than me anyway.'

'Yes. I suppose she would. Most unusual accent she has. Is that Jamaican patois?'

I stare at her. My mother has less of an accent than I do, and it's definitely more Brummie than Caribbean. 'I'm sure if you can't understand something she's said, she'll repeat it for you.'

She turns her back on me and walks away without another word. It's a relief to be on my own. All I want to do is crawl into bed and sleep my way through this entire weekend.

I turn back the blanket and check the bedding. I wouldn't put it past her to have snuck a funnel-web spider or a jam-jar full of bedbugs under the sheets instead of a hot water bottle.

Unless my hormones are making me paranoid?

They're at the door. Zombies. Knocking it down. I can't hear what they're shouting, but it's not good. Not good at all.

'Brains . . . hey, Brains? Wake up.'

226

I hear Toby's voice, smell his aftershave and I feel safe. But then when I open my eyes and realise where I am and remember all the bad stuff, the warmth leaves me again. 'Sorry. I was having a nightmare, I think.'

'So I gathered. You were thrashing about like a crazy woman. Anyway, it's dinner time.'

'Already?'

'Yep. You've been asleep for two hours.' He looks around the room. 'Ah, it's great to be up here again. I used to come up here all the time when I was a little boy. We still had live-in help then, well, a housekeeper, but she was in the other room. I used to tap on the wall and make ghost noises.'

'Charming.'

'Oh, she knew it was me. Funny, though. People would have died up here, wouldn't they? Servants? And I bet there were more than a few babies conceived, too. The master of the house popping up to take advantage of his *droit de seigneur*. Actually . . .'

He begins to kiss me and it's so tempting to let myself go with it, because in that kiss is everything that brings us together, and none of the tension that has kept us apart this last month.

But I can't let go. He might notice. 'Toby. Not here.'

'Oh, I think it's rather exciting. Won't you play along?'

I sit up. 'Right now I just want to get this dinner out of the way. That's enough play-acting for one evening.'

Grazia helped me choose the outfit for tonight. It's a tailored woollen dress – 'fantastic insulation against country house draughts, Sandie, and completely lined so nothing can show. Even though nothing is showing yet, of course' – in a deep copper-red. I've also put on my red garnet necklace, the first gift Toby ever gave me, long before we became an item.

I don't trust myself on the steep staircase, so I wear my slippers down to the first floor, clinging to the bare wall, before changing into the court shoes I bought to go with the dress. I'm even risking perfume. Nothing too heady – a quick spritz of Jo Malone's Grapefruit cologne – but enough to make me feel armed with my own personal fragrance force field.

Someone – Toby, perhaps, or the old family retainer – has lit the fire in the dining room, and so the space feels less like a mausoleum, though there's the thick, petrol smell of firelighters spreading through the air. There are candelabras, too, on the table, though no one's cleared out the wax for years, so the candles list dangerously. They make me think of Mrs G.

'. . . well, if you're too drunk to drive, can you at least sort out a taxi from the station?' Our hostess is in the kitchen, but her shrill voice carries like a fishwife's. Marnie's already downstairs, dressed in her version of country house chic, which involves lots of regal purple and fake fur. Tiger fur, rather than fox, but at least she's trying.

'Letty seems to be in a pickle. Apparently the hired help isn't in a fit state to pick up the last guest.'

I look at the place settings and realise she's right. The four of us, plus one. 'It's guess who's coming to dinner all over again.'

'Do you think we're the first *colonials* ever to be entertained at this dinner table?' she asks.

I decide not to mention the patois comment. Not that I want to protect Toby's mother, but tonight is going to be tough enough without parading the woman's bigotry.

My survival plan for the weekend is simple. Say nothing. Eat everything. The only thing I've been looking forward to about this trip is the food. I've imagined fresh nuts and mince pies on the hour, plus soups and devils on horseback and smoked salmon and a fat, golden turkey with all the trimmings and rib-sticking Christmas pudding with pounds and pounds of freshly made brandy butter . . .

OK, so the kitchen *did* look rather bare earlier, but I guess she must have a local lady coming in with supplies.

'Sandie Barrow, you look good enough to eat.' Toby is behind me, kissing my neck. 'All luscious and curvy. Have you put on a bit of weight?'

I wriggle away. 'No. What a thing to say to a woman on Christmas Eve.'

'I mean it as a compliment. The more of you there is the better.' He notices I'm still scowling. 'Within reason, of course. I don't want a fat girlfriend, but you're just—'

'Word of advice. Quit while you're ahead, boy,' says Marnie. 'Whatever men think, no woman wants to be told she's curvy.'

Mrs G. appears. She's changed out of her kimono and into a full-length emerald velvet evening dress, accessorised by a pearl choker, matching earrings, and a very manky looking cat draped over her shoulder.

'Hello, Sourpuss,' says Toby, stepping forward to take the tabby. 'Hanging on in there, eh, mate? Hope you're still nimble enough to get away from Monty or it could be a messy Christmas.'

Mrs G. snatches the cat back. 'Don't say that. Poor Sourpuss.'

She steps towards the table and for a moment I think she's going to put the cat down at its own place setting. But instead she crouches down and places Sourpuss in a corner. His paws give way like a folding chair, and he immediately falls asleep.

'Now,' she turns to us, 'I hope you're all hungry.'

That's the first sensible thing I have heard this woman say. I am utterly ravenous.

'Things should be ready in a couple of minutes,' she says. 'So. How about an aperitif? Gannet, would you do the honours?'

Toby doesn't hesitate, heading straight towards a drinks cabinet in the corner of the room. He pours her a drink before anyone else, a large brandy, which she almost snatches from his hand. I have a picture, then, of the way their Christmases must have been, since his father died. Maybe, too, of how the Christmases were when he was still alive: I suspect Laetitia Garnett has always got her own way.

'What can I get for my two other favourite girls?'

I'm aware of his mother watching, waiting for my answer. 'I'll have brandy too. A large one.'

She gives me a dirty look, then walks away, back into the kitchen. *Well, what do you expect me to do? Tell everyone my happy news, right here, right now?*

If she knows. I have to keep reminding myself that she might not . . .

Mrs G. returns with two large bowls, and two family sized packs of Walkers crisps. Not quite what I was hoping for, but it still counts as food, and it's all I can do not to snatch the bag before she tips the contents into the bowl. Better still, I can smell hot food coming from the kitchen. She disappears again, returning with a plate full of canapés. That's more like it.

I reach out for one and bite into it before I have a chance to work out quite what it is. Hmm. Salty. Cheesy. *Fishy?*

I examine the half-canapé left in my hand. 'Interesting. What is it?'

'Oh, just something I improvised . . .' she says vaguely, and tops up her own glass before sashaying back to the kitchen.

My mother takes the half off me and eats it. She pulls a face. 'At a guess, Ritz Crackers – stale ones – topped with Gentleman's Relish,' she whispers.

I peer at the plate. Ugh. I'm just reaching for crisps to take the taste away when the doorbell rings, a deep, dark bell that echoes in the kitchen. With no butler here, Toby goes to answer.

'The mystery guest,' says Marnie. 'Perhaps he's lined me up with some local hunk as my Christmas present. A blacksmith, maybe, or a farmer. Or . . . Oh.'

And I look around to see Gramma stepping into the room.

I feel my jaw dropping, and I close it again. But Gramma looks utterly composed, in her black raincoat with transparent plastic Rain-Mate hat.

'Marina. Sandra. You look surprised to see me.'

I step forward to kiss her and she accepts the kiss stiffly. 'You said you'd made . . . arrangements. But it's so good to see you. Merry Christmas, Gramma. It wouldn't be the same without you.' And I mean it.

She sniffs. 'If the mountain wouldn't come to Mohammed, then I decided to come to you . . . and thank goodness Toby has a stronger sense of family than my daughter and granddaughter.'

'Oh, I invited you because I knew Sandie wanted to see you,' he says, all effortless charm. 'Shall I get you something to drink?' He scoots towards the drinks cabinet. I think about what Marnie said. He *does* love me. He wouldn't have done this otherwise.

Gramma scowls. 'Some juice, if you have it, please.' She turns to me. 'And you'd be advised to stick to the water, young woman.'

I stare at her. 'Why?'

'Isn't it obvious? You've put on weight.' And she snatches the bowl of crisps away from me. 'Too many of these and not enough exercise. You don't want to end up like your mother, do you?'

I'm wondering whether now is the time to argue back, to say that nobody's perfect, that we all make mistakes. But before I have chance, Mrs G. appears wearing emerald green oven gloves – surely she can't have a pair to match every outfit? – and holding a large, deep baking tray.

'Ah, Mrs Barrow, I presume. Lovely to see you. And you've arrived just in time for supper.'

Our eyes follow the tray as she puts it down on the table.

Gramma speaks first. 'How . . . original. This is the first time I have had pizza for my Christmas Eve supper.'

The pizza is slightly undercooked, and the garlic bread she's done with it is on the charred side. Not that it stops me eating more than my share. Both Gramma and Mrs G. keep shooting me odd looks, but I'm past caring. I don't touch the brandy, though. It feels wrong.

Everything feels wrong about this Christmas.

After the pizza, Mrs G. serves nasty yellow soft-scoop ice-cream with strawberry sauce from a squeezy tube. Gramma's lips are already pursed with outrage when she offers to take the plates through – as Mrs G.'s eyes are drooping by this stage – and she beckons to me to follow her into the kitchen. I can't really refuse, but I feel sick, and not because of the ice cream. I am about to get the telling-off *of my life*. Though, in fact, a telling-off is probably the least worst thing that could happen. Better than her having guessed the truth . . .

She puts the plates on the marbled plastic worktop and looks around her.

'Oh, Lord,' she says. 'Where to start?' She begins opening cupboards, just as Marnie did.

'There's nothing in there, we've already looked.'

'But there must be food for lunch tomorrow?' She spots the glazed door in the corner and strides towards it. 'Aha. I knew it.'

I follow her inside and shiver. It's a utility room, entirely unheated, which is just as well, as a turkey is sitting on top of the washing machine. A dead turkey, as big as a pig. As well as the bird, there's a large crate of vegetables – sprouts, parsnips, carrots, earth-covered potatoes – and alongside it, ingredients in various bowls: dried fruit, suet, flour, candied peel, and a large bottle of brandy.

'So our hostess didn't get round to making her Christmas pudding.' Gramma sighs. Despite her diabetes, she refuses to deny her sweet tooth. 'Well, at least there's a dishwasher. I suggest you load that first, and then I'll make up the mix so at least it has the chance to steep overnight. Better than nothing.'

'Soak? In the brandy? But what about the Pledge?'

She gives me a withering look. 'The alcohol evaporates during the cooking process. Now. Hurry up, those dishes won't stack themselves, will they?'

It doesn't end with the dishwasher. Gramma finds a hundred other jobs, and I realise midway through peeling the parsnips that *this* is her punishment, and it's at least as effective as a telling-off, because I am dead on my feet.

Most infuriating of all, when we finally emerge from the kitchen, Toby, Marnie and Mrs G. don't seem to have noticed our absence. Sourpuss hasn't moved from his corner, and Monty is lying next to the fire, even though it's little more than embers now. But they haven't noticed that either, because alcohol is keeping them warm.

'Right, just in time for Midnight Mass,' says Gramma.

Toby grins. 'Very good, Mrs Barrow! But we have plenty of communion wine here.'

'I noticed a church by the station and I estimate it should only take us twenty minutes to walk there, a little longer on the way back because it's uphill. But of course by then we will have had our spirits raised.'

Toby gawps at her. 'But that's a Catholic church.'

'Yes. Well, I'm a Methodist myself, but it's the same God, and I have to confess I believe the Papists do the Christmas thing better than anyone else.'

Marnie and Toby exchange glances, but my grandmother is already harassing Mrs G. out of her chair and frankly the woman looks in no state to resist.

We wrap up against the cold, but oddly, when we get outside, it feels warmer than it did in the house, and by the time we get to the bottom of the hill, I have to take off my hat and tuck it in my bag. Marnie and Toby are singing *No Woman, No Cry,* while Gramma hums carols to herself, her arm firmly linked with Mrs G.'s.

We turn the last corner and the village appears, illuminated like the German Christmas ornaments we used to sell at Garnett's.

'Right. Much as I'd love to come to church, it'd be hypocritical as I don't believe in God,' says Toby, as we pass by the pub. 'However, I do believe in the Christmas spirit so how about we all go and worship at the font of beer?'

'I'm up for that,' says Marnie.

'Well, that doesn't surprise me. You were born with the devil inside you,' says Gramma. 'Sandra?'

I weigh up the benefits in my head. 'I'll come with you.'

Toby looks disappointed but reaches forward to kiss me. 'Happy Christmas for later, then. You're coming with us, aren't you, Mums?'

Mrs G. looks down at Gramma's arm in hers, confused. But she doesn't try to pull away. 'Actually, Gannet. I think I will join Mrs Barrow in church. Spiritual nourishment has been in short supply, lately.'

She barely slurs at all, even though she is trolleyed. I almost admire her for it.

The church is further away than I expected, and it's not a pretty limestone building like the rest of the village, but a modern brick one. Inside, though, it smells of incense and musty prayer books, and there are hundreds of nightlights on metal stands around the sides of the room. The church isn't busy – perhaps a dozen people – and they nod respectfully towards Mrs Garnett when we take our pews, near the back.

I don't *think* I believe, but there is something moving about this service. When I first went, as a little girl, the thrill of staying up past midnight was the big draw, and then gradually the magic of the ritual worked on me, until it seemed like the only way to begin Christmas.

But I can't have been thinking straight when I agreed to come with Gramma tonight, because this is not what I need to be doing now, not when I've already made my decision. I don't want to hear about the true meaning of Christmas. I try to block out the priest's softly spoken words, and think instead of Christmas at Garnett's: the decorations and the music and the smells and . . .

Then I hear sobbing and I look to my left, and it's Mrs Garnett, weeping openly. But before I can work out what to do, my gramma reaches into her handbag, retrieves her always-there packet of Kleenex, and then puts a stiff arm around the woman, who leans into her like a small child.

The pub is in darkness when we walk past it so Marnie and Toby must be back home already. None of us has said anything since the service finished. It's bitterly cold now, thanks to the clear, star-filled sky, but the walk uphill warms us up. Gramma says she'll put Mrs G. to bed, so I climb up to my attic room, only remembering how dangerous my heels could be on the loose carpet once I've actually got to the top.

I change into pyjamas, but the room's too cold and creepy for me even to attempt to sleep up here. I wait until Gramma has closed her door, and then climb back down the stairs, towards Toby's room. I don't care if this isn't the 'done thing' – I need the warmth of another human being. And at least if Toby's drunk, he won't notice the changes that have started in my body . . .

I hold my breath as I turn the door handle, which squeaks momentarily, and then I step inside. I can't see properly, but I can hear a slightly wheezy, drunken breathing from the four-poster. I approach on tiptoe, my hands extended until I touch the soft quilt. I sit on the bed, then crawl under the covers . . .

'I'm looking for the Lord of the Manor,' I whisper. No reply. 'It's your loyal servant girl here, reporting for duty.'

If that doesn't wake him up, surely nothing will. Finally I sense the warmth of another being and reach out . . .

To feel fur. And hard foot-pads. And a slightly rough, whiskery belly.

'Monty!'

I grope for a bedside light and blink as I switch it on.

Just me and the dog. Toby must still be in the pub, with my mother.

Merry Christmas, Monty . . .

And then, I can't help myself, and I can't explain why, but I wish the baby a Merry Christmas too, and then hate myself for making things worse.

Chapter Twenty-Four

CHRISTMAS DAY

❧

06:00 Emily

My first chance of a lie-in in weeks – the best present I could ever have – yet here I am, before dawn, wide awake. I'd hoped the bucketloads of booze Will and I drank last night might have knocked me out for the day, but instead I have a mind-melting hangover as well as a lifetime's worth of guilt over my first Christmas away from Freddie.

Will he be awake yet? I bet he is, he was so excited about it all this time around. Even last year he wasn't quite aware of what December the twenty-fifth meant, but now . . .

Has he tried to wake Duncan? God knows, waking my ex-husband can be a bloody difficult job at eleven o'clock, never mind now. I bet Duncan's snapped instead of inviting Freddie to snuggle up with him.

I'll kill him.

I sit up suddenly, then lie back because my head hurts. I know there's no point torturing myself like this, but then there's also precious little point in Christmas without my baby boy. I said as much to Will last night, in the brief pause between the first and second bottles of wine.

'I know it's rough on you, Em, but if you let him ruin our only bit of time off, then he's won.'

'He's won already.'

'I'm going to miss having the Fredster around too, you know.'

'But I'm his mother.'

Will sighed very deeply at this point. 'Please don't take this the wrong way, but is there any point in me being here?'

I should have taken the hint then but I had drunk most of that first bottle on my own and was way beyond self-awareness. 'Meaning what?'

'Meaning that sometimes it feels like there's only room for one male in your life. Meaning I wish you'd see that it is still possible for us to have a *nice time together*. OK, not the time we'd planned on having, but it's one single Christmas.'

'You don't get it, do you? He's my son.'

He nodded. 'And now it comes out, eh? You're right, Emily. How could I possibly know what it is to have a child? But let's not stop there. I can't know the meaning of love either, can I, if I haven't had a kid of my own? Or . . .' And then he got up from the sofa. 'What's the point?'

'Where are you going?'

'Dunno.'

At that moment, I didn't particularly care whether he was coming back, though I suspected he was off to the shed to play *Space Invaders* and seek solace in the small stash of Stella Artois he keeps hidden behind the toolbox. I was happy enough – well, not happy, obviously – to sit there with my wine, my self-pity, and Wallace and Gromit for company.

When he returned after half an hour, his skin outdoor-cold and his breath smelling of beer, we hugged briefly, as an apology, but we didn't talk about it. And even though we were both dizzy-pissed by the time we fell into bed, we didn't make love. The previous two Christmas Eves, we'd been all over each other, stifling giggles so we didn't wake the overexcited Freddie in the next room. How did it come to this?

Will is snoring. He won't be up for *hours*. I clutch my head with one hand, to stop the cells jarring any more than necessary against the inside of my skull, and use the other hand to pull myself up.

First light is appearing in Freddie's bedroom: I didn't close his curtains last night. Books about pirates and steam trains are scattered across his bed, from the panic-pack I did last night. Did I put enough pants in? He might wet the bed, as he doesn't know how to get to an unfamiliar loo in time.

I begin to tidy up, just for something to do, and then I see it.

The fucking spy teddy.

Freddie'd wanted Duncan to take it with them yesterday, but the boot in Duncan's ridiculous car was too full of the presents I'd wrapped so carefully.

'Right. That is *it*!'

I grab the monstrous toy and wrestle it out of the door, down the stairs, through the shop and into the back yard. It's almost as tall as I am and its stiff fur is spiky against the bare skin of my arms. I prop it up against the fence, and take aim at it, with a vicious kick to its satanic face. Its yellow eyes stare back, completely unscathed.

Something in me explodes, like a fire cracker. I punch the bear's nose, and then before I know quite what I'm doing I am pummelling and jabbing and tearing and wrenching and the intense pain in my head and limbs just spurs me on, because right now it feels like it's all the fault of the fucking teddy.

I only stop when I am so short of breath that I have to lean on the wall to avoid crumpling.

'Ugh.'

I look down. The bear is not recognisable as a bear any more. Bits of fake pelt lie in a shredded pile, topped by a single eye, which is connected to a wire itself connected to a circuit board. I can't see the transmitter, but it might be in that clump of twisted metal by the watering can. One bear leg is in the herb trough, the other by the bin.

The curtain just twitched at the window of one of the flats overlooking our yard. Who cares? Is the sight of a woman in a too short T-shirt, old pants and slippers kicking the shit out of a man-sized soft toy really that much of a big deal?

That'll be all round the village before a single Brussels sprout has been consumed.

I sigh. I don't care about the neighbours, but I hate to think what poor Freddie will say when he realises Big Ted has disappeared to the bear graveyard in the sky. And I *really* hate the fact that having destroyed the thing, I now have to pick up the bloody pieces.

Then again, isn't that what mothers always do?

07:00 *Kelly*

My dad snores but the Tube doesn't rumble. I already know this is going to the worst fucking Christmas I've ever had.

And it's not like I haven't had truly crap Christmases before. Even before Mum buggered off, it was usually a day of constant rows. Then once she'd decided that a lifetime of barbies on Bondi Beach was more tempting than argy-bargy in the Bush, Dad decided not to celebrate December the twenty-fifth because it's the same as every other day (except for the fact that the bookies are closed, which is not something to celebrate as far as he's concerned).

Downstairs Luis and his clan are already moving about and I can smell cake. He brought me one yesterday, 'pan dulce baked by my mother'. It smelled of cinnamon, and I had to put it out of sight in a cupboard, because I couldn't bear the thought of them all down there, laughing and mixing and cooking.

I'm not a good person, am I? Bad blood, that's what my mother's mother would have said. She hated my father. She had a point. But this time it's not Dad who is betraying someone's trust. It's me.

I did it. I had to. Reset the codes by phone, handed over my keys. Breaking and entering on a plate for Charlie's 'contractors'.

Not that it makes much sense to me that they need my codes – they're professionals, aren't they? But Charlie says it's because the place is like Fort Knox and it's easier this way, saves anyone getting hurt. 'They'll be there between three and four in the morning, because that's when the security guard nods off, according to this guy I had watching the place. Great timing for the lads, too. Twenty-four hours with the family over Christmas is just the thing to put my boys in the mood for a Boxing Day project.' He came round last night and drank tea in our flat while

239

his henchman got the keys copied, but wouldn't go into detail about what he's planning. 'Less you know the better, eh, sweetheart.' When the henchman returned, Charlie left a bottle of Scotch for Dad and a bottle of Victoria Beckham's perfume for me. 'Personal touch makes all the difference, eh, Kelly?'

I'm not kidding myself. The personal touch wasn't about politeness. It was a warning: I'd done my bit, now it's Charlie's turn to have his fun and I have to keep my nose out.

Dad's snores sound the same as they do every other day. But it's not just another day is it? Tonight I stop pretending I can change my life for the better.

08:20 Sandie

There are worse ways to be woken up, than by an enthusiastic kiss.

But Sleeping Beauty didn't have to contend with dog-breath.

'Monty, get off!'

I push away his paws without opening my eyes, and snuggle into Toby's warm body behind me. He has both arms around my waist, and I feel warm and cosy and . . .

And then, wide awake. I shouldn't be in his bed. And I definitely don't want to make love in daylight, when he's even half sober. What if he notices that I haven't put on weight all over, but in very particular places? My belly. My breasts.

'Oh, Sandie . . .'

'Merry Christmas, sunshine. Late one last night, was it?'

He pulls me tighter. 'Lovely surprise to find you here as my own personal bed-warmer. Couldn't wake you though.'

'Why, did I look too gorgeous to disturb?'

'Nah. I tried but you were out for the count. I really couldn't wake you.' He snuggles up more. 'You're awake now though. And so am I. And it appears that something else is waking up nicely too.'

I pull away. 'Yes. Monty.'

'Not what I meant, and you know it. And I *am* the Master of the House.'

'Hmm. But I'm more scared of the Lady of the House and I think she'll make me go without breakfast if she suspects anything. So I'm off back to my own quarters. And the Master of the House is just going to have to . . . hit the snooze button.'

I drag myself away reluctantly, and as I lift the covers the cold hits me, then the hunger. I am ravenous again.

I allow myself one yearning look back at Toby, and at Monty, who is lying in the dip left by my absence. Marnie's words about how Toby adores me come back to me, and I remember how much I adore him too. I want to lock the door from the inside, climb back in, stay here all day, ignore the calls and complaints from Mrs G. and Marnie and Gramma. Maybe even tell him the truth. See whether it really is such a disaster to be making a baby with a man who loves you . . .

Stop, Sandie. Don't get carried away. Look at the trouble I'm in. I know nothing about happy families, and, evidently, neither does Toby. The two of us wouldn't have a hope of bringing up a child properly, and it would be the baby that suffers the most. I am making the least worst choice for all three of us. That's all anyone can ever do.

09.00 *Grazia*

Forty-five years old, and I have never before had to put on a show to meet the boyfriend's parents.

Even though I have been planning my outfit since I accepted the invitation, I am still not certain I have chosen the right version of 'me' to put on show. It was clear immediately that my signature style would be too provocative, but to abandon red and black has ruled out nine-tenths of my wardrobe.

Equally I will not dress apologetically. I keep telling myself that this relationship is nothing to be ashamed of. The age difference (especially if they believe me to be thirty-seven) is not *so* dramatic and in any case is an accident of chronology, nothing more.

So my watchwords are: classic. Sophisticated. Effortless.

The latter, as every woman knows, takes *so much* effort that it almost makes one's eyes bleed, but now, as I drive with the roof down towards Nigel's parents, I hope it has been worth it. I can almost imagine that London's streets have been emptied just for me, and the lack of traffic means I seem to float through the city. I wear fawn cigarette pants, a silk top and a light jacket that billows in the cold breeze. And a headscarf to keep my hair under control. Nine-tenths Grace Kelly, with a hint of Sophia Loren. When another car comes into view near Hammersmith Bridge, I feel affronted that he is in my way, until he toots and waves and blows a kiss.

But as the city's flashier architecture melts away and is replaced by the upright ordinariness of her suburbs, I am losing my conviction. The sun has gone in and without its warmth my face is a curious mix of rough and smooth in the mirror: smooth where the Botox was injected, and rough where the pores show on my cheeks and chin.

The idea of turning back and spending my day walking around London's prettier squares and parks, as though they really do belong to me, is so tempting.

However, I am a woman of my word. And, if I truly want to turn my back on loneliness, then there is nothing else for it.

11:00 Emily

I have been staring at my mobile now for three-and-a-half hours. I even called it from the landline, to make sure there was no network problem.

Finally, I dial the number myself.

'Ugh?'

'Merry Christmas, Duncan! How are you and my lovely Freddie this festive morning?' OK, maybe now I sound like I've overdosed on happy pills, but I'm overcompensating.

'Not great, to be honest, Emily.'

I sit down on the sofa. 'What? Is Freddie all right? Is he hurt?'

'Oh, I love that. Thanks for the faith in my abilities. He's fine. Just grumpy.'

'Grumpy? How?'

'Oh, I dunno. Just the way kids are.'

But Freddie isn't 'just the way kids are'. He's one of the most even-tempered children at playgroup, probably because he's had to be, with me dragging him around shops for most of his life. 'Has he got a temperature?'

Duncan groans. 'Freddie. Come here, mate.' I hear rustling as the phone goes down, then fragments of unintelligible conversation. Duncan picks the phone up again. 'He's a bit warm, I suppose, but that'll be the excitement. Plus my mother has switched the temperature up to sauna levels because she doesn't want him to catch cold.'

'Have you got a thermometer in the house?'

'How the hell should I know? Look, if you were here, you'd see, he looks fine. Just grumpy.'

'If we'd stuck to the original plans, Duncan, he'd definitely be fine.'

'Don't start that. He has a right to be with his father.'

'Whose rights are we talking about, Duncan? Freddie's or yours?'

'Fuck's sake,' he hisses down the phone, 'not on Christmas Day. Remember, it was you who tried to cheat me into paying more than my share. I'm going to put the phone down now—'

'No, no, please. You're right. It's not the time. I'm sorry. Now, can I speak to him?'

'So long as you don't upset him. Freddie! Mummy's on the phone.'

More rustling, then heavy, rapid breathing down the phone. 'MUMMY?'

'Oh, my Fredster, happy Christmas, my darling. What did Santa bring for you?'

'Presents, Mummy.' His voice is loud but very uncertain. He hasn't quite got the hang of phones yet.

I laugh. 'Of course, presents. But what sort?'

'Don't know. Haven't opened them yet.'

'But it's eleven o'clock.'

'Daddy says wait till after dinner.'

'Oh. Well, maybe he'd let you open just one.' *Bastard Duncan.* My voice is cracking, and I hope Freddie can't tell.

There's a pause. 'Want to come home, Mummy. I'm tired. It's hot here in Sunnyset actually. Very hot.'

'Oh, sweetheart. You'll be home so soon, I promise. And if you're tired, ask Daddy if you can go and have a lie down before lunch. There'll be roast potatoes for lunch. You love roast potatoes, don't you?'

But now all I can hear is snuffling, and then Duncan grabs the phone. 'Well done, Emily. I hope you're happy.'

'It's not . . . I didn't . . . Put him back on, please, I'll calm him down. And Will wants to talk to him before he goes, too.'

'No way. I need to go now.'

'At least let him open one of his presents, that'll distract him.'

'When I need advice from you, Emily, I'll let you know.' And he rings off.

I throw the phone onto the sofa, and then batter my fists against the cushion out of frustration. Christmas wasn't meant to be like this.

'I've fucked everything up.'

'No you haven't.' Will appears from the bathroom, freshly showered and slightly less the worse for wear than I am.

I tell him what's happened. 'It's my fault.'

'Only if you're still blaming yourself for choosing to marry the wrong guy, way back when. This is Duncan's issue, not yours, Em. He's a scumbag to put himself first like this. But Freddie will be back with us soon, and he'll forget all about it. That's the beauty of kids, isn't it?'

'Duncan's going to use the Teddygate Tapes against us for ever.'

Will frowns. He knows enough about my ex to know there's no arguing with that. 'Let's focus on today, eh? Now, how about a Baileys?'

'It's too early.'

'There's no such thing as too early on Christmas Day. Baileys coming right up, together with some of those nice chocolate truffles you snaffled away in the shed.'

'You knew?'

He smiles. 'For a secret shopper, Em, you're really rubbish at keeping secrets.'

Chapter Twenty-Five

CHRISTMAS DAY

12:30 Kelly

'**H**appy birthday, baby Jesus!'

Dad raises his glass and the landlord laughs obligingly. Today only the hardcore are drinking in the Anchor. There's no gastropub Christmas lunch on offer to tempt in the middle-classes, just the stench of stale beer and the company of the desperate and the drunk and the desperately drunk.

Still, it's better than being at home. Downstairs, Luis and his family had started singing just before we left, and the cooking smells were too much to bear.

'Just like old times, eh, Kell?'

'You say that like it's a good thing, Dad.'

He picks up his glass of Scotch and swigs. 'You are sharp, aren't you? No surprise my girl hasn't found a man to take her off me hands yet, eh, Brian?'

Brian the landlord smiles vaguely. He doesn't get involved. Punch-ups are a nightly event in this particular pub.

'Mind you, there was a time when you were *very* popular with the boys, eh, Kell? Remember that.'

I stare at him. He wouldn't, would he? Not here.

He's not waiting for my reply, and takes his drink to a corner of the pub where a few of the cronies are already three sheets to the wind. Ken, Paolo and Woody are Dad's substitute family,

246

every bit as dysfunctional as he is. Ken's brain has been comprehensively addled by skunk. Paolo never had much of a brain to begin with, though he's sweet-natured enough. Woody's the worst of the lot: an evil fucker who makes his living fencing and dealing drugs of such low quality that they've been knocked back by the rest of the Shepherd's Bush's small-time dealers.

Dad likes them because when he's with them, he can pretend he's normal.

Now's the time to turn round, go home. But back at the flat, there's nothing to distract me from my badness.

I join them – Paolo budges up to make room for me – and I put my own vodka and orange down on the sticky table. 'Cheers, boys!'

Paolo and Ken grunt, but Woody fancies himself as a ladies' man. Which is absolutely not true unless you count ladies of the night. 'All right, Kell? Now, where did I put my mistletoe?' He leers at me over his pint, his gingery moustache flecked with foam.

'Forget the mistletoe, Woody. You'd need Rohypnol to get a kiss out of me.'

'Not a problem,' he says. 'I deliver whatever you want, three-six-five, twenty-four seven.'

'What's rohypnnotic?' asks Paolo.

'It makes women unconscious. It's the only way blokes like Woody have a hope of scoring with girls like me,' I say.

'Things have changed, eh, Kell?' says my father, smirking like a schoolboy.

'Fuck off, Dad.'

'No. I won't fuck off. You don't insult Woody and expect me not to say nothing. You're not exactly whiter than white yourself.'

Paolo looks bemused, Ken has the grace to look embarrassed, and Woody is watching me. Waiting.

'Meaning what, Dad? You've got something on your mind. Spit it out.'

'Ah, no, I'm only messing.'

'Well, don't. Not about something like that.'

We eyeball each other for a few seconds. He's the first to look away.

'So. Who's your money on for tomorrow then, Terry?' Ken asks eventually.

'Spreading my risk, Ken. One for City, one for United. Might add to the stake on United later, though.'

'How much have you put on?' asks Paolo.

Dad looks at me. 'Couple of hundred.'

'And the rest,' says Woody. Dad looks sheepish.

I groan. 'Dad. You promised.'

'When did I promise?'

'Er, when I sorted things out with Charlie for you, remember?'

'Charlie Flack?' Ken whistles. 'What are you doing messing with him?'

'You didn't sort out nothing,' he says. 'Take no notice, lads. I can handle him. Just doing him a favour, that's all.'

'You don't get it, do you, Dad? What I've had to do to try to save you from yourself.'

He stares at me. 'Who told you I wanted saving?'

I stand up now. I want to throw my drink at him, but it seems a waste of booze. Instead I swallow it in one swig. 'Sorry. My mistake. If you want to spend the rest of your life sitting in the Anchor, surrounding yourself with even bigger losers so you don't feel quite as shit as you really are, then be my guest.'

For a moment, I feel OK. Better than OK. Good. High on rage. Better than any drug Woody could get for me.

Dad's just given me my Get Out of Jail Free card, hasn't he? *Who told you I wanted saving?* What I should do now is call the cops to stop Charlie's boys and everything will be fine. All right, Dad might get a bit roughed up, but it won't be the first time. He'll survive. He always does.

Woody points his fat, grubby finger at me. 'Losers, are we? Better than being a filthy little slut who cries wolf, though, eh, darling?'

Ken puts a hand on Woody's arm. 'Not here, eh, Woods.'

'No. Someone needs to bring Miss High and Mighty down a peg. Because she seems to have forgotten a few things. Well, we have longer memories than you, darling. We *know* what you are.'

My legs are shaking. 'I never cried wolf.'

Woody smirks again: he senses weakness. 'No? Only that's not what I heard. And what half the Bush heard.'

I cover my ears with my hands but he's next to me, now, peeling back my fingers while he shouts at me. 'You're a whore, Kelly.'

And then his hands go limp and I see my father behind him, and my father's nicotine-stained fingers around Woody's neck, the thumbnail gouging into the space below his Adam's apple.

Woody wriggles free to face Dad, a look of outrage on his mottled face. 'What the fuck are you doing, Terry?' he says, his voice hoarse now. 'You were only talking about it yourself just now.'

Dad looks down at his hands. There's blood on Woody's neck, where Dad's nails broke the skin. It's only now that I realise I'm crying.

Just as Ken is standing up, ready to calm everyone down, Dad looks at Woody again. Then punches him, hard, in the face. I hear his nose crack, and my father pulls back his fist, rubbing his knuckles.

The landlord is already heading our way. It might be the first, but it won't be the only punch-up before closing time, that's for sure. I wonder why he opens on Christmas Day. Maybe he's got a family of his own he needs to escape.

'Let's go, Kell.' Dad picks up his coat and pushes me gently towards the exit. 'See you, boys.'

Blood is streaming down Woody's lips and chin, and he's touching his nose tentatively. 'You are mental, Wright. Totally mental.'

Out in the street, I see that the colour has drained from Dad's face.

'You didn't have to do that, Dad.'

He shrugs. 'Yeah, I did. Just like I had to last time. Friends are friends. But family's different. I just wish I'd finished my drink first.'

13:30 *Grazia*

How strange these suburbs are! I have only ever experienced villages and cities, and this in-between world has never appealed.

However, as a field trip into another world, this lunch is exceptional. An anthropologist would cherish every moment, and so would I if it were not for the fact that these suburbanites are scrutinising me as carefully as I am observing them.

And there is only one Grazia, but there are nine pairs of eyes following me. Nigel, Nigel's mother, Nigel's father, Nigel's sister, Nigel's sister's husband, an uncle, an aunt, and two elderly neighbours, the Oswalds. I am struggling with the names. Apart from Nigel and his sister Eleanor, they are all monosyllables. There is Mick and Jill, his parents, but the rest . . . pah! Bill, Bob, Lynn, Liz, Jim, John? I do not know.

Not that they are finding mine any easier, although they are trying their very best. They stumble over the different parts: Graaaazeea, Gracie-ay, Gra-tzeee. Only Eleanor has grasped it so far, 'because I buy the magazine as a treat on the way home on a Tuesday'.

But despite the name challenge, the welcome is surprisingly warm. OK, Nigel's mum cannot stop looking at me, but she does so with curiosity rather than malice. And I can see why she's staring. My Grace Kelly look seemed low-key in London, but here it is utterly decadent, if fawn can ever be described as decadent. Oh, the family and friends of Nigel wear colours, make no mistake, but they're happily uncoordinated, like the camp chorus line of a British pantomime.

Mick and Jill look like what they are: suburban parents. Mick is broad and tall, like his son, but wears loose trousers, to allow room for the Christmas lunch his wife is preparing loudly in the kitchen. Jill was clearly a pretty girl, but middle-age is just beginning to turn her stout, and her delicate features are lost in a round face, like currants in fruit bread as the dough rises.

But they're not unattractive. Not at all. There is something . . . well, bewitchingly real about them.

'Another Tia Maria?' Mick has the bottle ready to top me up.

'No, thanks. I will be driving home.'

'Ah, Nigel should have said. We'd have had you to stay over. Experience the entire British Christmas experience. It's not just the lunch, you know. There's the evening buffet, the midnight snack. Oh, and Jill always invites the whole close to the Boxing Day Brunch. It's an event.'

'I can imagine.'

I can, indeed, imagine. Strange. If Nigel had told me this before, I would have been quick to dismiss such a humdrum event as evidence of the desperate state of suburbia. I would have scoffed at the idea that a sideboard groaning with cold turkey and defrosted supermarket desserts is the highlight of the social calendar.

And yet, for a moment, I wish I had been invited to stay overnight.

'You enjoying yourself?' Nigel is next to me, but he's careful not to touch me. There are rules here. Rules you can see as restrictive or courteous, depending on your viewpoint. He wears a stripy shirt that must have been a gift, and too-loose jeans. Out of his well-cut suit he looks unfamiliar, but still unbelievably beautiful.

'It's so different.' And a little difficult, too: I am not used to having to accommodate the needs of others, to stay polite. Since Leon went, I have revelled in my selfishness.

'That's not what I asked, is it, Grazia?' He winks at me.

I smile back. 'I am having a delightful time,' I say, because it strikes me this is the kind of statement to make under such circumstances.

And then, to my utter astonishment, I realise that actually I am. Leon would laugh.

It strikes me how little I think about him now. Of course, he is always there, because he always was, for most of my adult life. But as to *specifically* thinking of him, of what he would think or say in a certain situation, no. People told me, when he was newly dead, that time would heal and that I would move on, and I nodded sagely and thought they were *fucking* crazy people.

They were right and I was wrong.

However, it is more than that. Though his voice and face are fading, in other ways I can see him more clearly now, and the life we had together: the good parts, yes, like the designer home, and the adoration, and the invitations.

But also the bad parts: for all its elegance and refinement, our lives had precious little warmth.

'. . . lunch is ready!' trills Jill.

'About time,' says Mick.

'We're both starving,' says Eleanor, patting her bump ostentatiously. She is due in April and cannot wait to give up work as a dental hygienist. When she smiles, she reveals pearly, even teeth.

The women head for the kitchen to bring out the food. I follow, because it seems to be the right thing to do, but when I reach out for the plate with the turkey on it, Jill tuts.

'That's Mick's job.'

I take in the carrots instead and follow Eleanor's example by spooning the vegetables into a built-in slot in a heated trolley. As they tumble in, the carrots coil around, limp as rubber bands, but they are coated in melted golden butter and my stomach rumbles.

Now here comes Mick, holding the bronzed bird aloft. The guests applaud, and I join in, as the turkey is placed at the end of the table and Mick holds a knife up for dramatic effect. Eleanor's husband, I forget his name, is making a hash of opening a bottle of Merlot, and I long to take it from him before he propels pulverised cork into our wine, but I sense this would not be welcome. And anyway, does it really matter, in the scheme of things?

The meat is perfectly moist, and the stuffing – a first for me – curiously tasty. The chestnuts are crunchy, and the chipolata sausages wrapped in bacon taste deliciously savoury. Even bread sauce is better than it looks.

With Leon, tradition was in short supply. We drank champagne and ate whatever we wanted at Christmas. He did buy me panettone, once, but though I made myself eat every single dry slice, I told him afterwards that I had not come to England to eat panettone.

Christmas pudding, alas, is no nicer to me than panettone, though it is palatable once Mick has poured brandy over it, set fire to it and then doused the flames in cream.

'Top-up, Grazia?' Mick has worked out how to pronounce it right.

'No, thanks. Remember, I'm driving.'

Though I wonder whether I might stay over, after all. Being in the bosom of someone else's family is both strange but also strangely pleasing.

14:00 Sandie

Gramma says she has never cooked such a huge turkey before.

'Of course, it's way too much, Sandra. For five people.'

'Don't forget the cat. And the dog.'

She doesn't smile. I can't blame her for being fed up. I bet she was expecting to be waited on hand and foot. I know I was. Somehow it's ended up being me and her, with chapped hands and sore feet, battling the elements in a kitchen with two micro-climates: the fat-spitting hot one radiating several metres from the range cooker, and the frozen wasteland everywhere else.

'It might only be another ten minutes,' she says. 'Or an hour, I just don't know.' She goes into the utility room and doesn't realise I can see her as she tastes a huge spoonful of leftover Christmas pudding mix. The *brandy*-laced Christmas pudding mix. So that's why she'd set aside a small bowlful when she put the pud on to cook first thing this morning,

I put the veg into the saucepans, and boil the water in the heavily scaled kettle for the third time. Nothing left to do, so I go into the living room, parlour, whatever the hell it's called, where Toby has lit a fire that doesn't smell of firelighters – he has hidden talents – and Marnie and Mrs G. are sitting as close to it as they can without actually scorching the flesh on their knees. This room would be beautiful in the summer: it has stunning floor-to-ceiling windows looking out onto the lawn and, beyond it, the village beneath. It explains a lot about Toby: how could you *not* grow up feeling a tiny bit superior when you do, literally, live so far above everyone else?

But it isn't summer. Outside, the fog still hasn't cleared and I swear it's seeping through the cracks in the glass. The dog, who can't sleep close to the fire because the cat's right next to it, is breathing out vapour with every wheezy snore. Poor Monty. As if it wasn't bad enough that Toby's present to him is a pair of doggy-antlers, kept in place by an elastic strap under his hairy chin.

I think I'd rather have had antlers than the scratchy nylon socks I got from his mother, or the evil-smelling candle from my mother. Toby has promised me my present later, when we're alone. 'Mum thinks flashy gifts are very non-U, so it's better to do in private.' I wish he'd told me that before I spent a day's net profit on a Youth Dew coffret and a pair of fawn suede driving gloves.

'. . . of course, Cannes was my favourite. The yachts were to die for, and the dresses. Exquisite.'

Mrs G. doesn't look at all hungover, or embarrassed by her behaviour last night. She is dressed in a floaty black Ghost dress, immaculately made up, and is holding court. I think she's forgotten that Gramma and I are slaving away making lunch for *her* guests, but then she's used to being waited on.

'Oh, when I was pregnant with Toby we had dinner with Joan Collins in Monaco, and she popped her hand on my stomach and said, "Darling, you're going to have a boy, and he'll go on to break a thousand hearts."'

Everyone laughs, except me. I'm kidding myself when I pretend I have this under control. The knowledge is there, all the time, just like the baby. I sicken myself.

Mrs G. moves seamlessly onto a story about Robert Wagner, and I return to the kitchen where Gramma is poking a hole in the turkey with a skewer. 'I think we may finally be there, thank the Lord!'

Not sure the Lord had much to do with it. I reheat the vegetables, and stir the bread sauce, and baste the sausages, and when tiny dots of hot fat hit my skin, I hardly feel their sting.

I look in vain for a dinner gong, but there's nothing, so instead I call out. 'Luncheon is served.'

'About time,' says Mrs G. as she takes her place at the head of the table. Yes, in her mind, we have evidently become the hired help.

Toby does at least have the grace to look embarrassed when Gramma appears with the sizzling turkey. 'It smells wonderful, Mrs Barrow. We can't thank you and Sandie enough for stepping into the breach, can we, *Mums?*'

His mother waves it off. 'I never have been able to cook, I'm afraid. Not how a man was caught in my circle.'

'Nor mine,' says Marnie, giggling.

'But then, you never did actually catch a man, did you, Marina?' says Gramma as she sits down. There's nothing casual about her tone. 'You got caught yourself.'

'Ma. Leave it, yeah?'

Gramma places the napkin on her lap. 'Shall we say grace?'

Toby raises his eyebrows at me across the table. He lowers his head and I do the same. I hear Marnie's ragged breathing as she tries to stop herself giggling.

As soon as Gramma reaches Amen, Toby leaps up. 'There's something missing!' He disappears into the hallway.

Mrs G. looks around her, then laughs. 'Do you know, I was waiting for my late husband to appear with his carving knife. Peculiar, isn't it, how you expect them to be here on high days and holidays, even though you know full well that they're dead. But at times like this it's as though they've been on an extended fishing trip and will pop up any moment with a pike that they've clearly just bought from the fishmonger's.'

'I know that feeling,' says Gramma, and I see the look that passes between the two widows, a moment of understanding that transcends class and race.

'The fact you made Pop's life a total misery so that death was probably a nice change is beside the point, huh, Ma?' says Marnie, trying to goad her.

I hold my breath.

'Bread sauce?' Gramma asks Mrs G. 'I made it from scratch.'

Toby reappears, blowing dust off a couple of bottles of red. 'Now then, this stuff is absolute nectar. Remember, Mums? Dad used to save it for Christmas. Didn't even realise we had any left.'

But Mrs G. is waiting for the next move from Marnie.

'You're not happy unless you're making someone else feel guilty, are you, Ma?'

'Marnie . . .' Toby's voice is soothing. 'Why don't we just enjoy the lunch your mother's worked so hard to make?' He begins to attack the turkey, hacking away and producing chunks rather than slices of the meat.

'She loves every minute of it. Playing the martyr, that's her thing. But try to challenge her, try to take away one of the crosses she loves to bear, that's where the problems start.'

I stare at my plate, which is still empty. I should step in to support Gramma.

'Do you think I *wanted* to bring up a baby when I was nearly fifty?' Gramma's voice is so quiet that for a moment I think perhaps I'm hearing things. 'Do you think I enjoyed it when they whispered behind our backs in church because they knew Sandra had no father?'

'Of course she has a father, Ma. I've got it down to a very short shortlist. Nothing to be ashamed of. Haven't you seen *Mamma Mia*? If it's good enough for Meryl Streep, it's good enough for me.'

I look down. *Not now.*

'You know what I mean, Marina. Children need both parents. And young parents, too, not out-of-touch pensioners. Oh, don't look so surprised, I am perfectly aware of my faults and I know that the values I hold – duty and honesty and morality – aren't fashionable. But you *chose* to let me hold the baby, didn't you? So it's as well that I do like to play the martyr, isn't it?'

The silence that follows is broken by the sound of the cork easing out of the wine, and of Toby pouring it into a glass. 'I hate to cut the discussion short, ladies, but I hope we can all agree that firstly, Sandie is a credit both to her mother and her grand-mother. And secondly, that Mrs Barrow has produced a most excellent Christmas lunch. I'd like to propose a toast . . .'

He moves up the table, pouring out wine the colour of my garnet necklace. He returns to his seat. 'A toast to family!'

We hesitate, perhaps for a fraction too long, but then we raise our glasses – the gaps between the place settings don't facilitate any clinking and I suspect Mrs G. would label it common. The wine is potent, so I push it away and settle down to eat dinner. I'm hoping for a thoughtful silence, interrupted only by the ring of cutlery against bone china . . .

'Of course, babies do have a habit of turning up when they're least wanted, wouldn't you agree?'

Uh-oh. It seems Mrs G. is not playing ball. Her tone is light but she looks straight at me as she says this.

'Certainly true in my case,' says Marnie, before winking at me. 'Still, you've turned out well, haven't you, Sandie?'

'Times *have* changed, of course,' continues Mrs G. 'These days, young women seem to think that they have some kind of god-given right to produce multiple babies by multiple fathers. And then expect to be supported by the state or the unwilling sperm donor. Or both.'

I focus on cutting my turkey into smaller pieces, though as both my mouth and the meat are bone dry, eating is beyond me.

Toby is smiling. 'Oh, Mums. That's not very politically correct, is it?'

'But true,' says Gramma. 'There's a lot to be said for the stabilising influence of shame on our society.'

Marnie spits out her food. 'Sorry! It was about to go down the wrong way. But honestly, Ma, you're crazy if you think we're better off in the dark ages when girls were expected to give their babies away and the men who made them pregnant got off scot-free. Or had to have backstreet abortions and hope they lived through it.'

'Such an interesting debate, abortion,' says Mrs G. 'Always divides people down the middle. What about you, Sandie? Which side of the fence do you sit on?'

'Mums? Hardly appropriate for dinner conversation, is it?'

'Oh, we're living in the modern world, now, Gannet, everything's appropriate. Sandie?'

'I think . . . it depends on the circumstances.'

'Ah, don't sit on the fence. Come, come. You're the only one of us here of an age to ever be affected directly, aren't you? You must have an opinion.'

'It's impossible to say unless you're in that situation.'

She continues to stare at me. 'Mmm. Maybe. Although we all have our own values.'

'All right, all right. I think that if a pregnancy is unwanted then a termination can be an acceptable choice.'

'Sandra!' Gramma throws down her fork. 'I cannot believe you'd say such a thing. And at *Christmas*.'

'I was only replying to our hostess. I had the feeling she wouldn't give up until she had an answer.'

Mrs G. smiles. 'Oh dear, here I go again. I'll never learn. Ask Toby, I have got this habit of pushing things. And all because of my insatiable curiosity about people.'

I sigh. 'What about you, Mrs Garnett? Where do you stand?'

'Ah, with apologies to Mrs Barrow – and I promise this will be the very last word on the matter – I tend to agree with you, Sandra. If a child is unwanted, and their financial future is uncertain, then a termination may be the best idea.' She takes a sip of wine and looks at me. 'Present company excepted, of course. You are a credit to your mother and your father. Whoever he was.' And she laughs lightly, to show she is making a joke.

No one joins in.

'More wine, anyone?' asks Toby at last. I'm about to shake my head, out of habit, when I realise I need all the help I can get to see this through without murdering someone.

I hold up my glass. 'Fill her up. To the top.'

Mrs G. leans back in her winged chair. I wish I could wipe the smug smile off her face, but instead I distract myself by counting the hours before we go home. Twenty-one hours down, forty-seven (*forty-seven?*) to go.

14:30 *Emily*

'Is this champagne all right?'

Will takes my glass from me. 'Let me try.' He drinks half the glass in one swig. 'You know, I'm not entirely sure. Better finish it off, just to be certain.' And he does.

'That was mine,' I protest.

'Have this one,' he says. 'It's already passed through my quality control checks.'

I sip the champagne. Definitely too many bubbles.

'What's wrong now, Em?'

'Nothing.'

And how could there be? This is the kind of Christmas we used to fantasise about, me and my schoolfriends, when we were teenagers. In bed with an incredibly handsome man and chocolate truffles. No need to make small talk with semi-continent relatives or eat Christmas pudding. Then there are the gifts this so-handsome man has bought me: soft, well-cut underwear the colour of crushed raspberries (not a thong in sight), and an adorable Victorian compendium of fairy tales, with full-colour plate illustrations. Not to mention an original photograph of *our shop* back in Edwardian times.

The boxed set of *Carry On* movies I've given him seems rather cheap in return, and I'm just not in the mood to don the naughty night-nurse uniform . . .

'Nothing?'

'Honestly, I'm fine.'

He leans forward and kisses me on the side of my neck. He moves down, kiss by kiss, until he's reached my collarbone and then I put my hand on his shoulder, and he gets the wrong idea, and eases me down onto the bed, and I spill my champagne and even before he has moved the chocolates onto the floor, he senses my reluctance. I hate myself for it.

'I'm sorry, Will. Really I am. You're being so good to me, and I know I have to grow up, I'll try, but I can't stop thinking about him.'

He nods, but I don't think he's nodding at me. He seems to have made his mind up about something. 'Em. Listen, I know the timing sucks here, but there was going to be no good time for this. I just . . . I just don't think—'

'Don't say it. *Please* don't.'

He closes his eyes. 'All right. All right, I won't. But living on top of each other, working together, living together, looking after Freddie . . . Perhaps we should have a few days to think.'

I'm the one nodding now, so furiously that my neck hurts. 'Thinking's good. We don't get time otherwise. Think and talk.'

He's already getting out of bed. 'No. Just think. And the best way to do that is . . . well, I was going to visit my parents tomorrow anyway, wasn't I? I think it's probably best if I bring it forward. They won't mind.'

'But I will.' My voice is small and irritating. I try again. 'You don't have to do that. We can give each other space.'

He smiles sadly. 'Space? Here? I don't think so.' He leans over to kiss me, but more carefully now, the way I kiss Freddie after he's had a bad dream. 'It's not an ending, Em. I'm not pretending I don't think we have problems, but going away, like I said, it'll give us a chance to think . . .'

As he pulls his weekend bag out from under the bed and begins to throw in underwear and T-shirts and jeans, I sink back down. I don't want to think. Or feel.

I just want everything to be OK, the way it's meant to be.

Chapter Twenty-Six

CHRISTMAS DAY

❧

15.00 Grazia

Nigel is a very good boy. He is in the kitchen, helping the women with the washing up. The Oswalds from next door left after Mr Oswald fell asleep onto his plate of mince pies. Eleanor's husband and Nigel's uncle whatever-he-is-called are smoking a cigarette in the back garden, and Mick and I are in the open-plan-diner-cum-lounge, admiring our expanding tummies and listening to a CD of Christmas hits, sung by Bing Crosby. On the television are gilt-framed photographs of Nigel and Eleanor in their graduation gowns, and the display cabinet is full of Lladro porcelain figurines, the ones of grey-and-white-hued young girls holding kittens or reading books. All is calm. All is bright.

I love it here. I feel on the edge of a snooze, and even more surprising, I feel relaxed enough to let myself drift sleepwards . . .

And then my mobile rings, and I leap halfway into the air.

I check the name on the screen – oh, I do not want to answer – but then realise I must. 'Sandie? Hello.'

'I can't take any more of this. I'm coming back to London.'

'What? Why? Where from?' I mouth *excuse me* to Mick, and head outside the house.

'Toby's mother knows. She keeps making all these digs at me, about babies and abortions and bastard children born to malingering women. And she's racist. And then there's my mother and my gramma going at it in the gaps in between. And—'

'Well, what has Toby said?'

'Nothing. It's obvious his mother spends most of her time at the manor house drunk, anyway, so he thinks it's normal.'

'Have you said something to him?'

'No. No.' Her voice is high-pitched and panicky, nothing like the calm businesswoman I know.

'Well, perhaps you should.'

'And then have him go to his mother and have her maybe say something about the bab— the pregnancy?'

'I doubt very much she would do that. Not if she wants rid of you.'

She hesitates, taking this in. 'All the same, I can't take that risk, Grazia. I'm coming back. I've got the car keys, I'll wait till they're all dozing after lunch, and then I'm driving back to London.'

'Without saying anything?'

'I know. I know. It's not big and it's not clever, and Toby will hate me for taking his car again, but I feel so trapped, Grazia. *So* trapped.'

'Will you feel less trapped once you are back in London?'

She laughs shortly. 'Very astute. Maybe not. But I have to try. In fact I was wondering if you fancied some company. I know, um, you like your Christmas in peace but I won't be any trouble and I just don't fancy going back to the flat. Too many reminders.'

I had not told any of the girls about Nigel's invitation. I do not know why. Perhaps I was so certain it would all go wrong. 'How long will it take you to get back?'

'Not sure. Two hours, maybe three?'

I turn to look back at the semi-detached house where the afternoon's entertainment consists of television, board games and, if I am lucky, a game of Blind Man's Buff. I was looking forward to it. But friends come first.

'Come home, Sandie. I will be waiting with the very best hot chocolate.'

I return to the house and find Mick has joined the rest of the party in the kitchen.

'Mick. Nigel. Jill. Thank you so much for a delicious lunch. I wish I could stay longer. Alas, I have received an emergency call from a friend in need and I must go back to London.'

'How awful. Is she ill?' says Jill, her sudsy hands flapping.

'Family trouble,' I say. 'If only everyone could have a day like yours, but unfortunately it is not the case.'

Jill glows. 'We're so glad you could come. It's been wonderful to meet you.' Mick puts an arm around her waist. I envy them.

After we say our goodbyes, Nigel joins me outside on the street. 'I can come with you, if you like.'

'Oh, you are a sweetheart. But it's girl trouble.' I lean forward to kiss him, then pull back. What if the neighbours are watching?

He kisses me full on the lips, for a delectable minute or more.

'Did I spot the twitch of a net curtain?' I say, slightly breathless, when we break apart.

'Now you see what I've escaped from.'

'It's lovely . . . but I suppose I can see it's not a place for the young. And now I understand where you come from, I understand you better.'

Nigel smiles. 'And I still don't understand you at all.'

'Woman of mystery.' I climb into my car.

'Can I see you tomorrow?'

I smile. 'I will call.'

I drive to the end of the close at suburban speed, turn left onto the main road and then hit the gas. I loved my taste of the sticks, but maybe it is not me after all. I never was one for family, was I?

On Battersea Bridge, where a little sunshine is falling on the Thames, *my* river, the telephone rings again.

'Grazia? Oh, Grazia, it's all gone wrong.'

'Emily, what is the matter? Not Freddie, surely?'

'Yes. I mean, no, he's fine, but I'm not. And neither's Will. Oh, Grazia, he's gone.'

'Gone?'

'To his parents. Early. He was meant to be going tomorrow anyway, but he went because I couldn't stop going on about Freddie, and I understand why he went but—'

'Hold on, hold on, Emily. I am losing track. Freddie is with you for Christmas, am I right?'

And then all I can hear is sniffling.

'Emily. Am I to understand you are on your own?'

I think I hear a *yes* in between sniffs.

'Not for much longer. You are cordially invited to the best Christmas supper in London.'

'But Will's got the car . . .'

'No problem. Have faith. Stand by your telephone.'

As I dial Sandie's number, to ask her to pick up Emily on the way, I have a sense of purpose. And something else I cannot quite put my finger on. Once I would have resented such calls. But now . . .

Ah yes. *Pride.* That is it. Both my secret shoppers called *me* first for a shoulder to cry on. And I am able to provide it.

16:55 Sandie

By the time I get to Heartsease Common to pick up a pale Emily (and several bags of goodies she insisted on bringing from the shop), I have had forty-three missed calls from Toby.

'Don't you think you should at least text him? He'll be worried,' says Emily when the phone rings for the forty-fourth time as we hit the Chiswick flyover.

'Raging at me for running away yet again, more likely.'

'He's not like that,' she insists.

'Look, Emily, no offence, but you don't know what he's like . . .'

She gives me a meaningful look. 'Anyone can see he's a good guy.'

I shake my head. She's always had so much invested in my relationship with Toby. She was the one who predicted that we'd get together, long before the two of us saw the light, and even now I'm sure she sees us as the characters in some Hollywood rom-com.

'A good guy who puts his mother first? A good guy who

disappears down the pub with my own mother every chance he gets?'

'Really? Are you sure he's down the pub? I mean . . .' she looks away for a moment. 'Did you watch the tape I sent? The one from the last assignment?'

'No. I never check your work any more. You're the best secret shopper I've got.'

Her eyes narrow. 'But . . .'

'But what? Look, Emily, I think we've both got more to worry about than your grotto filming, haven't we? All I know is, I can't rely on Toby to put me first. It's the same with Will, isn't it? First sign of trouble and men go right back to their mummies.'

She bites her lip. 'Hmm. I suppose so.'

And we lapse into a tense but still welcome silence for a couple more miles until my phone rings again.

'You ought to talk to him, Sandie.'

'Will you please stop meddling, Emily? If I want advice I will ask for it.'

She goes silent and when I look up, she's obviously upset. And I suppose she's right – I should tell him I am OK. Well, as OK as can be expected. I push my handbag towards her. 'Sorry, didn't mean to snap. If you want to text him on my behalf, feel free. Let him know what's what.'

She finds the phone, and as she tries to work out to use it, her breathing slows. Anything to take her mind off the situation with Will, not to mention Teddygate . . .

Christmas should be outlawed on the grounds of the catastrophic effect it has on relationships.

'How are you getting on, Emily?'

'The predictive text is different from on mine, but I'm nearly there.'

'Read it out to me, then.'

She scrolls down. 'Toby. Don't worry about me. I am fine. If you want to know why I've gone, ask your mother. Sandie.'

Shit. If he asks her, she might tell him about the baby. 'Whatever you do, don't press send on that one.'

'Why not? It's true, isn't it?'

I keep my eyes on the road. Driving is good for thinking. I

think about the lunch and the bickering and Mrs G.'s assumption that I am a free-loading parasite attempting to snare her beloved son in a financial trap.

And I realise Grazia was right earlier: there's no way the woman is going to tell him about the pregnancy, because all that matters to her is getting rid of *it* and me, and I also know that right now she'll be thinking she's managed it.

The thought makes that Barrow rage bubble inside me.

'You're right. Send it.'

Now Emily seems to be having second thoughts herself. 'Really? I mean, I suppose it is quite forthright. Can I put *love* Sandie, instead of just Sandie?'

'If you want. But send it.'

She shrugs and as we turn up Park Lane, she does as she's told. After a few seconds the mobile chimes, to show the message has gone on its way.

'That's that, then,' I say.

'Hmm,' she agrees.

We travel the last couple of miles to Grazia's flat in silence. I try to ignore the dread that has replaced the rage. *Temper, temper, Sandra, look where it gets you.*

But I had to do it, didn't I? He has to be willing to stand up for me, and if he can't, then surely it's better that I know now.

Sooner, rather than later.

'My girls! My lovely girls!'

Grazia seems merry when we arrive, though I don't think she's been drinking her way through Christmas: Italians don't, do they, as a rule? Her apartment is refreshingly free from festive décor, apart from the biggest scarlet and black wreath I have ever seen (almost as tall as I am) propped against a wall in the hall, and a handful of elegant cards on a high shelf. She sees me looking at them.

'Not many, ha? The good thing about moving house is I only gave my new address to the people who were real friends. A small, but select, group which includes you two, naturally. Now. Champagne.'

We follow her into the kitchen, and Emily drops bags full of stuff onto the floor. Just as well she's bothered, or we might go hungry: Grazia's is a playboy's kitchen, endless sleek white units with no handles and probably nothing inside the cupboards either. She pops open a bottle of Cristal, and though I feel Emily's censorious gaze on me as I take the first sip, I'm past caring.

'That is the spirit,' says Grazia, 'a little champagne is good for a baby. In Ireland, they drink Guinness, yes, so why not some Bubbles.'

'I'd rather not talk about babies, if that's OK,' I say.

She nods sympathetically, and leads the way into the dining room. It strikes me that she doesn't need decorations in here: the design is already as opulent as a ruby tiara. It's all about textures and richness in here, from the slightly flocked burgundy wallpaper, to the unforgiving clotted-cream coloured carpet (Freddie is *never* allowed in here when he visits). And then there's the inlaid mahogany table. Not that you can see it . . .

'Wow!' says Emily, shaken out of her misery by the table or, more accurately, what is on top of the table.

'Storecupboard essentials, and freezer items, mainly. If I had known you were coming then of course I would have ordered in more.'

More? I smile. I could hardly have been more wrong about going hungry at Grazia's. Her storecupboard essentials would put Fortnum's Food Hall to shame. I suppose the only reason she stays so thin is that she eats none of it, just hoards it like a fundamentalist preparing for the end of the world. Except I don't think a fundamentalist would be decadent enough to put aside such a feast: dill-marinated salmon and chicken liver pâté and caviar and tiny olives and even tinier capers and peppers stuffed with feta and mustard fruits and spiced truffles and cantucci biscuits and pomegranates split in half to reveal their crimson-jewelled seeds and white chocolate cookies and white meringues and . . .

And then I lose track because I am *so* hungry. I take a plate and begin to load it with a little of everything.

'Did you eat any of your Christmas lunch?' asks Emily.

'Not a lot. I was too busy trying not to slap Toby's mother from here to kingdom come.'

'Now I remember why I never want to get the wrong side of you,' she says.

Grazia returns with a tray heaped with the stuff Emily brought: a cooked turkey, a pack of pre-roasted chestnuts, a huge pack of cranberry and pistachio toffee, home-baked mince pies, cheeses, iced and unevenly cut star biscuits that Freddie must have made, pigs-in-blankets, and a big bottle of sunshine yellow egg nog. I have to get myself a second plate, because there's no room on the first, and when I've added a bit of everything, we retire to Grazia's lounge and sink into the squishy sofas next to her roaring open fire. It's not a real one, of course, but you'd never know. Grazia can afford the best. She would have been my ideal customer back at Garnett's: immaculate taste, unlimited budget.

'So. It is Christmas and we are all together,' our hostess says, topping up the champagne. 'It could be worse, yes?'

Our silence says it all.

'Sorry,' Emily says. 'I'm not my usual self. I need to snap out of it, but . . .'

Grazia tops up her glass. 'You like Christmas, is that true, Emily?'

'Can't get enough of it, usually. I remember . . . oh, it sounds stupid now.'

'What?' Grazia asks.

'I remember we used to have formal debates at school and when I was eleven I proposed that "this class believes it should be Christmas every day". Can you imagine? I never want another day like today.' She looks at her watch. 'I don't even know if that bastard Duncan has let Freddie open his presents yet. I should call . . .'

Her lip begins to tremble again.

'Yes. Call. But not yet,' says Grazia. 'He should not be allowed to believe that he has won. First, we must recapture the Christmas spirit.'

I sigh. 'How do you suggest we do that, then?'

'With stories! As you finish your food, you must think of memories to share of the best Christmas you have each celebrated.'

268

Emily and I exchange desperate glances. 'And you're joining in too, I take it?' I ask.

'But of course.'

My mouth is dry again now. Does the least worst Christmas count as the best, I wonder? We watch the flames and concentrate. Minutes tick by. A memory comes, that triggers another, and another. Smells, tastes, sounds.

'Got one!' says Emily. She seems to have perked up already.

'Then the floor is yours,' Grazia tells Emily.

19:10 Emily

'OK. Sitting comfortably? Then I'll begin. I was six. And the big event in my life that year was that I'd had measles. God, it was miserable. You're meant to forget how childhood illnesses feel, aren't you? Just like you're meant to forget childbirth. Well, I remember every contraction, and I also remember every pimple and every itch, and it was all terrible. Even worse, it happened right in the middle of the carnival season, in November, which meant I had to sit at home, under the supervision of various teenage babysitters, while Dad was on the float and my mum and sister were out there supporting him.'

Sandie looks outraged on my behalf. 'They left you behind?'

I nod. 'Yup. It could have been catastrophic if the measles had spread through the Madcap Knights, and anyway, it wouldn't have been much fun for me on the freezing cold processions with a hundred red spots and a temperature.'

'No. What I meant is, didn't they consider cancelling to stay at home with a sick child?'

I laugh. 'That just proves how little you know about my world, Sandie. My dad loves the bones of me, but missing carnival just wouldn't happen. Anyway, I got over the measles, just about, but then I picked up another couple of bugs, the way kids do . . .' I think of Freddie, but try to focus on my story, 'and all in all, I didn't get out of bed much that side of Christmas. I was completely sorry for myself by this point. So bored I wanted to go back to school except I didn't have the energy.

'I couldn't even summon up much excitement about Christmas, you know? As far as I was concerned, I'd missed the big event. Oh, and I haven't told you the worst bit. That was the year I was supposed to be the main character on our float. I was going to be Snow White. Red Pimple wasn't really the same, was it?'

The girls smile and so do I.

'Mum had even made my costume and I wore it around the house all the time. For a while it looked like the little girl who took my part, Josie, was going to get my costume too, until Dad said it might be infectious. After Christmas, Mum burned it, secretly, to be on the safe side. When I found out, I cried for days. It was all made of shiny polyester, you couldn't have washed it, but even so . . .'

I stop mid-sentence. 'Funny. You forget how important those things were, don't you? How disastrous it seemed at the time . . .'

'Emily?' Sandie says. 'You are going to deliver us a happy ending, I hope?'

'Yes, sorry. So, it's Christmas Eve. We had our rituals, like all families do. Mum used to sew this garland of carrots – carrots, can you imagine? – for the reindeers, and of course there was always sherry, which my father would taste, to check it was good enough for Santa. We'd have Rudolph's Red Nose cocktails – orange juice, with red food colouring – before going to bed.

'Mum seemed nervous this night. She broke two carrot garlands before managing to finish one, and spilled the colouring on the kitchen floor. And me and my sister Jane were just on the point of giving up on our fight to stay up, I was getting very tetchy because I was so tired, when there was a strange sound from outside. Like jingle bells . . .'

The girls are sitting forward in their chairs now, waiting for the end.

'I said, "Did anyone hear that?" but my mother and my sister both shook their heads. Then I heard the sound again, so I went to the window and I pulled the curtains, just a fraction, because I was actually a bit scared of the dark, and . . . well. It was them.'

'Them?' Grazia asks.

'The float. The Carnival float, complete with all seven dwarves and all four thousand light bulbs and the little model they'd made of the dwarves' cottage, and the forest and everything. It was the most beautiful thing I had ever seen. And then I saw Dad climb off the float and come into the house and he carried me out and onto the float, and then the music started, *Heigh Ho*, and they drove up and down our street *three times* and all the neighbours came out to wave and . . .' The memory is so clear, so colourful, that I feel the most intense longing to be back there, back then. 'I mean. For a little girl, can you imagine a better Christmas?'

'I would have loathed the attention,' Sandie says. 'I'd have preferred to be decorating the float or making the costumes while someone else is the star. But you'd still want that now, wouldn't you, Emily?'

I groan. 'You're probably right. Though of course it all went wrong the following year, when they gave me the starring role and everyone accused Dad of favouritism and I ended up having an accident on the float and forever earning the name of the Little Mermaid Who Wet Herself at Weston-super-Mare.'

Everyone laughs. 'A wonderful story,' says Grazia. 'And what is the lesson? The moral of the tale?'

I try to decide. 'Well, it sums up everything about our family. I can't imagine what it took for my father to get all the lads out, and in costume, on Christmas Eve. One of them even had to stay sober to drive the float. I guess that's the trouble with growing up. Who is ever going to be good enough to take the place of your dad?'

Grazia glances at me. No one says anything.

My hand darts to my mouth. 'Oh, fuck. I'm sorry, Sandie. What a tit I am. I didn't think . . .'

'No, it's fine, really. You don't miss what you never had.'

'Really?' I ask.

'Actually, that's bollocks. Of course I missed having a dad. I do now, when I hear about yours. But you can't rewrite history.'

'No . . . but you can make your own. You could do the family thing *your* way, Sandie. The baby could be your chance to make that dream happen.' I don't want to push her too far, but she's making such an awful mistake. Should I tell her about Toby's brilliant Santa act? Or have I meddled enough, like she said in the car?

'Oh, yes, because having a baby is the answer to lasting happiness and the perfect relationship, isn't it?'

I stare at her. 'Ouch.'

'OK. My turn to apologise, Emily. It's not your fault. It's just that we all know real life is no fairy tale, and that's why I've made my mind up. The fact I grew up without a dad around – or my mum – means I'm likely to make an even bigger hash of it, doesn't it? I don't want to discuss it any more. Come on, Grazia. Give us a tale of Christmas amongst the Young British Artists . . .'

19:33 Grazia

I shake my head, because my story has nothing to do with Leon and our life together. 'No. Our Christmases were not at all noteworthy. Too sterile. But there is something about this time of year that makes one think of childhood.'

'I can't imagine you as a little girl, Grazia,' Emily says. 'I think of you sitting in your pram with full make-up and perfect nails, eyeing up the talent and demanding only San Pellegrino in your water bottle.'

'Ah. If I had demanded anything, my mother would have put me firmly in my place. We were not, shall we say, an aspirational household.'

'You've never talked to us about your family before,' Sandie says.

'Even this story is not really about my family. Oh, they were not bad people, I suppose. But you know how every child has days when they are convinced they were adopted and that their real parents will be turning up any day in a limo to whisk them away?'

Emily and Sandie nod.

'That was me, all the time. Even now I have a suspicion I was swapped in the hospital bed. They were so . . . limited. Yes, that is the word, and limiting, too. Traditional. I was born in the sixties but it might as well have been the thirties as far as they were concerned. My father worked in the foundry, my mother kept him comfortable, though she moaned like a broken record. Even from my pram, I think perhaps I understood that we would never be happy, all together. That one day I would have to escape.

'But how would I escape? Where we lived in Liguria, the countryside seemed to go on for ever and for ever. Fields and fields, all the same shade of scorched brown, with the silver-grey of olive leaves. But no green. I longed for green.

'I was a monstrous child, I am sure. Frustrated beyond reason. By the time I was fourteen, I was all my parents spoke to each other about. The problem with Grazia and who was to blame. My father was uncommunicative at the best of times, a bad-tempered and judgemental bully who could not understand why things did not always go his way. But my mother was difficult, too, the kind of woman who would prod and poke and *spoil* several loaves of bread in the market before finding one that matched her exacting standards.' I smile. 'Maybe I am not as different as I would like to think. In any case, they deserved each other, and I grew up an unpleasant mix of the two.'

'Oh, come on, Grazia, I'm sure you weren't that bad,' says Emily.

'Kind of you to argue with me, but I was. My only good points were a strong bone structure, quality hair, and the first indications of a slender but womanly figure. But the boys who admired it were of no interest to me. Uncultured farmers or flash kids who talked of the city but I knew would never make it beyond the parochial limits. And then, just when I was on the verge of turning fifteen and picking one of them to sleep with, out of nothing but boredom and a determination to spite my parents by shaming them, Edith arrived.

'Edith was the most exotic thing to happen in our village for years, even though she was very short, with cropped grey hair she did not even bother to dye and appeared to cut herself, with a pudding basin. But somehow she had more style than any of the other women I knew. It would not be my idea of style now, I must say. Fitted tweed jackets and complicated pink blouses. Very Miss Marple.

'But she was exotic because of what she had done. In our village, widows wore black, and waited for death. Edith arrived from England speaking fluent and beautiful Italian, and instructed everyone to address her by her first name. Even me. I adored her immediately.'

'Why?' asks Sandie.

'She was the only person I had ever met who treated me as an individual. She arrived in the November and there was instantly this furious competition in the village about who would host her for the Christmas Eve dinner. Edith had read about the Feast of the Seven Fishes, even though the truth was that most people in our village could barely stretch beyond the feast of the seven sardines.

'But it became a matter of pride, and we won. Or rather, I won. She told me that she found me ten times more interesting than anyone else. Again, no one had ever called me interesting.

'Usually, dinner was painful. Only my father's mother was still alive, one of the more grotesque of the women in black. Because she had false teeth, she had stopped brushing her gums, and as they shrank, her false ones became looser and her breath became more and more foul. She always stayed the night in our apartment, and took my bed, and I swear I could smell her breath for several days after she left.'

'Apartment?' says Emily. 'I always imagined you lived in an amazing farmhouse.'

'No. Imagine the ugliest modern building you can, like a big concrete multi-storey car park, and we lived on the top floor. So. Where was I? Oh, yes. Christmas Eve. My father had only said yes to her coming to boost his status in the bar, but when the day came he was grumpy at the idea of having to change out of his pyjamas, but my mother insisted. Grandmother became agitated when she saw the fourth chair at the table, and because she was so deaf, it was difficult to explain what was happening.

'Edith arrived three minutes late. I saw her on the pavement outside, checking her watch, to ensure she did not catch us out.

Such consideration, you understand. I had never encountered this before.'

Sandie frowns. 'What, you're saying all the people in your village were ignorant peasants, Grazia?'

'Maybe I was not entirely open to the idea of intelligent life being present in Liguria,' I admit. 'As a surly teenager I was perhaps not in the best position to observe it.'

I take a sip of my champagne, and close my eyes. I am back there now, in that dark dining room that smelled of rotting gums and my father's hair cream, and of seven fishes. *Family life* . . .

'Edith came to lunch in an emerald green dress, very fitted, with puffy sleeves and very narrow cuffs, like deflated balloons. Yet she had this serenity about her. A confidence, but one that did not rely on putting others down, as my father's did. Within seconds of her arrival, my grandmother was soothed, my father was charmed and my mother over-awed. And I had this sudden revelation. That this woman could be my way out.

'We ate more slowly than usual, our pace led by our guest. There was salmon and eel and tuna and other seafood I cannot remember. My mother was a competent if uninspired cook, whatever my grandmother said, and Edith was delighted with every course, and the meal ended with Mama virtually force-feeding our guest torrone and pan dolce.

'But I hardly noticed the food. I was listening to Edith as she spoke about her late husband: their mutual love of all things Italian, his coin collection, his terrible piano playing. She briefly mentioned that his death from cancer had been prolonged, and had made her determined to live the rest of her life for both of them.

'I was watching her, too. She can only have been sixty at the time but seemed to me as old as God. Yet I was jealous of her. She had so much I wanted – the freedom, that profound happiness in her own skin – and I knew, suddenly, that there was somewhere better for me. England, I thought, this place where everything is that precise shade of emerald green, and women can do whatever they want and everyone is polite and graceful.'

Sandie laughs. 'It must have been a disappointment when you got here.'

I know she is joking, but I am not. 'No. England has been many things, but never a disappointment.'

'And the moral of the story is . . .' Emily thinks about it, 'if you invite strange women round for Christmas dinner, you never know where you're going to end up.'

'And you don't get much stranger than the two of us,' says Sandie.

'It's weird, isn't it?' Emily says. 'Because that's you now, isn't it, Grazia?'

'What is?'

'You're like this Edith woman. OK, I've never seen you in tweed or fussy pink blouses, and your hair is fabulous. But you're making your own way, aren't you? You've got what she had. You're a free spirit.'

I stare at her and Emily continues, 'I didn't know you when Leon was alive, obviously, but it never sounded like you had much freedom then. And now you do.'

'I had not thought about it like that . . .' But now I do. 'Like Edith? In a way, but I could not honestly describe myself as happy in my own skin. Otherwise, why would I have had poisons injected into my face, and spent hours looking for the changes in the mirror, like a crazy woman.'

Both Emily and Sandie scrutinise my face.

'Oh, Grazia, you kept that quiet,' says Emily. 'I hadn't noticed. I just thought that rosy glow of yours was down to all the sex you'd been having with your toyboy.'

'Maybe that helped a little. Cheaper than the doctor, and certainly more enjoyable.'

'You might not see yourself as happy in your skin, Grazia, but obviously you're giving off some kind of positive vibe to attract Nigel in the first place,' says Emily.

I consider this. Perhaps it is so. Though, as I think about Nigel and his family, I feel less sure about the future. He might be attracted to a free spirit, but in the end he will want what he grew up with: stability, security. Children.

'Grazia?'

'Sorry, Emily. Thinking is a dangerous pursuit at this time of year. But thank you. Being like Edith. The idea of that makes me happy.'

'And you changed our lives, too, like Edith changed yours,' says Emily, in full Pollyanna mode again. 'Now it's your turn, Sandie. We want to hear about a Birmingham Christmas.'

20:10 Sandie

'I still haven't been able to think of a single positive memory,' I lie, hoping to fob her off.

'What, nothing?' Emily asks. 'That's so sad.'

'OK. That's not quite true. What I mean is, I haven't been able to single out one memory. What I mostly remember is Gramma and me pretending that everything was fine, but longing for more. Well, I don't know for sure that Gramma was longing for more, but I was.'

'Oh, Sandie, you poor thing.'

'Not really. Half the girls in my class came from what Gramma called "broken homes" although most of them did at least get guilty conscience gifts at Christmas from their absent fathers. While I got something either practical or traditional from Gramma: shoes or a knitting set or sewing kit or something.

'And we had our traditions. She always cooked the proper dinner for us. the turkey, but with her candied yams, bought from the market, and then she made her own mince pies, too, with spices in the pastry. She tried so hard.

'It's just that I was always relieved when it was over, when I could get back to school and stop pretending not to care that my mother didn't want me and I didn't even know who my father was.'

The girls look away. I suppose it is all too raw. Not quite the kind of life-affirming story that Grazia had in mind.

'But what about the shops?' Emily says suddenly. 'You always loved the shops, didn't you?'

Of course, she's right. The shops were my Christmas present and, of course, there was the first trip to Garnett's, when I was very small, and fell in love with the building and the uniformed security guards and the glossy bags and the smells and the sounds and the theatre of it all . . .

'Thank you, Em, for reminding me. You know, it's funny, but even though kids have never been part of my plans, that's the only thing I imagined doing with a daughter. Taking her to the shops for the first time. Seeing her face. Not buying bath salts, like Gramma did for me, but buying her something beautiful that she'd always associate with that trip.'

'I'd love a daughter, too,' says Emily wistfully.

Grazia says nothing.

I shake myself out of it. 'The trouble is, kids don't do what you want, do they? If I'd followed Gramma's dreams for me, I'd be a respectable accountant or solicitor, married by now to another accountant or solicitor, or maybe even a doctor, and we might be considering starting a family in a year or two, when both our careers were firmly established. "No sense wasting your education, Sandra," she always says.'

'She's a women's libber on the quiet, your gramma,' says Emily.

'Hmm. And look at the good my education's done me. I'm a shop girl, knocked up by her ex-boss, and about to bring the wrath of the heavens down on me by doing what I've got to do.'

Emily opens her mouth and I shoot her a warning glance.

'OK. I won't say anything. I won't.' She looks at her watch and jumps a little. 'Shit. How did that happen? It's Freddie's bedtime and I haven't even wished him goodnight. Or found out whether bloody Duncan has let him open his presents yet. Excuse me. I have a phone call to make.'

She leaves the room.

Grazia looks at me. 'You know, if I had had a daughter, Sandie, I would have been delighted to have one like you. You are special. This is a black moment for you, certainly, but it will pass. Everything passes eventually.'

And she rests her hand on mine, and it feels warmer than I expected and I do believe her. I just wish I knew how long it would take before things improve.

Chapter Twenty-Seven

CHRISTMAS DAY

∾≈∾

23:22 *Kelly*

For the first time I can remember, the flat is quiet. Luis and his clan have laughed themselves to sleep downstairs, my father is so pissed that he's actually past snoring, and I miss that comforting rumble from the Tube.

This counts as absolute silence in the city, and it's keeping me awake. Well, it's not the only thing keeping me awake. There's the knowledge that Charlie's men are about to wreck Sandie's life, or at least mess it up badly. And then there are the memories that the incident in the Anchor has stirred up.

Not that they took all that much stirring up. They're always here, as much a part of Christmas as the tinsel and the queues and the sodding carols. I lie on my bed, fully dressed, and pretty pissed after polishing off Charlie's Scotch with my dad, and the only comfort is that it'll soon be over. Boxing Day is minutes away, then there'll be a few more endless bloody days until we're safely into the new year.

Not that I like New Year's Eve any better. Streets full of jolly people making stupid resolutions, reminding me of how far I *haven't* come.

No. I'm nowhere. I'm still in this shitty room, in my shitty life, staring at the same damp walls and Artexed ceiling.

Oh, fuck this.

I pull on my trainers and my coat and creep out of the flat. Well, I try to creep. I'm not at my most coordinated and I feel dizzy from the booze. But outside sobers me up. There's no cloud, and the pavements are frosted and slightly slippery. No one's about. Empty streets freak me out far more than busy ones. One of the only things I've ever rated about my part of London is the fact that it's throbbing, twenty-four hours a day: OK, so half of the people are Grade A head cases, but that means the other half will be there to witness what happens.

Or not.

I take the long way around, of course. Always do. Not that I think that any of that lot still live there – they left years ago, when the council and the police came and kicked them all out – but because I don't like seeing the house, or even the street name.

Maybe I'm kidding myself. I'm still trapped by what happened there, and by what people like Woody know or think they know about me and them and the whole fucking business.

I speed up. I want to get away from this place, from the litter and the estate agents and the kebab joints and the caffs and the snotty coffee shops and the charity shops and the yuppie shops and the endless signs for Westfield . . .

I'm running along the middle of the Green now, proper running, not like the fat sods who jog and pant their way around the crap-covered grass, fiddling with their shite iPods, like they're asking to be mugged.

And then I get to the roundabout, where the Bush ends and Holland Park begins, and I'm doubled up, no breath left, but I don't look back. I don't want to be here tonight. I don't want to be anywhere else, either, but I definitely don't want to be here.

I've walked the length of the Holland Road, and now I'm in Kensington. I've been pretending to myself that my route is aimless, but of course I know exactly where I'm going. Not why, though. To make myself feel even crappier about myself?

It's not like I'm going to try to stop them doing whatever they're doing. I'm guessing they're going to trash the place. Sandie'll live. You can replace stuff, and anyway it's not even her flat, it's Toby's, and no one's due there till tomorrow, not even that squat little dog of theirs.

Is that why I'm going? Just to make sure?

And, of course, knowing Sandie, they've got every kind of insurance going, so she'll probably end up even better off. New furniture. New décor. Those leather sofas of Toby's were looking a bit bloody last century anyhow.

Plus Charlie promised me Sandie would never be able to connect it back to me. 'My boys are professionals, sweetheart. We tidy up after ourselves. For everyone's sake. It's just having the electronic codes saves us having to get nasty with the security bloke on our way in, and the keys will stop us disturbing the neighbours.'

You see more, don't you, when you walk. I've been through the fancy bit of town down towards Kensington, past the big houses where they leave the curtains open so you can admire their gigantic trees. Then I cross the Cromwell Road, right down the middle. I even stand in the middle of the dual carriageway for a few seconds, like a kid playing chicken, because it's so empty. A weird, good feeling, like ruling the world.

Now I'm in Earl's Court, bedsit land, the bit where the Kiwis and Aussies go if they don't like Shepherd's Bush. The Christmas tree count is lower round here, and mostly the windows are dark, because the kids have sodded off back Down Under.

I suppose I could still do the same, couldn't I? Mum would be surprised but she said there'd always be a room for me if I changed my mind. That was before she had the twins, though. My half-brothers, and I've never even met them.

'There's a whole other life out here, Kelly,' she told me, in the days when she still bothered to call. Or when I still bothered to answer the phone.

I'm gonna have to do something, aren't I? I'll stick working at Sandie's for a few weeks after Christmas, help her clear up the mess and stop her getting suspicious, but I think there's a limit to how much guilt even I can hack.

One step in front of the other.

Chelsea's so much nicer without all the Sloaney types. I've been walking for an hour and a half and I've seen maybe half a dozen other people: a couple of pissed women who looked at me like I was a mirage, and a few minicab drivers wondering why they bothered to venture out.

Now there's another one, in a beaten-up shit-brown Ford of some sort. Even before it slows down, I know. I speed up. The car speeds up, too, then brakes at the last minute.

'Playing hard to get, darling?'

I can't see his face, but I can see his belly, spilling out over his seat belt. Nice to see that he's thinking about road safety even as he's trying to pick up a tart.

'And a merry fucking Christmas to you too.'

I turn around. He puts the car into reverse. Sweat pools on the back of my neck, under my arms, even my stomach. And it's below zero out here.

'Come on, darling.' He says darlink. I decide to try to remember this, and the bellies, in case I need to give evidence against him. 'You want business, I want business. I am very clean.'

'I'm not your darling and I don't give a shit if you're clean because this is the nearest you're getting to me. Fuck off home, will you, before I call the police and your wife disowns you.'

Dunno why I even bothered to mention the cops. They're never around when you need them.

Has the desired effect on Mr Brown Car, though. He zooms off. But I can still smell my own fear.

It takes me a few minutes to realise where I am, because I usually come from the opposite direction. The river is deep black to my left, and to my right is the apartment block.

So what the hell do I do now? Sit on a bench, watch the river, wait for the gang to arrive.

My fingers coil around the phone, warm in my pocket. I could call Sandie. Warn her. Or call the police and do the same. But then while I'm onto the cops I might as well ask for an ambulance for Dad, for when Charlie sets the dogs on him . . .

Now I've stopped I've begun to shiver. I look up at the apartment, trying to match the view I have from my desk with the windows. There are very few lights on anywhere – either the jet set have set off, despite the crunch, or the jet set are tucked up in bed, sleeping off the turkey.

'No.'

My voice disappears unheard into the dark. But it changes everything.

'No,' I say again, louder this time, because now I know I can't let this happen. Not to my friend.

Friend?

Is that what Sandie is? No, she's my employer, isn't she? And yet as I stand here, shivering and sweating, the bitter taste of Charlie's thank you whisky still in my mouth, I feel her vulnerability, and the misplaced trust she's put in me.

The security camera mounted on the wall of the building is slowly panning in my direction. I move the opposite way, and I pull the hood of my dad's jacket up over my head, and smell soap and smoke.

I have to stop this. The best way has to be changing the passcode, and if I use the riverside entrance, I don't have to pass the security guy. It's not one o'clock yet. I can be gone long before they show up at three . . . But even as I rehearse it in my head, I know something's wrong.

I turn around slowly and see first headlights, then a black van. Instinctively I edge backwards, until I'm hidden behind a phone box.

The van stops, and the lights go off.

I'm not breathing. I have to move my eyes as far to the left as they'll go to see what's happening, and it's starting to hurt.

Someone gets out of the driver's side. One . . . two figures climb out of the back. They're all dressed in black – seems like that's the dress code for henchmen these days – and they blend into the darkness. Except one, the fattest, is wearing trainers with a fluorescent stripe on the back. The twin stripes move at pavement level towards the pedestrian gate, and then disappear.

I let out my breath. The bastards are early. *Early.* Whoever heard of a bunch of thugs turning up early.

And then I realise. They're not early. How thick am I? There was no way that Charlie was going to tell me what time they were really due, was he, in case I did something stupid.

Something stupid like this.

It's too late now. I need to turn around, walk home, keep my nose out. Let's face it, it shouldn't be a surprise that Charlie is a lying, cheating, scumbag . . .

I realise something else. This isn't the end, is it? Charlie's like a sodding elephant. He never forgets. He never forgot about my father's weakness, and he knew just the moment to exploit it. He's hardly going to let go, now he's got this on me. All that business about the codes and the keys: that was as much about trapping me as it was getting into the flat.

And now I'm well and truly trapped.

I turn slowly to look up at the apartments. Is that the beam of a torch I can see moving up the stairwell? *Do something*, you useless tart. For once in your life, prove you've got some fucking courage.

I step towards the building but even as I do, I know I can't do anything on my own. I need back-up. Someone who does the right thing, no matter what.

Yeah, right, because you know loads of upstanding citizens, don't you, you loser, Kelly Wright? I slump against the wall, defeated.

And then I remember that I do know one upstanding citizen . . . if I can get him to believe what I'm saying.

It only takes Al eight minutes to get here from where he's staying in Fulham, but it is the second-longest eight minutes of my life.

He moves briskly but silently, like a tom cat, dressed in black like the men in Sandie's flat. When he's close enough to whisper, his face is questioning but he doesn't ask the obvious questions, which is just as well because my brain isn't functioning properly, thanks to booze and fear.

He didn't ask on the phone, either. He must have heard the panic in my voice.

I lean towards him and he whispers, right into my ear, 'They're inside?'

I nod. 'There are three of them.'

'Just my luck.' He sighs, shakes his head, then walks off in the direction of the gate. I can't hear his footsteps. I guess he learned how to do that in the Army.

I stand still. I really, really don't know what to do next.

'They're not messing about,' I call after him, but quietly, and he doesn't hear me.

I follow him, struggling to keep up. 'I said, they're not messing about. They're nasty.'

'I heard you. I didn't think they were collecting for Help the Aged.'

'And . . . the security code has changed.'

He turns round briefly. 'You've got a lot of explaining to do, haven't you? But I guess now isn't the time.'

I approach the gate and he stands back while I input the new code. He's not much taller than me, and suddenly he looks so vulnerable. This isn't the idea. The whole point is to make sure no one gets hurt: not me, not Dad, not Sandie, not the dog, not even Al.

'Would we be better off calling the police?' I whisper, words I never thought I'd say.

The gate shifts open and he shakes his head. 'They'd never make it in time.' He tiptoes through and then turns to make sure it doesn't slam shut again.

I slip into the gap.

Al stares at me. 'Is there anything else you need to tell me? Before . . .'

'No. I don't know who they are, but I know who sent them.'

He opens his mouth to say more, then shakes his head again. 'Later.'

We both look up to the penthouse. If I were a hired thug, I'd keep this nice and clean. Push us over the side. You don't survive if you fall six floors. Better still, there's no murder weapon.

I should turn back, make him do the same, but I can't. This is my mess and the whole reason I went along with it was to do the least harm. Flats can be fixed up, rebuilt. Dead people can't.

Low-level lights are on in the corridor – though this place is so posh that even the emergency lights are subtle and flattering. When Al turns round again, I see his surprise that I'm still there. His eyes are wide. Of course he's frightened. Who wouldn't be? But he's not slowing down.

'You sure?'

I nod.

'We'll take the stairs. They'll hear the lift starting up.'

My legs feel heavy by the third floor, even though I've had enough practice climbing stairs because the lift in our building is always out of order. So this heaviness must be fear. And there's a buzzing in my head, and my ears seem to be picking up every creak and scrape in London.

Fourth floor. Fifth floor. My legs are dead now.

'What's that?'

Al stops. 'I didn't hear anything.'

'Definitely something. A smashing sound . . .'

He speeds up, still barely making any noise. We're on the top flight now, and there's no doubt about it. The thugs are in there. They're trying to keep the noise down, but it's hard to trash a place in complete silence.

'What do we do now?' I whisper.

Al holds up his hand to stop me speaking. 'Wait.'

I'm about to say something else when I realise another of my senses has become extra sensitive.

'Al. Can you smell that?'

He nods. 'Fuck.'

It's petrol.

Chapter Twenty-Eight

BOXING DAY

❧

01:20 Emily

I keep counting the reasons why I shouldn't call him.

Because it's past one o'clock.

Because I'm quite drunk.

Because the girls think this is the kind of chat you should only have face to face.

Because he's the one who left so he should be the one to call.

Because I don't know what mood he's in.

Because I'll wake up his parents.

Because I have a tendency to get emotional and irrational on the phone.

And then I keep coming back to the single reason why I want to call.

Because I love him . . .

I turn over on the sofa bed. I'm sleeping in the living room, because I insisted Sandie take the proper bed as she's pregnant. She wasn't keen on special privileges, because she doesn't intend to be pregnant much longer, but I don't believe she's going to go through with it. I wouldn't be talking to her if I did. Any idiot can tell she's made for Toby, and he's made for her.

And I am made for Will and he is made for me. Telling that story about the float and the measles made me realise how impossible a task I'd set him, or any bloke: to be 'as good' as my father. Then I realised that Will has achieved exactly that, and the rest.

I pick up my phone. It's not really *that* late yet, is it? I mean, knowing Will and his brother, they're probably still up, playing backgammon and drinking port. That's what Army families do. They're big on tradition. Will once told me that when they were kids his father made him stand up all the way through the Queen's Christmas message.

The fake fire is still burning because I don't know how to turn it off. In the fairy-tale version of my life I'd see the future in those flames – Will and me with Freddie and a little girl, surrounded by our celebrity friends at the tenth anniversary party of the Emporium – and I'd know for sure that everything is going to turn out all right.

But all I can see are the carefully calibrated flames: even my imagination can't summon up Tom and Katie and Suri in between the flickers.

I press DIAL.

The phone rings once, twice, three times. Four, five, six . . .

'Emily?'

Will's voice is full of sleep.

'I woke you up, didn't I?'

'Errr. Yes.'

'I thought you were probably playing backgammon.'

'Is this an emergency, Em?'

'No. Yes. Well, not strictly a life-threatening moment. But maybe a life-changing one.' There's a silence from his end. 'Would it be better to leave it till later? When you're awake.'

He sighs. 'I'm awake now. Fire away.'

'OK. Thanks. OK.' I try to re-muster my thoughts. Before I dialled, those thoughts were neatly marshalled, an unstoppable force. Now they're . . . um, not. 'I owe you an apology, Will.'

'For what?'

I feel like saying *take your pick, name the crime, I'll confess: one apology, four hundred other offences to be taken into consideration.* 'For not appreciating you.'

He harrumphs. When he spends any time with his father, he always begins to sound like a retired brigadier.

I press on. 'I've been very stupid in not recognising how patient you've been with me. How exhausting it must be to live with me and my daydreams.'

He sighs. 'Look, I don't want you to apologise for the things that make you who you are, Em.'

'But . . .' Why does he sound so sad about it?

'I just need to get my head around whether the things that make you you, and the things that make me me, can work together. As a we.'

'Are you stoned?'

He laughs. 'No. I do sound like a self-help book, don't I? But I am serious. We both need to think about whether our expectations are, well, compatible.'

'Which means you think they're not?'

'You're jumping to conclusions.'

'So you don't deny it.'

Another world-on-his-shoulders sigh. 'We've obviously got issues, haven't we, or we wouldn't be apart like this. I'm tired now, Em and I've got a headache.'

There's a pause. I know I shouldn't say anything, but I can't help myself. 'I miss you.'

An even deeper sigh. 'I miss you too. And it's not that I don't appreciate the call, or the sentiment. I'll come back to Heartsease tomorrow. We'll talk about it then.'

My hope-o-meter goes up. 'You mean later today?'

'No. I mean tomorrow. Get some sleep, Emily. Sweet dreams.'

Chance would be a fine thing. The flames flicker away. I can't see the future in them, and I'm not sure I want to anyway.

02:43 Sandie

I know it's a dream, because my legs are thinner, and faster.

I'm running through a poppy field and behind me there's a small child in dungarees, either a boy with hippie hair or a tomboy girl. Toby is throwing something. A Frisbee? A football? A grenade?

I fall, the way you do from dreams, a stomach-whirling tumble, and as I hit the mattress at what feels like two hundred miles an hour, I realise my mobile's ringing.

It's Toby. I don't want to answer. He stopped calling after Emily sent that text. He must be drunk now, and ready for a row.

I let it go to answerphone. It rings again, straight away. I mute the sound and watch the phone, lighting up the room with every ring.

And then, without me telling it to, my hand reaches out and I answer.

'Hello?'

'Sandie? Oh God, oh, thank God. You're OK?' His tone isn't angry. It's desperate, almost hysterical.

'Yes.'

'Where the hell are you?' *Now* he sounds angry.

'At Grazia's.'

'You don't know, do you? Jesus. Sandie. I thought you were . . . I thought you'd gone up, too. That there'd been an accident or you'd fallen asleep or—'

'Slow down, will you, Toby? Just explain what's happening.'

'The flat's on fire. The police called. They've found a man, burned. And I'm fucking pissed and so is Marnie, and I want to set off but my mother won't give me her car keys and anyway you took my car but I don't care about that because I thought you were in the flat, and I thought you were . . . you were . . .'

And he starts weeping like a child after a nightmare.

'Toby. Toby? Listen to me. I'm fine. I'm nowhere near the flat. But I can be. I haven't been drinking, I'll go there straight away. This man . . . is he dead?'

'No. Well, he wasn't. They told me about finding someone and when I realised it wasn't a woman, I stopped listening.'

'Is it the whole building, or just our place?'

'I don't know. I don't know.'

Maybe I'm in shock myself, but I don't feel anything: no panic or dread, just a calm understanding of what needs to be done.

'I'm going to ring off now, Toby, so that I can go straight there. But I will call you as soon as I get there. Make yourself a

strong coffee and drink as much water as you can to sober up. I'm
OK. You're OK. Monty's OK. That's all that matters, surely?'

Now he's crying softly down the phone. 'Jesus, Sandie. Stay
safe, please, I couldn't bear it if anything happened to you . . .'

'It won't. I'm sure it's nothing like as bad as you're imagining.'

03:19 Sandie

It's worse.

Much, much worse.

'Fuck, Sandie. Thank God you weren't in there.' The expression on Emily's face makes it more real, somehow, than the line
of fire engines and police cars and the stench of burned plastic
and timber. A middle-aged gay couple I've never met before, who
live on the first floor, stand in their his-and-his dressing gowns,
clutching a cardboard box that keeps meowing pitifully.

I approach the first policeman I see. He looks at me suspiciously as I explain the situation.

'So you're not the owner, but you live with Mr Garnett. Do
you mind me asking why you're not together at Christmas?'

'I had to come back to London unexpectedly.' As I speak, I
realise how suspicious that sounds. I bet he's already got the
whole thing down as a domestic. 'The security guys will vouch for
me. Oh, and this is my key.' I pull it out of my handbag.

'Yeah, well,' he says, 'I'll have to take your word for that. We
could try it in the lock. If the door was still there.'

'Oh.' I look up at the top of the building. Some of the
windows have been blown out, and the ones that remain are
blackened from the inside. 'It's really that bad?'

He looks a bit more sympathetic now. 'Yeah. Sorry. The fires
are under control, but there's no way you can go up there.'

'Fires?'

'So they tell me.'

'I was hoping it might be an electrical fault.'

'More than one seat of fire. And it stinks of petrol up there. I
didn't tell you that, though.'

'Thanks. They told Toby . . . my partner, that they'd found someone.'

'Yep. He's in the ambulance. He's not talking, mainly because he can't breathe properly. Oh, and some of his teeth are missing.'

'Bloody hell.'

The policeman sighs. 'Between you and me, there are still persons reported.'

'What?'

'They're still looking. The lads are up there now, in breathing apparatus. The guy in the ambulance was incoherent but before they gave him oxygen he was rambling on about some girl . . .'

I'm trying to make sense of any of this when my phone rings again. I answer straight away, as honestly as I can. 'It's not good news, Toby. I think the place has been gutted, though they won't let me anywhere near. And they think . . . they think there might still be someone in there.'

'Who?'

I explain about the man who was found. 'Could it be squatters? Moved in over Christmas?'

'We only left on Christmas Eve. It makes no sense . . .'

'Look, I'd better see what else I can find out but there's no point racing down here, there's nothing you could do anyway.'

'Except be with you, Brains.'

The familiar nickname makes me feel very slightly less alone. 'I'll manage. I'll call you later.'

I find Emily and Grazia in the security office, setting up a production line of hot drinks and biscuits for the rescue services. They press a mug of tea into my hands and I'm about to step in, to suggest a more efficient way of organising themselves, when suddenly it seems real.

Someone might have died in there.

And that someone could so easily have been me.

'Drink your tea, Sandie. Three sugars. You need the glucose.' Emily holds the cup to my lips and the warm liquid drips into my mouth. It doesn't taste of anything.

I look through the glass. The familiar, too manicured court-yard is now more like a film set, with people in uniform tramping all over the grass. Good job it's plastic. Exhaustion smashes into me from nowhere, and I want to go upstairs, lie down on our huge bed, snuggle under the quilt that smells of Toby (and just a little bit of Monty, too) and sleep till New Year.

But the quilt isn't there any more. Or the bed. Or even, really, the flat. My brain attempts to process the things we've lost – our photographs, DVDs, everything in my office – and then I feel dizzy.

Outside, I see the ambulance doors open, and a man in black stumbles out. He's tearing the oxygen mask from his face, which is covered in soot. But there's something about him . . .

'Al?' I drop my cup, but hardly feel the hot liquid splashing down my body. I push past the girls, out into the courtyard. 'Al!' I shout.

His eyes turn, trying to work out where I am amongst the chaos. Finally he sees me. He's swaying.

'Don't move, Al.' I run over to him and take his arm. 'What are you doing here?'

He opens his mouth to speak, but what emerges isn't the confident, clipped tones I'm used to. Instead, it's the hoarsest sound you can imagine, as though he's attempting to speak through finely grated vocal chords.

'Yes . . . I couldn't . . . stop them . . .'

'Them? Who?'

He opens and closes his mouth but nothing comes out. Now I notice different things, beyond the darkened face: dried blood around his nostrils and mouth, a swelling on his right cheek, a gap between his lips where a tooth should be.

'What about the girl you said is inside?'

His eyes widen: the whites have turned a vivid cherry-red. 'They got . . . the wrong idea. I meant you.'

'So there's no one inside?'

'No one.'

'Wait there.' I find my policeman again. 'Excuse me. I've just spoken to the guy you found – I know him, he's a friend of mine – but he says there is no one inside the building. He was talking about me.'

He looks dubious. 'He seemed pretty worried earlier, but they haven't found anyone.'

I turn round to see two paramedics ushering Al back into the ambulance, and pushing the mask onto his face again. Nothing makes sense. What was he doing here? Who beat him up?

And who hates Toby enough to set fire to his home?

I feel a hand on my arm. 'You know, there's nothing more you can do here, Sandie.'

Grazia nods. 'Let's go home. Come back when it's light.'

'I should go to the hospital with Al.'

They look at one another. 'Don't you think there's something odd about the fact he was here?' asks Emily.

And, of course, she's right. And the implication of that strikes me and I don't know why I was too stupid to see it before. Al is *my* contact, not Toby's. Which means whoever did this wasn't trying to get at Toby at all.

But at me.

07:18 Emily

I've had quieter Christmases. And nicer Christmases. But I've never had one quite this dramatic.

OK, so my relationship is on the precipice, and my son is celebrating Christmas without me, and my ex has me over a barrel, and I have the kind of splitting headache I wouldn't even wish on Duncan, but at least *my* home hasn't been burned down.

I get up from the sofa. 'Anyone want more tea?'

Grazia and Sandie shake their heads. We all gave up on the idea of sleeping several hours ago. Instead, we're sitting huddled together in the living room, staring at the TV and nibbling on leftovers from last night's buffet. That seems like days ago, now. We're waiting for something to happen: Toby's finally been deemed sober enough to drive by his mother, so I suppose his arrival will be the next act.

I stand up and my headache hits me so hard I feel faint. Maybe that medicinal brandy when we got back wasn't the best idea. Even the prospect of making tea makes my brain feel scrambled.

Instead I turn on the tap and fill a glass with water so I can take another Nurofen.

'Emily! Your phone's ringing . . .'

Sandie brings it through. It must be Will, telling me he's slept on it, and I'm right and we're going to live happily ever after and . . .

It's not Will.

'Duncan. Is everything OK?'

'No, it bloody isn't.' His voice is echoey.

'Is Freddie all right? Where are you?'

'We're at the NHS walk-in centre and Freddie is not all right.'

It feels as though a building has fallen onto my chest: I can't breathe. 'What have you done to him?'

'Oh, for God's sake, Emily. It wasn't *me* that failed to spot the completely obvious signs that our son has chicken pox, was it?'

'Chicken pox?' I suddenly have the overwhelming urge to scratch my skin.

'Yep. The first red mark appeared on his face last night, after you spoke to him, and we brought him in first thing. Poor kid is itching for England. I can't believe that you hadn't spotted he was ill.'

'Can I talk to him?'

'No, he's nodded off. We're waiting for him to be double-checked before we can go home. You have had it, haven't you?'

'I've had the measles and the mumps, but I don't think I ever had chicken pox.' I try to remember. 'What are the symptoms?'

'Well, doh, spots! But before that, you get a headache, sore throat, temperature, which Freddie has had for several days, though you didn't notice. He was so fed up that he didn't even want to open his presents.'

'I—'

'If you haven't had it, you probably will have it now. Highly contagious, the doctor says.'

I run through the checklist of symptoms. *Bollocks* .'I think I might have it then, Duncan.'

'Bad luck,' he says, dismissively. 'Anyway, at least you have the wonderful Will to apply your calamine lotion. We'll be dropping Freddie back off later today, if that's OK.'

'What?'

'Well, a sick child needs to be with his mother, don't you think? I'm the first to admit that I'm really not much of a nursemaid.'

I'm speechless. He takes this as agreement. 'We'll get you the creams from the hospital pharmacy as a favour to help you out. Right, just spotted the doctor again, got to go, not even supposed to be on my mobile in here.'

He rings off. Sandie's watching me as I examine my arms for spots. 'Is everything OK?'

'Not really. Freddie's not well. I mean, it's not the end of the world, it's just chicken pox. Which means I've probably got it too. I mean, it's fine, isn't it? No one ever died of it, and it's only dangerous if . . .'

And then I stop. I look at Sandie and down at her belly, and up again at her face.

'Have you had it?' I ask.

'I don't remember. No. I don't think I have.'

'Oh. Oh, right. It's just . . . well, I'll have to check on the Internet or something, and it's probably nothing to worry about at all, but I have this feeling that chicken pox and early pregnancy aren't . . . the ideal combination.'

Sandie stares at me. 'What are you trying to say?'

'I think we need to stay calm.'

'Right. Then what?'

'Um. Well. See what your grandmother has to say. And put as much distance between the two of us as possible.'

'And if Gramma says I haven't had it?'

'Then – and only then,' she says, backing away from me, 'we might just allow ourselves to panic.'

London is slowly coming back to life again. The news addicts are buying papers full of Christmas crosswords and Boxing Day sport previews. Dog-walkers are out with their four-legged friends and their poop-scoops, and we're all blinking in the wintry sunshine.

I feel numb. I'm amazed that the city looks the same, after everything that's happened. I had to get out of the flat. Grazia keeps staring at me, waiting for my face to break out in livid spots, or possibly for me to start clucking like a chicken. Meanwhile, Emily keeps texting me messages of support from her self-imposed quarantine in the dining room. We called Gramma on Toby's mobile and she can remember nursing me through mumps and measles in vivid detail. But not chicken pox.

And Toby's now ten minutes' away and time's running out. I've had so long to make my mind up. I spent all that bloody time on the pier, weighing up the pros and cons, trying to imagine my life with or without Toby, and with or without a baby. I recognised the impossibility of my situation and came up with the least worst option.

Then the flat burned down, and then Al turned up, and before I'd absorbed any of what that means, Emily tells me that this pregnancy . . . no, this *baby*, might be at risk, and even though I really, truly thought I'd already decided to put a stop to it all, it's changed everything.

I swear I felt a shift inside me, like a tiny earthquake, changing everything. The idea that some virus could be working its way through my body, and then to the baby's, is so monstrous it makes me feel faint. However hard I try to convince myself that I should ignore what is clearly an emotional, illogical response to the shock of the last few hours, everything suddenly seems incredibly simple.

I want to protect the baby. Nothing else matters.

I see my reflection in the window of a bookshop. My eyes are tired, yes, but my face is deceptively calm and . . . a little rounder? Hormones, I suppose. So I am only human, even though it's taken me a long time to admit that.

My phone buzzes with a text message from Emily. HE'S HERE. WHERE ARE U. WHAT DO I TELL HIM.

I turn around, back towards the flat, and I know exactly what I have to tell him, though I have no idea where to begin.

'Before I say anything, please promise not to interrupt until I've finished.'

Toby and I are in Grazia's spare bedroom. When I got back to the flat, I found her playing the perfect hostess, serving tea and biscuits to Gramma, Mrs G., Marnie and Toby, while Monty scoffed finest prosciutto from a Wedgwood plate in the kitchen. Emily is still in quarantine, though at least there's no danger of her starving in the dining room, where yesterday's buffet is still going strong.

I beckoned to him and he followed me.

'Gannet, where are you going?' his mother called after him, but he ignored her. And now we're alone and I have to find the right words.

'Toby. What I'm going to tell you is going to be a shock, as it was to me. I've waited to tell you because . . . I thought I might get used to it.'

I pause.

'Is this about the chicken pox? Because I'll have you know, I'm very good at tending to the sick if you do turn out to have it. And I promise I'll still adore you, even if you're all poxy.'

'If only. You said you wouldn't interrupt.'

'Sorry. I thought you'd finished.' He smiles apologetically.

'No. No, I haven't really started yet. Toby, there's no way of dressing this up.' I take a deep breath. 'I'm pregnant.'

The smile fades slowly. His cheeks have gone a strange shade of grey. 'As in, a baby.'

'As in our baby, yes.'

'Bloody hell,' he mutters. 'Bloody hell.'

I wait for further reaction but nothing comes. 'What do you think?'

'Sorry, sorry. I was waiting for you to finish.'

'I have finished.'

'Oh. Yes. Of course you have. Um, right. Pregnant. Ah. How pregnant?'

I shake my head in exasperation. 'One hundred per cent.'

'Sorry. No, I meant, when . . . um?'

'According to my sums, the baby would be due in July.'

'My mother's birthday is in July,' he says, as though this is in any way relevant.

I bite my tongue. Of course he's going to say daft things, he's in shock. I've known for six weeks and I'm still in shock. 'Is that all you've got to say?'

He frowns. 'Um. What do the doctors say? Is everything . . . healthy?'

It's my turn to look away. 'I haven't seen a doctor. Not till now. I wanted to think, first. Although now that there's chicken pox to worry about, I'm going to try to see someone. Today. There might be a risk to . . . the baby.'

Toby is counting on his fingers. 'July. That means you're quite a bit pregnant, then, aren't you?'

I nod.

'How long have you known, Sandie?'

'Like I said before, I needed some time to think.'

'Did you know when you went away?'

I nod again.

'Before that?'

'Yes. Back in November. I was . . . confused. It wasn't supposed to happen, was it?'

'No, but . . .' he scowls. 'You've kept this to yourself since November?'

'I needed to work out what I felt about it. It's an emotional time. Especially with Marnie turning up. That opened up a lot of wounds for me. I didn't mean to leave it this long, but I couldn't work out what I should do.'

'And *you*'ve worked that out now, then, have you?' His tone is sarcastic.

'I know it's not just my decision, but it affects me most of all.'

'I see. And am I allowed to know what it is you've decided to do?'

'I haven't completely worked out what the best thing is. For a

300

while I was seriously thinking of termination and I'm not saying that isn't still an option, but the fire and everything, it's shaken my head up completely . . .'

He walks to the window. 'Give me a minute.' He taps his fingers on the ledge. 'So what you're saying is, if the fire hadn't happened, you were going to abort *my* baby? Have I read that right?'

'I'm not sure.'

'I'll make it simpler for you, shall I? If you'd had an abortion, were you intending to tell me that this baby had ever existed?'

I look away from him.

'You weren't going to say anything, were you?'

'I don't know. Listen, I love you, Toby. I know we don't say it, but I do. But I had to try to be logical. Sensible.'

He stares at me. His eyes are hard, as though he's suddenly noticed something revolting on his shoe. 'So do my feelings on this come into it at all?'

'Of course they do, Toby. I . . . I just needed time to adjust to the idea of being a mother.'

'Without the fire, how much longer would you have needed, do you think? A month? A *year*?'

I close my eyes. 'Things were different then. You haven't seen our flat yet. It changes everything.' I take a step towards him. 'You know, I want this to be a joint decision.'

'So if I say abort, you'll abort?'

'Is that a joint decision?'

'So it'll be a joint decision so long as I go along with whatever it is you happen to want at a particular moment . . . is that right?'

'Don't, Toby. Please.'

'Don't what? Am I going to be a father or not? It's fair enough for me to want to know the answer to that question, isn't it? Obviously I don't want to interfere with your women's rights or anything, but at the very least it'd be useful to know if I need to invest in a Spiderman costume and sign up for lessons so I can abseil down the side of the palace of Westminster.'

'You're in shock.'

'Very perceptive, Sandie. First my girlfriend steals my car and runs off for the second time in a fortnight. Next my home burns down. Then I hear that I'm going to be a daddy. Then I find out I might not become one. Oh, and into the bargain, the mother of the baby that may or may not be born has been keeping the glad tidings from me for weeks. Yes, I might be in shock.'

'I don't blame you for being angry.'

'Thanks for your understanding.'

'I didn't plan this. I've never even wanted children.'

'Haven't you?' He sounds astonished.

'Well, no. I mean, we've never talked about it, have we?'

'I thought all women wanted children. I mean, it's what you do, isn't it? Find someone. Settle down. Have babies. Bring them up. Send them to school. Try not to hate them when they're teenagers. Then wait a few years for the grandchildren. It's a no-brainer.'

'You want them, then?'

He looks flustered. 'Well, obviously. I mean, not now. Not right this minute, or next July, come to think of it. I'm a conventional kind of guy, I've been brought up to do things in the traditional order, get engaged, married and so on first of all.'

'As you know, we don't tend to do things like that in my family,' I say, but it doesn't sound light-hearted, as I'd intended.

'Is that meant to be an excuse for not telling me?'

'No. No. I'm sorry. There's no excuse. There are reasons, though. Like your mother's opinion of me.'

'I wondered how long it'd take you to bring her into this.'

'She really dislikes me, Toby. She'll never accept me.'

'She's just protective. Like all mothers. It's the maternal instinct, isn't it? Not that you seem to know much about that.'

'Toby—'

'Actually, I'd been planning to have words with her today. Your rather blunt text message did make me think and I was going to ask her to be kinder. Explain that if she couldn't adore you as much as I do, then the least she can do is to make more of an effort, because you are . . . were part of my future, whether she likes it or not.'

I look at him. 'Am I still part of your future?'

'I don't know anything any more.' He looks away. 'I ought to go to the flat now.'

'Will you come with me to the hospital, first? I need to find out what it means. About the chicken pox.'

'You've managed without me so far.'

I feel tears behind my eyes, but I grind my nails into my palms to stop them getting any further. 'I wouldn't say I've managed, exactly. But the least we can do for . . . well, whoever it is in here, is be there to hear what the options are.'

He hesitates. 'All right. I don't know what I'm going to tell Mother.'

I allow myself a half-smile. 'I think you'll find that won't be an issue.'

Chapter Twenty-Nine

DECEMBER 27

11:00 Kelly

You know who your mates are, times like these.

When I finally turned up on Tina's doorstep in Dalston yesterday, I was not looking my best. I stank of petrol and smoke, and when I passed all the happy families out for their Boxing Day strolls, the mothers backed away from me, and the fathers squared up. I must have looked like the kind of woman who bites the heads off babies.

I asked twenty people before I got a nod in the right direction to find Tina – this is a girl who doesn't want to be found by anyone – and tracked her down to a narrow two-up-two-down, sandwiched between an MOT garage on one side, and a funeral director on the other.

The curtain upstairs twitched as I opened the squeaky gate. Glad I saw it, otherwise I'd have given up when no one answered. Dunno what I'd have done, maybe just slumped down on the tiles in that porch and tried to sleep there and then. But as it was, I just leaned on the doorbell until I heard the baby crying, and then Tina opened the door by a couple of centimetres.

'Kelly. Bugger me. I wasn't expecting you.'

And that was all she said. No questions about the way I looked. No complaints about me being the shittiest friend in the world for not even realising she'd left the Bush. She just showed me into the kitchen, made me beans on toast and a massive vodka and orange, and then poured me a bath with half a bottle of her kids' bubble bath thrown in. The water was so near boiling point that I had to lower myself in, bit by bit, and then she got a sponge and scrubbed my arms and my face until my skin was hot pink and the bubbles had gone a dirty grey.

Then we sat in her front room, Lewis on the PlayStation, and baby Milly – who isn't really a baby any more, but a chubby toddler – on her lap, and Tina nattered on about nothing at all. She said that the woman who does her nails also read her palm and told her she was about to meet the love of her life. She said Lewis was definitely the best-looking of all the angels in the school nativity play. She debated which colour to dye her hair.

And then it went dark and she got out the Luxury Selection chocolate biscuits her mum had bought her, and we ate our way through the whole top layer, except for the manky ginger ones I didn't want, and then we dipped into the bottom layer, feeling like naughty kids. Still she didn't ask me anything.

It was only after she got Lewis and Milly to bed (in Tina's room, so I could sleep in Lewis's), and came down to find me gawping at Mario on the screen in exactly the same position she'd left me forty minutes earlier, that she said, 'If you want to tell me anything, you know it goes no further. And if you want to forget it all, I've got some pills that'll help.'

'Pills?'

'Well, I've got some weed too, but the pills are better for knocking you out. Prescription. Nothing dodgy.'

And they worked. Except, of course, that I woke up twenty minutes ago after thirteen hours of dreamless sleep and it was all back, every fucking detail, and there's sooty snot and tears all over the pillow because the smoke's in me and it's going to keep on coming out. Only it's not just the smoke that's coming out. It's everything I've always been afraid of.

I guess I'm safe here for today. But maybe not. It was Charlie told me that Tina had moved out this way in the first place. Then again, what would he want with me? He won't be asking for another favour quite so soon, will he? And he's got what he wanted, for now. Sandie will have got the message, I'd have thought, and I kept my side of the bargain. OK, I turned up, but it didn't stop them, did it? I reckon his blokes enjoyed our little encounter, anyway. They're the kind who love their work, and setting light to stuff is so soulless without the personal touch . . .

Then there's Al. He made it out OK; I know that because I made Tina put the local telly news on yesterday and it'd have been on there if someone had died. But I don't think he's going to be talking to the police, or looking too hard for me. Not if he's got any sense.

But does he have any sense? Going into that building made no sense either. Or what he did inside.

He stuck up for me, as though I was someone worth sticking up for.

I have to do what I did before. Train myself to forget. I remember it was impossible at first, the flashbacks kept coming, but then if I really concentrated on something else I could make them stop, for a minute, two, then ten, then an hour. And then in the end it was almost like it had happened to someone else or I'd seen it once in a movie, and forgotten the ending.

On the bedside table, next to Lewis's alien alarm clock and his spaceman mug, there's another one of Tina's magic pills. I weigh up my options: stay awake and remember, or go back to sleep and forget. No contest. I swallow the pill with the stale water in the bottom of Lewis's mug, and I watch the glow stars on the ceiling until they merge into a single, shimmering night sky . . .

This time I don't ease back gently into the world.

This time, I'm dragged back into it, kicking and screaming, but it's not me that's screaming, it's Tina.

'No way, sunshine! No fucking way! If you're here, then you played some part in getting her in this mess, and you ain't . . . hang on, no, you can't do that, my kids are in there—'

'Kelly? Kelly! I need to talk to you, all right?'

When I realise it's Al I feel relieved, but it's just the drugs, it must be, because the truth is I know how to deal with the Charlie Flacks of this world, but not with the Als, the men who behave according to the rules.

I clamber out of the boy-sized bed, but my legs give way under me. 'I'm in here,' I call out, and I hear the lightest of footsteps coming up the stairs, and I'm back there, inside the apartment building, racing towards the penthouse . . .

He steps into the room and I gasp.

'Jesus, Al.'

His face is black and blue, and purple and red. And extremely swollen: if I hadn't heard his voice, I might not have recognised him. But it's funny: he looks younger now, and so vulnerable.

'They were professional. Took it as far as they needed to, but no further. Couple of teeth gone but nothing else broken, amazingly. Not that it feels like that.' His voice is rough but almost amused.

'We didn't stop them, though, did we?'

'No.' He pats the bed. 'Mind if I sit down? It's been tiring, looking for you. But then, where does a girl like you go? Your dad had no idea at all.'

'You saw my dad?' I imagine Al in our squalid flat, and the thought makes me blush. 'I'm amazed he even realised I'd gone.'

Al doesn't say anything, and I realise Dad probably hadn't even noticed.

'And they haven't gone after him?'

Al shakes his head. 'No. Why would they? They had their fun with us . . .'

Tina appears at the door. 'I tried to stop him. Do you want me to call the cops? Or my neighbour would be quicker, he always looks out for me.'

'It's OK. Really.'

Tina gives him a seriously dirty look, but then leaves.

'You know, Kelly, I was that close to telling the police everything.'

'But you haven't?'

'Not yet. I haven't told them anything yet. I'm claiming amnesia, which does tend to accompany near-death experiences, I find. Call me an old softie, but I wanted to hear what you had to say for yourself first.'

'Why?'

He shrugs. 'I've been asking myself that question on the way over here. I don't trust you, Kelly. I know you must have sorted those thugs out with access to the building, despite what Sandie's done for you. But then you called me. And then with what happened inside . . .'

I flinch. I can't help it. 'It wasn't about *those* guys.'

He looks at me so closely that I feel naked. 'I didn't think it was.'

'I don't talk about it.'

'Even though whatever it is still affects you.'

'Only when I'm being threatened by a bunch of thugs in ski-masks.'

He's still looking at me. 'Except, I'm not sure that's really true, Kelly, is it? I've got this hunch that whatever happened is with you pretty much all the time.'

I guess it's the effect of those pills of Tina's because I feel so raw, even though I know he's talking bollocks. I'm a survivor. It's the only way to be. So why am I feeling like it was only yesterday that I stumbled out of that derelict house in Shepherd's Bush, knowing I'd never feel the same about anything ever again?

'I wasn't raped if that's what you're thinking.'

He doesn't react. He waits.

'Dad turned up before that happened. So, there's nothing to make a fuss about, really.'

'Kelly, I'm not a shrink, but I did learn a bit about post traumatic stress while I was in the Army. Sometimes it was the guys who saw their mates injured who had the biggest trouble dealing with it. So the worst doesn't have to have happened for you to be affected by it.'

The worst . . . like being pulled off the street and into the dark, rancid smelling house and being certain there was no one coming for me; or when my eyes adjusted to the lack of light and I saw the brother of the bloke that my dad had fallen out with, in the way he always falls out with people in the end; or when the brother said my dad needed teaching a lesson and outlined in detail what they planned to do to me, and in what order; or when I asked why this would teach *Dad* a lesson, and got a kick in the stomach for speaking. Or was the worst thing the sound of young carol-singers at the door – it was *Hark! The Herald Angels Sing* –

until they walked away, assuming no one was in, while the men cut away my clothes with a penknife, keeping up a graphic running commentary about my body, comments that stick with me till this day. Or when the first bloke stripped off, egged on by the others, and began touching me . . .

Or maybe when I heard the banging and my father broke in, with his mates, and they saw me there, naked, exposed, more frightened than I've ever been in my life.

Or when they led me out, my father's coat wrapped around me, but my feet bare against the cold pavement, and the neighbours peering out from their fairy-lit windows and pointing, and me knowing that I'd been saved, but not feeling grateful at all. And knowing already that I'd never feel safe again.

I'm not going to cry in front of Al, no way. I try to drag myself back from then, to now. 'Are you going to tell the police? About me calling you?'

'I don't know. I'm struggling to make sense of the last thirty-six hours. Back in the day, I used to try to live my life by the idea of doing the least harm. Right now I don't know how to achieve that, though if you trust me and explain, I might have a better idea about what to do.'

'I've never been big on trust.'

'That must be tough. It's one of the things I miss most, now I'm divorced, knowing there was someone there to tell, to thrash stuff out with. Not that I did that often enough when I was married, of course.'

'Is that a tactic?'

He looks surprised. 'What?'

'Telling me you're divorced. Sharing something very personal in the hope I'll feel I can trust you enough to tell you stuff back.'

He smiles. 'I didn't do it on purpose. But I haven't reported you yet, have I? That's the one reason why you should think about trusting me. Whatever your reasons, it's a massive burden to carry alone.'

It's the weirdest thing – the pills again, gotta be – because when he says that, I realise that's exactly how it feels. Like I can't even stand up straight, because there's always this weight on my shoulders. Like I'm carrying the lot of them; my dad, the gang,

Charlie, Sandie, every last one of them, whispering in my ear: 'you can't fight the system, Kell', 'they don't know you like I do', 'your dad means more to you than some stuck-up bitch', 'I trust you, Kelly, I really do . . .'

I make myself look at Al, trying to suss him out. It's true that once he knew where I was, it would have been so much easier for him to tell the cops. The post-traumatic stuff is bullshit, of course, but he's here.

The suddenness of my decision surprises me.

'OK. Try this out. If you'd lived in the same place your whole life . . . if everyone knew you backwards, knew what you'd done, what you were . . . and if your mother and brother had fucked off to Australia so all you had left was your dad, who is the original loser, but once did the right thing, when it really mattered. And then the world outside your shithole of an area opens up, just a little bit, and then closes down because some fucking wannabe gangster says that you have to choose between your family or the employer who took a chance on you, and you want to make the right choice, to turn your back on everything that happened before, but you can't. You don't. And then you don't know how to live with yourself . . .'

Al nods slowly. 'If that was me, I'd be confused. Angry.'

'No shit, Sherlock.'

'I think . . . I'd try to look ahead, not back. Maybe think about counselling some day, but right now, with a decision that has to be made, I'd try to work out what the future holds. If my father had been . . . resistant to change all his life, then I might consider whether any action I took would make a difference. Or whether now might be the time to withdraw from that crusade.'

'Leave him to it?'

'Maybe. Then in the case of the gang, I happen to hold my greatest contempt not for thugs, but for the men who choose not to get their hands dirty. I think they're the ones who need bringing to book.'

'Report Charlie Flack to the police?'

He smiles. 'I thought we were talking hypothetically?'

Shit. I didn't mean to name him. 'Forget I said that, please. Forget that name.'

He looks at me steadily. 'Kelly, I know him. I know Charlie.'

I shake my head. Al and Charlie are from opposite worlds. 'How?'

'Same way I know Sandie. I met her when she worked for Charlie on the undercover shopping. So did I, even though I loathed the man. But I was just out of the Army, building a business. Sometimes you can't make the right choices all at once. Once I got more clients I could afford to drop him. Sandie played a big part in that, I'll always be grateful for the work she put my way.'

'Did he threaten you when you dropped him?'

'A bit. But one of the benefits of being a he-man who can't relate to women unless they're stark naked and airbrushed on the inside of my locker door is that there's not much in the way of leverage. No wife, no kids to threaten. I've never been all that scared by pain, I give as good as I get, and so eventually he gave up. The thing was, he's funny about women and I just had this suspicion that he'd come after Sandie. Which is why I kept an eye on you. It felt wrong, somehow, you being there. I had a hunch you weren't all you seemed.'

'That obvious a lowlife, huh?' For a moment I feel like telling him the rest: the shoplifting and the second chance Luis gave me.

But before I confess the lot, he shakes his head. 'Not a lowlife, but I knew you were in trouble. And you still are, aren't you?'

'Some things aren't fixable.'

'That's not true, Kelly.'

'Go on, then. What would you do?'

'I'd focus on finding a place where I could feel safe again.'

I nod towards the bedroom and the glow stars. 'Not Dalston, then?'

'Maybe it's not about a physical place. Maybe it's about time. Money. Friendship. I might even ask myself whether justice could offer closure.'

'Go to the police? Yeah, right. Because they kept me safe last time, didn't they?'

'One question, Kelly. The guys who did what they did to you. Do you think they've done it to others since?'

'You don't get it, do you? In my world, people have to look after themselves.'

He stands up. 'And you wonder why the police can't keep you safe?'

'Where are you going?'

Al looks sad. 'Don't worry. I'm not going to report you. It's not going to help anyone for my memory to come back, is it, least of all Sandie. I can't identify the thugs, anyway.'

'Thank you.'

'Doesn't mean they won't make the connection to you without my help, Kelly. Especially if you don't turn up to work again in the New Year. I won't do anything to point the finger, but it won't necessarily save you.' He heads towards the door.

'Not sure I deserve saving, do I?'

He stops. 'Actually, I wouldn't agree with you there, Kelly. But until you think you're worth saving yourself, then what the rest of the world thinks isn't going to count for anything. Good luck.'

And he walks out of the house. On the way out I hear him apologising to Tina for barging in, and wishing her a happy new year.

Chapter Thirty

DECEMBER 27

12:00 *Emily*

Maybe there are better things to do between Christmas and New Year than examine your three-year-old's body for new spots. But at least it takes my mind off a) my own symptoms, and b) the tension of waiting for Will to arrive home.

'Are you all itchy-scratchy again, Freddie? Shall I rub on magic cream?'

'It isn't magic. It came from the hospital.'

'Of course. Silly me. Do you want me to put the hospital cream on, then?'

He starts to wrestle off his T-shirt, as a yes, and I help pull it over his head. It's horrible to see his soft skin scattered with red spots, but he's being terribly good, now he's home. When Duncan delivered him back yesterday, father and son were bickering more like little brothers and, if anything, Freddie was the more mature of the two. Duncan's eyes were bloodshot and he didn't stop for tea after unloading the Fredster's many presents, most of them still wrapped up.

We didn't wave Duncan off. Instead I stripped Freddie off, played 'count the spots', and agreed that he'd get one extra-special treat for each one I counted. He'll be sorted for treats till Easter at this rate.

Then we sat on the sofa together, eating spaghetti hoops with a topping of grated cheese, watching *Wallace and Gromit* again, and then the Muppet Christmas movie, and in between we've been singing made-up songs about chicken pox. This morning he was a bit more crabby and tired, but still a hundred per cent better company than his father. We even played shop downstairs, and brought the goodies we'd 'bought' back to the sofa for a midday feast.

'Hello! Is there a chicken in the house?'

I didn't hear the car and now I try to read Will's mood from his voice. But that's hardly a reliable indicator – he knows there's a poorly little boy up here with me and he's too sweet to let our argument impact on Freddie.

'Will's home!' Freddie leaps up from the sofa and I hear the craziest giggles coming from the hallway.

When I come out, I see why. Will's cheeks are covered in red spots. In fact, I think I recognise the shade as Lady in Red, my favourite lipstick, the one I lost in the van . . .

Will sees me and smiles, briefly, before turning his attention to Freddie. 'Where have you hidden the chicken? You can't have chicken pox without the chicken.'

'Where's *your* chicken?' says Freddie, before collapsing into giggles again.

Will looks behind him, then slaps his forehead. 'I must have left it behind. Oh dear. Oh dear, dear, dear.'

He pulls his bag upstairs and Freddie follows at his heels, brighter than I've seen him since he came home.

In the living room, Freddie checks the bag, just to be sure that the chicken hasn't snuck inside unnoticed. I stand close to Will and whisper in his ear: 'Have you thought any more about us?'

'I haven't thought about anything else,' he says, but his tone is careful.

'And?'

'No chickens,' says Freddie, crestfallen.

'Have you looked in here?' Will unzips the inner compartment.

Freddie peers inside. 'No chicken. Lots of chocolate!'

The two of them scramble onto the sofa together, Freddie nattering on about all his presents, and I think that if Will had

314

decided to leave, then he wouldn't be here, and yet he's deliberately not looking at me. The more I try to attract his attention, the harder he resists, until it's like a game of cat and mouse.

Finally Freddie falls asleep mid-sentence and Will carries him to bed and then returns.

'So.'

'So,' he replies.

'If it's bad news, can you get it out of the way nice and quickly, please? It's less painful that way, like waxing your legs.'

'Oh, Em.'

The way he says it makes me feel less brave. 'Actually, Will, scrub that. I don't want you to say anything until I've finished talking. I have to tell you now that I know where I've been going wrong, and it's all about floats.'

'Floats?'

'Yes. And carnivals and princesses and being the centre of attention. I'm too demanding, I know I am, and I like to pretend that there's some fairy godmother who'll appear from nowhere and make everything all right.'

'Right.' Will is frowning.

'I know what I need to do.'

'What's that?'

'Become a hard-nosed realist. Um . . . stop daydreaming, start acting, be a team, er, get tough, like on *The Apprentice* or something, dog eat dog—'

'Oh, Emily.' Will's shaking his head. 'You're doing it again. It doesn't always have to be about extremes. You don't have to get yourself a huge great suit with shoulder pads and a titanium-coated briefcase. It's about the everyday things.'

'Like?'

'Like taking it day by day. Being cautious but listening, too. Responding. Learning to compromise.'

'Are you talking about the shop, or us?'

'Both. Look, I know I've been guilty too, in some ways. I've wanted to protect you, which is why I used to keep the figures from you. But I realised while I was away that I was doing exactly the same as Duncan did, and your parents before him. You have this childlike quality, Em, that means people want to make sure it's all happy ever after all the time.'

'Exactly! That's why I need to grow up.'

'It cuts both ways, though. I love you because of that dreaminess. It's very attractive . . .'

My heart suddenly feels like a helium balloon. He loves me!

'. . . but it's also dangerous. It means you're down there playing shop, while I'm struggling alone with the bills. And then I get angry with you and myself, especially when you start on about babies and I know we don't have the money to pay the VAT bill, never mind bring a new person into the world.'

He loves me *not*?

'I've changed my mind again, Will. Please just get to the point where you say whether you want to split up or stay together.'

He looks at me. 'I want to make this work, but for that to happen, we both have to grow up a bit. Not so much that we turn boring, or lose the people we were when we fell for each other. But enough to stand on our own feet. And that also means standing up to Duncan.'

I love the *idea* of standing up to that pig of an ex, but the thought makes me feel a bit wobbly. 'In what way?'

'We need to stop relying on his money. Tell him where to stick it.'

'But we need that money.'

'Well, we shouldn't need it, should we? How do you think I feel, knowing I'm relying on that loathsome blackmailer to keep afloat? We have to pull away, even if it means losing the shop. In any case, he's going to stop paying us soon, whether we like it or not.'

I know Will's right: even yesterday, Duncan was dropping more hints about Teddygate and about how few jobs there were out there. And I don't think Heidi's about to rescue him: apparently she's staying put in the land of cuckoo clocks and fondue.

'Can we cope without him?'

He hesitates. 'You know, I had to stop myself then. I was about to tell you that it would all be OK, that we'd manage. But I can't promise that, can I?'

'No.'

'But I can say that if we're realistic and we work our hardest and we're honest with each other, then we stand as good a chance as anyone else.'

I bite my lip. I want to hear fairy stories, with that guaranteed happy ending. It's a hard habit to break, but break it I must.

'Is it too early to drink to that?'

14.00 Sandie

This hotel room is way too small for two people who want to avoid each other.

If Toby would stay in the bathroom, it would be just about OK. There's even a TV in there, and a phone. The insurance company have been very good about it all, paying for the hotel while we look for a flat, but London hotel rooms are barely big enough to swing a gerbil. I keep thinking I should just check out of here, of London, of our relationship. Head back up to Gramma's. But then there's still the small matter of the baby . . .

We did go to the hospital together, and the doctor said I probably had had chicken pox as a tiny child and everyone had forgotten, but he gave me anti-virals, so the risk would be minimal. But the scare switched on instincts I never believed I possessed. Toby didn't respond at all. He sat and stared at the casualty doctor, as though the man was speaking a foreign language.

In fact, he's barely said a word since then, beyond mumbling to the receptionist when we checked in here, and mumbling on the phone to the loss adjuster. Monty's had to go into kennels, which has upset him even more. Toby went to breakfast on his own, and I waited till he got back before I went myself, even though I'm still ravenous all the time (thank God for the twin-packs of biscuits that come with the complimentary tea and coffee).

I know that below the surface calm, he's beyond angry. I can see it in his eyes, when we accidentally look at each other. Now he's sitting at the desk making notes, lists, scribbling with a ferocity that fills the room with a scratchy sound of pen scoring through paper.

I need to be patient with him. After all, it's taken me six weeks to get used to the idea of being a mother, and he doesn't even have the choice about whether he wants to become a father, not now my hormones have kicked in and made up my mind for me.

He stands up, shuffles his paperwork into his briefcase, and puts on his coat.

'At least tell me where you're going, Toby.'

'The shop. It's sale day,' he says, still not looking at me. We used to spend the first day of the sales together, when we were at Garnett's. The best times. He slams the door behind him.

I sit back down on the bed and pick up a glossy magazine. I flick through the pages, taking nothing in. Every now and then it hits me that I've lost everything but the clothes I stand up in, and a few things I packed for the Christmas stopover at Bambourne Manor. My books, my business, and probably my relationship too. Maybe I can be forgiven for finding it hard to concentrate on the latest boutique ski resort, or the New Year's resolutions of society hostesses.

The phone rings. 'Hello?'

'Sandra? It's Laetitia Garnett. I want to come up and talk to you.'

The shock of hearing her acid-dipped voice makes me wince. 'What about?'

'Come, come. Don't be disingenuous.'

'Toby's not here.'

'I know. I just saw him leave.'

I don't want her near me. 'Look, I have nothing to say to you.' I put the phone down but within seconds there's a sharp knock at the door. I consider ignoring it.

'Sandra, open up. Let's be adult about this. The sooner you let me in, the sooner we can deal with this.'

She's not going anywhere. I check myself in the mirror – the best that can be said is that I look neat – and go to the door. She's immaculately dressed in a baby blue cashmere sweater and grey trousers. And she's not alone: behind her, there's a middle-aged man with the professionally depressed look of a funeral director.

She pushes past me, into the room.

'This is Arnold Noakes, our family solicitor,' she says, immediately sitting down on the one decent chair.

Mr Noakes nods at me, and follows her in. I perch on the edge of the bed: I'd prefer to stand up, but I feel unsteady. There's nowhere for Mr Noakes to go unless he joins me on the bed, and I'm guessing that might compromise his integrity.

'If you've brought a lawyer, shouldn't I have legal representation too?' Mr Noakes looks shifty, but Mrs G. glances at me for the first time.

'I wouldn't waste your money. The situation is quite clear.'

'Is it? I'd love to know what the situation is.' I force confidence into my voice. Confidence I am definitely not feeling.

'We simply want to explain what our position is,' says Mrs G. Her make-up is soft and subtle, just on the right side of wan. 'If you insist on having this baby then you need to realise that the child will not be part of the Garnett family. Nor will you. Dynasties like ours have had to protect ourselves from unwelcome gold-diggers over the years, and you will be no exception.'

'Does Toby have any say in this?'

'He's been emotionally hijacked, and he's not in any position to make a rational decision. Which is why I waited till he'd gone to discuss this with you.'

Mr Noakes is studying the retro-style swirled carpet.

'Don't you feel anything for your future grandchild?'

Mrs G. looks momentarily stumped, then disgusted. 'How am I supposed to feel? Every mother dreams of grandchildren, of the moment when she learns that the antique lace christening robe she mothballed all those years ago is ready to be brought out again.'

Is that really what grandmothers dream of? She really is the most extraordinarily mad person. But that means there's no telling what she might do.

'And to learn that the first grandchild is not just illegitimate but has been forced upon my only son, in such cynical circumstances . . . well, is it any wonder that I feel so distraught?'

I think about telling her it's not all about her, but decide it would be pointless. 'Why are you here?'

'To explain the situation. Arnold, take notes.' The man gets out his notebook and a small recording device. 'If you do intend to go through with the pregnancy, then we will not be in a position to offer financial assistance until we have proof that Toby is the baby's father, for obvious reasons.'

I shake my head. 'You're crazy.'

'I wouldn't expect you to understand the importance of maintaining the honour and bloodline of an influential family, Sandra. However, in the event that you are able to supply the appropriate evidence of a biological link, then the estate will, of course, pay the statutory maintenance required.'

'How generous,' I say.

'However, we may be in a position to increase that, in return for a concession from you, regarding inheritance.'

'Meaning?'

'Meaning that if you were willing to leave the birth certificate blank where the father's name is supposed to be, and were then willing to negotiate a final settlement that effectively renounces future inheritance rights, we would be in a position to make life extremely comfortable for you and the child. In a one-off payment.'

I stare at her. 'So, effectively, you'd want me to sign away the baby's right to say he or she's related to the Garnett clan, in return for money. Can you even do that?' I look at the solicitor.

'It's an entirely mutual agreement,' he says. 'There's no compulsion involved. Though you would be advised to seek legal advice yourself at the time.'

I want to lie down on the bed and be left alone. 'I need time to think.'

Arnold looks at Mrs G., who nods. 'Till tomorrow. No longer,' she says, and stands up. 'Arnold, give her the paperwork.'

I take the sheaf of papers. 'One question. What does Toby know about this?'

'The basics. He felt it would be uncomfortable to be here while this conversation took place, but he's fully aware of the implications.'

The dirty rotten *coward*. How could he? I might as well sign this now, if he's prepared to let me face his mother's threats alone. Yes. Me and junior are better off without him.

I see her to the door and into the corridor. 'I'll call you.'

She scowls. 'Oh. Talk to Arnold. He's paid to do the dirty work, aren't you?'

'Mums?'

We all look round at once. Toby has stepped out of the lift and is heading towards us.

'Come to hear my decision, have you?' I say. 'Well, you'll be pleased to know that I don't want anything to do with you, or your family.'

He shakes his head. 'What's going on?'

'You know, I always thought you were a cut above your spineless public schoolmates, Toby.'

His mother looks awkward. 'Gannet, ignore the woman. She's quite unhinged. She demanded a meeting, then wanted money out of me to go quietly. Can you believe it? Money, in return for getting rid of your bastard child.'

I stare at her, and at Toby. Then I realise. 'He doesn't know anything about this, does he?'

'I wish someone would tell me what's happening,' he says, and I thrust Arnold's paperwork at him.

'Read this. They want me to sign away any connection between the baby and the Garnett name.'

He begins to scan the document.

'Gannet, it's just a piece of paper. An excellent deal. If Sandie was careless with contraception, and rejects the most sensible option of a termination, then your life shouldn't be blighted, should it? Imagine having to spend time with her awful family instead of marrying the right kind of girl, with a similar background. This is your second chance.'

I wait for him to answer but he just keeps reading. In a strange way, maybe this is what needed to happen. If he believes that a baby will blight his life, then I'd do better to take the money and run. Perhaps it works both ways. Perhaps my child deserves a better father than this one.

Without thinking, I place my hand on my stomach, as though

the grape-sized being in there can give me a sign. At that moment, Toby turns around. He sees the gesture, but so does his mother.

'Oh, see what she's like,' she hisses. 'Playing with your emotions by pretending to feel the baby kicking. Which is ridiculous. At her stage, the foetus is no bigger than your thumbnail, incredibly easy to get rid of, of course, and certainly not capable of making its bastard presence felt. All this fuss over a bundle of cells.'

I almost feel sorry for her now. How can anyone live with all that bitterness inside them? 'It's OK, I wouldn't want to be part of a family that has you at the head of it. I'll sign it. But now I'm going home.'

I feel utterly calm as I walk back into the room, take the overnight bag from the wardrobe, and drag it into the bathroom. I fill my toilet bag, put it into the case, and then pull on my coat. I don't look back. I don't feel anything except relief at no longer sharing oxygen with that *witch*.

I step outside. An aproned woman is pulling her vacuum cleaner towards our room. She doesn't even seem to notice the odd little drama playing out on the landing.

Toby is being harangued by his mother. 'Gannet, you're just overwrought thanks to that silly girl. No, I will not leave. Not without you apologising for what you just said. Mr Noakes, you're my witness, I am not happy . . .'

I walk towards the lift.

'Sandie, stop.'

The lift door opens and there's a woman with a briefcase inside. She tuts at me. 'Are you coming or not?'

Before I can answer, Toby's at my side. 'Not,' he says, 'but these two are. Mother. Get in.'

The woman in the lift starts jabbing at the door close button, but Toby puts his shoe in the gap to keep the lift on our floor.

'I'll call security,' she threatens.

'No need,' says Toby. 'You don't want a scene, do you, Mother?'

'Really, Gannet, you're being very childish.'

'You want childish? OK, Mums. How's this then? You're the

gold-digger. Aren't you? You're the one who knows all about that, aren't you? Takes one to know one!' he shouts, and Mrs G. scurries towards the lift, with Mr Noakes in tow.

'I really am most dreadfully sorry,' she says to the woman in the lift. 'It's that terrible girl. I brought him up to have such lovely manners and all it's taken is . . .'

The lift doors close.

'Sandie?'

I look at him. 'What?'

'I can't believe this. My mother is crazy.'

'Yes, she is, isn't she?' I still feel peculiarly calm. Is this the hormones too?

'Come back to the room, please. We need to talk.'

'Actually, I think it's better if I give you time to yourself. Your mother's right about one thing. You're confused. It took me ages to get used to the idea, and I can't expect you to be any different. Ring me when you know what you want.'

I press the lift call button again.

'But I do know what I want,' he says, and his voice is quiet but determined. 'I have my mad mother to thank for that, but I know now.'

My calmness falters, a little. 'Which is?'

'Which is you.'

'And a baby?'

He smiles a nervous smile. 'I wouldn't say it was top of my Christmas list. It's going to take me a while, perhaps, to get used to the idea. But I want to get used to the idea, Brains, and that's what matters most, isn't it?'

He reaches out to touch my stomach.

'There's nothing to feel yet,' I say.

'I knew there was a little bit more of you, though, didn't I?' He kisses me, tentatively, on the cheek. 'And more of you can only be a good thing.'

323

16:09 *Kelly*

I still haven't told Tina what I'm planning, but I know she thinks I'm on the edge of losing it totally.

'You don't want to do anything hasty, Kell. Whatever that guy said to you, you don't need to listen.'

But I did listen to Al, and his words whirl round my head like rubbish down a windy alleyway. I have to get away from London, from everything I don't want to remember. The seaside, maybe. Or abroad. Abroad could be good.

Dad hasn't called me but I texted him to say I was OK and he texted back to say the same so at least I know Charlie's men haven't got him. And even though I jump every time the doorbell goes, the police haven't come after me yet about the fire.

Even so, I don't like to go out until it's dark, and by dusk each day I feel like I can't breathe unless I get out of my hiding place. How long can I go on like this? Tina hasn't once hinted that I'm not welcome, but it's a tiny house and I wouldn't want someone moping around it the way I am. Plus the kids will tire of camping in their mum's room before long.

'Just off round the block,' I call to Tina, but she's in the middle of playing pat-a-cake with Milly, so she doesn't answer.

Outside it's drizzling, and the temperature's falling, so perhaps this is the closest we're going to get to a white Christmas. There's no one else about. No one else stupid enough to take to the ugly streets of Dalston on a night like this.

Except ahead, I see that I'm not alone. There's a gang of kids, on bikes, as desperate to escape the dire festive entertainment as I am. They do wheelies and figures-of-eight in the glow of the street lamp, until they spot me. One of them shouts out – I can't hear what he says, but they're all looking now, and then they begin to move towards me.

I freeze. Not on purpose, but because my muscles simply refuse to work, even my eyes won't move and are fixed on these kids. Five, no, six of them, and they're cycling this way, very slowly. But they don't need to hurry, because I am going nowhere.

324

The terror churns inside me, as though someone has gripped my internal organs and is squeezing with all their strength.

The boys are next to me now. Closing in. All I can think is that this will be over, sometime, all I have to do is switch off, forget who I am, that I'm here . . .

They keep cycling. Simple as that. When I recover the use of my muscles I turn, slowly, and see them properly as they drift away.

And that's when I realise they're no older than seven or eight . . . If they jumped off their bikes, they wouldn't even reach my shoulder.

I walk in the opposite direction, my legs as tight and sore as if I'd been stock-still for hours, not seconds. There's a bus stop ahead, with a bench, and I sit on the plastic ledge, knowing I no longer have a choice. I could go to Brighton or Blackpool or fucking Timbuktu and I'd still be a hundred per cent fucked by my past. Some things you can't escape.

The number's already in my mobile. I hesitate for a few more seconds, then press dial. I hear half a ring before Al picks up.

'Kelly. Are you OK?'

'Yes . . . no. Not really. But I've made a decision.'

There's a pause. 'About the police?'

'I think so. If you come with me.'

'I'll be there in twenty.'

And after he rings off, I practise the words in a whisper: 'I want to report a crime.'

New Year's Eve:
Shopping Days to Christmas: 359

So. You survived. Older and wiser? Richer or poorer? Enjoy your
night off but remember, when the going gets tough, the tough go
shopping. Make sure they're shopping in your store, and you
might just survive to see another Christmas.

Chapter Thirty-One

DECEMBER 31

19.00 Grazia

I am dressed to the nines, but when I step into the Sanderson bar to meet Nigel, I do not feel confidence. I feel dread.

I see him before he sees me. He sits on a high white stool, and that body I know so well is a tiny bit hunched around his glass of champagne, like a small boy trying to make sure no one sees what he's drawing.

I tap him on the shoulder.

He jumps a little, and turns. His silvery eyes widen as he takes me in, from my high gold stilettos to my clingy scarlet dress and the matching lipstick. 'Wow, Grazia.'

'Wow, Nigel,' I say, and I mean it – that grey suit fits his body better than a wetsuit could. Which makes this moment even tougher.

He moves a bar stool out and I sit down. 'So tell me who is going to be here tonight?' he asks.

'People I have not seen for . . . a while.' I mean, since Leon died. This is my first outing with the old crowd, and what seemed like an inspired idea when the invitation arrived now seems foolhardy in the extreme. The invitation came from the professionally anorexic Selina, who organised the auction of Leon's paintings for me two years ago, and thereby helped me become financially my own woman, for the first time in my life. She had attached a Post-It to the invite: *Surely you have a man by now, my darling? Time for a public view, I am sure.*

'It'll be great to meet your friends,' he says, getting a glass and pouring me champagne, before toasting.

I sip my drink, and I think. Are they my friends? They are mainly the wealthy hangers-on, grabbing the coat-tails of talented artists, the kind of people Leon loathed. Even Selina is no real friend: she sold the paintings for commission, not to help me.

'They are more acquaintances.' I put down my glass and launch into the announcement I prepared earlier. 'In fact, Nigel, I don't think you should come with me. It has been fun, certainly, but it is time for you to find someone your own age. And this is possibly the best night of the year for that. Especially looking as you do tonight.'

He stares at me.

Perhaps my little speech was too brutal. It sounded better at home. Less of a brush-off, more of a valiant letting go.

'Are you dumping me? On New Year's Eve?'

'No.'

'It sounds like you are.'

I shake my head. 'This is not about me, Nigel. It is all about being fair to you. You deserve a girl of your own age, and with the best will in the world, I will never be that.'

'I'm catching you up,' he says, sounding more upset than I had anticipated. 'I'll be thirty next year and you'll be thirty-seven . . .'

I shake my head slowly. 'No, Nigel. I am forty-five. And next year I will be forty-six.'

I close my eyes now, because I do not want to see his reaction to the truth.

'I know, Grazia.'

My eyes pop open again. 'You know? How could you know?'

He shrugs. 'Google?'

'You went online to check up on me?'

'No, no, it wasn't like that. Not at all. But you've been acting like this woman of mystery for so long. You won't even let me come to your flat.

'Do *not* change the subject. You have been snooping about my age, making a fool of me.'

He sighs. 'I've never thought you're a fool. It wouldn't matter to me if you were sixty-five.'

I raise an eyebrow, or at least as far as the Botox allows me to.

'OK. Maybe sixty-five would be taking it a bit too far. But forty-five is nothing.'

'I cannot have children, Nigel.'

He shrugs. 'And?'

'You think it does not matter now, but it will. Believe me. I have met your family. I know that you will want your own kids one day.'

He shakes his head. 'One day? I don't plan my life on what ifs, but on how I feel. And what I know is that I want to be with you. You're beautiful with or without a few fine lines, Grazia. I know it's a cliché, but it's more than skin deep.'

I feel affronted on Dr Target's behalf. 'A line? Show me a line!'

'You don't have any.'

'No! I do not have any. But my face will not stay that way for ever, while yours will improve with age. It is one of the many injustices in life, but I have decided not to fight it any more.'

'You've lost me now.'

'This,' I pull at my cheek, 'is not natural. Nor are these lips or the smooth forehead. I am a fake.'

He leans forward just a touch to inspect me. He cannot help himself. 'You've had work done on your face? When?'

'Just after I met you.'

'Why?'

'Why do you think?' I look away. 'A one-off. I will not do it again, but that is my point, Nigel. I am ageing. It is normal. Perhaps if one is with a man who knew you as a young woman, then the process is bearable. But you have nothing to remember my beauty by.'

'You're talking rubbish.'

'No. No, I am not. I want to reach a stage where I can be proud of my wrinkles, to glorify in the experience that has produced them. But I am not there yet and I do not want you to witness my face's descent.'

And then he does something quite unexpected. He leans forward and places his hand on my forehead.

He shakes his head. 'I was just checking.'

'On my wrinkles?'

'On your temperature, because I am convinced you must have swine flu, Grazia. Either that, or some temporary insanity brought on by the festive period.'

'No, I am totally serious . . .' And I am. I cannot give him what he needs.

'Will you listen to *me* for once? I know you're older but it doesn't mean you're wiser.'

'The cheek!'

But he is smiling. 'I had to find some way of shutting you up, for however long. Let me finish. Please.'

I nod.

'Maybe at fifteen and thirty it would have mattered, Grazia.'

Is he trying to make me feel worse? But I stay silent.

'But what I see sitting opposite me now is a woman more beautiful than I could have wished for.'

'Nigel—'

'Be *quiet*! Honestly, the one thing that I would change about you is your tendency to interrupt me. *Like my mother does.*'

Ow. 'Sorry.'

'Neither of us can see the future, Grazia. I don't want a crystal ball or a palm-reader to guess if you'll end up with liver spots or I'll end up with gout. Even if you don't end up with me, you have to kick this habit of writing things off before they start. It's no way to live.'

'You have finished?'

'Mmm.'

'Maybe when you have more experience you will understand that things are not so simple.'

He gets off his bar stool. 'Right. You know, it's not me with the problem about age. It's you.'

'Are you going?' I ask.

'I don't know.' He paces on the spot. A few people are looking. 'Do you really want me to?'

I do not answer. He shrugs. 'That's clear then,' he says. He puts down cash for the champagne and walks out of the bar.

Fine. Good. That is what I had planned. He took it fairly well,

I think. So much easier to go to this party on my own, no behind-my-back-whispers or tricky explanations. Simply me and the old gang.

Why am I feeling nauseous?

My mobile phone buzzes with a message. As I look at the screen, I realise I am hoping it might be Nigel. How ridiculous. In fact, I can still see him through the thin gauze curtain on the street outside, trying to hail a cab, never an easy task on December the thirty-first. I am sure he has a better party to go to. Somewhere more age-appropriate . . . I turn my back on him, to read the text.

The message is from Emily, sent to me and to Sandie:

I WANT YOUR NEW YEAR RESOLUTIONS BEFORE MIDNIGHT, GIRLS. AND I WILL HOLD YOU TO THEM NEXT YEAR! LOVE EM XXX

I do not do resolutions. Life is too random, too unpredictable to pretend that one can influence the way life goes. And what could I do anyway? Look where one single *resolution* to have sex again has landed me. Alone at a bar on New Year's Eve.

I turn back and watch as, in slow motion, a cab finally answers Nigel's call. It pulls up by the icy pavement.

'Grazia! Darling?' I follow the voice to see Selina walking towards me. She is even more frozen-of-face than the last time I saw her, and as she approaches I see her examining my features to see whether I have joined her 'club'.

I peer through the gauze again and Nigel turns back and looks at me. He is right. Age is my hang-up, not his.

I look at Selina.

Then I run, tripping over my umbrella. I leave it there. I can buy another umbrella.

I cannot buy another Nigel.

I reach the cab and find him holding the door open for me.

'Where to, Grazia?'

'My place,' I say, and give the address to the driver. 'I am sorry.'

'Apology accepted, on one condition.'

'What?'

'That you get through tonight without mentioning your age, or mine.'

I smile. 'It will be a challenge. I will need help.'

'I can certainly remind you. Or we could set up a system of fines, like a swear box?'

'I had something more direct in mind,' I say, leaning forward to kiss him.

Now I feel like a teenager, 'snogging' in the back of a taxi. I can think of no better way to stop myself thinking about the march of time.

20:30 Emily

Is it possible to burst with happiness?

I am having the scabbiest of New Year's Eves. I *did* have chicken pox, after all, though mine is a day or so behind Freddie's, so he is proudly showing off the first signs of his recovery, while I scratch and squirm and mourn the temporary loss of my smooth skin.

And yet, I'm happy. It takes a near-miss to make you thankful for what you have and I am seriously, ecstatically thankful.

'More calamine?' Will approaches with a tube of lotion in one hand and a bottle in the other. 'Or more champagne?'

'Both, please?'

He fills my glass then lifts my T-shirt to rub the lotion into the marks on my back, as tenderly as I soothed Freddie's. There is no better man on this planet than Will (with the possible exception of my dad). Which must mean that for all of my silly tendencies, I have done some good things in this life to deserve him.

Or maybe he's my reward for putting up with Duncan for so long. Though I've definitely burned my bridges with my ex now. Once we'd decided we could cope without him and his money, I was all for driving down to Somerset for a massive showdown, but then my first poxy spot appeared and Will vetoed it. Which forced me to be more . . . imaginative.

OK. So the courier cost a few quid, but it was worth it. I

332

retrieved the pieces of Satanic teddy from the bin and packaged them up neatly into a parcel, along with a label marked 'Open on delivery to confirm contents received safely' and a note inside that didn't mince words.

THIS IS YOURS, YOU SNOOPING BASTARD. AND YOU CAN PAY YOUR WAY WITH FREDDIE, NO MORE, NO LESS. IT'S CALLED BEING FAIR. HAPPY NEW YEAR.

When the courier called to confirm delivery, I asked him to describe Duncan's reaction when he opened it.

'He kind of did this dance on the spot.'

'A happy dance?'

'Nah. More like . . . you know that bloke from *Faulty Towers*? Like that. Only worse.'

It won't be easy, I know that much. Will's going to take me through the figures once I've stopped itching, and I'm not looking forward to the truth. But I've spent too long going 'la-la-la' with my fingers in my ears. And we *did* make a profit in the run-up to Christmas, and I've had this brilliant idea of taking over the empty chemist next door and turning it into a kind of craft centre for the newly impoverished, where we'll teach budget cookery and mending and dressmaking. We could even have a knitting masterclass with Jean.

Will has even bigger plans: he wants to set up a local bank and our own currency, the Heartsease Pound, which we could use for bartering and services in the area, and could attract all sorts of publicity and grants.

Really. We could be the new Richard Briers and Felicity Kendal. Except, actually, I quite like us being the old Emily Cheney and Will Powell.

'How's that?' says Will, putting his finger on a particularly irritating spot and massaging it so expertly that it stops itching.

'Absolutely perfect.'

I'm not, generally, an emotional person. But the last few days have been awash with bucketfuls of feelings.

Like when we left the hotel, after the scene with Mrs Garnett, and sprung Monty from kennels, and both the dog and Toby were so thrilled to be reunited that I had more than one tear in my eye.

And then there was the moment when Emily texted me to remind me to watch her final grotto assignment, and I uploaded the back-up copy and did a double take when I realised that Toby was standing in as Santa all the time I'd assumed he was pissing it up with the rest of the board. I saw how tenderly he spoke to Freddie in the footage and I felt ashamed that I could have doubted his potential as a daddy.

And, most emotional of all, was the moment when we both drove up to Birmingham to see Gramma.

She took the news of the baby stoically.

'I presume you'll get married?' she said, ever direct.

Toby and I looked at each other. In fact, he'd already suggested it and I'd said no. Not no never, but no, let's see. Apart from anything else, I have quite enough on my plate dealing with the aftermath of everything we own going up in flames, without trying to organise a wedding.

Though the practical aspects of the fire seem trivial compared to what we've learned since about *why*. Al called when he got out of hospital and asked to meet, though I took Toby with me because I couldn't get my head around Al having been involved in the fire somehow.

And then Kelly was there too, looking more waiflike than ever, and the way they sat so close to each other in the nondescript café, I assumed at first they were a *couple*, and that perhaps they'd wanted to tell us face to face. Until she started speaking . . .

As we listened, Toby put his hand on mine, obviously expecting me to get angry. But there was no rumble from my inner grizzly bear. Maybe it's the pregnancy hormones. Or maybe I knew from her face that no one would judge her more harshly than she judges herself.

Not that I'm having her back. Gramma always says 'To err is human, Sandra, but to forgive is divine', but none of the Barrow women do forgiveness all that well.

I won't forgive Mrs G., either. Not just a monster but a hypocrite too. When she met Mr G., she was poorer than I am, approaching the end of an unspectacular career as a chorus girl in musical comedy. *The Retail Prince and the Showgirl* . . .

I might not be able to forgive her, but she has to stay a part of my life, as the baby's grandmother. I'm trying not to think about that right now. Tomorrow is, after all, another year.

'Hey, honey? You're managing to stay awake till the bongs, then?' Marnie is here staying at Gramma's until she's worked out what her next move will be.

'Just about.'

'So next year I'm gonna be a grandma, huh?' She shakes her head. 'But I'm still just a child myself. That's not going to help me find a man.'

'Don't have to tell them,' I say. 'They'll never find out in Jamaica.'

She takes a swig of port. 'I'm not going back, Sandie. Not running away this time.'

I stare. 'You sure?'

'Time I stopped pissing about. I have responsibilities now, huh? We are going to be a grandmother.'

She reaches out to hug me and I don't feel awkward, though I do feel short of breath after a while.

'There's something else, too. I can't promise anything, but if you want me to, I can make some inquiries about . . .' she hesitates, 'about your father.'

I don't move, or speak.

'You see, Sandie, I know exactly who he is. I told Ma I didn't because . . . well, it was easier. He's not what you'd call a pillar of society and I knew as soon as it happened that he'd have been no use to you whatsoever. It's why I left the island before anyone could find out. But we've all changed. Hell, I'm gonna be a granny. Maybe he's changed, too . . .'

I still don't say anything. *Too many surprises.* I hate surprises.

She looks anxious. 'Sorry. I screwed up again, didn't I? Now is not the time. But think about it.'

Toby is here now. He has a sixth sense for knowing when to rescue me. Now he's used to the idea of being a dad-to-be, he's going for it in a big way. He'd have bought the whole of Garnett's toy and baby department already if I hadn't pointed out that a) it's bad luck and b) we don't actually have anywhere to put it.

'How are you doing, mother of my heir?' he whispers.

'Good. Looking forward to the new year, and a bit of peace and quiet.'

He reaches forward, to touch my tummy. There is definitely a bump beginning to appear now, and his hand on there feels comfortable. He speaks into my belly button. 'Peace and quiet. You hear that, baby?' Then he sits up, kisses me. 'Do you have a resolution this year, Brains?'

I remember Emily's text. She'll never forgive me if I don't reply.

'Still working on it. Pass me the phone, would you, Toby?'

'Your wish is my command.'

23:59 *Kelly*

In Trafalgar Square the lions look like they're shitting themselves. Despite the netting and the coppers and the cold, there are hundreds of people who want to take an early bath in the fountains.

I shiver at the thought of it. I don't know what I'm doing here, really. I'm Kelly Louise Wright, I fucking hate happy people. I hate celebrations. I hate the singing and the big gangs of mates. And I especially hate that bloody great tree from Norway, with all the lights on it. Can't they take it down? Christmas is over and done with.

Oh, and I hate London, too. First chance I get, I'm out of here. Trouble is, where do I go? Not Australia, that's for sure. Don't think I could handle all the sunshine and the nasty weak beer and the g'days.

Besides, I can't leave, not till the coppers have finished investigating. I hadn't expected them to take me seriously, to be honest, but they did the whole thing with the soft sofa and the smiling lady officer. Still not convinced they'll get anywhere, not now. But what surprised me more than them listening was how I felt after they listened.

Lighter.

'Here we are. Just the thing to warm us up.' Al has worked his way through the party-goers without spilling the two hot chocolates. Is that what they teach in the Army – advanced drink carrying? Crowd navigation? Whatever it is, it's nice to see his familiar, mellow face, among so many strangers.

'Thanks.' I clutch the paper cup, and my frozen hands begin to thaw. I don't have gloves. I don't have much. I haven't been home – or any further west than here – since the fire. When Al offered to put me up, I thought he wanted to get into my knickers, even though at the same time, I couldn't see why anyone would want to.

Anyway, it's all above board. He has a renovated ex-council place over near Vauxhall, and I've got my own room, and he's given me a shelf for bathroom stuff, though of course I haven't got anything except a new toothbrush to put there, and he says I can stay as long as I like, until I decide what to do.

I asked him why, that first night.

'Because I've seen where you came from, Kelly, and now I think I understand you.'

He's barking. I told him so. No one understands me, they wouldn't want to. But when he said that I felt nice. Like maybe I was a person who had something going for her.

The countdown's beginning now, and the crowd are shouting out the numbers all the way from sixty. They're hugging and snogging and crying and laughing. Suckers. Like this minute means anything different from the minute before or the minute afterwards.

So I don't know why I feel jealous of them. Or why I feel warm again when Al takes my hand as they're counting thirty-two, thirty-one, thirty, or why by twenty-five I'm beginning to think it would be nicer still if he'd put his arm around me, or why by twelve-eleven-ten-nine-eight I've realised that actually he's bloody good looking and there's nothing I'd like more right now than a New Year's kiss.

Even though, you know, I don't rate kissing, generally.

Six

Five

Four

Three

Two

One

And as everyone else cheers and as the fireworks go off and turn the sky psychedelic, I turn to him and I tilt my face a bit, like they do in films, which always makes the hero go in for the kill.

And he does tilt his head down towards mine . . .

And kisses me on the cheek.

The sodding cheek!

But, what's even weirder, is that that kiss on the cheek is about the loveliest thing that anyone's done to me for years. Literally years. There's something in his dark eyes, the eyes that I know have seen all sorts you wouldn't want to see, just like mine have, that says *no hurry*.

And I realise that maybe I was wrong about that minute being the same as every other. Because for the first time in I don't know how long, I feel I've got something to look forward to. However long it takes.

00:37 Emily

The mobile wakes me. I'm lying on the sofa, my head in Will's lap, and he's stroking my hair. I turn his wrist and look at his watch.

'I missed midnight! I missed the bongs!'

'I couldn't bring myself to wake you,' he says, 'though to be honest I'm glad you've woken up now. I'm getting cramp.'

I shift myself to upright, feeling pissed off. I wanted to welcome in this year, to make my resolutions. The phone's on the table and I pick it up: the texts have all come though at once, later than they were sent. There's the usual from Mum and Dad, my sister, the old gang down in Somerset, but I'm not looking for them . . .

Here we are.

I RESOLVE TO COME OUT OF MY DEEP FREEZE, EMBRACE MY TOYBOY AND NEVER TOUCH BOTOX AGAIN. FELICE ANNO NUOVO, GRAZIA X

Fabulous. I was worried I'd never get to meet the wonderful Nigel.

I scroll down again.

MY RESOLUTION IS TO DO MY LEVEL BEST TO LIKE MY FAMILY, TO TOLERATE TOBY'S FAMILY, TO COOK A LOVELY BABY, AND TO CHERISH MY FRIENDS. SANDIE X

I show the messages to Will and he smiles. 'What about you, Em?'

I pretend to think about it, though of course I've spent hours deciding what my resolution should be.

'This year, I'm going to stop expecting my life to be a fairy-tale. But I'm never giving up on miracles.'

'Very Emily,' Will says. 'And very lovely, too.'

'What are you looking forward to this year, Will?' I ask.

'Health and happiness, obviously,' he says, then leans forward to kiss my (thankfully pox free) neck. 'A successful shop and no more financial worries. Quality time with Freddie. But you know what I'm looking forward to most of all?'

I shake my head.

'I can't wait to see you in that nurse's uniform. My Christmas present is well overdue.'

And as we both collapse into helpless giggles on the sofa, I decide that happy endings are overrated. Happy beginnings are so much more exciting . . .

Acknowledgements

It was a real treat to return to the characters from *The Secret Shopper's Revenge* – and now I know how much fun it can be writing a sequel, I might just have to do another one . . .

Of course, it's also a treat because I'm lucky enough to work with lots of talented people who help turn a vague idea into the book you're holding. Thank you to Angela McMahon and Sophie Mitchell for publicity expertise, to Jade Chandler for making sure everything happens at the right time, to the sales teams for getting the book into the stores, to Ami Smithson for a terrific cover, and to Juliet Ewers, Susan Lamb, Lisa Milton, Genevieve Pegg and Jon Wood for so much support along the way. Special thanks to Kate Mills for editing brilliance and morale-boosting enthusiasm!

Thanks to all at LAW, but especially Araminta Whitley, queen of deals, ideas and hosiery wisdom.

Hello to my precious writing friends, including members of the Romantic Novelists' Association, the Novel Racers, the Bloggers with Book Deals and everyone on The Board. Special thanks to Linda Buckley-Archer, Giselle Green, Jacqui Hazell, Jacqui Lofthouse, Meg Sanders, Louise Voss and Stephanie Zia. Also to my fellow New Romantics (www.thenewromantics.org): Lucy Diamond (aka Sue Mongredien), Sarah Duncan, Veronica Henry, Milly Johnson, Jojo Moyes, and especially to Matt Dunn (and Tina Patel) for helping us settle into our latest adventure.

Lots of love to friends and family, especially David and Diana Carter, Geri Lewis, Jenny Eden, my sister Toni, my parents, and Rich . . . and many apologies to anyone I might have forgotten.

Finally, and most importantly, many thanks to you for reading. The response to the first Secret Shopper book was very exciting, and I hope this one is worth waiting for. I'd love to hear from you via my website, www.kate-harrison.com.

Kate Harrison
August 2009